初級英文文法

Dennis Le Boeuf & 景黎明

目錄

1 單數和複數名詞

1

名詞有單數、複數之分，兩者的用法如下：

單數名詞用來指「單一個」的人／事物／地點：

「一個」人	**an actor**（一個演員）
「一隻」動物	**a tiger**（一隻老虎）
「一個」地點	**a room**（一個房間）
「一件」物品	**a towel**（一條毛巾）

複數名詞指「多個」的人／事物／地點：

「多個」人	**actors**（多位演員）
「多隻」動物	**tigers**（數隻老虎）
「數個」地點	**rooms**（多個房間）
「數件」物品	**towels**（幾條毛巾）

one baby
一個嬰兒

three babies
三個嬰兒

one dog
一隻狗

two dogs
兩隻狗

a dress
一件洋裝

four dresses
四件洋裝

a toothbrush
一把牙刷

five toothbrushes
五把牙刷

2　複數名詞的構成方式

1　大多數名詞 ＋ s

| camera | ▶ | cameras | 相機 |
| egg | | eggs | 雞蛋 |

2　字尾為 s、x、sh、ch 的名詞 ＋ es

boss		bosses	老闆
fox	▶	foxes	狐狸
wish		wishes	願望
church		churches	教堂

3　字尾為「子音字母 ＋ y」的名詞 ↝ 去 y ＋ ies

body		bodies	身體
city	▶	cities	城市
family		families	家庭
story		stories	故事

4　字尾為 f/fe 的名詞 ↝ 去 f/fe ＋ ves

knife		knives	刀子
leaf	▶	leaves	葉子
wife		wives	妻子

5　字尾為「子音 ＋ o」的名詞 ＋ es

| hero | | heroes | 英雄 |
| potato | ▶ | potatoes | 馬鈴薯 |

| tomato | ▶ | tomatoes | 番茄 |

例外

piano ▶ pianos 鋼琴
yo-yo ▶ yo-yos 溜溜球

3　不規則名詞的複數形

不規則名詞（**irregular**）的複數形，並不是加 s 或 es，由於沒有固定的規則，須一一牢記。

a man	→	two men	男人
a woman	→	two women	女人
a child	→	two children	孩子
a mouse	→	two mice	老鼠
a tooth	→	two teeth	牙齒
one person	→	two people	人
a deer	→	two deer	鹿
one fish	→	two fish	魚
one sheep	→	two sheep	綿羊

- **Sally is a nice person.** 莎莉是一個好人。

- **Sally and her parents are nice people.**
  莎莉和她的父母都是好人。

4

在英語中，下列物品總是以複數形式出現，這些東西多有「成對」的特色，因此沒有單數形。

scissors 剪刀

glasses 眼鏡

pants (trousers) 長褲

jeans 牛仔褲

shorts 短褲

pajamas 睡衣褲

這類名詞要搭配複數動詞（are）、複數代名詞（them）。

- **Where are my glasses? I can't find them.**
  我的眼鏡在哪裡？我找不到。

- **I'm going to buy a new pair of jeans.**
  我要買一條新的牛仔褲。

這類名詞可以用 a pair of（一條、一把、一副）來修飾，表示「單一」的概念，或用 some（一些）來修飾，表示複數概念。

1 寫出下列單數可數名詞的複數形。

1 sheep	_____	**6** video	_____	**11** box	_____
2 copy	_____	**7** dress	_____	**12** bus	_____
3 birthday	_____	**8** brush	_____	**13** zoo	_____
4 leaf	_____	**9** child	_____	**14** goldfish	_____
5 hero	_____	**10** church	_____	**15** piano	_____

2 糾正錯誤。

1 Dan and Stan are two man from Japan.

Dan and Stan are two men from Japan.

2 Lori's mom told us two Christmas storys.

_____

3 Your child are in my house.

_____

4 She has three wishs.

_____

5 Grandpa has two bad tooths.

_____

6 There are a lot of fishes in the pond.

_____

7 Where is my blue pajama?

_____

3 根據中文提示，完成下列英文句子。

1 Sally 在刷牙。　　　　　　Sally is brushing her _____ .

2 那些箱子裡面有小狐狸嗎？　Are there any baby _____ in those _____ ?

3 那兩個男孩喜歡機器人玩具。Those two _____ love robotic _____ .

4 Hive 先生的貓有九條命。　Mr. Hive's cat has nine _____ .

5 Joe 的 Rose 姨媽常栽種馬鈴薯和番茄。Joe's Aunt Rose always grows lots of _____ and _____ .

6 那箱溜溜球放在那兩台鋼琴之間。The box of _____ is between those two _____ .

4 請在圖中找出下列單字的複數形（文字可能由上往下、由下往上、或斜的）。

```
  w w g         s s s
 s e o i m     n e e e o
s o c f m v     e o v o x v
s e e l o o e e   s r t e r e g s
o h d s i p x n s e d a i e n e s
s s i e q b i e f v l m h h o o d
c i v s u b r e s i i o t t i a t
w h s i a s a s n h t a d n y
g e z b e s r k c t a h f
f r z i i e s i o r i h y
  d e e d v o p e d r z
  s s o a n q b s k
    b e a w t
    l i b
      p
```

1 baby ____ 12 piano ____
2 body ____ 13 potato ____
3 child ____ 14 quiz ____
4 copy ____ 15 radio ____
5 dress ____ 16 thief ____
6 fox ____ 17 tomato ____
7 hero ____ 18 video ____
8 knife ____ 19 wish ____
9 leaf ____ 20 wife ____
10 library ____ 21 woman ____
11 ox ____

Chapter 2 不定冠詞 a/an

1

在**單數可數名詞**前面，通常要加不定冠詞 a 或 an（或 one、my、the 等）。

- **Tomorrow I'll give Ms. Tower** a flower. 明天我要給陶爾小姐一朵花。

- **Ruth is looking for** an elephant tooth. 露絲在找一顆象牙。

- **Do you want to become** a teacher? 你想當老師嗎？

2

a 用於「字首發音為子音的字」之前：

a **b**all
一顆球

a **c**ar
一輛車

a **h**ouse
一棟房子

a **r**abbit
一隻兔子

a **s**chool
一所學校

a **u**niversity
一所大學

an 用於「字首發音為母音（a, e, i, o, u）的字」之前：

an **a**pple
一顆蘋果

an **e**gg
一個雞蛋

an **i**dea
一個主意

an **e**lephant
一頭大象

an **o**range
一個柳橙

an **u**mbrella
一把傘

遇到「數字」時的用法

採用一樣的規則：以子音發音開始的數字用 a，以母音發音開始的數字用 an。

a **10**-year old house
一棟十年的老房子

10 的發音為 /tɛn/，是子音開頭，因此前面用 a。

an **8**-year-old artist
一名八歲大的藝術家

8 的發音為 /et/，是母音開頭，因此前面用 an。

遇到「縮寫」時的用法

以字母 F, H, L, M, N, R, S, X 開始的縮寫字，都是以母音發音開頭，要用 an。

an **F**BI agent
一名聯邦調查局官員

F 的發音為 /ɛf/，因此 FBI 是一個以母音開頭的字，要用 an。

an **X**-ray machine
一台 X 光機

X 的發音為 /ɛks/，因此 X-ray 是一個以母音開頭的字，要用 an。

3

要用 a 還是用 an，關鍵在於字首的發音（母音還是子音發音），而不在拼寫。

有些字的拼寫雖以母音字母 eu、u、o 開始，但字首發音為子音，要用 a。

a European	/ˌjʊrəˈpiən/	一個歐洲人
a university	/ˌjunəˈvɜsətɪ/	一所大學
a one-day-trip	/wʌn/	一天的旅程

h 位於字首：有些字的字首 h 不發音，要用 an。

| an hour | /aʊr/ | 一小時 |
| an honor | /ˈɑnɚ/ | 一件光榮的事 |

4

複數名詞前，不用 a 或 an。

- She is a dancer, not a teacher.
  ┌─ 單數名詞
  她是一名舞蹈家，不是教師。
- They are dancers, not teachers.
  ┌─ 複數名詞
  他們是舞蹈家，不是教師。

5

「a/an + 單數可數名詞」不用來指整個類別，整個類別通常用複數名詞。

- "I don't like apples," said Mike.
  邁克説：「我不喜歡吃蘋果。」

  "I don't like an apple," said Mike.
  └─ 這是錯誤用法

a **t**eacher 一名教師

a **z**ebra 一匹斑馬

a **s**andwich 一個三明治

a **d**oor 一扇門

a **u**niform 一件制服

a **h**orse 一匹馬

a **E**uropean 一個歐洲人

a **m**ouse 一隻老鼠

a **1**0-hour bus drive
一趟十小時的公車旅行

an **a**rtist 一名藝術家

an **e**agle 一隻老鷹

an **i**ce cream cone 一支蛋捲冰淇淋

an **o**pen door 一扇敞開的門

an **u**ncle 一位叔叔／伯伯

an **h**onor 一件光榮的事／一個光榮的人

an **E**gyptian 一個埃及人

an **M**BA degree 一個企業管理碩士學位

an **1**1 a.m. meeting 一場上午 **11** 點的會議

6　a/an 和 one 的用法比較

用 one 強調確定的數量是「一個」，而不是兩個、三個等。如果沒有特別要強調數量，就用 a。

- I asked you to buy one pair of blue shoes, not two.
  我要你買一雙藍色的鞋，而不是兩雙。

- She would like to have a cup of coffee, not tea.
  她想喝一杯咖啡，不是茶。

PRACTICE

1 請在下列表示各項職業的名詞前加 **a** 或 **an**。

1 _____ engineer
2 _____ businessperson
3 _____ editor
4 _____ singer
5 _____ doctor
6 _____ artist
7 _____ firefighter
8 _____ waiter
9 _____ actress
10 _____ ballet dancer

2 在空格內填上 **a** 或 **an**。

1 _____ classroom
2 _____ uniform
3 _____ eye
4 _____ door
5 _____ ear
6 _____ pizza
7 _____ strawberry
8 _____ airplane
9 _____ MBA degree
10 _____ ice-cream cone
11 _____ honor
12 _____ mouse
13 _____ arrow
14 _____ honest student
15 _____ artist
16 _____ upstairs bathroom
17 _____ UFO
18 _____ accident
19 _____ object
20 _____ invitation

3 在空格內填上 **a** 或 **an**。

1 a banana and _____ orange

2 _____ apple and a pear

3 an ostrich and _____ monkey

4 an airplane and _____ pilot

5 a school and _____ teacher

6 _____ elephant and a tiger

4 請用 **a**、**an** 或 **one**，以及下面的綠色字彙，完成下列句子。注意句首的第一個字母要大寫。

hour   one-horned   FBI   X-ray   bookstore

passenger   Egyptian   cup   university

1 Gus said, "Only _____ was injured when that truck hit the bus."

2 Would you like _____ of coffee or tea?

3 _____ agent is talking to Ann.

4 Does she have _____ degree?

5 Amy Tower and I waited for our bus for _____ .

6 Ellen is a European, and Alan is _____ . They both love ballet.

7 Is this _____ of _____ deer?

8 Mr. Door works in _____ .

5 從 A 框和 B 框裡選擇詞語並造句，必要時加 **a/an**。

A	B
I can't ride	old house
Her mom is	horse
I'd like to play	computer game
Jenny never wears	university
They live in	engineer
He works at	bikini

1 *I can't ride a horse.*

2 _____

3 _____

4 _____

5 _____

6 _____

Chapter

3 可數和不可數名詞

1

可數名詞是可以用**數量**表示的人、事物、地點或動物的名稱。可數名詞具有**單數**和**複數**形式，可以用 a、one、two、three 等修飾。

a bus
一輛公車

a computer
一台電腦

an egg
一顆蛋

two buses
兩輛公車

two computers
兩台電腦

three eggs
三顆蛋

2

不可數名詞不可以用數量來表示，不可以用 a、one、two、three 等修飾；不可數名詞都是**單數名詞，沒有複數形式**。以下的名詞都是不可數名詞：

money
錢

water
水

milk
牛奶

tea
茶

coffee
咖啡

oil
油

rice
米

butter
奶油

cheese
乳酪

bread
麵包

rain
雨

weather
天氣

snow
雪

hair
頭髮

furniture
傢俱

homework
家庭作業

traffic
交通

work 工作
advice 建議
information 資訊
knowledge 知識
news 新聞

3

可數名詞因單數或複數的不同，可與**單數**或**複數**動詞連用；**不可數**名詞後面只能接**單數**動詞。

• My brother Roy loves that robotic toy. 我兄弟羅伊喜歡那個機器人玩具。→ 單數可數名詞（brother）
用單數動詞（loves）

• Those boys love robotic toys. 那些男孩喜歡機器人玩具。 → 複數可數名詞（boys）
用複數動詞（love）

• "Your hair is lovely," said Claire. 克萊兒說：「你的頭髮好漂亮。」 → 不可數名詞（hair）
用單數動詞（is）

4

有些名詞可以是可數名詞，也可以是不可數名詞，但意思不同。

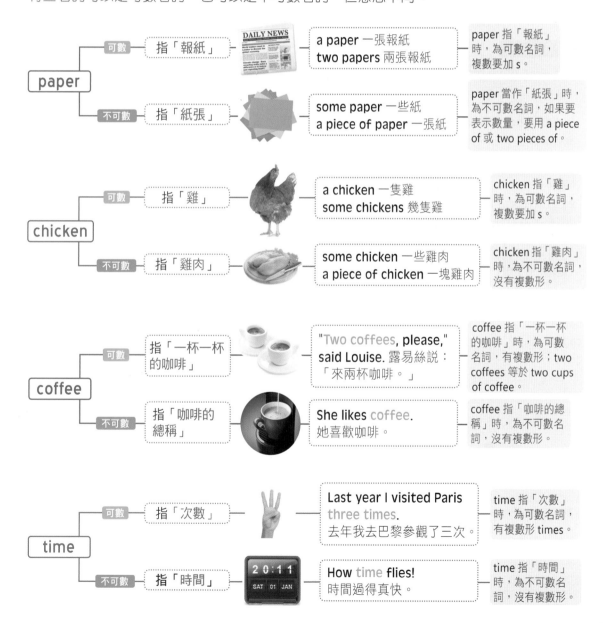

| paper | 可數 | 指「報紙」 | DAILY NEWS | a paper 一張報紙
two papers 兩張報紙 | paper 指「報紙」時，為可數名詞，複數要加 s。 |
| | 不可數 | 指「紙張」 | | some paper 一些紙
a piece of paper 一張紙 | paper 當作「紙張」時，為不可數名詞，如果要表示數量，要用 a piece of 或 two pieces of。 |

| chicken | 可數 | 指「雞」 | | a chicken 一隻雞
some chickens 幾隻雞 | chicken 指「雞」時，為可數名詞，複數要加 s。 |
| | 不可數 | 指「雞肉」 | | some chicken 一些雞肉
a piece of chicken 一塊雞肉 | chicken 指「雞肉」時，為不可數名詞，沒有複數形。 |

| coffee | 可數 | 指「一杯一杯的咖啡」 | | "Two coffees, please," said Louise. 露易絲說：「來兩杯咖啡。」 | coffee 指「一杯一杯的咖啡」時，為可數名詞，有複數形；two coffees 等於 two cups of coffee。 |
| | 不可數 | 指「咖啡的總稱」 | | She likes coffee. 她喜歡咖啡。 | coffee 指「咖啡的總稱」時，為不可數名詞，沒有複數形。 |

| time | 可數 | 指「次數」 | | Last year I visited Paris three times. 去年我去巴黎參觀了三次。 | time 指「次數」時，為可數名詞，有複數形 times。 |
| | 不可數 | 指「時間」 | 20:11 SAT 01 JAN | How time flies! 時間過得真快。 | time 指「時間」時，為不可數名詞，沒有複數形。 |

5

單數可數名詞前，通常要加 a/an（或 one、the、my 等）。

參見 Chapter 2（不是冠詞 a/an）

- Jenny has a purple bikini. 珍妮有一件紫色的比基尼。

6

複數可數名詞和**不可數名詞**前，不能加 a/an，但經常會加 some 或 any 等修飾語。

＊ some 通常用在肯定句中，any 通常用在疑問句和否定句中〔參見 Chapter 9〕。

複數可數名詞

- Paul Powers bought me some flowers. 保羅・鮑爾斯買了一些花給我。
  → flowers 是複數可數名詞，前面不能加 a，但在肯定句中經常加 some。

- "Are there any cookies?" asked Penny. 潘妮問：「有沒有餅乾？」
  → cookies 是複數可數名詞，前面不能加 a，但在疑問句中經常加 any。

不可數名詞

- Ms. Rice gave me some good advice. 萊斯小姐給了我一些好建議。
  → advice 是不可數名詞，前面不能加 an，但在肯定句中經常加 some。

- I didn't borrow any money from Penny. 我沒有向潘妮借過錢。
  → money 是不可數名詞，前面不能加 a，但在否定句中經常加 any。

7

有些不可數的物質名詞，可以用量詞來表示數量，句型為：「量詞 + of + 不可數名詞」。
如果要表示「兩瓶水」、「三張紙」等這類複數概念，「量詞」要用複數形。

量詞 + of + 不可數名詞

bar（條、塊）
bottle（瓶）
carton（盒）
glass（杯）
jar（罐）
loaf（條）
piece（塊、張、片）

a glass of ＋

a loaf of ＋

two bars of ＋

a jar of ＋

four bottles of ＋

three pieces of ＋

使用量詞

- Louise, would you like a piece of cheese? 露易絲，你想吃塊起司嗎？

- Midge put two cartons of milk in the fridge. 米姬在冰箱裡放了兩盒牛奶。

使用 some/any 等修飾語

- Louise would like some cheese.
  露易絲想吃一些起司

- "There's some milk in the fridge," said Midge. 米姬説：「冰箱裡有牛奶。」

a glass of milk 一杯牛奶　　a loaf of bread 一條麵包
two bars of soap 兩塊肥皂　　a jar of honey 一罐蜂蜜
four bottles of water 四瓶水　three pieces of chalk 三支粉筆

1 請根據圖片，從綠色字彙中選出正確的名稱填入空格，並視需要加上 a 或 an。

table milk bread student tie snow

1 _____ 2 _____ 3 _____ 4 _____ 5 _____ 6 _____

2 請判斷下列句子是否正確，正確打 ✓，不正確打 ×，並寫出正確句子。

1 You have told me that story five times. □ _____

2 "Would you like an apple juice?" asked Mike. □ _____

3 Lily, your hairs look lovely. □ _____

4 Ted just ate a piece of bread. □ _____

5 "Does Mom have a lot of butters?" asked Tom. □ _____

6 A knowledge is power. □ _____

7 Mabel put some money on the table. □ _____

8 Times fly when we're having fun under the sun! □ _____

9 "Is there any students absent today?" asked Kay. □ _____

10 My parents is going to visit Norway in May. □ _____

11 Mort saw a heavy traffic near the airport. □ _____

3 用 is 或 are 填空，完成下列句子，在必要的地方補充 a 或 an。

1 "There _____ some good news," said Claire.

2 There _____ strawberry on my apple pie.

3 These _____ tasty strawberries.

4 There _____ too much noise on Neat Street.

5 Ted, there _____ puppy under your bed.

6 Midge, there _____ still some eggs in your fridge.

7 There _____ little dog behind that log.

8 "There _____ three kittens in this basket," said Clair.

9 "There _____ still some milk in the bottle," said Liz.

10 "That _____ expensive cellphone!" exclaimed Pat.

Chapter 4 the 的基本用法

1

the + 隨後再次提及的名詞

單數可數名詞被初次提及時，會用不定冠詞 a/an，隨後再次提及時，則用定冠詞 the 來修飾。

同一隻

這裡的肥鼠是剛剛提過的那一隻，再次提及時改用 the。

- That is a big fat rat. Look, my little cat is chasing the big fat rat.
  那是一隻大肥鼠。瞧，我的小貓在追趕那隻大肥鼠。

不可數名詞被初次提及時，不須加冠詞，但可以用 some 等修飾語；隨後再次提及時，就要加定冠詞 the。

彼麵包即是此麵包

這裡的一些麵包是剛剛提過的那些麵包，再次提及時改用 the。

- Dad bought some bread yesterday, but today the bread has gone bad.
  爸爸昨天買了一些麵包，可是那些麵包今天壞了。

2

the + 已知的東西（已經清楚是哪個東西或哪個人）

- **Louise, lock** the door, **please.** 露易絲，請鎖門。
  → 聽者知道提及的是哪一道門。

- **Dwight, please turn on** the light. 杜威特，請開燈。
  → 聽者知道提及的是哪盞燈。

- Sam **Where is Mom?** 媽媽在哪裡？

  Ann **She's in** the garden. 她在花園裡。
  → 聽者知道提及的是哪個花園。

the + 獨一無二的東西

- I should try to count all the stars in the sky. 我應該數數看天上的星星有多少。

- The sun was too hot, so I sat under my beach umbrella.
  太陽太大了，於是我在我的海灘陽傘下面坐了下來。

the sun 太陽	**the moon** 月亮	**the stars** 星星	**the sky** 天空	**the weather** 天氣
the universe 宇宙	**the solar system** 太陽系	**the planets** 行星	**the Earth** 地球	**the earth** 人類／人間
the world 世界	**the Atlantic Ocean** 大西洋	**the president** 總裁		

比較下面句子 a/an 和 the 的用法。

有趣的城市很多，倫敦只是其中一個，所以用不定冠詞 an。

- **London is an interesting city.**
  倫敦是一個有趣的城市。

英國的首都只有一個，所以用定冠詞 the。

- **London is the capital of Britain.**
  倫敦是英國的首都。

天底下的老師何其多，布萊克先生只是其中一個，所以用不定冠詞 a。

- **Mr. Black is a teacher.**
  布萊克先生是一名老師。

我們學校最老的老師只有一個，所以用定冠詞 the。

- **Mr. Black is the oldest teacher in our school.** 布萊克先生是我們學校年紀最大的老師。

1 | 請在空格內填上 **a**、**an** 或 **the**。

1 This is _____ walnut. _____ walnut is delicious.

2 She is _____ singer. _____ singer is pretty.

3 This is _____ owl. _____ owl hunts at night.

4 He is _____ artist. _____ artist is hardworking.

2 | 請選擇正確答案，填入空格中。

1
| a picture |
| the picture |

ⓐ Joan, look at _____ of Lady Gaga on my cellphone.

ⓑ She showed us _____ of her home in Hawaii.

2
| a sofa |
| the sofa |

ⓐ Look, there is a black cat on _____ .

ⓑ Mr. Broom has a TV, a phone, and _____ in his bathroom.

3
| a shower |
| the shower |

ⓐ You can't take a shower here because there isn't _____ in this bathroom.

ⓑ You can't take a shower today because _____ is broken.

4

| a dog |
| the dog |

a Did you use to have _____ ?

b Yes, but _____ ran away with a big hog.

5

| a gate |
| the gate |

a "Is there _____ to the backyard?" asked Claire.

b Dwight locked _____ and left for the night.

6

| an ocean |
| the ocean |

a In 1492 Columbus sailed _____ blue. He never knew what land he'd come to.

b We gave Grandma Glove _____ of love.

---

3 改錯：請將下列句子改寫為正確的句子。

1 Margo locked door and closed window.

_____

2 I have to pick up Mort at airport.

_____

3 The BBC report was about the huge new wind farm in North Sea.

_____

4 Mary learned a lot about world in the library.

_____

5 Why do stars twinkle in dark sky?

_____

5 泛指與特指名詞，以及 the 的用法

1

當所談論的複數名詞或不可數名詞是「**泛指人或物的總體**」時，**不用 the**。

└── 複數名詞 pandas，泛指所有的熊貓。

- **Are** pandas **dangerous?** 熊貓會很危險嗎？

└── life 為不可數名詞，泛指生活。

- Life **is difficult without a nice wife.** 如果沒有一個好妻子，日子會很難過。

└── pop music 為不可數名詞，泛指流行音樂。

- **Does Rick love** pop music? 瑞克喜歡流行音樂嗎？

2

談論「特定的人或物」（無論是複數名詞、單數可數名詞、不可數名詞）時，**用 the**。

泛指柳橙這種水果

- I love oranges.
  我喜歡柳橙。

特指放在桌子上的那些柳橙

- The oranges **on the table look great.**
  桌上的柳橙看起來很不錯。

泛指雨傘這種物品

- **Please lend me** an umbrella.
  請借我一把雨傘。

特指某一把雨傘

- **Please put** the umbrella **on the porch.**
  請把雨傘放在陽臺上。

泛指錢這種交易媒介

- Is money **important?**
  錢很重要嗎？

特指桌子上的那些錢

- **Please pass me** the money **on the table.**
  請把桌上的錢遞給我。

在下面這類的天氣用語或相對的地理用語中，雖然有泛指的意思，但通常要加 the。

in the rain 在雨中

in the snow 在雪中

in the mountains 在山裡

the city 都市（生活）

the country/
the countryside 鄉下

the coast 沿海地區

the ocean 海洋

the sea 海洋

- **Coco loves to walk in** the snow.
  可可喜歡在雪中行走。

- **We take most of our vacations on** the coast.
  我們大部分的假期都是在沿海地區度過。

- **She prefers** the mountains **to** the sea.
  她喜歡山勝過大海。

- **I'm going to** the countryside **next weekend to visit Nancy Wu.**
  下週末我要去鄉下看望南西 ‧ 吳。

1 請用下面的綠色字詞彙，造句談論你喜歡（I like）或不喜歡（I don't like）什麼，來練習下列不加 the 的詞語。

pop music *soccer* *golf* *computer games*
Japanese food *fast-food restaurants* *ice cream* *pears*

1 _____

2 _____

3 _____

4 _____

5 _____

6 _____

2 請選擇正確答案，填入空格中。（注意：句首的第一個字母要大寫）

1 | carrots
the carrots

a My sister doesn't like _____ .

b Louise, pass me _____ , please.

2 | French toast
the French toast

a Every Sunday morning I eat
_____ .

b I like _____ in that restaurant.

3 | children
the children

a _____ over there are having fun.

b That movie about exploring the moon is popular with both _____ and adults around the world.

4

| salt |
| the salt |

ⓐ Walt, where is _____ ?

ⓑ Too much _____ is not good for you.

5

| bread |
| the bread |

ⓐ _____ was warm and fresh.

ⓑ She loves to eat _____ and butter.

6

| pandas |
| the pandas |

ⓐ _____ are animals with black and white fur.

ⓑ _____ have helped our zoo attract more tourists.

7

| a country |
| the country |

ⓐ I love living in _____ , but Kitty loves living in the city.

ⓑ Mr. Love is from _____ that most people have never heard of.

8

| rain |
| the rain |

ⓐ Lots of _____ is coming our way.

ⓑ Jane loves to walk in _____ .

9

| a city |
| the city |

ⓐ Where would you prefer to live, in _____ or the countryside?

ⓑ I live in _____ along the coast.

10

| people |
| the people |

ⓐ I like to meet _____ from different countries.

ⓑ Who are _____ in our classroom?

11

| a |
| the |

ⓐ Dee likes to swim in _____ sea.

ⓑ Does _____ wild sea require a skilled sailor?

6 不加 the 和要加 the 的習慣用語

1 不加 the 的習慣用語

使用下列慣用語時，**不加 the**。

1 用「**by+ 交通工具**」來表達交通方式時，不加 the。

```
go        交通
     + by +
travel    工具
```

bike（自行車）
car（汽車）
taxi（計程車）
bus（公車）
train（火車）
airplane（飛機）
air（空路）
land（陸路）
sea（海路）
water（水路）

go by bike	騎腳踏車去
go by car	坐汽車去
go by taxi	坐計程車去
go by bus	坐公車去
go by train	坐火車去
go by airplane	搭飛機去
travel by air	經由空路
travel by land	經由陸路
travel by sea	經由海路
travel by water	經由水路

走路的用法也不用 the

走路去 **go on foot**
　　　travel on foot
(on foot = walking)

- **Gus went there** by bus.
  加斯搭公車去那裡。

- **Will Jane travel** by train?
  珍要搭火車旅行嗎？

2 有些地點名詞接在 to、at、in 等介系詞後面時，多半表達該地點的**功能**，或人們前往該地點的**目的**，此時也**不加 the**。

go to +
school　去上學 —— 學校的功能是上課，此時不加 the，表示是去上學。
college　去上學院
work　去上班
church　去教堂做禮拜
prison　進監獄 —— 強調的是監獄的功能，表示進去服刑。
bed　去睡覺

be at +
school　在學校上學
college　在學院上學
work　在上班
church　在教堂做禮拜 —— 強調的是教堂的功能，表示在做禮拜。

be in +
bed　在睡覺 —— 強調的是床的功能，表示睡覺，而不是在床上看書等。
prison　在監獄

go + home　回家
be at + home　在家裡 —— go home 不用介系詞。

- Is he at home now?
  他現在在家嗎？

3 不加 the 的**時間用語**：

　at **night** 夜晚
　at **midnight** 半夜
　by **day** 白天
　by **night** 夜間

- **The dog often barks** at midnight.
  那隻狗常會在半夜吠叫。

❹ 「吃三餐」不加 the：

have eat	+	breakfast	吃早餐
		lunch	吃午餐
		dinner	吃晚餐

have something for eat something for	+	breakfast	早餐吃……
		lunch	午餐吃……
		dinner	晚餐吃……

• **What do you usually have** for lunch?
  你午餐通常吃什麼？

❺ 一些**成雙重複的慣用語**，不使用 the：

arm in arm 臂挽著臂
day after day 日復一日
face to face 面對面
hand in hand 手牽手
side by side 肩並肩
year after year 年復一年

2

表示「週、月、年、夏天、星期」等的名詞前面如果接 next 或 last，則不加 the。

next	+	week	下週
		month	下個月
		year	明年
		summer	明年夏天
		winter	明年冬天
		Sunday	下週日

last	+	week	上週
		month	上個月
		year	去年
		spring	去年春天
		fall	去年秋天
		Friday	上星期五

• **I'm going to India** next week.
  我下星期要去印度。

3

「語言」和「學科名稱」前不加 the。

• **Trish speaks**	+	English.	翠希講英文。
		Spanish.	翠希講西班牙文。
		Polish.	翠希講波蘭話。

• **Her major is**	+	chemistry.	她主修化學。
		history.	她主修歷史。
		art.	她主修藝術。

4

體育活動前不加 the。

baseball　basketball　golf　skating

• **My favorite sport is** water-skiing.
  我最喜歡的運動是滑水。

TV 這個字指「電視節目」時，不加 **the**；指「電視機」時，要加 **the**。

Does he like to watch TV?
他喜歡看電視嗎？ └ 喜歡看電視節目而非喜歡看電視機。

Did you watch the royal wedding on TV yesterday?
昨天你看了電視上播放的皇家婚禮沒有？ on TV 指的是電視節目，不加 the。

Please turn off the TV.
請把電視關了。 └ the TV 指的是電視機，不是電視節目。

5 要加 the 的習慣用語

在下列的慣用用法中，**要加 the。**

❶ 要加 the 的**地點**或**活動**用語：

go to ＋ the theater　去電影院／去劇院
be at ＋ the theater　在電影院／在劇院
listen to ＋ the radio　聽廣播／聽收音機
be on ＋ the radio　在廣播中

- Ms. Star usually listens to the radio
  when she's driving her car.
  塔爾小姐開車時通常會聽廣播。

❷ 要加 the 的**時間**用語：

in the ＋	morning	在上午
	afternoon	在下午
	evening	在晚上
	day	在白天
	daytime	在白天

- Bing walks his dog in the evening.
  賓晚上溜狗。

❸ 要加 the 的**方向位置**用語：

the ＋	top	＋ (of)	頂端
	end		末端
	beginning		開端
	middle		中間
	left		左邊
	right		右邊
	bottom		底部
	north		北方
	south		南方

- In our country we drive on the right
  side of the road.
  在我們國家，開車要靠右。

- My girlfriend's house is near the
  end of this street.
  我女朋友家就在這條大街的街底。

❹ 「演奏樂器」要加 the。

play the violin　play the guitar　play the piano
拉小提琴　　　　彈吉他　　　　彈鋼琴

- At the age of three, Lynn started to
  play the violin.
  琳恩三歲時開始拉小提琴。

❺ 一些表示「**集體**」、「**整體**」的名詞，
常加 the 使用。

the police 警察
the fire brigade 消防隊
the army 軍隊

- Amy is in the army. 艾咪在陸軍服役。

❻ 表達「**相同**」或「**最……**」的用語，
要加 the。

the same 相同的　　best 是形容詞 good 的最高
the best player 最優秀的運動員　級〔參見 Chapter 59〕。

- Where is the nearest post office?
  這裡最近的郵局在哪裡？
  　　　　　　nearest 是形容詞 near 的
  　　　　　　最高級〔參見 Chapter 59〕。

❼ 序數詞（first 第一、second 第二……）
要加 the。

the first floor 一樓
the second floor 二樓

❽ 與某些形容詞連用，以表示一類人或
物，要加 the。

the old 老人
the young 年輕人
the disabled 身障人士

PRACTICE

1 完成下列問句：請在需要加 **the** 的空格處填上 **the**，如果不需要加 **the**，則劃上斜線「/」。

1. Does Gus go to _____ school on _____ foot or by _____ bus?
2. Do bats sleep in _____ day and come out to hunt for _____ food at _____ night?
3. What time does Ted usually go to _____ bed?
4. Does Joe play _____ piano?
5. Let's plant this little tree in _____ countryside.
6. Do you prefer traveling by _____ airplane or _____ train?
7. Does Jane like to walk in _____ rain?
8. Does June watch _____ TV in _____ afternoon?
9. Coco, why don't we get together for _____ dinner tomorrow?
10. Are your favorite sports _____ basketball and _____ soccer?
11. Is _____ English used in many countries?
12. Are they walking _____ arm in _____ arm around the farm?

2 完成下列句子：從綠色詞彙中選出適當的辭彙填空，並在必要的地方加 **the**。

breakfast   midnight   bed   police   prison TV
eleventh   movie theater   home   guitar   morning

1. Ann Car can play _____.
2. It's getting late, and Jerome and I have to go _____.
3. Somebody was trying to break into her house, so she called _____.
4. Ms. King, you will have some health problems in the future if you don't eat _____ in _____.
5. Last night she went to bed at _____.
6. "There are some good movies on at _____ this weekend," said Clair.
7. Is your manager's office on _____ floor?
8. I enjoy watching _____ while I am taking a bath.
9. Peter's ex-wife will be locked up in _____ for the rest of her life.
10. The sun is up. Are you still in _____, Ted?

Chapter

7 普通名詞和專有名詞

1

「非特定」的人、事物或地點的名稱，是**普通名詞**。普通名詞包括**單數可數名詞**、**複數名詞**、**不可數名詞**。

單數可數名詞	複數名詞	不可數名詞
actor 演員	actors 演員	gas 汽油
car 汽車	cars 汽車	gold 金
park 公園	parks 公園	water 水
friend 朋友	friends 朋友	money 錢

2

「特定」的人、事物或地點的名稱，是**專有名詞**。專有名詞的首字母一定要**大寫**，且通常**不加冠詞**。常見的專有名詞類別如下：

1 人名

Jenny has a new bikini.
珍妮有一件新的比基尼泳裝。

2 節日

Kay flew home on Christmas Day.
凱耶誕節那天搭飛機回家了。

3 語言

Can Trish speak Spanish?
翠希會講西班牙語嗎？

4 星期

Today is Sunday, and I don't need to get up early.
今天是星期天，我不用早起。

5 月分

Ray will go to New York in June.
雷六月要去紐約。

6 城市鄉鎮

Margo lives in Chicago.
瑪歌住在芝加哥。

7 國家

Ann is from Egypt.
安是埃及人。

 例外 1

國家名稱如果是複數形式，須加 **the**。

the Netherlands 荷蘭
the Philippines 菲律賓

 例外 2

國家名稱如果帶有 **states**、**kingdom** 或 **republic** 等詞彙，須加 **the**。

the United States 美國
the United Kingdom 英國
the Irish Republic 愛爾蘭共和國

8 州、省

She lives in Michigan.
她住在密西根州。

9 大洲

Which is bigger, Africa or Australia?
非洲和澳洲，哪一洲大？

10 山名

Mount Fuji is the highest mountain in Japan.
富士山是日本最高的山。

11 街道廣場

My shop is on Fifth Street.
我的商店在第五街上。

Is Times Square in New York?
時代廣場在紐約嗎？

12 大學、公園、機場名

Is he studying at Oxford University?
他在唸牛津大學嗎？

This Sunday we are going to Central Park in New York City.
這個星期天我們要去紐約市的中央公園。

He will pick me up at Tampa International Airport.
他會來坦帕國際機場接我。

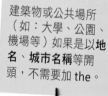

> 建築物或公共場所（如：大學、公園、機場等）如果是以**地名、城市名稱**等開頭，不需要加 the。

3

專有名詞當中若包含「**of . . .**」片語，須加上 the。

┌─ 「倫敦大學」帶有 of，所以最前面要加 the。
- Is she a student at the University of London?
  她是倫敦大學的學生嗎？

┌─ 「倫敦塔」帶有 of，所以最前面要加 the。
- The Tower of London is one of Britain's most popular travel destinations.
  倫敦塔是英國最受歡迎的一個旅遊景點。

4

下列的專有名詞（地理、建築、姓氏），須加 the：

1 海洋

2 運河

3 河川

4 沙漠

- She loves to swim in the Mediterranean Sea.
  她喜歡在地中海裡游泳。
- The Grand Canal of China is the longest one in the world. 京杭大運河是世界上最上的運河。

- The Mississippi is the fourth longest river in the world. 世界上第四長的河是密西西比河。
- The Sahara is the largest desert in the world.
  撒哈拉沙漠是世界上最大的沙漠。

5 山脈

6 電影院 劇院

7 飯店

8 餐廳

- The Rockies are a major mountain range in North America. 落磯山脈是北美洲的一個主要山脈。
- She's going to watch a ballet at the Playhouse Theater. 她要去普利豪爾劇院看一場芭蕾舞。

- Del lives close to the Royal Hotel.
  戴爾住在皇家飯店附近。
- She is working as a waitress at the Star of India*.
  她在「印度之星」當服務生。〔＊餐廳名稱〕

9 博物館 美術館

- Have you ever visited the British Museum?
  你參觀過大英博物館嗎？

10 姓氏複數名（表示一家人）

- The Browns are going to visit Paris this summer.
  布朗一家人今年夏天要去巴黎旅遊。

PRACTICE

1 自右欄選出與左欄同類的普通名詞，填入空格中。

- **1** police officer, doctor
- **2** puppy, tiger
- **3** aunt, cousin
- **4** cellphone, bookcase
- **5** apple, banana
- **6** hallway, kitchen

- a nephew, uncle
- b computer, table
- c monkey, owl
- d living room, library
- e mango, grape
- f dentist, teacher

2 自右欄選出與左欄同類的專有名詞，填入空格中。

_____ ① Mary, Mike
_____ ② Egypt, India
_____ ③ London, Moscow
_____ ④ Florida, California
_____ ⑤ Africa, Asia
_____ ⑥ March, Saturday

ⓐ New Delhi, Taipei
ⓑ Europe, North America
ⓒ Michigan, Texas
ⓓ Emma, Ben
ⓔ Sunday, January
ⓕ Indonesia, Singapore

3 將下面的字彙依照類別填入空格中，並在必要的地方加 the。

Atlantic	Hilton	Mount Everest	British Museum	Dubai
Arabian Sea	Sahara	Rhine	Indian Ocean	Africa
Holiday Inn	Gobi Desert	National Gallery	Mediterranean	Tokyo
Himalayas	Netherlands	North America	Germany	Mississippi

① Continents _____ _____
② Countries _____ _____
③ Capital cities _____ _____
④ Oceans _____ _____
⑤ Seas _____ _____
⑥ Rivers _____ _____
⑦ Museums/Galleries _____ _____
⑧ Famous hotels _____ _____
⑨ Mounts/Mountain ranges _____ _____
⑩ Desert _____ _____

4 在下列空格中需要 the 的地方填上 the，如果不需要 the，則用斜線「/」表示。注意句子的首字母要大寫。

① Ray and I go to the movies every _____ Saturday.
② I am going to leave _____ Malaysia next _____ Sunday and drive right across _____ Asia.
③ _____ Tower of London is a historic castle on the north bank of _____ River Thames in central _____ London.
④ She is studying the history of _____ United Kingdom of Great Britain and Northern Ireland.
⑤ Clark and I will go swimming at _____ Sun Park.
⑥ Del lives behind _____ Hilton Hotel.
⑦ Kay is going to visit _____ British Museum today.
⑧ My home is in _____ Rome.

Chapter

8 名詞所有格

1

名詞所有格用以表示「所有權」，意思是「……的」。

- I sent her out of Dan's tent. → Dan's tent 指「丹的帳篷」，
  我請她離開丹的帳篷。　　　　　說明此物屬於丹的。

- Kay's friends love to go to the movies on Sundays. → Kay's friend 指「凱的朋友」，
  凱的朋友們星期天時喜歡去看電影。　　　　　　　　表示凱所擁有的朋友。

- "Where is your sister's house?" asked Clair. → your sister's house 指「你妹妹的房子」，
  克萊兒問：「你妹妹的房子在哪裡？」　　　　　　表示「你姊妹所居住的房子」。

2

名詞所有格可以單獨使用，省略後面的名詞，來代替重複提及的名詞。

- That's not my cellphone; it's Pat's. → Pat's 等於 Pat's cellphone，
  那不是我的手機，那是派特的。　　　　省略了後面的名詞，避免重複。

- Sally's hair is shorter than Emma's. → Emma's 等於 Emma's hair，
  莎莉的頭髮比艾瑪的頭髮短。　　　　　省略了後面的名詞，避免重複。

---

3 名詞所有格的構成方式

❶ 單數名詞 + 's

Mary's grandmother
瑪麗的奶奶

my brother's socks
我弟弟的襪子

Dickens's novels
狄更斯的小說

the dog's house
(= the doghouse)
狗屋

❷ 複數名詞

▸ 字尾非 s 的複數名詞 + 's

a children's book 一本童書
the women's changing room 女更衣室

▸ 字尾是 s 的複數名詞 + '

the bosses' plan 老闆們的計畫
my brothers' airplane 我兄弟們的飛機

→ sister's 是單數名詞的所有格，
表示「一個姊姊的」。

• **That is my** sister's **car.** 那是我姊姊的汽車。

→ sisters' 是複數名詞的所有格，
表示不只一個姊姊，是
「幾個姊姊共同擁有的」。

• **That is my** sisters' **car.** 那是我姊姊們的汽車。

4

「of 片語」也常拿來表示所有權，「of 片語」和所有格「's」用來表示所有權的用法是
有區別的。

❶ 生物的所有格使用 's 或 ' ：有生命的人和動物，通常使用所有格「's」或「'」。

Sue's electric car
蘇的電動汽車

our grandpa's birthday
我們爺爺的生日

Mr. Black's wife
布萊克先生的妻子

❷ 無生物的所有格使用 of ：常用「the + 所有物 + of + 無生物名詞」的句型。

the	+ 所有物	+ of	+ 無生物名詞

the	door	of	the school library	校圖書館的門
the	end	of	the vacation	假期的尾聲
the	back	of	the car	汽車的後面

1 請寫出下列詞語的英文。

1　女性雜誌（「雜誌」用複數）

2　我奶奶的眼鏡

3　Liz 的電腦

4　Doris 的學校

5　那個（the) 兔子的頭

6　她的頭頂

7　我父母的房子

8　那個（the) 農夫的妻子

9　我數學老師的名字

10　我家鄉的名字

2 將括弧中的正確答案畫上底線。

1　Those flies are on (the boss'/the boss's) pies.

2　Did Pat see the (children's/children') robotic cat?

3　"Where is (the women/the women's) room?" asked Ms. Bloom.

4　Are there any foxes near (the Coxes's/the Coxes') boxes?

5　Are (Peter's/Peter') new pants on the chair?

6 Are you invited to (the birthday party of Jane/Jane's birthday party) this Saturday night?

7 His car stopped at (the end of the street/the street's end).

3 請依括弧裡的提示，在空格內填入正確的名詞所有格。

1 Tricia's junk might be _____ (另一個人的) treasure.

2 Lori's _____ (姨媽的愛情故事) are very interesting.

3 (Dawn Knox 的兩隻貓) _____ like to play on those boxes.

4 "Is there any money inside _____ (Joy 的口袋)?" asked Penny.

5 The _____ (鳥籠) is small.

6 (Jane 的玩具) _____ are in the box.

7 That is _____ (Sherlock Holmes 的帽子).

trunk

8 A skunk is hiding in _____ (Mona 的汽車行李箱裡) .

Chapter

9 some, any, no, every, all

1

當名詞數量不確定的時候，經常會使用 some（一些）或 any（任何；一些／絲毫）來修飾。some 和 any 後面可以接**不可數名詞**或**複數名詞**。

some 一些
any 任何

+

不可數名詞

複數名詞

some apples 一些蘋果
any apples 任何蘋果
some games 一些遊戲
any games 任何遊戲
some eggs 一些蛋
any eggs 任何蛋
some cellphones 一些手機
any cellphones 任何手機

some apple juice 一些蘋果汁
any apple juice 任何蘋果汁
some beef 一些牛肉
any beef 任何牛肉
some money 一些錢
any money 任何錢
some help 一些幫助
any help 任何幫助

2

some 和 any 指「一些；任何／絲毫」時，用法是相對的。any 常用在**疑問句**和**否定句**中，some 常用在**肯定句**中。

肯定句的用法：表示冰箱裡有一些柳橙汁。
- There is some orange juice in the refrigerator. 冰箱裡有一些柳橙汁。

否定句的用法：表示冰箱裡沒有任何柳橙汁。
- There isn't any orange juice in the refrigerator. 冰箱裡一點柳橙汁也沒有。

肯定句的用法：表示桌子上有一些梨子。
- There are some pears on the table. 桌上有一些梨子。

疑問句的用法：用來詢問桌子上有沒有任何梨子。
- Are there any pears on the table? 桌上有梨子嗎？

- There are some fish in the pond. 池塘裡有一些魚。 → 肯定句

- There aren't any fish in the pond. 池塘裡沒有魚。 → 否定句

- Are there any fish in the pond? 池塘裡有魚嗎？ → 疑問句

3

some 也常用來表示「請求」或「提供某物」，這兩種情況的**疑問句**要用 some，不用 any。

Can/Could I have . . .?

用來表示「請求」
（疑問句用 some）

April "Could I have some cheese, please?"

Raul "Sure. Help yourself."

愛波爾 「我可以吃一些起司嗎？」

勞爾 「可以啊，自己拿吧。」

Would you like . . . ?　　用來表示「提供某物」（疑問句用 some）

Dan Would you like some bubble gum?

Ann Yes, please.

丹　你要不要吃泡泡糖？

安　好啊，請給我一些吧。

4

any 可用在**肯定句**中，後面接**單數名詞**，表示「任何一個、每一個」，泛指所有的人或所有的物（everyone 或 everything）。

- Any teacher would be glad to have students like Jenny and Penny.
  任何一個老師都會很高興有像珍妮和潘妮那樣的學生。

- I am sure any student can pass that test.
  我確定任何一個學生都可以通過那個考試。

5

some 和 **any** 也可用作不定代名詞，代替重複的名詞，即後面不帶名詞。

Rita I have some strawberries.
Would you like some?　┌ = some strawberries

Rick No, thanks. I don't want any. I'm on a diet.　┌ = any strawberries

瑞塔　我有一些草莓。你要不要吃？

瑞克　不用，謝謝。我不想吃，我在節食。

6

no 表「否定」，等於「not any + 名詞」或「not a + 名詞」。no 後面一定要接名詞，可接**單數名詞**、**不可數名詞**或**複數名詞**。「no + 名詞」常用在 have/has 與 there is/are 之後。

no **garden** 沒有花園 →單數可數名詞（= not a garden）

no **cheese** 沒有起司 →不可數名詞（= not any cheese）

no **mistakes** 沒有錯誤 →複數名詞（= not any mistakes）

┌ 「no + 複數名詞」=「not any + 複數名詞」

- She has no friends in New York City.
  = She doesn't have any friends in New York City. 她在紐約市沒有朋友。

┌ 「no + 不可數名詞」=「not any + 不可數名詞」

- There's no soap in the bathroom.
  = There isn't any soap in the bathroom.
  洗手間裡沒有肥皂。　「no + 單數可數名詞」=「not a + 單數可數名詞」

- It's a beautiful house, but there is no swimming pool.
  = It's a beautiful house, but it doesn't have a swimming pool.
  那幢房子很漂亮，但是沒有游泳池。

7

every（每一個）和 **all**（全部的）的用法不同：

every ＋ 單數名詞 ＋ 單數動詞

- Every house on Tenth Street looks the same.
  第十街上的每一幢房子看起來都一樣。

- Does every country have earthquakes?
  每一個國家都會地震嗎？

all ＋ 複數名詞 ＋ 複數動詞

- All the houses on Tenth Street look the same. 第十街上所有的房子看起來都一樣。

- Do all countries have earthquakes?
  所有國家都會地震嗎？

Dean How often do you surf the Internet?

Anne Almost every day.

狄恩　你多久上網一次？　every day 表示「頻率」，意思是「每一天」。

安　幾乎每天。

Judy How long did you surf the Internet yesterday?　all day 表示「延續時間」，意思是「整天」。

Leo Almost all day.

茱蒂　你昨天上網多久？

李歐　幾乎整天都在網上。

1 請自右欄中選出正確的答案，完成句子。

_____	**1**	There is an	**a** any sugar in my coffee.
_____	**2**	There isn't	**b** some beef in the fridge.
_____	**3**	There are	**c** any apples on the tree?
_____	**4**	Are there	**d** orange on the table.
_____	**5**	There is	**e** some tomatoes in the basket.

2 請用括弧內的詞彙，改寫句子。

1 There isn't any good news about our nation's economy. (no)

_____

2 There are no hangers in the closet. (any)

_____

3 There isn't any evidence to prove she was involved in the crime. (no)

_____

4 She has put no money in the bank. (any)

_____

3 用 **no**、**any** 或 **some** 填空（有些句子可能有兩個答案）。

1 Dee, would you like _____ milk tea?

2 Kirk needs _____ help with his math homework.

3 "Are there _____ grapes left?" asked Clair.

4 Joan never reads _____ text messages on her cellphone.

5 I have _____ good news about Ms. King's diamond rings.

6 There aren't _____ green leaves on the tree in my backyard.

7 Ed can make _____ great French bread.

8 Ann Could I have _____ milk, please?

Dan Sorry, there is _____ milk in the fridge.

9 Oh, we need _____ gas.

10 Do you have _____ tomatoes and potatoes?

4 用 every 或 all 填空。

1 Kay usually drinks three cups of coffee _____ day.

2 "How often do you visit your grandma in Paris?"
   "_____ year. Usually in July."

3 Should _____ the countries in the world seek peace?

4 I didn't sleep well last night because the dog next door barked _____ night.

5 _____ room in our hotel has a balcony and an oceanfront view.

6 Yesterday it snowed _____ day.

Chapter

10 much, many, a lot of, (a) little, (a) few, enough

---

1 much, many（很多）

much 和 many 是表示「很多」的數量形容詞，常用在**疑問句**和**否定句**中。
much 修飾**不可數名詞**，**many** 修飾**複數名詞**。

much + 不可數名詞   much money 很多錢

many + 複數名詞   many books 很多書

	疑問句	否定句
不可數	How much milk is there in the fridge? 冰箱裡還有多少牛奶？	→There isn't much milk. 沒有多少牛奶了。
可數	How many eggs do we have? 我們有多少雞蛋？	→There aren't many eggs left. 剩下沒幾個雞蛋了。

---

2 a lot of（很多）

❶ much 不用於肯定句。**肯定句**通常用 **a lot of**，可修飾**複數名詞**或**不可數名詞**。

a lot of + 複數名詞 / 不可數名詞

a lot of books 很多書

a lot of money 很多錢

	疑問句（用 much 或 many）	肯定句（用 a lot of）
不可數	How much orange juice is there in the fridge? 冰箱裡有多少柳橙汁？	→There's a lot of orange juice. 還有很多柳橙汁。
可數	How many tomatoes are there in the fridge? 冰箱裡有多少番茄？	→There're a lot of tomatoes. 有很多番茄。

「a lot of + 不可數名詞」（food）→使用單數動詞 is
• There is a lot of **food** in the fridge. 冰箱裡有很多食物。

「a lot of + 複數名詞」（people）→使用複數動詞 were
• There were a lot of **people** at the party. 聚會上有很多人。

❷ a lot of 除了用於肯定句取代 much 和 many 之外，也可以用於**否定句**和**疑問句**。
  many 則有時也可以用於肯定句。

┌─ 肯定句
- Amy is not lonely. She has many / a lot of friends. 艾咪不孤單，她有很多朋友。

┌─ 疑問句
- Did Sue ask you many / a lot of questions? 蘇問了你很多問題嗎？

┌─ 否定句
- He doesn't have many / a lot of supporters. 他沒有很多支持者。

3

a little（一點） 為肯定意義，表示「有一點」。	┌→ some money, but not much • I have only a little money to spend on the trip to Egypt. 我只有一些錢，去埃及旅遊的時候可以用。
a few（一些） 為肯定意義，表示「有一些」。	┌→ some friends, but not many • She has only a few friends at school. 她在學校只有幾個朋友。
little, few（幾乎沒有） 為否定意義，表示「幾乎沒有」。	┌→ almost no money • Amy has little money left after paying all of her bills. She is almost bankrupt. 艾咪繳了所有的帳單後就沒什麼錢了，差不多破產了。 ┌→ almost no friends • He has few friends and often feels lonely. 他沒有什麼朋友，常感到孤單。
a few/few + 複數名詞	• Dinner will be ready in a few minutes. 再過幾分鐘晚餐就準備好了。
a little/little + 不可數名詞	• Trish knows a little English. 翠希只懂一點點英文。
enough（足夠的） enough + 複數可數名詞 enough + 不可數名詞	• We've got enough tomatoes. 我們有足夠的番茄。 • There isn't enough time for Clair to cut your hair. 克萊兒沒有足夠的時間幫你剪頭髮了。

4

too much 和 **too many**（太多）可以用於**肯定句**。

┌→ too much + 不可數名詞（traffic）
- There was too much traffic on Highway 75 today.
  今天 75 號公路上很塞。

┌→ too many + 複數可數名詞（spelling mistakes）
- Pam made too many spelling mistakes on her English exam.
  潘姆在英文考試中拼錯很多字。

much、many、a lot、a little、a few、enough 可以用來替代重複出現的名詞，當代名詞使用，在句中作主詞和受詞。

→ a lot = a lot of ice cream
- We have some ice cream, but not a lot. 我們有一些冰淇淋，但不多。

→ enough = enough trouble
- We don't need any more trouble. We've already got enough.
  我們不需要更多的麻煩，我們的麻煩已經夠多了。

→ much = much snow
- There's some snow on the roof, but not much. 屋頂上有一些雪，但不太多。

- A lot of time has been wasted. 浪費了許多時間。→ a lot 作主詞時，若指複數名詞，動詞用複數；若指不可數名詞，動詞用單數。

- Many of us are bilingual. 我們中間許多人會說兩種語言。
  └→ many 作主詞時，動詞用複數。

- Much/Little is expected from you if you join that club. → much 和 little 作主詞時，動詞用單數。
  如果你加入那個俱樂部，對你的期望會很高的／對你沒有什麼期望的。

PRACTICE

1 選出正確的答案。

_____ **1** "Don't worry. There is _____ food for everyone," said Clair.
  a enough b a few c much d many

_____ **2** She asked too _____ questions during the movie.
  a much b enough c a few d many

_____ **3** Sue doesn't watch TV because almost every evening she has too _____ homework to do.
  a little b much c many d a lot of

_____ **4** I only knew _____ people at the party last night.
  a a little b a lot of c many d a few

_____ **5** Sue still has too _____ homework to do and too _____ new words to teach Lulu.
  a much, much b many, much c much, enough d much, many

_____ **6** We have only _____ tea, two frozen pizzas, and a few eggs. Let's go to the supermarket.
  a a few b many c a little d much

7 Ann How _____ money do you have with you?

Dan I've _____ cash and three credit cards.

a much, a lot of b many, a lot of c much, a few d many, enough

8 "I want to travel around the world after I graduate from college."

"It will cost you _____ money to do that."

a much b many c a lot of d little

9 I'm very hungry now. I didn't eat _____ this morning.

a much b many c a lot of d little

10 Lee isn't healthy. He watches too _____ TV

and doesn't get _____ exercise.

a many, a lot of b much, a little

c much, enough d little, a few

---

2 請依括弧內的中文提示，在空格內填入正確的英文。（有些句子可能有兩個或多個答案。）

1 Do you have _____ Australian friends?（很多）

2 Kay caused _____ trouble today.（太多）

3 _____ students in my class can read more than 300 English words per minute.（幾個）

4 Would you like _____ sugar in your tea?（一點）

5 She has a lot of female pals but doesn't have _____ male friends.（很多）

6 She doesn't get _____ fresh air and sunshine.（充足的）

7 _____ roses do you want to buy for your girlfriend?（多少）

8 There was _____ milk in the container. It was almost empty.（少的）

9 _____ many stores in this city that sell that type of cellphone.（有）

10 Lynn, don't let _____ UV sunlight damage your skin.（過量的）

Chapter 11 both, either, neither, most, several

1

both、either、neither 都用來指「兩件事或物，或是兩個人」。

both（兩者都）

both + 複數名詞（+ 複數動詞）

- Both his eyes were injured. 他的雙眼都受傷了。

- Both my headlights stopped working.
  我的兩個前車燈都壞了。

  注意 both 修飾兩個人或物；all 修飾三個或三個以上的人或物，
  也可以修飾不可數名詞。
  - both students 這兩位學生都
  - both Mary and Larry 瑪麗和勞瑞都
  - all students 所有學生都
  - all the time 無時無刻不

either（兩者之中任一的）

either + 單數名詞（+ 單數動詞）

- "There are two roads from here to the airport.
  Which road should we take?"
  "Either road is fine with me."
  「從這裡去機場有兩條路可以走，我們應該走哪一條？」
  「哪一條都可以。」

neither（兩者都不）

neither + 單數名詞（+ 單數動詞）

Mary Do you want to go to school in Britain or America?
Larry Neither country appeals to me. I want to study
in Canada.
Mary 你想去英國還是美國念書？
Larry 這兩個國家我都不是很想去。我是想去加拿大念書。

2

most（大多數的／大部分的）

most + 複數名詞 + 複數動詞

most + 不可數名詞 + 單數動詞

- Most universities have their own admissions policy.
  多數大學都有自己的入學政策。

- Are most stores open in downtown Chicago on
  Christmas Day?
  芝加哥商業區大多數的商店，耶誕節那天都有營業嗎？

- He thinks most gambling is based on luck.
  他認為大部分賭博都靠運氣。

- Most money is contaminated with germs.
  大部分錢都被細菌污染了。

3

several（數個）

several + 複數名詞（+ 複數動詞）

- Several **people were** injured in the bus accident **yesterday.** 昨天的公車事故中有好幾個人受傷。

- **The Eagle Airline strike lasted for** several **days.** 老鷹航空公司的罷工持續了好幾天。

> 注意 both、either、neither、most、several 與 all、some、any、many 等一樣，既可作形容詞，修飾名詞，也可作不定代名詞，起名詞的作用，後面常接「of + 名詞」，在句中作主詞或受詞〔參見 Chapter 19 和 Chapter 20〕。

4

總結：數量形容詞與不可數名詞、可數單數名詞和複數名詞在一起時的用法：

| a lot of / enough / most | + | 不可數名詞 | → | a lot of traffic 交通擁擠 / enough money 足夠的錢 / most traffic 大部分交通 |

| a lot of / enough / most | + | 複數名詞 | → | a lot of people 很多人 / enough eggs 足夠的雞蛋 / most people 多數人 |

| much / a little | + | 不可數名詞 | → | much juice 許多汁 / a little time 一點時間 |

| many / a few | + | 複數名詞 | → | many robotic toys 許多機器人玩具 / a few female friends 幾個女性朋友 |

| every / either / neither | + | 單數可數名詞 | → | every student 每一個學生 / either boy（兩者中）任一個男孩 / neither city 兩個城市都不 |

| both / several | + | 複數名詞 | → | both boys 兩個男孩 / several students 好幾個學生 |

both boys
兩個男孩

several students
好幾個學生

| all / no | + | 複數名詞 | → | all nations 所有的國家 / no cars 沒有汽車 |

| all / no | + | 單數可數名詞 | → | all night 整夜 / no garden 沒有花園 |

| all / no | + | 不可數名詞 | → | all the time 始終 / no time 沒有時間 |

all the time
始終

no time
沒有時間

1 | 用 **both** 與 **neither**，根據圖片完成下列句子。

my brothers

1 _____ strong.

2 _____
any hair on his head.

to the train station

3 _____
going to the train station.

9 x 8 x 3 = 79
9 x 8 x 3 = 89

4 _____ correct.

5 _____
filled with food.

6 _____ swollen.

2 選出正確答案。

1 _____ of calming down quickly.
- a There is much way
- b There are most ways
- c There are several ways
- d There are a little ways

2 _____ in the United States saw a drop in unemployment during May.
- a Every cities
- b Most cities
- c Both cities
- d Neither cities

3 _____ my blog and email account have been hacked.
- a Enough
- b Most
- c Several
- d Both

4 _____ sister is tall.
- a Neither
- b Both
- c All
- d Several

5 Dan Which city do you like better, San Francisco or Honolulu?
- Ann _____ city impresses me. I like London.
- a Most
- b Both
- c No
- d Neither

6 Applications for this management position are welcome from _____ sexes.
- a both
- b neither
- c either
- d every

7 His huge house has eighteen rooms, and the police searched _____ one of them.
- a both
- b a lot of
- c all
- d every

8 You can exchange your money in _____ banks.
- a enough
- b every
- c much
- d most

9 I have trouble with _____ feet.
- a neither
- b either
- c most
- d both

Chapter 12 主格代名詞

1

❶ **主格代名詞**是在句中作**主詞**用的代名詞。主格代名詞依人稱、單複數而有不同，共有下列幾種：

	單數		複數	
第一人稱	I	I talked to Jim.	we	We talked to Jim.
第二人稱	you	You talked to Jim.	you	You talked to Jim.
第三人稱	he	He talked to Jim.	they	They talked to Jim.
	she	She talked to Jim.		
	it	It is a wonderful idea.		

❷ **主格代名詞**在句中做主詞。主格代名詞不能省略。

- He **bought a new computer.** 他買了一台新電腦。
- She **needs help from Lily.** 她需要莉莉的幫忙。
- They **informed me about what happened to Kay.** 他們把凱發生的事告訴了我。
- Jerome **isn't in the office today.** He's **at home.** 傑羅姆今天不在辦公室，他在家裡。
- She's **a lovely puppy.** 她是一隻可愛小狗。
  └── he 或 she 也可用來指動物或非生物，表示說話人的感情。

2 主格代名詞 it 的用法

❶ it 當作**虛主詞**使用：在說明「時間、日期（包含星期幾）、天氣、氣溫、距離」的句子中，常用 **it** 作為虛主詞。

1 時間
"What time is it?"
"It's 9 p.m."
「幾點了？」
「晚上九點。」

2 日期
"What day is it?"
"It's Monday."
「今天是星期幾？」
「星期一。」

3 天氣

• Isn't it a beautiful rainy day!
多美的下雨天啊！

4 氣溫
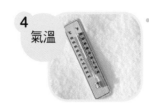

• It's below zero, and Lily is cold and hungry.
氣溫零度以下，莉莉又冷又餓。

5 距離

• It's five miles from here to the mall.
從這裡到購物中心有五英里遠。

❷ 如果某個人、事、物在上文中「已經被提及過」，或是「很明顯知道指的是哪一個」時，可以用 **it** 來指稱。

Ann　Who's that by the pond?
Dan　It's Mary Bond. ←它可以指人。
安　池塘旁邊的那個人是誰？
丹　是瑪麗・龐德。

● 它可以指動物。
↓
• It is a polar bear.
那是一頭北極熊。

● 它可以指物。
↓
It is his new electric car.
這是他的新電動車。

它可以指地方。
• Welcome to Bali for the sailboat race —it's a beautiful place.
歡迎來到峇里島參觀帆船比賽，這是一個美麗的地方。

❸ **it** 可用來辨認身份。

• It's your girlfriend on the phone. 你的女朋友打來的電話。

• Hi, it's me. 喂，是我。
└ 電話上表明身分時用它。

❹ **it** 可用作形式主詞；還可用在強調句型中，起強調作用。

┌──── 作形式主詞
• Is it possible to get there on time? 有可能準時到達那裡嗎？
┌──── 起強調作用
• It was Tom who gave you that nickname, not me.
是湯姆給你取的綽號，不是我給你取的。

1 請在空格處填上正確的主格代名詞。句首字母要大寫（有些題目的答案不只一個）。

☑ Are _____ hungry?

② Bali is an Indonesian island. _____ is a lovely tourist destination.

③ Margo is my girlfriend. _____ lives in Chicago.

④ Dennis is my brother. _____ loves to play tennis.

⑤ I haven't seen my old friends Coco and Sam for a long time. _____ moved to Italy five years ago.

⑥ _____ is Chicago that she's going to, not New York.

2 請在空格處填上 I、you、he、she、it、we 或 they。句首字母要大寫。
（有些題目的答案不只一個）

① _____ is snowing.

② _____ is expensive.

③ _____ are old but healthy and happy.

 4 _____ have a headache.

 5 _____ is climbing that tall tree.

 6 Look! _____ are mad at each other.

 7 _____ is playing a computer game again.

 8 _____ are a lot stronger than me.

Chapter

13 代名詞所有格限定詞／代名詞所有格形容詞

1

❶ 「限定詞」是放在名詞前面，修飾名詞用的詞彙，相當於形容詞的意思。
代名詞所有格限定詞依人稱和單複數分為下列幾種：

		單數		複數
第一人稱	my	I like my cat.	our	We like our cats.
第二人稱	your	You like your cat.	your	You like your cats.
第三人稱	his	He likes his cat.		
	her	She likes her cat.	their	They like their cats.
	its	The cat is playing with its toy. 那隻貓在玩牠的玩具。		

❷ **代名詞所有格限定詞**用於名詞前面，表示「物品的主人」或「人與人之間的關係」。
因為具有形容詞的作用，也稱為**代名詞所有格形容詞**（或「形容詞性物主代名詞」）。

• **That is her cat.** 這是她的貓咪。

　　　　　　　┌→ your cellphone，即是指「Joan 的手機」。
• **Joan, may I use your cellphone?** 裘安，我可以用你的手機嗎？

　　　　　　　┌→ his grandma，即是指「Jerome 的奶奶」。
• **Jerome and his grandma are going to fly to Rome.** 傑羅姆和他的奶奶要搭飛機去羅馬。

　　　┌→ our 指「我們的」。
• **These are our suitcases.** 這些是我們的手提箱。

　　　　　　　　┌→ its 在這裡指「狗狗的」。
• **What does that little dog have in its mouth?** 那隻小狗嘴裡咬的是什麼？

　　　　　　　　　　　┌→ their 在這裡指「我朋友們的」。
• **Those are police officers, and they are my friends. That's their car.**
那些是警察，他們是我的朋友。那是他們的車。

❸ whose 是**疑問所有格限定詞**，意思是「誰的」。

Paul	Whose dirty socks are those?
Lisa	They are Tom's .
保羅	那些是誰的髒襪子？
麗莎	是湯姆的襪子。

Tom's = Tom's socks

2

代名詞所有格限定詞的後面一定要接**名詞**，其拼寫方式不會因後面接的名詞是單數或複數而有所不同。

┌─my 不會因為後面是接單數或複數名詞而變化─┐

單數   複數

my friend 我的朋友   → my friends 我的朋友們

her cute puppy 她的可愛小狗   → her cute puppies 她的可愛小狗們

單數   複數

└─ her 不會因為後面是接單數或複數名詞而變化 ─┘

- Our <u>friend</u> gave us a purple beach umbrella.
  我們的朋友給了我們一把紫色的海灘傘。

- Our <u>friends</u> gave us a used electric motor scooter.
  我們的朋友們給了我們一輛中古的電動摩托車。

3

注意 he's 和 his 以及 it's 和 its 的區別。

his 「他的」	┌ his 是限定詞。 • His car is over there. 他的車在那裡。
he's = he is「他是」	┌ he's 是縮寫詞（= He is）。 • He's a police officer. 他是一名警察。
its 「它的」	┌ its 是限定詞。 • Its tail is short. 牠的尾巴很短。
it's = it is「它是」	┌ it's 是縮寫詞（= It is）。 • It's a dog. 牠是一隻狗。

1 在空格內填入 her、his、its、our、my 或 their。

1. I can't go out with Dirk tonight, because I haven't finished _____ homework.

2. Mike is a taxi driver, and this is _____ car.

3. Jean is a violinist, and that is _____ violin.

4. That horse belongs to Mr. Crown, and _____ tail is brown.

5. Mabel and I are table tennis players, and this is _____ new ping-pong table.

6. This is May and _____ husband Ray on _____ wedding day.

2 在空格內填入正確的所有格限定詞。

My first name is Lulu. **1** _____ last name is Waterloo. I'm fifteen years old. I'm from London. **2** _____ parents are both pilots. I don't have any sisters, but I have two brothers. **3** _____ names are Tom and Sam. Tom is an artist, and Sam is an English teacher. They are both married. **4** _____ wives are identical twins. **5** _____ names are Tina and Tia. They are Italians. How about you? What's **6** _____ first name? What's **7** _____ last name? Could you tell me something about **8** _____ family?

3 自右欄中選出與左欄相應的句子，填入空格中。

_____ 1 Jason is my brother.

_____ 2 We are taxi drivers.

_____ 3 They're police officers.

_____ 4 She's a singer.

_____ 5 This is my rabbit.

a Her name is A-mei.

b Their car is black and has a big red light on its roof.

c Our cars are yellow.

d Those are his students.

e Its ears are big.

4 請選出正確的答案填入空格中（句首字母需大寫）。

1 | its | it's |

a I like New York because _____ an exciting city.

b That big dog is wagging _____ tail.

2 | his | he's |

a Mike is my older brother. _____ a graduate student at Harvard University.

b _____ new electric car is very inexpensive to drive.

3 | her | my |

a I saw Mary walking _____ dog.

b My parents are divorced, and I live with _____ paternal grandparents.

4 | his | its |

a Look at that beautiful tree. _____ leaves are beginning to fall. Summer is truly over.

b I met our neighbor Bret Black yesterday, but I haven't met _____ wife yet.

Chapter

14 受格代名詞

1

❶ **受格代名詞**依人稱和單複數分為下列幾種：

		單數		複數
第一人稱	me	Jim talked to me.	us	Jim talked to us.
第二人稱	you	Jim talked to you.	you	Jim talked to you.
第三人稱	him	Jim talked to him.		
	her	Jim talked to her.	them	Jim talked to them.
	it	I like it.		

❷ **受格代名詞**在句中做**動詞**或**介系詞**的受詞，因此必須放在**動詞**或**介系詞**的後面。

介系詞 + 受格代名詞

at（在）
for（為）
to（對；到）
with（和）
……

動詞 + 受格代名詞

help（幫助）
like（喜歡）
see（看到）
teach（教導）
……

┌→ 動詞 let 後面接受格代名詞 me。
　┌→ 動詞 introduce 後面接受格代名詞 you。
　　┌→ 介系詞 to 後面接受格代名詞 her。

• **Here comes my sister Mary.** Let me introduce you to her.
我的妹妹瑪麗來了，讓我把你介紹給她。

┌→ 動詞 take 後面接受格代名詞 them，them 指雙胞胎 Jim 和 Tim。

• **The twins Jim and Tim Sun are very healthy, and every day their parents** take them **to the gym.**
孫家雙胞胎吉姆和迪姆很健康，他們的父母每天都會帶他們去體育館。

┌→ it 用作形式受詞。

• **I find** it **strange that Mary has fallen in love with that lazy Lee.**
我覺得很奇怪，瑪麗居然愛上了那個懶惰的李。

❸ **受格代名詞**可以指代前面提及的人、物、地方等,用來**避免重複**名詞。

┌─── him 在這裡指 Jim ──┐
- Where is Jim? We are looking for him . 吉姆在哪裡?我們在找他。

┌────── them 在這裡指 my parents ──┐
- My parents are flying to Florida. I'm going to see them off at the airport.
  我的父母要飛往佛羅里達,我要去機場給他們送行。

┌─── her 在這裡指 my wife ──┐
- My wife is fixing our car. I'm helping her. 我太太在修我們的車,我在幫她。

┌ them 在這裡指 those monkeys ┐
- Those monkeys seem cold. Look at them. 那些猴子看起來好像很冷,瞧瞧牠們。

❹ 受格代名詞通常不可以省略。

┌─► 不要省略 me。
- That bee stung me. 那隻蜜蜂叮了我。

┌─► 不要省略 you。
- The presents will be given to you on Christmas Day. 聖誕節那天就會把禮物拿給你了。

2

it、they 和 them 可以指物。
- It's beautiful. I want to buy it. 好漂亮喔,我想買這件。
- They are beautiful. I want to buy them. 這些好漂亮,我全部都想買。

3

it、them 如果在動詞之後作直接受詞(物)時,it 和 them 後面要加介系詞 to,再接間接受詞(人)。

動詞 + **it / them** + to + 人
　　　　↳ 物(直接受詞)　　　　↳ 間接受詞

　　　　　　　　　→ it 指「物」,是直接受詞。
- I'd like to read this novel. Can you lend it to me, please?
  我想看這本小說,你可以借我嗎?
　　　　　　　　　　→ me 指「人」,是間接受詞。

　　　　　　　　　　→ them 指「物」,是直接受詞。
- Louise would love to read these novels. Can you lend them to her, please?
  露易絲想看這些小說,你可以借她嗎?
　　　　　　　　　　↳ her 指「人」,是間接受詞。

4

在口語中,受格代名詞可作**主詞**,或用在連綴動詞後面作**主詞補語**。
- "I like sports." "Me too." 「我喜歡運動。」「我也是。」
- "Who broke the window?" "It was her, not me." 「是誰打破了窗戶?」「是她,不是我。」

1 請用下列句型，看圖回答問題。

I + like / don't like + him / her / it / them

1 Do you like Lady Gaga?

....

....

2 Do you like basketball?

....

....

3 Do you like pizza?

....

....

4 Do you like potatoes?

....

....

5 Do you like Superman?

....

....

6 Do you like jazz?

....

....

2 把括弧裡的中文翻譯成英文，完成下列句子。

1 Can Dee help _____? (我)

2 "_____ like to play computer games," said Mike. (我)

3 _____ needs a little help from me. (他)

4 Gus, please help _____. (我們)

5 This coat is for _____, and it's made out of artificial fur. (她)

6 Why is Kim going out with _____? He is such a lazy guy. (他)

3 選出正確的答案。

1 Kim told me | I that she did not like he | him.

2 You | Your can count on they | them to help us find Sue.

3 Coffee appeals to both Jenny and I | me.

4 They invited my | me wife and I | me to their | them party.

5 Mary and I | me will share an apple pie.

6 Jim is rude. I don't like him | them.

7 I can't find my glasses? Have you seen them | they?

8 Who is the woman in the pink dress? Do you know she | her?

9 We | Us can see Gus, but he | him can't see our | we | us hiding behind the bus.

10 I | Me love you | your. Do you love I | me?

4 將下列句子改寫為正確的句子。

1 I need copies of your pictures of the International Moon Base. Please email me.

   _____

2 Ann doesn't like dogs. She is afraid of it.

   _____

3 I want to talk to Gus, but he doesn't want to talk to her.

   _____

4 That's my money. Please give it back me.

   _____

5 "Does Bob like its new job?" "No, he doesn't like him."

   _____

Chapter 15 獨立所有格代名詞

1

獨立所有格代名詞有：

	單數	複數
第一人稱	mine	ours
第二人稱	yours	yours
第三人稱	his hers	theirs

2

獨立所有格代名詞（也稱為「名詞性物主代名詞」）用來替代重複出現的單數名詞和複數名詞，等於「代名詞所有格限定詞 + 名詞」，因此後面不需要再接名詞。

代名詞所有格限定詞 ＋ 名詞 → 獨立所有格代名詞（不接名詞）

It's my car.   It's mine.
It's our car.   It's ours.
It's your car.   It's yours.
It's his car.   It's his.
It's her car.   It's hers.
It's their car.   It's theirs.

獨立所有格代名詞用來替代重複出現的名詞。

His = His sports car

• **This is my sports car. His is black.**
這是我的跑車，他的是黑色的。

yours = your toothbrush

• **This toothbrush is yours, not mine.**
這把牙刷是你的，不是我的。

mine = my toothbrush

ours = our pears

• **Those pears are ours, not theirs.**
那些梨子是我們的，不是他們的。

theirs = their pears

mine = my teddy bears

• **These teddy bears are mine, not theirs.**
這些泰迪熊是我的，不是他們的。

theirs = their teddy bears

Maria Is this his cellphone or hers? 這是他的手機還是她的？

┌→ hers = her cellphone

Brian It's his. 是他的。

└→ his = his cellphone

his 是代名詞所有格形容詞（his cellphone），也是獨立所有格代名詞（It's his.），兩種用法的拼寫相同。

Carol Is that your suitcase? 那是你的行李箱嗎？

Daniel No, this brown one is mine. 不是，這個棕色的才是我的。

└→ mine = my suitcase

Karen Whose USB memory stick is this? 這是誰的隨身碟？

Jeff It's mine. 是我的。

└→ mine = my memory stick

- I have my passport with me, but Mike doesn't have his.
我有帶護照，但是邁克沒有帶。

└→ his = his passport

3

獨立所有格代名詞也常用在「. . . of + 獨立所有格代名詞」的句型裡，of 前面的名詞可以是單數，也可以是複數。

| 名詞（複數或單數） | + | **of** | + | 獨立所有格代名詞 |

a friend				mine
some friends		of		his
this lovely puppy				hers
these lovely puppies				yours
				ours

- A friend of <u>mine</u> asked me to take care of her kids for a week.
我的一個朋友要我幫忙照顧她的孩子一個禮拜。

- Amy introduced me to <u>some friends of hers</u>.
艾咪介紹我給她的一些朋友認識。

1 請依括弧內的提示，用正確的獨立所有格代名詞填空，完成下列句子。

1. That is Anna's problem, not _____. （他的）

2. This frog of _____ can hop over that dog. （我的）

3. Is this new electric car really _____? （我們的）

4. I have an electric motor scooter, and so does Mary. Mine is a year old, and _____ is new. （她的）

5. This is my wallet, not _____. （你的）

2 用獨立所有格代名詞改寫下列句子。

1. That is his sports car.

   That sports car is his.

2. This is our apartment.

   _____

3. "This is my new house," said the dog.

   _____

4. That is not my backpack. I left mine at home.

   _____

[5] This isn't our room. Ours is 504, not 404.

_____

[6] Those are her cows.

_____

[7] Is this your coat? —No, it isn't mine.

_____

3 請判斷下列句子是否正確，正確打 ✓，不正確打 ×，並寫出正確句子。

[1] Sue went out for dinner with some friends of her.

☐ _____

[2] It's yours problem, not mine.

☐ _____

[3] I'm going on a trip to Australia with a friend of me.

☐ _____

[4] My hands were very cold, and his were warm.

☐ _____

16 指示代名詞 this, that, these, those

1

this、that、these、those 是**指示代名詞**。當某物或某人在說話者的**附近**時，用 this 或 these 表示；某物或某人距離說話者**較遠**時，用 that 或 those 表示。this、that 用於**單數名詞**前面，these、those 用於**複數名詞**前面。

所指的對象就在這裡或在附近。

this 單數

that 單數

所指的對象在較遠處或不在附近。

• This **is a gray dog.**
這是一隻灰狗。

• That **is a white dog.**
那是一隻白狗。

所指的對象就在這裡或在附近。

these 複數

those 複數

所指的對象在較遠處或不在附近。

• These **are gray dogs.**
這些是灰狗。

• Those **are white dogs.**
那些是白狗。

• That **is a boat.**
那是一艘船。

• This **is my friend Joe.** 這是我朋友喬。

Greg **Who is** this? →靠近說話者的那個人。
Amy This **is my baby Liz.**
桂格 這位是誰？
愛咪 這位是我的寶寶莉茲。

- These **cheese sandwiches** are for our lunch. 這些起司三明治是我們的午餐。→靠近說話者的那些三明治。
- Is **that** a police officer in that car? 那輛車子裡的人是警察嗎？→遠離說話者的那個警察。
- **Those** are Paul's baseballs. 那些是保羅的棒球。→遠離說話者的那些棒球。

2

this、that、these、those 可以作**指示形容詞**，放在名詞前面，也可以作**指示代名詞**，後面沒有名詞。

指示形容詞（放在名詞前）
- **This pizza** is delicious. 這個披薩香噴噴的。
- Who is **that girl**? 那個女孩是誰？
- How much are **these shoes**? 這鞋子多少錢？
- **Those teddy bears** are cute. 那些玩具熊很可愛。

指示代名詞（後面沒有名詞）
- → **This** is delicious. 這個好香啊。
- → Who is **that**? 那是誰？
- → How much are **these**? 這些多少錢？
- → **Those** are cute teddy bears. 那些是可愛的玩具熊。

- **This** is a clock. **This clock** wakes me up. 這是一座時鐘，這座鐘叫我起床。

Joan Who is **this little girl**?
Bill **This** is my little sister Kris.
瓊安 這個小女孩是誰？
比爾 這是我的小妹克麗絲。

3

that 可以指「已經發生的某件事」或「某人剛才說話的內容」。

- **That** was really a wonderful trip. 那真是一次絕妙的旅程。

Jim I'm sorry to be so late. 對不起，我遲到了。
Mary **That**'s all right. 沒關係。

Ruth Are you in love with Sue? 你愛上蘇了嗎？
Jay No, I'm not. Where did you get **that** idea? 沒有啊，你怎麼會這麼想？

Jill Tom and I are going to get married next week. 湯姆和我下週要結婚了。
Tim Oh, **that**'s great! 喔，太好了！

4

「this is . . .」（我是……）和「is that . . . ?」（你是……嗎？）是常見的**電話用語**。this 表示「這一方」，that 指「對方」。

- Hello, **this** is Dan. 喂，我是丹。
- Hello, is **that** Mary Black? My name is Jane Brown. 喂，你是瑪莉・布萊克嗎？我是珍・布朗。

在美式英語中，常講：
Hello, are you Mary Black? My name is Jane Brown.

5

為避免重複，that、those 可用在比較級中，指代上下文提到過的物或事。

- Mangoes are more delicious here than **those** in my hometown. 這裡的芒果比我家鄉的芒果味道更美味。
- The climate in Florida is definitely warmer than **that** in Michigan. 佛羅里達的氣候當然比密西根的氣候暖和。

1 請將左欄句子的前半與右欄句子的後半連接，構成完整句子。

1. This is a •   • ⓐ alligator.
2. That's •   • ⓑ is a picture of Mars.
3. That •   • ⓒ pine tree.
4. This is an •   • ⓓ robot.
5. This is a •   • ⓔ a houseboat.

2 依提示用 **this**、**that**、**these** 或 **those** 填空。

1.

_____ is my friend. He loves to play his guitar.

2.

"_____ is Mt. Fuji," declared Pat.

3.

Sid asked me, "Are _____ tall things over there pyramids?"

4

_____ picnic table belongs to Sue.

5

Joe's mom said, " _____ are two very nice cars."

6

_____ are my cats.

7

Are _____ your yo-yos?

8

_____ is a nice cow.

Chapter 17 代名詞 one, ones, none

1

one 用來替代前面已經提及的某個**單數可數名詞**，目的是為避免重複那個名詞。此時：

$$one = \frac{a}{an} + 單數可數名詞$$

- I need an excuse for why I am late. Can you come up with one?
  我需要一個遲到的理由，你能幫我想一個嗎？
  = an excuse

- I am making a peanut butter sandwich. Would you like one?
  我在做花生醬三明治，你要不要吃一個？
  = a peanut butter sandwich

2 **one 的常見用語**

this one or that one

- Which skirt do you want? This one or that one?
  你要哪一件裙子？這一件還是那一件？

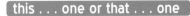

this . . . one or that . . . one

- Which motor scooter is yours? This blue one or that red one?
  哪一輛速可達摩托車是你的？這輛藍色的還是那輛紅色的？

the one
Alex Which hotel are you staying at? 你住在哪家飯店？
Andrea The one next to the hospital. 醫院旁邊的那一家。

the . . . one
- Do you like the pink dress or the green one?
  你喜歡這件粉紅色的洋裝，還是那件綠色的？

a/an . . . one
- After checking eight hotel rooms, we finally found a clean one.
  我們看過飯店的八個房間之後，終於找到一間乾淨的。

another one
- That piece of cheesecake was very tasty. I'm going to have another one. 那塊起司蛋糕很好吃，我還想吃一塊。

3

ones 用來替代重複出現的**複數名詞**。

ones = stores / apples/flowers . . .
- They are going to replace those small stores with large ones.
  他們要修建大商店來取代那些小商店。

| these/those
（通常不接 ones） | • **Which flowers do you want?** These or those?
你想要哪些花？這些還是那些？ |

| the ones | Lisa **Which** DVDs **are yours?** 哪些 DVD 是你的？
Kevin The ones **in the bookcase are mine.** 書櫃裡的那些 DVD 是我的。 |

| these/those . . .
ones
= the . . . ones | Mark **I would like to buy 15 pounds of** apples. 我想買 15 磅蘋果。
Pearl **Do you want** the **red** ones **or** the **green** ones?
= Do you want these **red** ones **or** those **green** ones?
你想要這些紅的還是那些綠的？ |

| some . . . ones | • **My blouses are all old. I'm going to buy** some **new** ones.
我的上衣都舊了，我要買一些新的。 |

4

one 和 **ones** 只能替代**可數名詞**，如果是不可數名詞，還是必須重複出現。

• **The store didn't have any fresh milk, so I bought some canned** milk.
那家商店沒有賣鮮奶，於是我買了一些罐裝牛奶。

⌐ milk 是不可數名詞，
所以要再重複出現。

5

疑問句中用 **which one** 或 **which ones**。

⌐→ = Which flavors

• **We have ice cream in eight flavors.** Which ones **do you want for your children?**
我們的霜淇淋有八種味道。你想要給你孩子們買哪一些味道的霜淇淋？

• **Look at these three dresses. Aren't they pretty?** Which one **do you like best?**
你看那三條裙子，好好看喔！你最喜歡哪一條？

⌐→ = Which dress

---

6 ┤ none 與 no one 比較 ├

❶ **none** 的意思是「一點也沒有」、「一個也沒有」，可以指**物**或人。

Betty **How many friends did you make while traveling in India?**
你在印度旅行時交了多少朋友？
Joseph None. 一個也沒有。
⌐→ 指人

Betty **How much money do you have on you?** 你身上有多少錢？
Joseph None. 沒有半毛錢。
⌐→ 指物

❷ **no one** 表示「沒有人」，等於 **nobody**，只能指人，不能指物〔參見 Chapter 18〕。

Betty **Who wants to go to a movie with Jim tonight?** 今晚，誰想跟吉姆一起去看電影？
Joseph No one. 沒有人想去。
⌐→ = Nobody.

為避免同一名詞重複，可用 one 和 it 來代替前面提及的某個**單數可數名詞**。it 代替上文提及的那件**特指**的事物，**one** 則指前面提及的**同類**事物，但不是同一件。

it 代替前一句中提到的 beautiful dress。

- This is a <u>beautiful dress</u>. I want to buy it. 這件洋裝很漂亮，我想買下來。

one 指前面提及的同類物品，但不是同一件洋裝。

- <u>Your dress</u> is lovely. I want to buy one like yours.
  你這件洋裝真漂亮，我也想買一件像這樣的洋裝。

PRACTICE

1 請用 **one** 或 **ones** 填空，完成對話。

1 Dan　Those are my DVDs.

　　Ann　Which _____? The _____ on the couch?

　　Dan　No, the _____ on the desk.

2 Dan　Look at these swimsuits. Which _____ do you like best?

　　Ann　Well, I guess I like the blue and green checkered _____ .

　　　　The black _____ is also pretty good.

　　Dan　I think this blue and white stripped _____ would look great on you.

2 請用 **one** 或 **ones** 填空，並寫出 one 或 ones 指代的單字。

1 Do you like these long dresses more than you like those short _____ ?

2 The envelope is too small. I need a big _____ ?

3 Of these four singers, which _____ do you like the best?

Madonna　　　　Rain　　　　A-Mei　　　Leehom Wang

4 Among those three famous movies stars, which _____
do you admire the most?

---

3 請判斷下列句子是否正確，正確打 ✓，不正確打 ✗，並寫出正確句子。

1 We have 5 types of juice. Which ones do you want for your birthday party?
☐ _____

2 "Small mistakes tend to lead to large ones," said the American novelist
David Baldacci.
☐ _____

3 I prefer artificial fur. I never get my wife anything made of real one.
☐ _____

4 "Would you like to have a sports car?"
"No, I don't need one sports car."
☐ _____

5 "Waitress, these cups are not clean."
"Oh, sorry! Here is a clean one."
☐ _____

6 She asked for some more coffee, but there was no one left.
☐ _____

Chapter 18

不定代名詞 something, anything, somebody, anybody 等，以及不定副詞或名詞 somewhere, anywhere 等

1

		some-	any-	no-	every-
代名詞（人物）	-body	somebody 某人	anybody 任何人	nobody 沒有人	everybody 每個人
代名詞（人物）	-one	someone 某人	anyone 任何人	no one 沒有人	everyone 每個人
代名詞（事物）	-thing	something 某事／物	anything 任何事／物	nothing 沒有事／物	everything 每件事／物
副詞／名詞（場所）	-where	somewhere 某處	anywhere 任何地方	nowhere 任何地方都不	everywhere 到處

通常用於肯定句

通常用於否定句和疑問句

* 這兩組詞彙的用法區別，跟 some 和 any 的用法區別一樣〔參見 Chapter 9〕。

- **There's** somebody **at our door.**
  門口有人。

- **I've** something **important to tell Sue.** 我有很重要的事要告訴蘇。
  → something、anything、nothing 等被形容詞修飾時，形容詞要放在其後面。

- **Don't depend on** anyone **for** anything.
  無論什麼事都不要依靠任何人。→ 否定句

- **Have you seen Claire** anywhere?
  你有沒有在哪裡看到克萊兒？→ 疑問句

2

somebody、someone、something 用於疑問句時，表示「請求」或「提供支援或物品」。

- **Could** somebody **help us?** 有沒有人能幫我們？ → 表示「請求」

- **Would you like** something **to eat?** 你想吃點什麼嗎？ → 表示「提供物品」

something、anybody、nowhere 等字後面，經常接這種「**to + 動詞**」的不定詞形式，如：

anybody to talk to 任何可以說話的人
nowhere to go 沒有可以去的地方

3

anybody、anyone、anything、anywhere 如果用於**肯定句**，是表示「無論什麼人、什麼事、什麼東西、哪裡都可以」的意思。

- I am so thirsty that I'll drink almost anything. 我渴死了，什麼都可以喝。

- Anyone can solve this puzzle. 任何人都可以解出這個謎題。

4

字尾 -body 或 -one	→ 表示人物（使用 -body 和 -one 的意義完全相同）
字尾 -thing	→ 表示事或物
字尾 -where	→ 表示地方

└──→ -body 或 -one 的結尾，表示「人」。
- Everybody likes you. = Everyone likes you. 大家都喜歡你。

└──→ -thing 結尾，表示「事」。
- Dad looks sad. Is there anything wrong? 爸爸看起來很傷心，發生了什麼事？

└──→ -where 結尾，表示「地方」。
- My doll is nowhere to be found. 我的洋娃娃不見了。

5

everybody、everyone、everything、nothing、nobody 和 no one 等作**主詞**時，要用**單數動詞**。

- Is anybody hurt? 有人受傷嗎？
  └──────→ 使用單數動詞

- Everybody knows Daisy is a bit lazy. 大家都知道黛絲有點懶惰。

6

nobody、no one、nothing 屬於否定詞。在英語中，一個句子只能使用一個否定詞，不能使用雙重否定的句型，因此，nobody、no one、nothing 不能與其他否定詞（never、not 等）連用。

nobody = not + anybody

no one = not + anyone

nothing = not + anything

nowhere = not + anywhere

- There is no one in the office now.
  = There isn't anybody in the office now.
  現在辦公室裡一個人也沒有。

- "There's nowhere for me to go," cried Sue.
  = "There isn't anywhere for me to go," cried Sue.
  蘇說：「我沒有地方可以去。」

"There isn't nowhere for me to go," cried Sue.
這是錯誤用法，不可使用雙重否定。

1 請判斷下列句子是否正確，正確打 ✓，不正確打 ✕，並寫出正確句子。

1 I am not going anywhere.

☐ _____

2 There isn't nothing in our fridge.

☐ _____

3 I don't want to talk to nobody right now.

☐ _____

4 Jane thinks anybody can learn to fly an airplane.

☐ _____

5 Are everything OK with Kay?

☐ _____

6 Something terrible happened to Sue.

☐ _____

7 She isn't nowhere to be seen.

☐ _____

8 I have anything important to do today.

☐ _____

2 請用框內的詞彙填空，完成下列段落與會話。

1

| somewhere |
| anywhere |
| nowhere |
| everywhere |

Where is my dog Lulu? She is ❶_____ to be seen. I have been looking for her ❷_____ in the neighborhood, but I can't find her ❸_____ . I'm tired. I need to find ❹_____ to sit down and rest.

2

something
anything
nothing
everything

M = Mother
J = Jenny

M Would you like ❶_____ to eat or drink?
   I've got pizza, sandwiches, milk, orange juice, coffee,
   and tea.

J No, thanks. I don't want ❷_____ to eat
   or drink right now.

M Is there ❸_____ wrong? You've had
   ❹_____ to eat or drink the whole
   afternoon. You have been at the computer for hours.
   And you seem to be worried.

J ❺_____ is fine. I'm not hungry or
   thirsty at the moment. I am just busy with my school
   assignments.

M At least drink ❻_____ . Your school work
   is important, but you need to take care of your health.

3

somebody
anybody
nobody
everybody

W = Woman
O = Operator

W Hello! May I speak to ❶_____ in the
   principal's office?

O Sorry, Ms. There's ❷_____ in the office
   now. It's already 6:30 p.m. ❸_____ has
   left the office.

W But I must speak to ❹_____ today.
   It's important.

O I'm really sorry. There isn't ❺_____ here.
   Please call back tomorrow morning.

Chapter 19 all, some, most, any, none 搭配 of 片語的用法

1

all、most、some、any 和 no 可以作**數量形容詞**用，後面直接加**名詞**。這些形容詞的後面要接**複數名詞**或**不可數名詞**〔參見 Chapter 9 和 Chapter 11〕。

泛指的用法，是不限定特定範圍或對象；特指的用法，則是限定某一個範圍內的某一些人、事、物。

泛指的用法

| all most some any no | + | 複數名詞 不可數名詞 |

- All children **need to feel safe in school.**
  所有的孩子在學校都需要感到安全。

- Most cities **face the same problems.**
  多數城市面臨同樣的問題。

- Some books **are not worth reading.**
  有些書不值得一讀。

- She doesn't have any friends.
  她一個朋友也沒有。

- I have no money **on me.** 我身上沒有錢。

all 後面的 of 經常省略，常用「all the . . .」或「all my . . .」。

- She has lived in Rome all her life. 她一生都住在羅馬。

- You can fool all the people some of the time and some of the people all the time but you cannot fool all the people all the time. —Abraham Lincoln

  你可以偶而愚弄所有的人民，或是從頭到尾愚弄部分的人民，但你無法從頭到尾愚弄所有的人民。
  （美國第 16 任總統林肯）

all、most、some、any 也可以作**代名詞**用，而 no 的代名詞是 **none**。這些代名詞常和 **of** 連用，of 之後須先接 **the**、**this**、**those** 或所有格 **my**、**our** 等，再接**名詞**。

特指的用法

| all (of) most of some of any of none of | + | the this that these those my your her | + | 名詞 |

- All (of) the students **in my class passed the English exam.**
  我班上所有的學生都通過了英文考試。

- Most of the cities **on the list have one thing in common—terrible air pollution.**
  這張表所列出的城市多有一個共同點：空氣污染嚴重。

- Some of these books **are out of print.**
  這些書有一些已經絕版了。

- She doesn't want any of your money.
  她不想要你的任何一毛錢。

- None of her classmates **like/likes her.**
  她的同學沒有一個喜歡她。

「none of + 複數名詞」做主詞時，動詞可以用單數形式，也可以用複數形式。

2 no 與 none 的比較

no（數量形容詞）→ 修飾名詞，後面不接 of〔參見 Chapter 9〕。
none（代名詞）→ 不作形容詞，可單獨使用〔參見 Chapter 17〕，也可以與 of 連用。

• Should I marry a woman who has no friends? 我應該跟一個沒有朋友的女子結婚嗎？

• None of my friends have/has visited India. 我的朋友沒有人去過印度。

3

| all
most
some
any | + of + | the
my | + 複數
名詞 | → 作主詞時，動詞要用**複數動詞**。 |

└─ 複數動詞

• Most of my friends have traveled around the world.
我的朋友多數都到過世界各地旅行。

| all
most
some
any
none | + of + | the
his | + 不可數
名詞 | → 作主詞時，動詞要用**單數動詞**。 |

└─ 單數動詞

• Some of the money has been spent foolishly. 有一些錢被亂花了。

| none | + of + | the
her | + 複數
名詞 | → 作主詞時，動詞可以用複數動詞，也可以用
單數動詞（美式英語較常用複數動詞）。 |

└─ 複數動詞或單數動詞都可以

• None of the answers are/is correct. 沒有一個回答是正確的。

4

all、most、some、any 和 none，可以接 of，再接**複數人稱代名詞**或 it。

| all
most
some
any
none | + of + | us
them
you
it | | Mark Do you know all these people at the party?
Linda I know most of them, but not all of them.
馬克 你認識聚會上的所有人嗎？
琳達 大多數我都認識，但不是全部。

Mark Have you read any of these books? 你讀過這些書嗎？
Linda None of them. 都沒有讀過。 |

| all
~~most~~
some
any | + of + | us
them
you | → 作主詞時，動詞要用**複數動詞**。 |

┌→ *複數動詞*
• Do any of you **want** to go to the movie theater tonight? 你們今晚有人想看電影嗎？

| none | + of + | us
them
you | → 作主詞時，動詞可用**複數動詞**，也可以用**單數動詞**。
（**美式英語**較常用**複數動詞**。） |

┌→ *複數動詞或單數動詞都可以*
• None of us **are/is** perfect. 我們沒有一個人是完美的。

| all
most
some
any
none | + of + | it | → 作主詞時，動詞要用**單數動詞**。 |

Mark Didn't she tell an exciting story about her trip to Tibet?
Linda Yes, she did, but some of it **was** not true. └→ *單數動詞*

馬克 她不是說過她去西藏的一件趣事嗎？
琳達 她是講過，但其中一些內容不是事實。

PRACTICE

1 選出正確答案。

1 Most people｜Most of people **think life is beautiful.**

2 All students｜All the students **failed the math exam.**

3 Some of the questions｜Some of questions **on the college entrance English exam were very difficult.**

4 "Do you know all the people｜all people **in the house?"**
"No, I have never seen any of these people｜any people **before."**

5 I didn't sleep well last night, because the dog next door barked most night｜most of the night.

6 None of her money was｜were **spent foolishly.**

7 Do most of you｜most of the you **want an Apple iPad?**

8 All them｜All of them **are making good money now, so they all should be happy.**

2 請依據圖片，用 **all**、**most**、**some**、**none** 搭配 **of them** 或 **of it** 回答問題。

1

How many of these police officers are women?

_____

2
These are my robots.

How many of these robots are yours?

_____

3

How many of the students are standing?

_____

4

How many of your friends are overweight?

_____

3 用括弧裡的單字填空，並視情況加上 **of**。

1 She enjoyed _____ the movie though she didn't like the scary parts. (most)

2 She doesn't like _____ her brother's friends. (any)

3 _____ people love to talk. (Some)

4 She thinks _____ children love ice-cream. (all)

5 _____ his friends came to the airport to see him off. (None)

6 The weather was awful while I was on a one-week trip to London. It rained _____ the time. (most)

7 He has saved _____ money. (no)

8 _____ my friends are still single. (Some)

Chapter

20 many, several, both, either, neither 搭配 of 片語的用法

1

many（許多）、several（數個）、both（兩者都）、either（兩者之任一個）、neither（兩者都不）可以作**數量形容詞**用，後面直接加**名詞**〔參見 Chapter 10 和 Chapter 11〕。

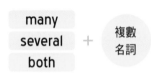

- Sue has many friends in Honolulu. 蘇在檀香山有很多朋友。
- Lily lives several miles away from me.
  莉莉住的地方離我有好幾英里。
- Last month Sue visited Paris and London, and she enjoyed both cities. 上月蘇參觀了巴黎和倫敦，她兩個城市都喜歡。

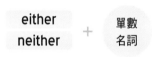

- There are willow trees on either side of the river.
  河的兩邊都有楊柳樹。
- Neither statement is true. 兩個陳述都不是事實。

2

many、several、both、either、neither 也可以
作**代名詞**，常和 **of** 連用。

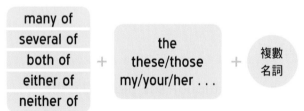

many、several、both、either、neither 後面所接的 of 片語，of 之後一定要加 the、these、my 等限定詞，才能接名詞，不能省略。
- Both of my brothers are married.
  我的兩個哥哥都結婚了。

of 後面的 my 不能省略。

- Many of her friends have a college education. 她的許多朋友受過大學教育。
- Several of the employees went home sick. 員工中有好幾個生病回家了。
- Yesterday she broke both of her legs. 她昨天摔斷了兩條腿。
- Have you read either of these books? 這兩本書你讀過其中一本嗎？
- Neither of my sisters has ever been abroad. 我的兩個姊姊都沒有出過國。

3

要注意，一個句子不能有雙重否定。neither 是否定詞，因此不能用在否定句中，
否定句中要用 either。

動詞否定式 doesn't like 加上 either，表示否定含意。
- Liz doesn't like either of these books. 這兩本書莉茲都不喜歡。
- Neither of these books is interesting to Liz. 這兩本書沒有一本引起莉茲的興趣。

neither 加上動詞肯定式 is，表示否定含意。

4 both 的用法

❶ both 表示「兩者都……」，只能用在**肯定句裡**。要表示「兩者都不……」，
不能用 both not，要用 neither。

- Neither of them is here. 他們兩個都不在這裡。
  Both of them are not here. → 錯誤用法

❷ 在「both of + the/these/my . . .」的句型裡，of 可以省略，僅用「both + the/
these/my . . .」，甚至，連 the/these/my 等修飾語都可以省略。

- Both of my sisters **are single.** 我的兩個姊姊都是單身。
  = Both my sisters **are single.** → 省略 of
  = Both sisters **are single.** → 省略 of my

- I enjoyed both of those movies. 那兩部影片我都喜歡。
  = I enjoyed both those movies. → 省略 of
  = I enjoyed both movies. → 省略 of those

5

| many
several
both | + | of | + | the
these
my | → | 這整個片語作主詞時，動詞要用**複數動詞**。 |

| either
neither | + | of | + | the
these
my | → | 這整個片語作主詞時，正式用語會用**單數動詞**。 |

- 複數動詞
  Several of my friends **have a master's degree in education.**
  我的朋友中有好幾個獲得了教育碩士學位。

- Neither of my sisters **is married.** 我的兩個姊姊都沒有結婚。
  單數動詞

6

many、several、both、either、neither 可以接 **of** 再接**複數人稱代名詞**。

| many
several
both
either
neither | + | of | + | us
them
you |

作動詞 like 的受詞

- Look at these two pictures on the wall. I <u>like</u> both of them.
  瞧瞧牆上的這兩張照片。兩張我都喜歡。

作介系詞 about 的受詞

- My two dogs have been missing for a week. There is still no news <u>about</u> either of them.
  我的兩隻狗已經失蹤一個星期了，仍然下落不明。

many			us	
several	+ of +		them	→ 作主詞時，動詞要用**複數動詞**。
both			you	

either			us	
neither	+ of +		them	→ 作主詞時，動詞要用**單數動詞**。
			you	

複數動詞

- Several of us **are going to attend the Fifteenth International Space Station Conference.** 我們中有好幾個要去參加國際太空站第十五屆會議。

單數動詞

- Neither of them **was chosen to do research at the International Space Station.** 他們倆沒有一個被選上去國際太空站做學術研究。

PRACTICE

1 用括弧裡的單字填空，並視情況加上 of（如：either of、several of）。

1. "Which bikini do you like, this one or that one?"
   "I don't like _____ them." (either)
2. She has introduced me to _____ her relatives. (several)
3. _____ foot is swollen. (Neither)
4. It happened _____ years ago. (many)
5. "You look tired."
   "Yes, I'm tired. _____ my children are hospitalized." (Both)
6. _____ them will win. (Neither)
7. Applications for this research position are welcomed from people of _____ sex and any age. (either)
8. _____ my friends will be going on to college. (Many)
9. _____ buildings in the village were damaged by the earthquake. (Several)
10. Sally sends _____ you her love. (both)

2 用 **both**、**either** 或 **neither** 填空，並視情況加上 of（如：**both of**、**either of**）。

1 _____ my parents are software programmers.

2 Dan Which country would you like to visit during the summer vacation, Greece or Italy?

  Ann _____ country is fine with me. Both countries have a lot of great places to visit.

3 Dan Did you enjoy those two movies we saw yesterday?

  Ann No, I didn't like _____ them. Both of them had too much violence.

4 Dan Which bus did you take to come here, number 1 or number 5?

  Ann _____ them. I took the subway.

5 Dan Can Mike and Mark speak Chinese?

  Ann No, they can't, but _____ them have decided to learn the language.

3 將下列錯誤的句子改寫為正確的句子。

1 Both of my sisters likes reading and motorcycle riding.

_____

2 These both oranges are bad.

_____

3 Both of them are not coming tomorrow.

_____

4 She doesn't like neither of her math teachers.

_____

5 Both of the children is good at playing the piano.

_____

6 Neither my sisters can dance.

_____

7 Both us saw it happen.

_____

Chapter 21 反身代名詞（-self/-selves）

1

反身代名詞依人稱和單複數分為下列幾種：

	單數	複數
第一人稱	myself	ourselves
第二人稱	yourself	yourselves
第三人稱	himself	
	herself	themselves
	itself	

2

反身代名詞用來指代**主詞**。當主詞和受詞是一樣時，就用反身代名詞。

• **These women trained** themselves **to play soccer.** 這些女子訓練自己踢足球。
  └ 指代 these women ┘

• **Jane is very proud of** herself. 珍感到自豪。
  └── 指代 Jane ──┘

• **Sam loves only** himself. 山姆只喜歡自己。
  └── 指代 Sam ──┘

• **I am going to buy** myself **an electric car.** 我要給自己買一輛電動車。
  └── 指代 I ──┘

  ┌─ 指代 Claire ─┐
• **Claire admired** herself **in the mirror while brushing her hair.**
  克萊兒一邊梳頭髮，一邊欣賞鏡中的自己。

  受詞 yourself 指代祈使句
  中的主詞 you（祈使句中的
  主詞 you，通常被省略）。

• **Be careful getting the knife off the shelf, and don't cut** yourself.
  從架上把刀拿下來時要小心一些，不要割傷了自己。

- Jim is looking at Kim.
吉姆在看金姆。

- Sue is looking at herself in the mirror. 蘇在照鏡子。

- I would like to talk to you.
我想跟你談一談。

- Sometimes he talks to himself.
有時他會自言自語。

3

反身代名詞可以用來進行**強調**，加強語氣。

用來強調，意思是「本人」。
- President Nancy Day herself spoke to me today. 今天南西‧戴總裁本人跟我談了話。

用來強調，意思是「親自」。
- My grandma built this cottage herself. 這幢別墅是我奶奶自己蓋的。

4

慣用語「**by oneself**」的意思是「獨自」或「不用他人幫忙」。

by myself
by yourself
by herself
by himself
by itself
by ourselves
by themselves

→ ① 獨自（alone）
② 不用他人幫忙（without help）

指獨自一個人，沒有別人做伴。

- She likes to spend time by herself.
她喜歡獨自消磨時光。

- I can't carry this bookcase into the office by myself. — 指獨力完成某事，沒有人幫忙。
我無法靠我自己把這個書櫃搬進辦公室。

5

反身代名詞的其他固定慣用語：

teach oneself 自學
enjoy oneself 盡情享受
help oneself (to something) 請自便
for oneself 為自己

1 | 請用下列詞彙填空，完成句子。

myself
yourself
himself
herself
itself
ourselves
yourselves
themselves

1 Trish is teaching _____ English.

2 I am going to the shop to buy _____ a necklace.

3 They will learn to rely upon _____ to finish difficult tasks.

4 We are enjoying _____ at the Christmas party.

5 He made _____ a cup of coffee.

6 Be careful! Don't cut _____ .

7 Jane and Ted, did you build this house by _____ ?

8 The robot can open the door by _____ .

2 | 選出正確的答案。

_____ **1** Please help _____ to the food on the table.
     a yourself   b themselves
     c myself   d herself

_____ **2** Mom began to cough, so she decided to give _____ a day off.
     a himself   b myself
     c herself   d yourself

_____ **3** Can they learn this dance by _____ ?
     a myself   b themselves
     c yourselves   d ourselves

_____ **4** The little boy carried in all his packages by _____ .
     a himself   b myself
     c herself   d themselves

_____ **5** Why does your sister Jane always talk about _____ ?
     a himself   b itself
     c yourself   d herself

6 The house _____ is nice, but the backyard is too small.
- a himself
- b myself
- c itself
- d herself

7 Alaska is very cold in the winter, and I do not want to live there by _____ .
- a himself
- b myself
- c herself
- d yourself

8 We will solve that problem _____ .
- a myself
- b themselves
- c yourselves
- d ourselves

---

3 請判斷下列句子是否正確，正確打 ✓，不正確打 ×，並寫出正確句子。

1 Enjoy yourself at the party, and give my best wishes to Joy.

☐ _____

2 On the long dinner table is the sign "Please help you."

☐ _____

3 Tonight she finished her homework by herself.

☐ _____

4 Why are you laughing at you?

☐ _____

5 The students ourselves invited Marty and me to their party.

☐ _____

6 She is very proud of herself.

☐ _____

Chapter

22　連綴動詞

I **連綴動詞的定義與類別**

大多數動詞用來表達行為或動作，但有些動詞是用來「描述或確認句中主詞的**狀態**」，這種動詞稱為**連綴動詞**。連綴動詞連接**主詞**和**表語**（現代英文文法把表語稱為「主詞補語」）。常見的連綴動詞如下：

1 be 動詞（最常見的連綴動詞）　→

　→ be 動詞的用法，參見 Chapter 25 be 動詞的現在式，以及 Chapter 34 be 動詞的過去式。

　→ be 動詞也可以作**助動詞**，參見 Chapter 24 短語動詞和助動詞。

2 感官動詞（作連綴動詞用）

　→ 感官動詞的詳細用法，參見 Unit 10 感官動詞和使役動詞。

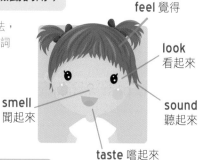

feel 覺得
look 看起來
smell 聞起來
sound 聽起來
taste 嚐起來

3 表示狀態或狀態變化的詞

seem 似乎	become 開始變得
prove 證明是	turn 變得
get 成為	go 變成
grow 漸漸變得	run 變得
remain 保持	appear 看起來好像
keep 保持	

---

2 **連綴動詞的用法**

主詞 + 連繫動詞 + 主詞補語（名詞／代名詞／形容詞／介系詞片語／子句）

→ 連綴動詞連接句子的主詞（名詞或代名詞）和主詞補語。主詞補語可以是名詞、代名詞、形容詞、介系詞片語或子句，用來修飾句中的主詞。

• **Those young people** are **all college students.** 那些年輕人都是大學生。
　→「連綴動詞（are）＋主詞補語（名詞 college students）」，用來說明主詞 those young people 的身分。

• **That bottle of milk** has gone **sour.** 那瓶牛奶酸掉了。
　→「連綴動詞（has gone）＋主詞補語（形容詞 sour）」，用來描述主詞（that bottle of milk）的狀態。

• **His room** smells **bad.** 他房間的氣味難聞。
　→ smells 是連綴動詞，形容詞 bad 作主詞補語，修飾主詞 his room。連綴動詞後面不接副詞。

• **She is** still **in bed.** 她還在床上睡覺。　→ 主詞 ＋ 連綴動詞 ＋ 介系詞片語

• **That's** how you can milk a cow. 就是這樣給奶牛擠奶的。　→ 主詞 ＋ 連綴動詞 ＋ 子句

3

有些詞既可以作**連綴動詞**，又可以作**普通動詞**，該如何區分呢？

可以用 be 動詞取代　→　這些動詞就是連綴動詞。

不能用 be 動詞取代　→　這些動詞就是普通動詞（即行為動詞）。

- **Dee looked angry with me.** → ≈ Dee was angry with me.
  蒂看起來在生我的氣。
  → 用 was 取代 looked 後，語句通順，語意不變，
  則 looked 是連綴動詞。

- **Donna looked at the sky.** → ≠ Donna was at the sky.
  唐娜望著天空。
  → 用 was 取代 looked 後，語意改變，語句不合邏輯，
  則這裡的 looked 是普通動詞。

PRACTICE

1 | 指出下面的動詞是連綴動詞（A）還是普通動詞（B），並把 A 或 B 填入空格中。

1. _____ Art felt a great pain in his heart.
2. _____ This red blanket feels soft under my head.
3. _____ Mitch felt along the wall for the light switch.
4. _____ The hungry child ran wild.
5. _____ She ran all the way back home.
6. _____ Despite the troubles that came their way, they remained friends anyway.
7. _____ Pam felt nervous even though she was well prepared for the exam.
8. _____ Come and smell these roses.
9. _____ The tired Girl Scouts were in a happy mood as they tasted all the wonderful food.
10. _____ The wine tasted fine.

2 | 請判斷下列句子是否正確，正確打 ✓，不正確打 ×，並加以更正。

1. The red meat tasted badly and caused me to vomit in my bed. _____
2. Scot is thirsty and hot. _____
3. We tasted the fine wine. _____
4. The little girl first got madly and then later became sadly. _____
5. Sally's face turned red, and she said, "I won't marry Ted." _____

3 | 把下列短語翻譯成英文。

1. 聞起來很香 _____
2. 聞聞這些花 _____
3. 品嚐這魚肉 _____
4. 嚐起來好吃 _____
5. 感覺柔軟 _____

Chapter

23 及物動詞與不及物動詞

---

1 及物動詞

❶ 動詞可分為**及物動詞**和**不及物動詞**。及物動詞不能單獨使用，須搭配一個名詞、代名詞或子句作為受詞。

主詞 + 及物動詞 + 受詞（名詞/代名詞）

┌→ 吉姆愛誰呢？動詞 love 後面要加受詞。

• Jim loves **Kim.** 吉姆愛金姆。
  主詞　及物動詞　受詞

　　　　　　　　┌→ 及物動詞（help）+ 受詞（one another）

• Ray and his friends help <u>one another</u> every day. 雷和他的朋友們每天都互相幫助。
　　　　　　主詞　　　　　　及物動詞　　受詞

❷ 有些及物動詞可以接兩個受詞：**直接受詞**和**間接受詞**。「你給某人的**東西**，或你為某人做的**事**」，叫做直接受詞；「接受該物品的**人**」，叫做間接受詞。

主詞 + 及物動詞 + 間接受詞 + 直接受詞

　　　　┌→ 請給我什麼？動詞 give 後面要加一個直接受詞（the money）和一個間接受詞（me）。

• Please give me <u>the money!</u> = Please give <u>the money</u> to me! 請把錢給我！
　　　　　及物動詞　間接受詞　直接受詞　　　　　及物動詞　直接受詞　間接受詞

　　　　　通常把間接受詞（us）放在
　　　　┌→ 直接受詞（song）前面。　　　　　　　　　間接受詞放在直接受詞後面
　　　　　　　　　　　　　　　　　　　　　　　　→ 時，需要一個介系詞連接。

• Please sing us a <u>song.</u> 請為我們唱一首歌。
　　　　　及物動詞　間接受詞　直接受詞

---

2 不及物動詞

不及物動詞可以單獨使用，不用接受詞。如：
come（來）、go（去）、fall（跌倒；落下）、
smile（微笑）等，都是不及物動詞。

主詞 + 不及物動詞 + 受詞

不及物動詞，不接受詞。

　　　　　　┌→ 不及物動詞 jog 單獨使用，不接受詞。

• Do you jog every day? 你每天都慢跑嗎？

• A giant bee is hiding behind that big oak tree.
  一隻巨大的蜜蜂躲在那棵大橡樹後面。

3 ── 兼作及物和不及物動詞的詞

一些動詞既可以當及物動詞，也可以當不及物動詞。

- **Rae** sings **every day.** 芮每天都要唱歌。 →不及物動詞 sings 單獨使用，不接受詞。

- **Rae** sings <u>spirituals</u> **every day.** 芮每天都要唱聖歌。 →及物動詞 sings 接受詞（spirituals）。

- **She** studied **hard for the test.** 她努力地準備了考試。 →不及物動詞

- **Midge** studied <u>Spanish</u> **in college.** 米姬大學時學過西班牙語。 →及物動詞

PRACTICE

1 用底線標記出括弧中的正確答案。

1. Please help me (open/open the door).
2. Jake and his jazz music (gave me a headache/gave a headache me).
3. Please (give me/give me the money)!
4. Mona (runs a hotel/runs me) in Arizona.
5. Ms. Birch (gave $5,000 to the church/gave the church).
6. Midge (has left me/has left me some food) in the fridge.

2 根據句意及所給的中文，用現在進行式完成句子。
〔現在進行式的用法，參見 Chapter 30。〕

1. Miss Peach＿＿＿＿＿＿＿＿＿＿＿ along the beach.（溜狗）
2. Miss Reach ＿＿＿＿＿＿＿＿＿＿ along the beach.（快樂地散步）
3. Joe ＿＿＿＿＿＿＿＿＿＿.（放風箏）
4. The huge kite ＿＿＿＿＿＿＿＿＿.（在天空中高高飛翔）
5. Faye Star ＿＿＿＿＿＿＿＿＿.（駕駛一輛新跑車）
6. Faye ＿＿＿＿＿＿＿＿＿ today.（小心翼翼駕駛）
7. Paul and Saul ＿＿＿＿＿＿＿＿＿.（打籃球）
8. Mark and Clark ＿＿＿＿＿＿＿＿＿.（在公園玩）

3 請判斷下列句子是否正確，正確打 ✓，不正確打 ×，並寫出正確句子。

1. I do the crossword puzzle every day with my Uncle Stew.
2. Ray bought some roses Kay for her birthday.
3. "That will do," said Andrew.
4. Joan Flowers talked on her cellphone for two hours!
5. Mom is reading a funny story my little brother Tom.

24 助動詞和短語動詞

I 助動詞（Do/Have/Be）

助動詞本身無意義，必須與行為動詞連用，用來構成動詞的時態、疑問句、否定句、被動式或簡略回答。常見的助動詞有三類：

do → （do, does, did）：用來構成否定句和疑問句或代替主要動詞或做簡略回答。

- **Do** you and Rae go swimming every day?
  你和芮每天都要去游泳嗎？→ *疑問句*

- I **did**n't eat anything this morning.
  今天早上我沒有吃東西。→ *否定句*

- "Do you take this woman to be your wife?" "Yes, I **do**." ⌐ *簡略回答*
  「你要選這個女人當你的老婆？」「對，沒錯！」

- She speaks English as fluently as you (**do**).
  她的英文講得和你一樣好。└─ *代替主要動詞 speak（也可省略 do）。*

have → （have been, has been, had been）：用來構成完成式。

- Sue Flowers **has been** jogging for over two hours. → *現在完成進行式*
  蘇‧弗勞爾斯已經慢跑了兩個多小時。

be → （am, is, are, was, were, being, been）：用來構成進行式與被動式。

- Dad **is** making dinner. 爸爸正在做晚餐。→ *現在進行式*

- Last night two people **were** injured in a car accident.
  昨晚的車禍中有兩人受傷。→ *被動式*

比較 do、**does**、**did** 除了當助動詞用，也可以作**行為動詞**，談論行為動作。

Usually Mom **does** the shopping, Kirk **does** the cooking, and I **do** my homework. 通常是媽媽負責採購，柯克做飯，而我做功課。

比較 have、**has**、**had** 也可作**行為動詞**或表示「**擁有**」〔參見 Chapter 27〕。

have breakfast 吃早餐
have coffee 喝咖啡
have a good time 玩得很愉快
have a baby 生孩子
have a headache 頭痛

注意 除了助動詞 be、have、do 外，**will** 也可作助動詞，用來構成簡單未來式。在英式英語中，**shall** 也可以作助動詞，與第一人稱代名詞連用，構成簡單未來式〔參見 Chapter 41 簡單未來式〕。

🇺🇸 美式英語 | Joe thinks it **will** be warm and clear tomorrow.
喬認為明天會是晴朗暖和的日子。

🇬🇧 英式英語 | I **shall** probably leave for New York tomorrow.

🇺🇸 美式英語 | I **will** probably leave for New York tomorrow. 明天我可能要離開去紐約。

2　短語動詞

短語動詞由一個動詞接一個介系詞或副詞組成，短語動詞可能是**不及物動詞**，也可能是**及物動詞**。

不及物動詞
- She likes to show off. 她喜歡炫耀。

及物動詞
- Mr. Keating called off the meeting. 濟廷先生取消了會議。

3　短語動詞的構成法

| 動詞 | + | 介系詞 | → | 相當於**及物動詞** |

agree with 一致　　　　depend on/upon 依靠
arrive in/at 到達　　　get to 到達
ask for 請求　　　　　look for 尋找
begin with 以⋯⋯開始　laugh at 嘲笑
belong to 屬於　　　　run into 偶遇、撞到
believe in 信任、信仰　wait for 等待

- The clown suit belongs to the richest man in town.
  那件小丑衣是城裡最富有的男人的。

| 及物動詞 | + | 副詞 | → | 相當於**及物動詞** |

blow up 炸毀　　　　pick up 拾起
bring up 養育　　　　point out 指出
carry out 執行　　　put on 穿上
fill out 填寫　　　　put off 推遲
find out 發現、查明　set up 建立
give up 讓出　　　　take off 脫下
hand in 交出　　　　turn off 關掉
hang up 掛斷電話　　turn on 打開
look up 查（字典）　think over 考慮

- Fill out this application form, and give it to Jill. 填寫這張申請表，然後交給潔兒。

Note 代名詞作受詞時，須放在動詞後、副詞前；當名詞作受詞時，常放在副詞後，但也可放副詞前。

She looked it up in her cellphone dictionary.
她在她的手機字典裡查詢這個字。

| 不及物動詞 | + | 副詞 | → | 相當於**不及物動詞** |

get up 起床　　　　set out 出發
give in 讓步　　　　stand up 起立
go on 繼續　　　　take off 起飛
grow up 成長　　　turn away 轉過去
look out 小心　　　turn up 出現
run out 用完　　　wake up 醒來
show off 炫耀　　　watch out 小心

- My ex-girlfriend unexpectedly turned up at the party.
  我的前女友出人意料地出現在聚會上。

| 動詞 | + | 副詞 | + | 介系詞 | → | 相當於**及物動詞** |

get along with 與⋯⋯相處
catch up with 趕上
go on with 繼續
keep up with 跟上
look down on/upon 瞧不起
look forward to 盼望

- Mary Straw gets along well with her mother-in-law.
  瑪麗・斯特勞和她婆婆相處融洽。

| 動詞 | + | 名詞 | + | 介系詞 | → | 相當於**及物動詞** |

keep an eye on 注意、照看
take part in 參加
make fun of 取笑
make use of 利用
make friends with 交朋友
pay attention to 注意、關心
get hold of 抓住
lose hold of 沒有抓住
shake hands with 和⋯⋯握手
take care of 照顧

- Please pay attention to your pronunciation. 請注意你的發音。

除了本單元討論的動詞外，動詞還有情態動詞和使役動詞，參見 **Unit 9** 和 **Unit 10**。

1 選出所屬的動詞類別（A, B, C），填入空格中。

[A] 行為動詞
[B] 連綴動詞
[C] 助動詞

_____ **1** My brother told me a story about a little girl called Pearl who was bullied by her stepmother.

_____ **2** I had fish for dinner tonight.

_____ **3** Why are you unhappy today?

_____ **4** Brook is reading a book.

_____ **5** Kay and Rae are not belly dancers, but they are studying ballet.

_____ **6** Lee and his girlfriend Dee had been canoeing down the river for three days.

_____ **7** What did you do last night?

_____ **8** Where did you hide my bunny bank filled with money?

2 根據句意及所給的中文，從下面表格裡選出短語動詞完成句子。
（動詞的形式須依句意作變化。）

agree with	get up	look for	run into
bring up	hand in	look it up	take off
call off	hang up	look out	turn away
find out	keep up with	make fun of	watch out

1 What is she _____ ?（在找什麼）

2 Our referee _____ the game because of the cold and snow.（取消了）

3 Jake and I can't _____ each other about which path to take. （意見不一致）

4 Ray's dad sighed, "It isn't easy to _____ children nowadays." （養育）

5 My brother Rod and I _____ our term papers and then left for Cape Cod. （交出了）

6 Dee _____ her wet boots and went into her RV. （脫下了）

7 Kay _____ and started to cry. （轉過去）

8 Please _____ when our bank loan is due. （查明）

9 She _____ the phone. （掛斷了電話）

10 If you don't understand this phrasal verb, please _____ in a dictionary. （查字典）

11 Kate's hard work helps her to _____ her classmates. （跟上）

12 It's time to _____. （起床）

13 _____, Chet, or you'll get wet. （小心）

14 Rae _____ her English professor in the hallway. （碰到了）

15 Don't _____ his strong Russian accent. （取笑）

Chapter

25 be 動詞的現在式

1

be 動詞是表示「是」或「在」的動詞，共有下列八個，本章將說明 be 動詞當作**連綴動詞**的現在式用法。

現在式	am is are
過去式	was were
不定詞	(to) be
現在分詞和動名詞	being
過去分詞	been

---

2 be 動詞的句型

be 動詞也可以當做助動詞，構成進行式或被動式〔參見 Chapter 24〕。

主詞 + be 動詞 → 肯定句

主詞 + be 動詞 + not → 否定句

be 動詞 + 主詞 → 疑問句

肯定句

• Look! This is a bow and this is an arrow! 你看！這是一把弓，這是一支箭！

肯定句

• They are basketball players. 他們是籃球員。

否定簡略回答

• "Is Paul tall?" "No, he isn't." 「保羅很高嗎？」「不，他不高。」
  疑問句

肯定簡略回答

• "Is Ms. Letter a writer?" "Yes, she is." 「雷特小姐是作家嗎？」「是的，她是作家。」
  疑問句

be 動詞現在式句型一覽表

	肯定句	肯定縮寫	否定句	否定縮寫	疑問句
單數	I am	I'm	I am not	I'm not	am I?
	you are	you're	you are not	you're not = you aren't	are you?
	he is	he's	he is not	he's not = he isn't	is he?
	she is	she's	she is not	she's not = she isn't	is she?
	it is	it's	it is not	it's not = it isn't	is it?
	this is	無縮寫	this is not	this isn't	is this?
	that is	that's	that is not	that's not = that isn't	is that?
複數	we are	we're	we are not	we're not = we aren't	are we?
	you are	you're	you are not	you're not = you aren't	are you?
	they are	they're	they are not	they're not = they aren't	are they?
	these are	無縮寫	these are not	these aren't	are these?
	those are	無縮寫	those are not	those aren't	are those?

肯定的縮寫形式**不能用於簡答**：
✓ Yes, they are.
× Yes, they're.

否定的縮寫形式**可以用於簡答**：
No, they aren't.
= No, they're not.
= No, they are not.

3　be 動詞現在式的用法

be 動詞的**現在式**為 **am**、**is**、**are**，用法如下：

Hi, I am Pam.

┌── am 只搭配代名詞 I 使用。

I + **am** → • Hi, I am **Pam.** 你好，我是潘姆。

he / she / it / this / that / 單數名詞（Mom, Jerry . . .） + **is** →

┌── is 搭配代名詞 it 使用。
• It's **sunny and warm today.** 天陽光燦爛，天氣溫暖。
• This is **my sister Liz.** 這是我的妹妹莉茲。
└── is 搭配代名詞 this 使用。

we / you / they / these / those / 複數名詞（parents, trees . . .） + **are** →

疑問句把 be 動詞
┌── 放在主詞前。

否定句把 not 放在
┌── be 動詞後。
= No, they're not.
= No, they are not.

• "Are they **Chinese?**" "No, they aren't. They are **Japanese.**"
「他們是中國人嗎？」「不是，他們是日本人。」

= Yes, they're my Keys.
= Yes, they are my Keys.
• "Are these **your keys?**" "Yes, they are."
「這些是你的鑰匙嗎？」「是，是我的鑰匙。」

• Trish and I are British. 翠希和我都是英國人。
└── 兩個或兩個以上的名詞用 and 連接，
當作主詞用時，動詞要用 are。

1 請用 **am**、**is** 或 **are** 完成下列句子。

1 Paul _____ a basketball player.

2 The trees _____ tall, the walls _____ high, and the clouds _____ above them all.

3 Bart and his little sister Liz _____ both smart.

4 These _____ busy bees.

5 She _____ hungry.

6 I _____ not Japanese. I _____ Taiwanese.

7 Lee _____ not happy with me.

8 Basketball and soccer _____ my favorite sports.

2 選出正確的答案（斜線表示不需要任何文字）。

1 This _____ Liz, and that woman in the red dress _____ Pat.
   ⓐ is, are   ⓑ is, is   ⓒ am, is   ⓓ are, are

2 _____ Trish and Violet British?
   ⓐ Are   ⓑ Is   ⓒ Am   ⓓ /

3 Joe, _____ the Sears Tower in Chicago?
   ⓐ are   ⓑ is   ⓒ am   ⓓ /

4 "_____ you an astronaut?" asked Sue. "No, I _____," replied Joe.
   ⓐ Are, are not   ⓑ Is, am not   ⓒ Are, am not   ⓓ Is, is not

5 Mort asked, "_____ soccer your favorite sport?"
   Liz replied, "Yes, it _____."
   ⓐ Am, is   ⓑ Are, is   ⓒ Is, is   ⓓ Are, are

6 "What color _____ my eyes?" Kim asked Jim.
   ⓐ is   ⓑ are   ⓒ am   ⓓ is not

7. "Who _____ your friend, Liz? And _____ your friend British or Polish?" asked Trish.

    a is, am   b is, is   c is, are   d are, are

8. "_____ your parents artists?" asked Omar. "Yes, they _____ ," replied Kay.

    a Are, aren't   b Am, are   c Are, are   d Are, is

9. I sometimes play baseball and football, but my favorite sport _____ basketball.

    a is   b are   c am   d aren't

10. Tom _____ a Canadian, but his mom _____ a Singaporean and his dad _____ a Korean.

    a is, is, is   b is, are, are   c is, are, is   d are, is, is

---

3 用正確的 be 動詞現在式，完成下列問句，並寫出簡答（如「**Yes, they are.**」、「**No, they are not.**」）。

1. Ruth _____ Ann and Dan from Japan?
   Jason Yes, they _____.

2. Ruth _____ you a football player?
   Jason No, I _____.

3. Ruth _____ they British?
   Jason No, they _____. They are Spanish.

4. Ruth _____ she Korean?
   Jason No, she_____. She's Singaporean.

5. Ruth _____ your sister a teacher?
   Jason Yes, she_____.

6. Ruth _____ he Italian?
   Jason No, he_____. He's Indonesian.

7. Ruth _____ Kim and Jim interested in politics?
   Jason No, they _____. They are interested in economics.

8. Ruth _____ you hungry?
   Jason Yes, I _____.

Chapter

26 there is, there are（某處有某物）

在 there is 和 there are 的句型中，**there** 是**語助詞**，用來引導一個句子。動詞用 is 還是 are，要視後面所接的**主詞之單複數**來決定。

there + is / are → 表示「某處有……」

there + is / are + not → 表示「某處沒有……」

• There are **two strong men over there.**
They are sumo wrestlers.
那邊有兩個壯漢，他們是相撲選手。

> There are 要接複數名詞（men）；也可以用縮寫形式 There're。

There is 要接單數名詞（a cellphone, a couch）或不可數名詞（water）；也可以用縮寫形式 There's。

• There is **some water under that otter.**
那隻水獺下面有一些水。

Sandra Are there **any cars in the parking lot?**

Jason Yes, there are.

珊卓 停車場裡有車嗎？

傑森 有。

    1. Are there 接複數名詞（cars）。
    2. 疑問句要把 be 動詞 is 或 are 放在 there 之前。
    3. 肯定簡答不能用縮寫形式：
      × Yes, there're.
      × Yes, there's.

Sandra Is there **a dog under the table?**

Jason No, there isn't.

珊卓 桌子下面有一隻狗嗎？

傑森 沒有。

    1. Is there 接單數可數名詞（dog）。
    2. 否定簡答通常用縮寫形式：
      ✓ No, there isn't.
      ✓ No, there aren't.

there is 和 there are 的句型

	單數		複數	否定縮寫
肯定句	there is = there's	• There is a picture on the wall. = There's a picture on the wall. 牆上有一張照片。	there are = there're	• There are two pictures on the wall. = There're two pictures on the wall. 牆上有兩張照片。
疑問句	is there?	• Is there a picture on the wall? 牆上有一張照片嗎？	are there?	• Are there two pictures on the wall? 牆上有兩張照片嗎？
否定句	there is not = there isn't	• There is not a picture on the wall. = There isn't a picture on the wall. 牆上沒有一張照片。	there are not = there aren't	• There are not two pictures on the wall. = There aren't two pictures on the wall. 牆上沒有兩張照片。

* 否定句更常用縮寫形式：there isn't 和 there aren't。

2

there is/there's 和 it is/it's 不同，**there is** 表示「某處有……」；**it is** 表示「是……」。

there + **is** → 表示「某處有……」

• There's too much spice on this pizza.
這個披薩上面的香料放太多了。

it + **is** → 表示「是……」

• I don't like this pizza. It's too spicy.
我不喜歡這個披薩，太辣了。

PRACTICE

1 用 **There is** 或 **There are** 填空。

1. _____ a TV at the corner of the room.
2. _____ two boats in the water.
3. _____ four sandwiches on the table.
4. _____ a big dog in our yard.

2 依圖示，用 **Is there** 或 **Are there** 填空，然後回答問題。

1. _____ a puppy in the box?

_____

2. _____ four people in the car?

_____

3. _____ a fish in the cat's mouth?

_____

4. _____ two kites in the sky?

_____

3 連連看：自右欄選出適當的詞語與左欄連接，完成句子或對話。

1 There is •

2 There are •

3 Are there two telephones in that room? •

4 Is there a white dress on the bed? •

5 There isn't •

• a three ladies at our door.

• b Yes, there is.

• c a new car in our garage.

• d a cloud in the sky.

• e No, there aren't.

4 選出正確的答案。

1 Ted, is｜are there a cat under your bed?

2 Midge, is｜are there any milk in our fridge?

3 Gary Are｜Is there anyone absent today?
Donna Yes, there are｜is two students absent. Their names are Fay and Rae.

4 Gary Is｜Are there anyone in your class from Iran?
Donna No, there isn't｜aren't anyone from Iran.

5 Gary Is｜Are there any teachers in your family?
Donna Yes, there is｜are two: my sisters, Millie and Lilly.

6 Is｜Are there any clouds in the sky?

7 How many nickels is｜are there in a dollar?

8 Is｜Are there an Italian restaurant near your school?

9 Gary What's that noise?
Donna There's｜It's a jet airplane.

10 Gary Why are you rubbing your eye?
Donna There is｜It is something in my eye.

Chapter

27 have, has（擁有）

1

have 是「擁有……」的意思，其第三人稱單數形式是 has。美式英語直接把 have 和 has 當動詞使用，英式英語會在口語中使用 have got、has got 來取代 have 和 has。

🇺🇸 美式英語 ｜ Scot has a houseboat.

🇬🇧 英式英語 ｜ Scot has got a houseboat.
史考特有一個船屋。

2 否定句的構成

🇺🇸 美式英語 ｜ 主詞 + do not / does not + have → 美式英語以助動詞 do/does + not 搭配 have〔參見 Chapter 29〕。

🇬🇧 英式英語 ｜ 主詞 + have / has + not + got → 英式英語在 have 或 has 的後面加上 not，構成否定句。

┌ = don't have
🇺🇸 美式英語 ｜ Look, I do not have much hair.

🇬🇧 英式英語 ｜ Look, I have not got much hair. 你看，我的頭髮不多了。
└ = haven't got

3 疑問句的構成

🇺🇸 美式英語 ｜ do / does + 主詞 + have → 美式英語以助動詞 do 或 does 搭配 have〔參見 Chapter 29〕。

🇬🇧 英式英語 ｜ have / has + 主詞 + got → 英式英語直接將 have 或 has 移到主詞前面，構成疑問句。

┌ = Yes, I have. → 否定簡答：No, I don't.
🇺🇸 美式英語 ｜ "Do you have a canoe?" "Yes, I do."「你有獨木舟嗎？」「我有。」

🇬🇧 英式英語 ｜ "Have you got a canoe?" "Yes, I have."「你有獨木舟嗎？」「我有。」
└ 無論是肯定還是否定回答，英式簡略回答時，不能用 have got/has got 或 have not got/has not got。
→ 否定簡答：No, I haven't.

4　have 和 has 的句型

🇺🇸 美式英語

	單數	複數
肯定句	I have	we have
	you have	you have
	he has	they have
	she has	
	it has	
	Joy has	Joy and Roy have
疑問句	do I have?	do we have?
	do you have?	do you have?
	does he have?	do they have?
	does she have?	
	does it have?	
	does Joy have?	do Joy and Roy have?
否定句	I do not have	we do not have
	you do not have	you do not have
	he does not have	they do not have
	she does not have	
	it does not have	
	Joy does not have	Joy and Roy do not have

* 縮寫：do not = don't
　　　does not = doesn't

* 本書之範例以美式英語為主。

🇬🇧 英式英語

	單數	複數
肯定句	I have (got)	we have (got)
	you have (got)	you have (got)
	he has (got)	they have (got)
	she has (got)	
	it has (got)	
	Scot has (got)	my parents have (got)
疑問句	have I got?	have we got?
	have you got?	have you got?
	has he got?	have they got?
	has she got?	
	has it got?	
	has Scot got?	have my parents got?
否定句	I have not got	we have not got
	you have not got	you have not got
	he has not got	they have not got
	she has not got	
	it has not got	
	Scot has not got	my parents have not got

* 縮寫：have not got = haven't got　　has not got = hasn't got

* 注意：英式這種用 got 的形式，不能用在簡略回答中。簡略回答的形式是 haven't 和 hasn't。

* 範例："Has Mary got a sports car?"
　　　"No, she hasn't." (Not: ~~No, she has not got.~~/~~No, she hasn't got.~~)
　　　"Yes, she has." (Not: ~~Yes, she has got.~~/~~Yes, she's got.~~)

5

have 或 have got 也可以用來表示「生病」、說明「症狀」。

🇺🇸 美式英語 | I have a sore throat.

🇬🇧 英式英語 | I have got a sore throat. 我喉嚨痛。
　　　　　　└─→ = I've got

6　there is/are 與動詞 have/has 比較

there + is / are + 主詞 → 指「某處有……」

　　　　　　　　　　　　　　┌─ 某處有……
　　　　　　　　　　　　　　• There are three cellphones on the desk. 桌上有三支手機。

主詞 + have / has → 指「某人有……」

　　　　　　　　　　　　　┌─ 某人有……
　　　　　　　　　　　　　• My sister has two cellphones.
　　　　　　　　　　　　　我姊姊有兩支手機。

動詞 **have** 還用在下面這些片語中（吃、喝，體驗、進行、從事）。

have 不可用 have got 替代。

| 吃吃喝喝 | have breakfast 吃早餐
have lunch 吃午餐
have dinner 吃晚餐
have a sandwich 吃三明治
have a pizza 吃披薩
have a cup of tea 喝茶
have a glass of milk 喝牛奶
have something to eat 吃……
have something to drink 喝…… | 體驗、進行、從事某些事 | have a baby 生孩子
have a rest 休息
have a vacation 度假
have a party 開派對
have a meeting 開會
have a good time 度過愉快時光
have a nice trip 旅遊愉快
have a dream 做夢；夢想
have an accident 發生意外 |

• **She usually has two cups of coffee in the morning.** 她早上通常會喝兩杯咖啡。

PRACTICE

1 用 **have** 或 **has** 填空。

1. I _____ a horse.
2. He _____ a dog and a hog.
3. Joy and Roy _____ a girl and a boy.
4. Meg's friends are sumo wrestlers and _____ strong legs.

2 使用美式英語，用現在式填空完成句子。

1. "_____ your sister have big eyes?" "Yes, my sister _____ big eyes."
2. "_____ you and Sharon _____ any children?"
"No, we _____ any children."
3. "_____ you _____ a sister named Sue?" "No, I _____."
4. "_____ Bess _____ a new dress?" "Yes, she _____."
5. "_____ Lulu and Sue _____ a canoe?"
"Yes, they do, and they like to canoe every day."

3 連連看：自右欄選出適當的詞語與左欄連接，完成句子或對話。

1 I have _____ • • a Yes, she has it.

2 Does she have your key? • • b No, we don't.

3 He has a _____ • • c strong arms.

4 Do you and Lee have a baby? • • d beautiful garden.

5 Does he have black hair? • • e No, he doesn't.

4 Tom 要去露營，下圖列出了他有的物品和沒有的物品。請依提示句型，用美式英語寫出他有什麼、沒有什麼，並在必要之處加 **a** 或 **an**。

Tom has · · ·
Tom doesn't have · · ·

✗ jacket

✗ sleeping bag

✔ tent

✔ knives and forks

1 _____

2 _____

3 _____

4 _____

5 將下列句子改寫為正確的句子。

1 Do rabbits has big ears?

_____

2 Does Claire has black hair?

_____

3 Does Scot Oat got a nice houseboat?

_____

4 "Does the fox have a long tail?" "Yes, it has got."

_____

5 Do you got a headache?

_____

6 She usually has got a sandwich for lunch.

_____

Chapter 28 簡單現在式：肯定句的用法

1

簡單現在式的主要用法有兩種：

❶ 說明**慣例**（**重複的事件或動作**）的時態，常與 every day、usually、often、sometimes 連用。

- **Tom** usually goes **to the movies on Saturday night with his sisters, Jenny and Penny.**
  湯姆星期六晚上通常都會跟他的姊姊珍妮和潘妮一起去看電影。

❷ 描述**事實**（永久為真的事）。

- **The moon** goes **around the earth, and the earth** goes **around the sun.**
  月亮繞著地球轉，地球繞著太陽轉。

---

2 ── **簡單現在式的肯定句句型**

| 第一、二人稱代名詞（I、we、you）
複數代名詞（they）
複數名詞 | + | 原形動詞
（不加 s） |

| 第三人稱單數代名詞（he、she、it）
單數名詞 | + | 須變化
動詞形式 | → | 使用第三人稱單數動詞（字尾加了 s 或 es 的動詞，如 jogs、goes）。|

簡單現在式肯定句的句型

	單數	複數
第一人稱代名詞	I jog every day.	We jog every day.
第二人稱代名詞	You jog every day.	You jog every day.
第三人稱代名詞	He jogs every day. She jogs every day. It jogs every day.	They jog every day.
名詞	Ray jogs every day.	Ray and May jog every day.

┌ 單數名詞用第三人稱單數動詞。　　　┌ 複數名詞使用原形動詞。

• Coco lives in New York City, and her parents live in Tokyo.
可可住在紐約市，她的父母住在東京。

┌ 第一人稱使用原形動詞。　　　　┌ 單數名詞用第三人稱單數動詞。

• I work in a restaurant, and my sister works in a university.
我在一家餐廳工作，我妹在一所大學工作。

┌ 單數不定代名詞 everybody 和單數人稱代名詞 he，使用單數動詞。

• Everybody loves Andy, and he loves the sea. 大家都喜歡安迪，而安迪喜歡大海。

3 第三人稱單數動詞的拼寫規則

大多數動詞 在字尾加 s	字尾是 s、ch、sh、x、 z、o 的動詞，加上 es	字尾是子音＋y 的動詞 刪除 y，加 ies
eat → eats	pass → passes	cry → cries
play → plays	watch → watches	fly → flies
sell → sells	finish → finishes	marry → marries
walk → walks	fix → fixes	carry → carries
win → wins	buzz → buzzes	study → studies
work → works	do → does	worry → worries

4 動詞 have（單數三人稱用 has）

	單數	複數
第一人稱	I have	we have
第二人稱	you have	you have
第三人稱	he has she has it has	they have

* 動詞 have 的用法，
參見 Chapter 27。

┌ = drinks

• Ted has a glass of milk every night
before he goes to bed.
泰德每晚上床睡覺之前都會喝一杯牛奶。

• She has a toothache.
她牙疼。

1 | 寫出下列動詞的第三人稱單數動詞。

1 drink _____ **5** carry _____ **9** study _____

2 sit _____ **6** cook _____ **10** wish _____

3 go _____ **7** rest _____ **11** march _____

4 kiss _____ **8** brush _____ **12** hurry _____

2 | 將括弧裡的字用正確的簡單現在式，填入空格中。

1 Dwight _____ to work at night. (like)

2 We _____ window shopping every Sunday morning. (go)

3 Claire _____ the clean country air. (love)

4 Her cat _____ a small bowl of milk every morning. (drink)

5 Every weekday Grandma Card _____ as a crossing guard. (work)

3 | 自圖片中選出正確的詞語搭配，並將詞語組合，以簡單現在式填空，完成句子。

a

play | the drums

b

sing | pop songs

c

teach | English

d

drive | a school bus

e

make | bread

1. Gus is a bus driver. He _____ .
2. His dad is a drummer. He _____ .
3. His mom is a baker. She _____ .
4. My sister is a teacher. She _____ .
5. We're singers. We _____ .

4 用 **have** 的正確形式填空，完成下列對話。

1. What's the matter with you?—I _____ a stomachache.
2. What's the matter with Sue?—She _____ a headache.
3. What's the matter with Stew?—He _____ a backache.

5 自下列綠色文字中選出正確的詞彙，並以簡單現在式填空。

wash   love   speak   sleep   close   teach

1. This restaurant usually _____ at midnight.
2. Jim _____ his mom and dad, and they _____ him.
3. Ann _____ English in Japan.
4. He _____ his car once a week.
5. My mom is a trilingual. That means she _____ three languages.
6. Dwight _____ eight hours a night.

Chapter

29 簡單現在式：否定句和疑問句的用法

I 否定句的構成

主詞 + do not / does not + 原形動詞 → 簡單現在式的否定句是使用 **do not** 或 **does not** 加上原形動詞。do 和 does 是助動詞〔參見 Chapter 24〕。

簡單現在式否定句的句型

	單數	複數
第一人稱代名詞	I do not jog every day.	We do not jog every day.
第二人稱代名詞	You do not jog every day.	You do not jog every day.
第三人稱代名詞	He does not jog every day. She does not jog every day. It does not jog every day.	They do not jog every day.
名詞	Ray does not jog every day.	Ray and May do not jog every day.

* 縮寫：does not = doesn't　　　　* 縮寫：do not = don't

---

2 疑問句的構成

疑問句是在主詞前使用助動詞 do 或 does，動詞也是要用原形動詞。

do / does + 主詞 + 原形動詞 → 疑問詞 + do / does + 主詞 + 原形動詞

簡單現在式疑問句的句型

	單數	複數
第一人稱代名詞	Do I jog every day?	Do we jog every day?
第二人稱代名詞	Do you jog every day?	Do you jog every day?
第三人稱代名詞	Does he jog every day? Does she jog every day? Does it jog every day?	Do they jog every day?
名詞	Does Kay jog every day?	Do Kay and May jog every day?
疑問詞	What time does he get up?	What do they usually do on weekends?
	How much does it cost to fly to New York?	Where do you come from?

Sharon Does **she** sew? 她做針線活嗎？

Edward No, she doesn't. 不，她不做。

           └──► = No, she doesn't sew.
                 = No, she never sews.

          ┌──► 使用疑問詞的問句

• **When** does **Ted** usually **go** to bed?
泰德通常什麼時候上床睡覺？

never ＋簡單式動詞

這個句型也可構成否定句。
主詞若為第三人稱單數，就
要用第三人稱單數動詞：

• She never cries.
她從不哭的。

會話範例
專訪籃球員

This is Paul. He plays basketball, and he is an excellent basketball player.
這位是保羅。他打籃球，是一名優秀的籃球員。

★ Interviewer 訪問者
★ Paul 保羅

Interviewer	Paul, may I ask you some questions?	保羅，我可以問你一些問題嗎？
Paul	OK.	好啊。
Interviewer	Do **you** smoke?	你抽菸嗎？
Paul	No, I don't.	我不抽菸。
Interviewer	Do **you** drink **coffee**?	你喝咖啡嗎？
Paul	No, I don't. I drink **green tea**.	我不喝咖啡，我喝綠茶。
Interviewer	Does **your sister, Sue,** play basketball, too?	你的姊姊蘇也打籃球嗎？
Paul	No, she doesn't. She plays **the piano**.	不，她不打籃球，她彈鋼琴。
Interviewer	Do **your parents** watch **your basketball games**?	你父母會看你的籃球比賽嗎？
Paul	Yes, they do.	他們會看。
Interviewer	Do **you** like **ice cream**?	你喜歡吃霜淇淋嗎？
Paul	No, I don't like **ice cream**.	不，我不喜歡吃霜淇淋。
Interviewer	**What kind of dessert** do **you** like?	你喜歡吃什麼樣的甜點？
Paul	I love **apple pie**.	我喜歡吃蘋果派。
Interviewer	Thank you, Paul.	謝謝你，保羅。
Paul	You're welcome.	不客氣。

1 用 **Do** 或 **Does** 填空。

1. _____ Dwight work at night?
2. _____ Gus and you go to school by bus?
3. _____ she play computer games on weekdays?
4. _____ they take the subway to school?
5. _____ you practice ballet every day?
6. _____ Bing usually walk to school in the morning?

2 用 **don't** 或 **doesn't** 填空。

1. Bing _____ get up early in the morning.
2. I _____ watch TV very much.
3. Kay's mom and dad _____ work on Sundays.
4. Pete _____ eat meat.
5. Three of my friends _____ eat meat.
6. Jerome _____ live in London. He lives in Rome.

3 將括弧裡的動詞以簡單現在式填入空格中，然後改寫成疑問句，再根據提示簡答。

1. Bing _____ to church every Sunday morning. (go)

   _____ ?

   Yes, _____ .

2. Kay and Lee _____ their electric car every Sunday. (wash)

   _____ ?

   Yes, _____ .

3. Trish _____ Polish. (speak)

   _____ ?

   No, _____ .

4 Kay and May _____ basketball every day. (play)

_____ ?

No, _____ .

5 Ming and you _____ out to eat every Friday evening. (go)

_____ ?

No, _____ .

6 She never _____ computer games at home. (play)

_____ ?

No, _____ .

4 利用下列詞彙，搭配 **do** 或 **does** 寫出疑問句。

1 ice cream ｜ Mr. and Mrs. Dream ｜ like

_____

2 how much ｜ to fly from London ｜ it ｜ cost ｜ to Singapore

_____

3 want ｜ he ｜ what ｜ for breakfast

_____

4 you ｜ go to school ｜ usually ｜ how

_____

5 often ｜ snow ｜ here ｜ it

_____

6 soccer ｜ like ｜ your brother Mike

_____

Chapter

30 現在進行式：肯定句的用法

I

現在進行式用來描述**講話當下正在進行的**（或沒有在進行的）**動作和狀況。**

〔現在進行式也可用來表示未來，參見 Chapter 39。〕

- Claire is combing her long hair.
  克萊兒正在梳她的長髮。

- It's 4 p.m. We are having our afternoon tea.
  現在是下午四點，我們正在喝下午茶。

- I can't go shopping now because I'm doing my homework.
  我現在不能去購物，因為我正在做功課。

- Look, your dog is swimming in the lake.
  你看，你的狗在湖裡游泳。

---

2 ── 現在進行式的肯定句句型

主詞 + am / is / are + 動詞的現在分詞 → 動詞 be（am, is, are）除了當作連綴動詞外，還可以當作助動詞，構成現在進行式。

現在進行式肯定句的句型

▼ 主詞	單數	複數
第一人稱代名詞	I am working. = I'm working.	We are working. = We're working.
第二人稱代名詞	You are working. = You're working.	You are working. = You're working.
第三人稱代名詞	He is working. = He's working. She is working. = She's working. It is working. = It's working.	They are working. = They're working.
名詞	Ming is working.	Ming and Tom are working.

---

3 | **動詞現在分詞的構成方式**

〔參見附錄二〕

❶ 大多數動詞，在字尾加 ing。

→ do → doing
　study → studying

❷ 字尾是 e 的動詞，刪除 e，加上 ing。

→ have → having
　smile → smiling

❸ 字尾是 ie 的動詞，將 ie 改成 y，再加 ing。

→ die → dying
　lie → lying

❹ 單音節動詞，並且是「短母音 + 子音字尾」，先重複字尾子音，再加 ing。

→ run → running
　sit → sitting
　swim → swimming

❺ 雙音節或多音節動詞：

　① 重音在最後一音節上，則重複字尾的子音，再加 ing。

→ begin → beginning
　[bɪˋgɪn]

　② 重音不在最後一音節上，則直接加 ing。

→ listen → listening
　[ˋlɪsn̩]

1 寫出下列動詞的現在分詞。

1 rain _____	**6** make _____	**11** stop _____
2 swim _____	**7** come _____	**12** control _____
3 tie _____	**8** drive _____	**13** run _____
4 jog _____	**9** put _____	**14** lie _____
5 die _____	**10** happen _____	**15** sit _____

2 依圖示,利用下列詞彙寫出現在進行式的句子。

1

Ted | stand on his head

_____
_____

2

I | do the splits

_____
_____

3

the baby | cry

_____
_____

4

the girls | run

_____
_____

5

she | cook

_____
_____

6

Dad | sleep

_____
_____

7

the kites | fly

_____
_____

8

she | try on | her new dress

_____
_____

9

I | read | a novel on my cellphone

_____
_____

3 重組句子：將下列詞彙重組為正確的句子。

1 reading | I | an | am | storybook. | English

_____

2 girls | swimming | now. | are | the

_____

3 is | the | at | looking | she | birds | in the tree.

_____

4 peace. | is | for | praying | she | world

_____

5 giving | Rose | he | red rose. | a | is

_____

6 to | not | you | listening | me. | are

_____

7 the | are | on | Internet. | chatting | they

_____

8 you | in | seat. | sitting | my | are

_____

9 playing | and Dennis | are | tennis. | Ming

_____

10 walking | street. | across | Uncle Pete | the | is

_____

4 自下列的綠色詞彙中選出適當的詞彙，以現在進行式填空。

swim   stay   cook   do   wear

1 "Where is Dad?" "He's in the kitchen. He _____."

2 Please be quiet. Dirk _____ his math homework.

3 Look at Tess. She _____ her new blue dress. Doesn't she look beautiful!

4 June and Don are on their honeymoon. They _____ at the Day Motel in Green Bay.

5 Look! Jake _____ in Cold Lake.

Chapter 31 現在進行式：否定句和疑問句的用法

1 否定句的構成

主詞 + be 動詞 (am, is, are) + not + 動詞的現在分詞 → be 動詞在這裡起助動詞作用，與主要動詞的現在分詞形式搭配，構成進行式。

現在進行式否定句的句型

▼ 主詞	單數	複數
第一人稱代名詞	I am not working. = I'm not working.	We are not working. = We're not working. = We aren't working.
第二人稱代名詞	You are not working. = You're not working. = You aren't working.	You are not working. = You're not working. = You aren't working.
第三人稱代名詞	He is not working. = He's not working. = He isn't working. She is not working. = She's not working. = She isn't working. It is not working. = It's not working. = It isn't working.	They are not working. = They're not working. = They aren't working.
名詞	Ming is not working. = Ming's not working. = Ming isn't working.	Ming and Tom are not working. = Ming and Tom aren't working.

肯定句
- She is running now. 她現在正在跑步。

否定句
- She is not running now. = She isn't running now. = She's not running now.
  她現在沒有在跑步。

2 疑問句的構成

be 動詞 (am, is, are) + 主詞 + 動詞的現在分詞 → be 動詞在這裡起助動詞作用，與主要動詞的現在分詞形式搭配，構成進行式。

be 動詞在這裡起助動詞作用，與主要動詞的現在分詞搭配，構成現在進行式。

句型的疑問詞包括 who、what、when、where、why 和 how，疑問詞的後面仍須使用疑問句的句型。

```
疑問詞  +  be 動詞
           (am, is, are)  +  主詞  +  動詞的
                                     現在分詞  →
```

現在進行式疑問句的句型

▼ 主詞	單數	複數
第一人稱代名詞	Am I working?	Are we working?
第二人稱代名詞	Are you working?	Are you working?
第三人稱代名詞	Is he working?	Are they working?
	Is she working?	
	Is it working?	
名詞	Is Ming working?	Are Ming and Tom working?
使用疑問詞的問句	What's she reading?	Where are they ice-skating?
	Who's she talking to?	Why are you yelling at Sue?

┌── 疑問句

Laura Is she running now?　她現在正在跑步嗎？
Jose Yes, she is. →簡答　對，她在跑步。
No, she isn't. →簡答　不，她沒有在跑步。

Eric What is Aunt Liz telling those boys?
Carol She's telling them not to make so much noise.
艾瑞克 莉茲姑姑正在跟那些男孩說什麼？
卡蘿 她在叫他們不要太吵鬧。

Debra Is Jane driving to Spain right now?
Scott No, she isn't driving. She's flying her airplane to Spain.
黛博拉 珍正在開車去西班牙嗎？
史考特 沒有，她沒有在開車，她正駕著自己的飛機去西班牙。

Peter Is Mike sleeping now?
Sarah No, he isn't sleeping. He's talking to Mom on Skype.
彼得 邁克正在睡覺嗎？
莎拉 沒有，他沒在睡覺，他在跟媽媽用 Skype 聊天。

Peter Is it raining there?
Sarah No, it's not raining. The sun is shining brightly.
彼得 那裡正在下雨嗎？
莎拉 沒有下雨啊，現在陽光正燦爛呢。

1 重組下列詞彙，寫出現在進行式的肯定句，然後改寫成疑問句和否定句。

1 He | write | an email | to Lily

a) 肯定句 _____

b) 疑問句 _____

c) 否定句 _____

2 She | think about | food

a) 肯定句 _____

b) 疑問句 _____

c) 否定句 _____

3 They | jump | on | the big bed | now

a) 肯定句 _____

b) 疑問句 _____

c) 否定句 _____

4 She | jog | in the fog

a) 肯定句 _____

b) 疑問句 _____

c) 否定句 _____

2 看圖回答問題（註明 ★ 的題目請使用簡答）。

sing

1 Is Paul playing basketball?

★ _____

2 What is Paul doing?

_____

read a newspaper

3 Is your dad writing an email?

★ _____

4 What is your dad doing?

_____

sleep in our classroom

make cupcakes

talk on the phone

watch TV

5 Is Sue counting her money?

★ _____

6 What's Sue doing?

_____

7 Are they eating pizza in the kitchen?

★ _____

8 What are they doing?

_____

9 Is Joan driving?

★ _____

10 What's Joan doing?

_____

11 Is Lee listening to the BBC?

★ _____

12 What is Lee doing?

_____

3 利用下列詞彙，搭配助動詞 **is** 或 **are**，組成正確的疑問句。

1 waiting | you | for | who

_____

2 to me | you | listening

_____

3 you | that woman in the miniskirt | staring at

_____

4 staying | your relatives | at a hotel

_____

Chapter

32 比較：簡單現在式和現在進行式

1

簡單 現在式 →	用來談論**習慣**或**經常、不斷發生的事**，也可以談論**偶爾發生的事**或**從未發生的事**。	• Does **Kay practice the piano** every day? 凱每天都要練鋼琴嗎？ • **Bing** takes **a shower** every morning. 賓每天早上都要沖個澡。 • **It** often snows **in Michigan during the winter.** 密西根冬天常下雪。
現在 進行式 →	用來描述**說話時正在發生的事**。	• It's 8 p.m. **Joe** is practicing **the piano.** 現在是晚上八點，喬正在練鋼琴。 • **Oh, look!** It's snowing. 啊，瞧！下雪了。

2

下面的詞彙和片語常用於**簡單現在式**：

always 總是	**every day** 每天	**every weekend** 每個週末
never 從不	**every year** 每年	**once a day** 每天一次
often 經常	**every decade** 每十年	**twice a week** 一週兩次
sometimes 有時	**every morning** 每天早上	**twice a year** 一年兩次
usually 通常	**every Sunday** 每個星期天	**all the time** 一直；始終

3

現在進行式也可以用來描述「**目前發生的事**」，但並不一定指此時此刻正在發生的事。

指目前處在找工作的狀態，
└─ 而非此時此刻正在發生的事。

• **Bob** is looking **for a job at the moment.**
目前鮑勃正在找工作。

I'm almost in the mood to look for a job.
我再差一點點就有心情去找工作囉。

┌─► 指每天都會做的一件事。

- **Every day** my little brother Ted **jumps** up and down on my bed.
  我的小弟泰德每天都要在我的床上跳上跳下。

┌─► 指此時此刻正在做的事。

- My little brother Ted **is <u>now</u> jumping** up and down on my bed.
  我的小弟泰德正在我的床上跳上跳下。

┌─► 指每天生活中的一種習慣。

- **Every day** Rich **eats** a sandwich. 瑞奇每天都要吃一個三明治。

┌─► 指此時此刻正在做的事。

- It's 1:30 p.m. Rich **is eating** a sandwich. 現在是下午一點半，瑞奇正在吃三明治。

┌─► 指每年習慣性會做的一件事。

- **Every summer** I **go** to Chicago to see Uncle Joe. 我每年夏天都要去芝加哥看喬叔。

┌─► 指此刻正要做的事。

- I **am leaving** <u>now</u> for Chicago to see Uncle Joe. 我正要出發去芝加哥看喬叔。

┌─► 指每天晚上都會做的一件事。

- **Every night** Trish **listens** to English for an hour. 翠希每天晚上都要聽一個小時的英文。

┌─► 指此時此刻正在做的事。

- **At the moment** Trish **is listening** to some English. 此刻，翠希正在聽英文。

詢問所從事的職業。
(= What is your job?)

`Juan` **What do you do?** 你從事什麼工作？

`Janet` I **work** as a waiter. 我是服務生。

詢問此時正在
做什麼事情。

`Anna` **What are you doing?** 你在做什麼？

`Carl` I'**m having** a sandwich. 我在吃三明治。

- Mark **is** a salesperson. He **sells** computers. At the moment he **is not** at work. He **is** at home. He **is playing** a Facebook game called "Happy Farm."
  馬克是一名銷售電腦的業務員。此刻，他沒有在上班，他在家裡玩臉書的「開心農場」。

- Jane **is** a teacher. She **teaches** English and Spanish. At the moment she'**s not** in school. She'**s** at home. She'**s watering** the plants in her backyard garden.
  珍是一名教師，她教英語和西班牙語。此刻，她沒有在學校，她在家裡的後花園澆花。

1 利用動詞 swim，寫出簡單現在式和現在進行式的句型，完成下表。

簡單現在式	現在進行式
1 I _swim_	I _am swimming_
2 you _____	you _____
3 he _____	he _____
4 she _____	she _____
5 it _____	it _____
6 we _____	we _____
7 you _____	you _____
8 they _____	they _____

2 選出正確的答案。

1 Why is Meg carrying | Why are Meg carrying **an egg?**

2 Kay and I go | is going **to play baseball almost every day.**

3 Is she using | Does she use **her cellphone right now?**

4 I usually do | I am usually doing **my homework in the evening,** but tonight I play | I'm playing **a computer game.**

3 用簡單現在式或現在進行式完成下列疑問句，然後根據事實回答問題。
(Q = Question: A = Answer)

1 you | often | wear | sunglasses?
> Q _Do you often wear sunglasses?_
> A _Yes, I do./No, I don't._

2 you | wear | sunglasses | now?
> Q _____
> A _____

3 it | often | snow | in your city?
> Q _____
> A _____

4 it | snow | now?

Q _____

A _____

5 you | usually | listen to English | in the evening?

Q _____

A _____

6 you | listen to English | now?

Q _____

A _____

7 you | sometimes | play chess | in the afternoon?

Q _____

A _____

8 you | play chess | now?

Q _____

A _____

9 you | often | make tea | for your mom?

Q _____

A _____

10 you | make tea | for your mom | now?

Q _____

A _____

4 用 **am**、**is**、**are** 或 **do**、**don't**、**does**、**doesn't** 填空。

1 "Where _____ you come from?" asked Sue.

2 My sister is a taxi driver. She _____ not driving right now.
She _____ playing the piano.

3 He _____ play computer games very often.

4 "Excuse me, _____ you speak Japanese?" "No, I _____."

5 How often _____ she surf the Internet?

6 What's the matter? Why _____ you crying?

Chapter

33 不能用於進行式的動詞

有些動詞通常只用於**簡單式**，不用於**進行式**，這些動詞叫做**非進行式動詞**或**非動作動詞**，主要分有以下四大類：

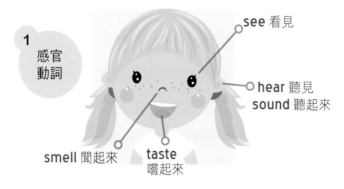

1 感官動詞

see 看見
hear 聽見
sound 聽起來
smell 聞起來
taste 嚐起來

2 連綴動詞

be 是
appear 好像是
look (= seem)
　　看起來；好像
seem 好像

・ I can see Lee, but he can't see me.
我能看見李，但他看不見我。

> see（看見）、hear（聽見）
> 等動詞，常與 can 連用。
> 不可用進行式。

　不可用進行式。
・ She seems to be very confident of herself. 她好像非常有自信。

3 心理狀態和感情的動詞

believe 相信；信任	know 知道	see 理解 (= understand)
doubt 懷疑；不相信	like/dislike 喜歡／不喜歡	suppose 猜想；認為
feel 覺得；相信；認為	love 愛	think 認為
(= have an opinion)	need 需要	(= have an opinion)
forget 忘記	prefer 更喜歡	understand 理解
guess 認為；推測	realize 意識到	want 想要
hate 仇恨；不喜歡	recognize 認識；認出	wish 希望；想要
imagine 猜想	remember 記得	

　不可用進行式。
・ I don't believe her. 我不相信她。

　不可用進行式。
・ I feel that I can win the speech contest. 我覺得我能贏這場講演賽。

　不可用進行式。
・ "I like this music," said Mike. 邁克説：「我喜歡這個音樂。」

　不可用進行式。
・ I don't understand this word. 我不懂這個字的意思。

4
其他

agree 同意　　have (= possess) 擁有　　owe 欠債；應感激　　possess 擁有
belong 屬於　　include 包括　　own 擁有

┌─ 不可以用進行式。
• I agree with you. 我同意你的看法。

2

上述非進行式動詞當中，有些同時也是描述**動作**的一般**行為動詞**，在當作行為動詞、描述一個動作時，就**可以用進行式**。

此句的 think (= believe)，描述「相信、認為」這種心理狀態，
┌─ 不是行為動詞，只能用簡單式。

think
• She thinks money is everything. 她認為金錢是最重要的。
┌─ 此句的 think (= use the mind)，描述
• Please don't talk to me now. I'm thinking.　「思考」這個動作，可以用進行式。
此刻請不要跟我說話，我正在想事情。

┌─ 意思是「擁有」（= possess），不是動作，只能用簡單式。
have
• I have an electric car. 我有一輛電動小汽車。
┌─ 意思是「吃」（= eat），是動作，可以用進行式。
• I'm having dinner with Pam. 我正在跟潘姆一起吃飯。

┌─ 意思是「嚐起來……」，是感官的感受，只能用簡單式。
taste
• The fish tastes good. 這條魚嚐起來味道不錯。
┌─ 意思是「品嚐」的動作，可以用進行式。
• Mom is tasting the chicken soup now. 媽媽正在品嚐雞湯。

┌─ 意思是「理解」（= understand），不是動作，只能用簡單式。
see
• Do you see what I mean? 你明白我的意思嗎？
┌─ 意思是「會見」（= visit），是動作，可以用進行式。　→ 有些進行式動詞可以
• Are you seeing Joe tomorrow? 你明天要去找喬嗎？　　　用來表示未來〔參見
　　　　　　　　　　　　　　　　　　　　　　　　　　　　　Chapter 39〕。

意思是「有多重」（= have weight），
┌─ 不是動作，只能用簡單式。
weigh
• How much does Kay weigh? 凱的體重是多少？
┌─ 意思是「秤重量」（= determine the weight of），是動作，可以用進行式。
• Lily is weighing a box of books. 莉莉在秤一箱書的重量。

3

但是 **feel sick**（感覺生病）或 **feel tired**（感覺疲累）的片語，可以用簡單式，也可以用進行式〔參見 Unit 10 感官動詞和使役動詞〕。

• I'm feeling tired. = I feel tired. 我覺得好累。

1 將提示的動詞用簡單現在式或現在進行式填空，完成句子。

1. I _____ (need) your help today.

2. Sue _____ (think) highly of you.

3. Your puppy _____ (look) at the kitten.

4. _____ (you/want) any tea or coffee?

5. I _____ (see) what you mean.

6. _____ (the baby/smell) bad?

7. What _____ (you/think) about right now?

8. What _____ (your dad/think) about your boyfriend?

9. Why _____ (Mom/smell) the milk?

10. She _____ (have) a cottage near the old stone bridge.

11. Dad, the milk _____ (taste) bad.

12. At the moment we _____ (have) a wonderful time on the beach.

13. I _____ (know) that girl in the fancy hat, but I can't remember her name.

14. I _____ (not/understand) his English.

15. It's getting late and I'm tired. I _____ (want) to go home.

16. She _____ (prefer) the quiet and clean countryside to the noisy and polluted cities.

2 請判斷下列句子是否正確，正確打 ✓，不正確打 ×，並寫出正確句子。

1. This flower is smelling so good!

   ☐ _____

2. I am loving ice cream.

   ☐ _____

3 Do you believe me?

4 I think about you every day.

5 Be quiet, please. I think hard.

6 Bob is having a good job.

7 They're having a good time at the party.

8 Are you knowing my friend Sue?

9 Dan is feeling that time is very precious.

10 Why are you smelling my armpit?

11 Is Mom seeing the doctor this afternoon?

12 "What are you doing?" "I'm weighing myself."

13 Are you seeing what Mom means about Tom?

14 How much are you weighing?

15 I am loving my dog very much.

Chapter

34 be 動詞的簡單過去式

1

be 動詞的**簡單過去式**是 was 和 were，代名詞 I 一定搭配 was，you 一定搭配 were 使用。除了這兩種固定用法之外，其他單數代名詞（he, she, it）和單數名詞（例如：Mary, my mother）都用 was，複數代名詞（we, they）和複數名詞（例如：my parents）都用 were。

be 動詞過去式句型一覽表

	肯定句	否定句	疑問句
單數	I was	I was not	was I?
	you were	you were not	were you?
	he was	he was not	was he?
	she was	she was not	was she?
	it was	it was not	was it?
複數	we were	we were not	were we?
	you were	you were not	were you?
	they were	they were not	were they?

* 否定縮寫　was not = wasn't
　　　　　　were not = weren't

2

當作**連綴動詞**用的 **be** 動詞的簡單過去式，用來談論「**過去存在的事或狀態**」，與表示**過去時間**的詞彙連用。表示**過去時間**的詞彙有：

last week	上週
a minute ago	一分鐘前
yesterday	昨天
last night	昨晚
in 2009	在 2009 年

疑問句的句型，be 動詞（was/were）放在主詞前面。

Henry Where were you in 2012? 2012 年你在哪裡？

Jean I was in Berlin. 我在柏林。　代名詞 you 用 were；代名詞 I 用 was。

Doris Where was Joe six months ago? 六個月前喬在哪裡？

Keith He was in Rome. 他在羅馬。

單數名詞（如：Joe, Mom）和單數代名詞（he, she, it）用 was。

Adam Where's our dog? She was here a few minute ago.

Julie I don't know. Oh, look, there she is! She's under the bed.

亞當 我們的狗狗呢？幾分鐘前牠還在這裡呀。

茱麗 我不知道。哦，你看，牠在那裡！在床下面。

複數名詞（如：my parents）和複合名詞（如：Sue and Lulu）用 were。

Roy Where were Sue and Lulu last week? 蘇和露露上週在哪裡？

Judy They were in the countryside. 她們在鄉下。

複數代名詞（如：they, we）用 were。

疑問句把 be 動詞（Was/Were）置於主詞前面。

Rose Were you at the zoo last Sunday? 上個星期天你在動物園嗎？

Terry No, I was not. I was at the circus. 沒有啊，我在看馬戲表演。

否定詞 not 要放在 be 動詞後面（was not/were not）。

3

現在式用 **am** 或 **is** 的句子，過去式就用 **was**；現在式用 **are** 的句子，過去式就用 **were**。

現在式　　　　　　　　　　過去式

- I am full of energy today. → I was very tried yesterday.
  我今天精力充沛。　　　　　昨天我很累。

- Where is Claire now? → Where was Claire yesterday morning?
  克萊兒現在在哪裡？　　　克萊兒昨天上午在哪裡？

- You are late again. → You were late yesterday.
  你又遲到了。　　　　　你昨天遲到了。

- They are not in school today. → They were not in school yesterday.
  他們今天沒有上學。　　　　　他們昨天沒有上學。

1 參照插圖，用正確的 **be** 動詞填空，完成對話。

1. Lori Who _____ Michael Jackson?
   Fred He _____ an African American singer and dancer.

2. Lori Who _____ Lady Gaga?
   Fred She _____ an American pop singer-songwriter.

3. Lori Who _____ Sylvester Stallone?
   Fred He _____ an American actor, screenwriter, and film director.

4. Lori Who _____ John F. Kennedy?
   Fred He _____ the 35th President of America, and he began the Apollo Moon Program.

2 用 **was** 或 **were** 填空完成問句，再根據事實回答問題。

1. Where _____ you at eight last night?

   _____

2. _____ your mom sick yesterday?

   _____

3. _____ the weather bad the day before yesterday?

   _____

4. _____ you and your parents at the seaside last Sunday?

   _____

3 選出正確的答案。

_____ 1. Kay _____ with me yesterday.
   a wasn't   b isn't   c weren't

_____ ② Mom, where _____ you and June last Friday afternoon?
a are　　b were　　c was

_____ ③ There _____ still a lot of snow on the top of Mount Fuji last month, but today there _____ none.
a is, is　　b was, is　　c were, are

_____ ④ Last night Joe and I _____ in Paris, and now we _____ in Chicago.
a were, were　　b are, were　　c were, are

_____ ⑤ There _____ lots of orange juice in this big bottle an hour ago, but now there _____ none.
a were, is　　b was, was　　c was, is

_____ ⑥ _____ Mom and Dad at a party last night?
a Were　　b Are　　c Was

_____ ⑦ "Happy birthday to you, Margo!" "Thanks a lot. But my birthday _____ a month ago."
a is　　b were　　c was

_____ ⑧ "Where _____ Lulu in 2010?" "That is an odd question. She _____ born until 2011."
a were, weren't　　b was, wasn't　　c is, wasn't

_____ ⑨ I feel great today, but yesterday I _____ tired and depressed.
a was　　b am　　c were

4　用 **was** 或 **were**，搭配下列詞彙，重組出正確的「疑問句」。

① at home ｜ Jerome ｜ last night

_____

② Kay ｜ why ｜ yesterday ｜ upset

_____

③ why ｜ late ｜ you and Bing ｜ this morning ｜ for school

_____

④ born ｜ you ｜ when

_____

Chapter

35 簡單過去式

| |

肯定句 主詞 + 過去式動詞 → 簡單過去式必須使用簡單過去式的動詞。過去式動詞，除了 be 動詞外，通常在原形動詞後面加上 -ed 或 -d（例如：watch → watched）。

否定句 主詞 + did not = didn't + 原形動詞 → 簡單過去式的否定句句型，是在述語動詞前面加上 did not 或者縮寫 didn't，述語動詞要用原形動詞。did 是助動詞。

疑問句 did + 主詞 + 原形動詞 → 簡單過去式的疑問句句型，是在主詞前面加上助動詞 did，述語動詞使用原形動詞。

疑問詞開頭的疑問句 疑問詞 + did + 主詞 + 原形動詞 → 如果有疑問詞（what、where 等），則疑問詞要放於句首。

簡單過去式的句型

		肯定句	否定句	疑問句
單數		I played	I did not play	did I play?
		you played	you did not play	did you play?
		he played	he did not play	did he play?
		she played	she did not play	did she play?
		it played	it did not play	did it play?
複數		we played	we did not play	did we play?
		you played	you did not play	did you play?
		they played	they did not play	did they play?

* 肯定形式的簡略回答：
Yes, I/we/you/they/he/she/it did.

* 否定形式的簡略回答：
No, I/we/you/they/he/she/it didn't.

* 縮寫：did not = didn't

動詞的**簡單過去式**用來描述**過去曾經存在或發生的事**，句中通常會有**表示過去時間的詞彙**，如：yesterday（昨天）、a minute ago（一分鐘前）、last week（上週）等。

Tim　What did you and Sue do last night? 昨晚你和蘇做了什麼？

Sara　We watched TV. 我們看了電視。

Lois　Where did Kay go for a bicycle ride yesterday? 昨天凱去哪裡騎自行車了？

Jack　Yesterday she went for a bicycle ride in the countryside. 昨天她去鄉下騎自行車。
　　　　└→ went 是 go 的過去式，屬於不規則變化的動詞。

Bob　Did Joe snore quietly a while ago? 剛才喬是不是有小聲打鼾？

Tina　No, he did not snore quietly. He snored loudly. 不，他不是小聲打鼾，而是鼾聲大作。
　　　　└→ he did not snore quietly = he didn't snore quietly

Diana　Did Kay sing in the choir last Sunday? 上個星期天，凱有去參加聖歌合唱嗎？

Randy　Yes, she sang in the choir last Sunday. 有，上個星期天她有去參加聖歌合唱。
　　　　└→ sang 是 sing 的過去式動詞，屬於不規則動詞。
　　　　　　這裡也可以做簡略回答「Yes, she did.」。

Emily　Did you cook for Lulu last night? 昨晚你有煮飯給露露吃嗎？

Steve　No, I didn't cook, because she cooked for me. 我沒有，是她煮飯給我吃。
　　　　└→ didn't = did not

Laura　What did you do yesterday afternoon? 昨天下午你在做什麼？

Craig　I played tennis and I won. 我去打網球，而且贏了。
　　　　└→ won 是 win 的過去式，屬於不規則動詞。

3　動詞過去式的構成方式

❶ 大多數動詞，在字尾加 ed
→
start → started
wash → washed

❷ 字尾是 e 的動詞，在字尾加 d
→
hate → hated
like → liked

❸ 字尾是「子音 +y」的動詞，將 y 改成 ied
→
reply → replied
try → tried

❹ 單音節動詞，並且是「短母音 + 子音字尾」，先重複字尾的子音子母，再加 ed
→
plan → planned
stop → stopped

❺ 不規則動詞〔參見附錄四：不規則動詞表〕
→
do → did
read → read

1 將括弧內的單字，用簡單過去式填空，完成句子。

1. Kay _____ (cut) her finger yesterday.

2. A few minutes ago Mabel _____ (set) the table.

3. Dwight _____ (sleep) very well last night.

4. Bing _____ (get) up late this morning.

5. Last night Ted _____ (hit) his head when he fell out of bed.

6. Yesterday evening Lori _____ (read) us an interesting story.

2 重組下列詞彙，寫出正確的「疑問句」，再依據事實做「簡答」。
(Q= Question; A = Answer)

1. new pink silk dress | a | yesterday | you | wear

   Q. *Did you wear a new pink silk dress yesterday?*

   A. *Yes, I did./No, I didn't.*

2. last night | have a good time | you

   Q. _____

   A. _____

3. study English | you | last night

   Q. _____

   A. _____

4. you | last night | eat | any pizza

   Q. _____

   A. _____

5. night | snow | it | last

   Q. _____

   A. _____

3 根據下面的文字，再觀察圖片（Jane 昨天真正做的事），來回答 Jane 昨天所做過或沒做過的事，請為每一事件寫出「疑問句」，並依據圖片做出回答（答句請寫出完整句子）。（Q= Question; A = Answer）

yesterday

1 get up at 6:30

2 go to see a movie

3 do lots of homework

4 play table tennis

5 climb a mountain

1 Q: *Did Jane get up at 6:30 a.m.?*
A: *No, she didn't get up at 6:30.*

2 Q:
A:

3 Q:
A:

4 Q:
A:

5 Q:
A:

Chapter 36 過去進行式

I ── 過去進行式的構成方式

過去進行式用來表示「**過去某個時間正在進行的動作**」。

主詞 ＋ was / were ＋ 現在分詞 → 〔現在分詞的構成，參見 Chapter 30〕

┌ were doing 表示過去進行式。

Kathy What were you doing at 8:30 this morning?　你今天早上八點半在做什麼？
Felix I was walking happily to school.　我正高高興興地走路去上學。
Kathy Was the sun shining?　那時有太陽嗎？
Felix Yes, the sun was shining.　有啊，陽光燦爛。
Kathy Were the birds singing in the trees?　樹上有鳥兒在唱歌嗎？
Felix Yes, they were.　有喔。
　　　└ 簡答

過去進行式的句型

	單數	複數
肯定句	I was walking	we were walking
	you were walking	you were walking
	he was walking	
	she was walking	they were walking
	it was walking	
疑問句	was I walking?	were we walking?
	were you walking?	were you walking?
	was he walking?	
	was she walking?	were they walking?
	was it walking?	
否定句	I was not walking	we were not walking
	you were not walking	you were not walking
	he was not walking	
	she was not walking	they were not walking
	it was not walking	

* 縮寫：
was not = wasn't
were not = weren't

2 | 過去進行式和簡單過去式的比較

過去進行式 → 過去某個時刻正在進行的動作

┌─ 指明昨晚九點正在進行的動作。

❶

Bess **What** was **Sue** doing **at nine last night?**
昨晚九點蘇在做什麼？

Adam **She** was text messaging **me.**
她在跟我傳手機簡訊。

簡單過去式 → 過去發生過的事件

┌─ 指昨晚做過的事，未指明時刻。

Eva **What** did **Dwight** do **last night?** 昨晚杜威特做了什麼事？

Pat **He** read **the news on the Internet and**
wrote **an email.**
他上網看了新聞，還寫了一封電子郵件。

過去進行式 → 過去持續時間比較長的動作

┌─ walk（走路）是較長時間的行為動作，所以用過去進行式。

• I was walking **to town when I** saw **the accident.**
我走路去城裡的路上，目睹了那場交通事故。 saw（看見）是短暫的行為動作，
所以用簡單過去式。

┌─ read（閱讀）是較長時間的行為動作，所以用過去進行式。

❷

• She was reading **when somebody** knocked **on the door.**
有人敲門時，她正在看書。 └─ knock（敲門）是短暫的行為動作，
所以用簡單過去式。

• Dad fell asleep while **he** was watching **TV.** 爸看電視看得睡著了。
→ 一般過去式：較為短暫的行為動作（fell asleep）。
→ 過去進行式：較長時間的行為動作，即延續性動作（was watching）。
→ while 引導的子句，須用延續性動詞。

簡單過去式 → 過去持續時間較短暫的動作

┌─ stop（停止）是短暫的行為動作，所以用簡單過去式。

• She stopped reading **when somebody** knocked → 「stop + 動詞 -ing」
on the door. 她聽見有人敲門，就不看書了。 的用法，參見
Chapter 54。

3

不能用於**現在進行式**的動詞，也沒有**過去進行式**〔不能用於進行式的動詞，參見 Chapter 33〕。

┌─ 連綴動詞 seem 不能使用現在進行式，也就沒有過去進行式，

• Last year Bob seemed **to be very happy with his job.**
去年鮑勃好像對他的工作很滿意。

143

PRACTICE

1 利用下列詞語，設定「昨天晚上九點」（**at nine last night**），用過去進行式寫出完整句子。

1 listen to | the BBC | Dee

_____

2 a | Brooke | cookbook | read

_____

3 on | big bed | bounce | Ted | his

_____

4 Kim | jog | in | gym | and Jim | the

_____

5 Paul | his | how | a ball | to catch | dog | teach

_____

6 Uncle Ed | get | to go | ready | to bed

_____

2 依據括弧提示回答問題。

1 What were Kay and May doing around 9:30 yesterday morning?
(play basketball)

_____

2 What was Kay doing around eleven yesterday morning? (cook)

_____

3 Around eleven yesterday morning, what was Bing doing? (practice singing)

_____

4 What were Kate and her brother Dwight doing around eight last night?
(walk their dog)

_____

5 What were you doing at nine last night? (teach my dog Lulu how to roll over.)

_____

6 Around 2:30 this morning, what was your dog Lulu doing? (bark at my cat Lily)

_____

7 What was Scot doing at nine last night? (write an email to his friend Dee)

_____

8 What were Bing and June doing the whole afternoon? (argue about nothing)

_____

9 What was your sister doing at King Beach at ten yesterday morning?
(build a huge sand castle)

_____

10 What were Gwen and Dwight doing when you arrived home last night?
(eat by candlelight)

_____

3 | 選出正確答案。

_____ 1 Last Saturday night, Brad [   ] a lot of wine and [   ] bad.
　　　a drank, was smelling　　　c drank, smelled
　　　b was drinking, was smelling　d drinked, smelled

_____ 2 [   ] May [   ] at 5 p.m. yesterday?
　　　a Was, cooking　b Did, cooking　c Were, cooking　d Was, cook

_____ 3 What [   ] Pam and Bing [   ] at 9:30 this morning?
　　　a was, doing　　b were, doing　　c do, did　　d did, doing

_____ 4 When Brook's sister was four years old, she [   ] to read comic books.
　　　a is liking　　b was liking　　c liked　　d likes

_____ 5 "What was Lori doing when you [   ] into the library?"
　　　"She [   ] a story."
　　　a were coming, was reading　　c comes, is reading
　　　b came, read　　　　　　　　　d came, was reading

_____ 6 Last night you [   ] Sue.
　　　a were surprising　b surprises　c are surprising　d surprised

_____ 7 What were you doing when the phone [   ] ?
　　　a is ringing　b ringed　c rang　d were ringing

_____ 8 I broke my left leg yesterday. It [   ] when I [   ] the roof.
　　　I fell off the ladder.
　　　a happened, was fixing　　　c happened, fixed
　　　b was happening, was fixing　d was happening, fixed

_____ 9 How fast [   ] you [   ] when the police [   ] you?
　　　a did, drive, stopped　　　c were, driving, was stopping
　　　b were, driving, stopped　　d did, drive, was stopping

Chapter 37 簡單現在完成式

I 簡單現在完成式的構成方式

簡單現在完成式用來表達「從過去一直延續到現在的事件或狀態」。

主詞 + 助動詞 have/has + 過去分詞

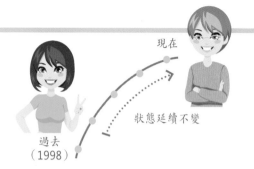

現在

狀態延續不變

過去（1998）

┌─ 使用現在完成式，表示從 1998 年開始當律師，直到現在仍然是律師。

- She has been a lawyer since January 1, 1998.
  她從 1998 年一月一日起就一直在當律師。

- She has been a lawyer for many years. 她當律師好多年了。
  └─ 使用現在完成式，表示多年來都在當律師，直到現在仍然是律師。

動詞過去分詞的構成方式

①	規則動詞的過去分詞變化方式，與過去式一樣。	call → called dance → danced cry → cried stop → stopped
②	不規則動詞〔參見附錄四：不規則動詞表〕。	do → done eat → eaten begin → begun see → seen

簡單現在完成式的句型

	單數		複數	
肯定句	I you	have worked	we you	have worked
	he she it	has worked	they	have worked
疑問句	have	I you worked?	have	we you worked?
	has	he she it worked?	have	they worked?
否定句	I you he she it	have not worked	we you	have not worked
		has not worked	they	have not worked

* 縮寫：
I have → I've
you have → you've
we have → we've
they have → they've
he has → he's
she has → she's
it has → it's

* 縮寫：
have not → haven't
has not → hasn't

2

簡單現在完成式中，常用 for 和 since 來表示「**事情延續的時間長度**」。

for
- I've waited **for Jane** for two hours. 我已經等珍兩個小時了。
  └─ for + 一段時間
- She's lived **in Ireland** for 15 years. 她已經在愛爾蘭住了 15 年了。

┌─ since + 持定的時間點

since
- I've waited **for Jane** since 2 p.m. 我從下午兩點起就一直在等珍。
- She's lived **in Ireland** since she was born. 她從出生就住在愛爾蘭。
  └─ since + 子句（子句要用過去式）

3

簡單現在完成式用來描述「**對現在產生影響的過去行為動作**」，常會使用到 just、already、yet 等字。（yet 用在**否定句**和**疑問句**中。）

┌─ 還未完成的過去動作→顯示喬此時不在華盛頓特區。

- Joe has not yet arrived in Washington D.C. 喬還沒有抵達華盛頓特區。
  └─ yet 用於否定句中。

┌─ yet 用於疑問句中。

Max Has he started his new job yet? 他開始他的新工作了嗎？

Jill Yes, he has already started his new job. 他已經開始他的新工作了。
  └─ 已經完成的過去動作→顯示他現在已經在做新的工作了。

┌─ 簡單現在完成式常用句型「How long have you/has she + been...?」。

Ida How long has she been in Paris? 她在巴黎有多長時間了？   顯示她現在已經在巴黎了。

Dave Let me see. She arrived in Paris last Friday. Today is Tuesday. She has been in Paris for five days.
讓我想一想。她上個星期五到巴黎，今天是星期二，她在巴黎五天了。

4

簡單現在完成式用來談論「直到目前為止的人生經歷」，常用到never（不曾）和ever（曾經）這兩個副詞。（ever = at any time，常用於**疑問句**和**否定句**。）

┌─ ever 用於疑問句。

- Have **you** ever met **Sue?** 你見過蘇嗎？

- Have **you** ever ridden **a horse?** 你騎過馬嗎？

┌─ 用 never 構成否定句。

- Coco has never seen **snow.** 可可沒有看過雪。

- Claire has never traveled **by air.** 克萊兒還沒有坐過飛機。

been（去過）和 gone（去了）的用法比較

| 主詞 | + | **have/has been to** | + | 地點 | → | 某人曾經到過某個地方，但是現在已經離開那裡。 |
| 主詞 | + | **have/has gone to** | + | 地點 | → | 某人去了某個地方，而且現在還在那裡，或是在路途中。 |

┌ 我以前去過巴西，但我現在不在那裡了。

- I have been to **Brazil three times.** 我去過巴西三次。
- She isn't at home. She has gone to **Brazil.** 她不在家，她去巴西了。

└ 她現在在在巴西，或是在前往巴西或回來的路途上。

PRACTICE

1 將下列句子改寫為疑問句和否定句。

1 Jim has met Lenore before

➡ *Has Jim met Lenore before? Jim hasn't met Lenore.*

2 Ann has arrived in Pakistan.

➡ _____

3 She has already told me about her vacation in Paris.

➡ _____

4 They have knocked down all the old houses in this neighborhood.

➡ _____

5 Dirk has finished his math homework.

➡ _____

2 將括弧內的單字以簡單現在完成式填空，並在第二個空格內填入 for 或 since。

1 Today is my parents' golden wedding anniversary. They _____ (be) married _____ fifty years.

2 Ann is a computer programmer in Japan. She _____ (work) there _____ May 10, 2011.

3 My sister Kay loves the sea, but she _____ (not be) to the seaside _____ last May.

4 My grandparents are in South Africa. They _____ (live) there _____ two years.

3 將括弧內的單字搭配 **ever** 或 **never**，用簡單現在完成式填空，完成句子。

1 Lily doesn't seem to like me. She _____ (smile) at me.

2 Joe _____ (be) to Tokyo.

3 _____ you _____ (play) table tennis with Dennis?

4 _____ you _____ (cheat) on an exam?

4 用 **been** 或 **gone** 填空，完成句子。

1 Sally has _____ to Disney World five times and the Kennedy Space Center eight times.

2 Has she ever _____ to the International Space Station?

3 "May I speak to Ms. Brown?"
   "She's not here. She's _____ to Greece on a two-week tour.

4 "How long has she _____ in Nigeria?"
   "She has _____ there since August 4, 2011.

5 Mom has _____ to the market. She should be back soon.

6 Monica doesn't believe that I have ever _____ to Antarctica.

7 Our maid has _____ away for a two-week vacation, but she'll be back tomorrow.

8 You'll have to wait a few minutes. My friend has _____ to get you some help.

5 將括弧裡的詞語用「簡單現在完成式」填空。

1 Amy, you _____ (already do) a lot for me.

2 His flight _____ (not yet take) off, so Mort must still be at the airport.

3 The war _____ (already begin).

4 _____ Dirk _____ (finish) writing his story yet?

Chapter
38 簡單現在完成式和簡單過去式

I

簡單現在完成式用來描述從「過去一直延續到現在」的事，
簡單過去式用來描述「過去發生過，而且現在已經結束」的事情。

使用現在完成式，
表示現在還住在羅馬。

- Jerome has lived in Rome for ten years.
  傑羅姆在羅馬住了十年了。

使用過去式，表示現在沒住在日本了。

- Ann lived in Japan for two years.
  安曾經在日本住過兩年。

2

❶ 句中有「尚未結束的時間副詞」，使用**現在完成式**。

| ·today 今天 | ·this week 這星期 |
| ·this year 今年 | ·lately 最近 |

- Have you seen Kay today? 你今天有看到凱嗎？
- Have you talked to Sue lately? 你最近有跟蘇說過話嗎？

❷ 現在完成式用來描述「到目前為止尚不確定」什麼時候發生的事情，常用 ever、never。

- Has she ever been to South Africa? 她去過南非嗎？
- Paul has never played football. 保羅沒有打過橄欖球。

❸ 句中有「已經結束的時間副詞」，使用**簡單過去式**。

·yesterday 昨天	·last week 上週
·last year 去年	·then 那時
·ago 之前	·in 2012 在 2012 年

- I saw Kay last week. 我上星期見過凱。
- Did you talk to Sue on the phone last night? 你昨晚有跟蘇講電話嗎？
- Paul played table tennis with Kay yesterday. 保羅昨天跟凱打乒乓球。
- Did she go to South Africa last year? 她去年有去南非嗎？

---

3 ── 簡單過去式的用法

❶ 指「過去的某一特定時間」，要用**簡單過去式**。

then（當時），指過去的某一特定時間，要用簡單過去式。

- What did Ben do then? 班那時候在做什麼？

某年某月某日，為過去的某一特定時間，要用簡單過去式。

- Kate was born in Thailand on January 8, 2008. 凱特於 2008 年 1 月 8 號在泰國出生。

十分鐘之前，為過去的某一特定時間，要用簡單過去式。

- Coco went home ten minutes ago. 可可十分鐘前回家去了。

❷ 詢問「事情發生的時間」（what time、when），要用**簡單過去式**。

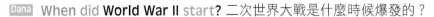

└→ what time（何時），要用簡單過去式。

June **What time** did **you** get **up this morning?** 你今天早上幾點起床？

Ivan I got **up at 6 a.m.** 我六點起床。

└→ when（何時），要用簡單過去式。

Bart **When** did **you last** see **Coco?** 你最後見到可可是什麼時候？

Holly I last saw **her two years ago when she married Joe.**
我最後見到她是兩年前她嫁給喬的時候。

Dana **When** did **World War II** start? 二次世界大戰是什麼時候爆發的？

Andy **World War II** started **in 1939.** 二次世界大戰是在 1939 年爆發的。

4　　簡單現在完成式的用法

「過去發生的動作，對現在還有影響，眼前就可以看到結果」，這時要用**簡單現在完成式**。

└→ 用簡單現在完成式，表示現在腿傷還沒好。

• **Poor Peg! She** has broken **her right leg.** 可憐的佩格！她摔斷右腿了。

└→ 用簡單過去式，表示摔斷腿發生在過去，但現在腿傷已經好了。

比較 **Ted** broke **his right leg last year. Now he can run very fast.**
泰德去年摔斷了右腿，但現在可以跑很快了。

└→ 用簡單現在完成式，表示與現在的狀態有關連，表達「我對俄國很熟悉」。

• I have traveled **a lot in Russia.** 我到過俄國的很多地方。

└→ 用簡單過去式，只強調是一個過去的事件。

比較 **Last year Sue** traveled **a lot in France.** 蘇去年去了法國的很多地方。

└→ 用簡單現在完成式，表示與現在的狀態有關連，表達「現在不在這裡」。

• **She's not here. She's** gone **home.** 她不在這裡，她回家了。

└→ 用簡單過去式，只強調是一個過去的動作。

比較 **She** went **home ten minutes ago.** 她十分鐘前回家了。

5　　比較 ago 和 for

ago 指「在……之前」，要用**過去式**。　→

Erin **When** did **you** start **to study English?**
你是什麼時候開始學英文的？

Ken I started **to study English three years ago.**
我三年前開始學英文。

for 指時間的持續，可以用於完成式，也可以用於簡單過去式。　→

Erin **How long** have **you** studied **English?**
你學英文學多久了？

Ken I have studied **English for three years.**
我學英文學三年了。

比較 **She** studied **Russian for two years while in high school.**
她在高中時學了兩年的俄語。→用簡單過去式只強調過去發生的事，
對現在沒有影響，很可能現在她已經沒有學俄語了。

151

1 寫出下列動詞的過去式和過去分詞。

1 rob _____ _____ **10** meet _____ _____

2 help _____ _____ **11** wait _____ _____

3 nod _____ _____ **12** see _____ _____

4 rain _____ _____ **13** say _____ _____

5 write _____ _____ **14** worry _____ _____

6 believe _____ _____ **15** speak _____ _____

7 hurry _____ _____ **16** stay _____ _____

8 take _____ _____ **17** sleep _____ _____

9 dance _____ _____ **18** enjoy _____ _____

2 選出正確答案。

_____ **1** Daryl _____ to Lily lately?

Ken Yes, I have. Yesterday I went to visit Lily and Sue.

ⓐ Have you spoken　　ⓑ Did you speak

_____ **2** There is a big fire downtown. When _____ ?

ⓐ has it started　　ⓑ did it start

_____ **3** My dad is retired now. He _____ as a pilot for 40 years.

ⓐ has worked　　ⓑ worked

_____ **4** There has been a traffic jam for a few hours. It _____ around
seven in the morning.

ⓐ has started　　ⓑ started

_____ **5** Last week he _____ Alice a lovely pearl necklace.

ⓐ has given　　ⓑ gave

_____ **6** Sue is a Spanish teacher in London. She _____ Spanish for
more than five years.

ⓐ has taught　　ⓑ taught

_____ 7 Kate _____ in Brazil since 2008.
　　　　 a has lived　　 b lived

_____ 8 When _____ married?
　　　　 a has Ms. Reed got　　 b did Ms. Reed get

_____ 9 Kay _____ at the picnic yesterday.
　　　　 a has not been　　 b was not

_____ 10 Her birthday is April 15. She _____ in 2010.
　　　　 a has been born　　 b was born

3 自下列綠色詞彙中選出適當的詞彙，用簡單過去式填空，完成句子。

travel　　occupy　　continue　　ring　　refuse　　study

1 She _____ to give her name and address to the police and is still in jail.

2 The puppy _____ the best sofa chair in the living room.

3 She _____ to Austria and Switzerland last year with me.

4 Dell _____ the church bell.

5 She _____ the questions carefully before answering them.

6 After the interruption, Mom _____ with her story.

4 自下列綠色詞彙中選出適當的詞彙，用簡單現在完成式填空，完成句子。

climb　　break　　have　　explore　　go　　see

1 We _____ many interesting dinosaurs in this museum.

2 Bob _____ his left arm and right leg and has to quit his job.

3 Dirk is not at home; he _____ to work.

4 Sue _____ the Great Barrier Reef off the coast of Queensland in northeast Australia.

5 I'm not hungry. I _____ my lunch.

6 Kay _____ that hill every Sunday since last May.

Chapter

39 表示未來的現在進行式和簡單現在式

現在進行式一般表示「某事現在正在進行」，但也可以用來談論「未來事件」。

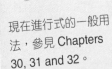現在進行式的一般用法，參見 Chapters 30, 31 and 32。

Coco White's schedule for tomorrow
可可・懷特的明日行程（從早上八點半到晚上九點）

時間	行程
8:30 go to church 上教堂	用現在進行式來說明計畫未來要做的事。 • **What** is **Coco doing** tomorrow? 可可明天要做什麼？
1:40 see the dentist 看牙醫	• **She's going** to church at 8:30. 她八點半要上教堂。 • **She's seeing** the dentist at 1:40. 她一點四十分要去看牙醫。
4:00 ~ 5:00 have a yoga class 上瑜伽課	• **She's having** a yoga class from 4:00 to 5:00. 她四點到五點要上瑜珈課。
5:30 have dinner with Mark at the Double Happiness Restaurant 跟馬克一起到雙喜飯店吃晚餐	• **She's having** dinner with Mark at the Double Happiness Restaurant at 5:30. 她五點半要跟馬克去雙喜餐廳吃晚餐。
9:00 go to the airport to pick up Jane 去機場接珍	• **She's going** to the airport to pick up Jane at 9:00. 她九點要去機場接珍。

2

現在進行式談論未來事件，指「**已經計畫好要做的事**」。

┌─ 我已經和Kay約好今天要見面，這是計畫好的事，使用現在進行式。
* I'm visiting Kay today. 我今天要去找凱。

┌─ 你已經安排好要去哪裡了嗎？
* Where are you going this spring? 你今年春天要去哪裡？

┌─ 邁克已經安排好要做什麼了嗎？
* What is Mike doing this summer vacation? 邁克今年暑假要做什麼？

┌─ 你已經安排好晚飯吃什麼了嗎？
* What are you having for dinner? 你晚餐要吃什麼？

┌─ 指已經安排好要做的事，使用現在進行式。

Kent	Where are you going this summer?	你今年夏天要去哪裡？
Sue	I'm going to Norway to experience the midnight sun.	我要去挪威體驗午夜的太陽。
Kent	That sounds great! When are you leaving?	真不錯！你什麼時候出發？
Sue	I'm leaving on June 20.	我 6 月 20 號出發。
Kent	How are you getting there?	你要怎麼去？
Sue	I'm flying there.	搭飛機囉。
Kent	When are you coming back?	你什麼時候回來？
Sue	I'm coming back on July 5.	我 7 月 5 號回來。

3

簡單現在式也可用來談論「**未來事件**」，用於時間表、節目單、火車、航班時刻表等。

┌─ 指時間表、節目單等，使用簡單現在式。
* The concert starts at 8 p.m. 音樂會晚上八點開始。

┌─ 指人的未來計畫時，使用現在進行式。
比較 We're going to a concert tonight. 我們今晚要去音樂會。

┌─ 指時刻表時，使用簡單現在式。
* What time does her plane take off? 她的飛機什麼時候起飛？

┌─ 指人的未來計畫時，使用現在進行式。
比較 What time is she leaving for Los Angeles? 她什麼時候離開去洛杉磯？

1 依據你的真實情況，重組下列詞彙為肯定句或否定句，並以現在進行式寫出句子。

1 go to | Malaysia | this summer | for a vacation
➡ *I'm going to Malaysia this summer for a vacation.*
➡ *I'm not going to Malaysia this summer for a vacation.*

2 meet | a friend | on the Internet | tomorrow night
➡ _____
➡ _____

3 go to | the multiplex movie theater | on Saturday night
➡ _____
➡ _____

4 have | a private English class | on Sunday afternoon
➡ _____
➡ _____

5 play | some computer games | on Sunday morning
➡ _____
➡ _____

2 依據 **Sally** 的日程表，用現在進行式重組詞語，完成下列問句，並作出回答。

Saturday night	visit Dwight
Sunday night	go to a dance with Vance
next Monday morning	go on a business trip to Los Angeles fly from New York Airport
next Monday night	stay at the Holiday Inn
at 9:20 next Friday night	come back home/arrive in New York

1 What | Sally | do | on Saturday night?
➡ _____
➡ _____

2 Where | Sally | go | on Sunday night?

➡ _____

➡ _____

3 What | Sally | do | next Monday morning?

➡ _____

➡ _____

4 Where | Sally | fly | from?

➡ _____

➡ _____

5 Which hotel | Sally | stay | at?

➡ _____

➡ _____

6 How long | Sally | stay | in Los Angeles?

➡ _____

➡ _____

7 When | Sally | come | back | home?

➡ _____

➡ _____

8 What | time | Sally | arrive | in New York?

➡ _____

➡ _____

3 │ 利用括弧內提示的詞彙，用現在進行式或簡單現在式填空，完成對話。

Carl What 1 _____ (you/do) tonight?

Ruth I 2 _____ (go) to a movie tonight.

Carl What time 3 _____ (the movie/start)?

Ruth It 4 _____ (start) at 7:30.

Chapter

40 用 be going to 談論未來事件

1 be going to 句型的構成方式

主詞 + **be going to** + 原形動詞

be going to 的句型

	肯定句			否定句			疑問句		
單數	I	am	going to play	I	am not	going to play	am	I	going to play?
	you	are		you	are not		are	you	
	he	is		he	is not		is	he	
	she			she				she	
	it			it				it	
複數	we	are		we	are not		are	we	
	you			you				you	
	they			they				they	

* 縮寫：I'm, you're, he's, she's, it's, we're, they're
is not = isn't, are not = aren't

2

be going to 常用來表達「意圖」或「先前的決定」，在某人做出一個明確的計畫或具體的安排之前，可以用 be going to 這個句型來表達打算做什麼或不打算做什麼；**現在進行式**則是用來表示「已經做了具體安排的未來事件」(參見 Chapter 39)。

- **June** is going to show **her new cellphone to her friends at noon.**
  茱恩中午要把她的新手機秀給朋友們看。

- **Tonight he** is going to chat **with his African friends on the Internet.**
  他今晚要上網和非洲的朋友們聊天。

- **Tomorrow is my mom's birthday.** I'm going to give **her a flower.**
  明天是我媽媽的生日，我打算送她一朵花。

- **After graduation from college, Alice** is going to be **a fashion model and actress.**
  艾麗絲大學畢業後打算去當時裝模特兒和演員。

Happy birthday, Mom!

現在式 → 用於習慣做的事

Every day

Every morning

Every night

- I usually take a bus to school. 我通常搭公車去上學。
- Mom usually walks to work. 媽媽通常走路上班。
- Dirk usually does his homework.
德克通常都會做功課。

現在進行式 → 用於正在進行的事

Today (at the moment)

This morning (at the moment)

Tonight (at the moment)

- I'm taking the subway.
我正在搭地鐵。
- She's riding her bicycle.
她正在騎自行車。
- He's playing a computer game. 他正在玩電腦遊戲。

be going to → 用於將要進行的事

Tomorrow

Tomorrow morning

Tomorrow night

- I'm going to ride my motor scooter. 我要去騎我的速可達摩托車。
- She's going to stay at home. 她要待在家裡。
- He's going to chat with a friend on Skype. 他要用 Skype 跟一個朋友聊天。

4

be going to 的句型也可以用來表示「**可預見馬上要發生的事**」。

┌─ 用 be going to 句型，表示眼見要從樹上掉下來了。
- Watch out! You're going to fall off that branch!
小心！你快要從樹枝上掉下來了！

用 be going to 句型，
┌─ 表示眼見要遲到了。
- Oh! It's already 8:00, and I haven't had my breakfast. I'm going to be late for school.
啊！已經八點了，我還沒有吃早餐。我上學要遲到了。

- Look at the dark sky. It's going to snow.
你看天色好暗，快要下雪了。 └─ 用 be going to 句型，表示眼見要下雪了。

1 依照括弧裡的中文提示，用 **be going to** 句型完成下列句子，用來表達畢業之後想做的事情或想從事的工作。

1 Mary _____ the captain of a ferry. （當）

2 Jim _____ his mother to run a gym. （幫助）

3 Andrew _____ in Honolulu. （工作）

4 Dan _____ English in Japan. （教）

5 We _____ around the world. （旅遊）

6 I _____ to Australia. （搬遷）

2 你這個星期天打算做什麼？有以下計畫嗎？依據你的選擇，用 **be going to** 句型搭配下列片語造句。

1 put some pictures on my blog

2 chat with my friends on Skype

3 watch some DVD movies

4 play badminton

5 visit my friends

6 go for a hike in the countryside

1 _____

_____

2 _____

3 _____

4 _____

5 _____

6 _____

3 根據圖片內容，用「She's going to . . . on Sunday morning.」的句型造句。

1 go to church
2 fly to Paris
3 play soccer
4 chat with her parents on Skype

1 _____ on Sunday morning.

2 _____ on Sunday morning.

3 _____ on Sunday morning.

4 _____ on Sunday morning.

Chapter 41 簡單未來式：用 will 談論未來事件

I 簡單未來式句型的構成方式

主詞 + 助動詞 will + 原形動詞 →

在第一人稱 I 和 we 後面，有些人用 shall 來代替 will，表示將來要發生的行為動作，意思不變，不過 will 在現代英語中較為常用。

- I think we will win. = I think we shall win.
  我想我們會贏。

- Kate will be late. 凱特會遲到。
  └→ 除了第一人稱外，其他人稱都要用 will。

肯定句		否定句		疑問句		
I		I			I	
You		You			you	
He		He			he	
She	will be there.	She	will not be there.	Will	she	be there?
It		It			it	
We		We			we	
They		They			they	

* 縮寫：I'll, you'll, he'll, she'll, it'll, we'll, they'll   will not = won't

---

2

「will + 原形動詞」稱為**簡單未來式**，用來表示「**預測未來將發生的事**」。

└→ 用 will，表達「預測未來將發生的事」。

- Someday thousands of people and robots will live and work on the moon and build a civilization there.
  有朝一日，成千上萬的人類和機器人將在月球上居住、工作，在那裡建立文明。

3

will 常與 probably（可能）或 perhaps（或許）連用，用來「預測未來」。

- Tonight Coco will probably go for a boat ride with her sister Margo.
  可可今晚可能會和她妹妹瑪歌去划船。

- Perhaps I will not go to his party on Saturday night.
  我星期六晚上可能不會去參加他的派對。

4

(I) + [think / expect / wonder / suppose] + ······ + (will) + (原形動詞) → 用來表達自己對未來的預測

- I think **there** will be lots of changes in my little sis when she learns to walk.
  我想，等我小妹學會走路之後，她會有很多變化。

- I don't think **it** will rain **tonight.** 我覺得今晚不會下雨。

- We expect **Brazil** will win **the next World Cup.**
  我們預測巴西將贏得下一屆的世界盃。

5

❶ 如果這個未來事件是「**已經安排好要做**」或「**打算做的事**」，而不是預測的，那就要用「**現在進行式**」或「**be going to**」，而不使用 will〔參見 Chapter 39 和 Chapter 40〕。

└─ 已經安排好要做的事，不用 will。

- I'm going **to the theater tonight. I've already bought the ticket.**
  我今晚要去看電影，票已經買好了。

❷ 如果這個未來事件是「**在說話當下才做出的決定，不是預先安排好的**」，就要用 will。

└─ 面臨當下突發的狀況，臨時決定要做的事，要使用 will。

- Get out of my house or I'll call **the police.** 離開我的房子，否則我要報警了。

Beth　Look, there is a fire! 啊，失火了！

Kirk　I'll call 911. 我來打 911。

└─ 遇到突發狀況，當下決定要做的事，要使用 will。

6

「**there will be**」的句型，用來表示「**預測未來將會有……**」。

肯定句 → There will be **a lot of rich countries by 2110.**
到了 2110 年，將會有很多富有的國家。

└─ = There won't be

否定句 → There will not be **a lot of rich countries by 2110.**
到了 2110 年，將不會有很多富有的國家。

疑問句 → Will there be **a lot of rich countries by 2110?**
到了 2110 年，將會有很多富有的國家嗎？

1 五十年後，人類生活會是什麼樣？用 **will** 的簡單未來式重組下列詞彙。

1 humans | live | on Mars 50 years from now?
Will humans live on Mars 50 years from now?

2 there | be | any | global wars?

_____

3 polar bears | be | extinct?

_____

4 life | be | better?

_____

5 the Internet | be | the same?

_____

6 there | be | more schools | than now?

_____

7 people | live | longer?

_____

8 humans | speak | the same language?

_____

9 there | be | a big gap | between the poor and the rich?

_____

10 there | be | any | cities and farms | on the moon?

_____

11 robots | do | all the farming?

_____

12 there | be | any | cars, trains, buses, and RVs | on Mars?

_____

2 依據你自己的看法，用 **will** 或 **won't** 回答上述問題。

① *Humans will live on Mars 50 years from now.*
Or: Humans won't live on Mars 50 years from now.

②

③

④

⑤

⑥

⑦

⑧

⑨

⑩

⑪

⑫

3 自右欄中選出適合左欄會話的回應，連線完成對話。

① Alice, I've been robbed. •   • [a] I'll turn on the heat.

② Joan, telephone! •   • [b] I'll buy a new one for you.

③ Bing, it's so cold here! •   • [c] I'll make it tidy right away.

④ Kay, your room is messy. •   • [d] I'll call the police.

⑤ Mom, my cellphone is broken. •   • [e] I'll get it.

⑥ Sue, how can I reach you? •   • [f] I'll give you my email address.

4 選出正確的答案。

① Will | Shall Coco be at the office tomorrow?

② Do you think they will | shall be on time?

③ I can't go to your party tonight. I'll work. | I'm working.

④ I believe it is snowing a lot | it will snow a lot next winter.

Chapter

42 will 和 be going to 用法比較

I

未來簡單式 will ── 表示「決定」 → 突然決定要做的事

── 表示「未來」 → 單純預測未來

be going to ── 表示「決定」 → 事先決定要做的事

── 表示「未來」 → 確定事情馬上就要發生（或已經在發生）

2　表示「決定將要做的事」

表示突然決定

Seth Sue, how can I reach you? 蘇，我要怎麼跟你聯絡？

Sue Well, I'll give you my cellphone number. 喔，我給你我的手機號碼。

└→ will 指「在說話的時刻做出的決定」，乃「突然的決定」。

┌→ be going to 指「之前就做好的決定」。

表示事先決定

• I'm going to give Erica my cellphone number, so she can reach me when she comes to South Africa.
我要把手機號碼給艾芮卡，這樣她來南非時就可以跟我聯絡。

表示突然決定

Elsa Have you washed the RV? 你洗休旅車了沒？

Rene Oh, no! I forgot. I'll wash it now. 啊，糟糕！我忘記了，我馬上去洗。

└→ 在說話的時刻做出的決定。

表示事先決定

• I'm going to wash the RV. 我要洗休旅車。

└→ 之前就做出的決定。

3　表示「未來要發生的事」

┌→ will 也用來單純預測未來，表示「認為或知道未來將要發生的事」。

單純預測未來

• I think she will be homesick while studying in Ireland.
我想她在愛爾蘭讀書時會想家的。

• According to the TV weather broadcast, it'll rain tomorrow.
電視氣象預報說，明天會下雨。

┌→ 表示「按目前狀況，馬上就要發生的事，或已經在發生的事」。

馬上就要發生

• Oh, no! I'm going to be airsick! 哎喲，不好了！我要暈機了！

• Look at the dark clouds. It's going to rain. 你看那些烏雲，要下雨了。

1 請用 **will** 或 **be going to** 填空，完成句子。

1 Oh, no! It's starting to rain! I _____ get wet.

2 Look out! That tree _____ fall!

3 Don't go out now. You _____ get wet.

4 Hold on! We _____ crash.

5 Don't climb the tree. You _____ fall down.

6 Sue, don't go close to that dog. It _____ bite you.

2 依據提示，用 **will** 或 **be going to** 填空，完成句子。

1 Tonight I _____ study English for two hours with Trish.
（已經做好的決定）

2 Don't touch that sharp knife. You _____ cut yourself.
（單純預測未來）

3 Dan Do you have Mike's phone number?
Ann Wait, I _____ look it up for you.（突然做出的決定）

4 Gus, those dogs _____ bite us.（確定事情馬上就要發生）

5 Dan We are lost.
Ann I _____ go and ask someone the way.（突然做出的決定）

6 Next month she _____ have a baby girl.（明顯快要發生的事）

7 Bye-bye! I _____ call you tonight.（突然做出的決定）

8 Coco _____ see the dentist tomorrow.（之前做好的決定）

9 Oh, dear! It's already 10:30. We're not ready yet. We _____ miss our flight.（明顯快要發生的事）

10 Do you think the English exam _____ be difficult?
（單純預測未來）

Chapter

43 can 和 could 的用法

---

1 — **can 和 could 句型的構成方式**

「情態動詞」又稱「情態助動詞」，是一種用來輔助述語動詞的詞類，而情態動詞本身也是帶有意義的。can 和 could 都是表示「能力」、「可能性」、「允許」和「請求」的**情態動詞**。

主詞 + can / could + 原形動詞

肯定句	否定句	疑問句
I / You / He / She / It / We / They can drive. could drive.	I / You / He / She / It / We / They cannot drive. could not drive.	Can / Could I / you / he / she / it / we / they drive?

縮寫：
cannot → can't
could not → couldn't

---

2 —

can 可以表示「**能力**」（ability）或「做某事的**可能性**」（possibility），意為「能夠、可以，會」（= know how to; be able to）。

表示能力　**Ross** Can **that little girl** count? 那個小女孩會數數嗎？

　Tara No, she can't. 不行，她不會。
　└→ 簡略回答

　Stacy Can **Trish** speak **Spanish**? 翠希會講西班牙語嗎？

　Neil Yes, she can. 會，她會講。
　└→ 簡略回答

The dentist will be able to see you . . .;
└→ It's possible for the dentist to see you . . .

表示做某事的可能性　• **The dentist** can see **you around ten tomorrow morning.**
牙醫明天上午十點左右可以幫你看診。

┌→ I will not be able to come . . .; it's not possible for me to come . . .
• Sorry, I can't come **to your wedding this Sunday because I will be in South Africa.**
對不起，我這個星期天無法參加你的婚禮，因為我那個時候人在南非。

3

could 也用來表示「**能力**」和「做某事的**可能性**」，但只能用於**過去式**。

- She could read in English when she was three. 她三歲就會閱讀英文了。→過去的能力

- He couldn't drive until he was 60. 他到六十歲時才學會開車。→過去的能力

- I had a birthday party last night, but my boyfriend could not come.
  我昨晚辦了一個慶生會，但是我的男朋友沒有辦法來參加。└─ he was not able to come . . .;
  it was not possible for him to come .

4

can 和 could 表示「**推測**」，意為「**可能**」（be likely)，用於**疑問句**和**否定句**中。

Dan	Yesterday Kay heard she was adopted when she was a baby.	凱昨天得知自己是在襁褓中時被領養的小孩。
Ann	Can/Could that be true? →疑問句	這有可能是真的嗎？
Nan	That can't/couldn't be true. →否定句	不可能是真的。

5

❶ 「**Can you . . .?**」、「**Could you . . .?**」句型用來表示「**請他人做某事**」或「**邀請**」。
在口氣上，使用 could 比使用 can 更為客氣。

| 請求對方做某件事 | Can you . . . ?
Could you . . . ? | • Can you please babysit Bill? 你能幫忙顧照一下比爾嗎？
= Could you please babysit Bill?
　└─ 使用 could，語氣較客氣。 |
| 邀請對方做某件事 | Can you . . . ?
Could you . . . ? | • Can you come over for dinner tomorrow?
= Could you come over for dinner tomorrow?
你明天能過來吃晚餐嗎？ |

❷ 「**Can I . . .?**」、「**Could I . . .?**」句型用來「**向他人索取某物**」或「**請求允許**」。
在口氣上，could 比 can 更客氣。（也可以用「**May I . . .?**」〔參見 Chapter 44 第 4 條〕）

| 向他人索取物品 | Can I . . . ?
Could I . . . ? | • Can I have a cup of coffee, please? 給我一杯咖啡，好嗎？
= Could I have a cup of coffee, please? |
| 請求對方的許可 | Can I . . . ?
Could I . . . ? | • Can I use your computer to check my email?
= Could I use your computer to check my email?
我能用你的電腦收一下我的電子郵件嗎？ |

6

can 也可以用來表示「**許可**」；can't 表示「**不許可**」。（不能用 could/couldn't。）

┌─ 請求許可，用 can 或 could 都可以。

| Cory | Can/Could I have some beer? | 我可以喝點啤酒嗎？ |
| Ella | No, you can't. You have to drive us home. | 不行，你要開車送我們回家。 |

└─ 表示不許可，只能用 can't，不能用 couldn't。
表示許可，也只能用 can，不用 could，例如「Yes, you can.」。

1 利用圖片中的片語，寫出問句詢問對方（**you**）是否會做這些事，再調換角色，依據你自己的實際情況，用簡答回答這些問題。

① touch your toes

② play the violin

③ stand on your head

④ drive a bus

⑤ ride a horse

⑥ dance a ballet

1 Can you touch your toes?   Yes, I can. Or: No, I can't.

2 _____   _____

3 _____   _____

4 _____   _____

5 _____   _____

6 _____   _____

2 用 **can** 或 **can't**，搭配下列綠色詞彙的動詞填空，完成句子。

go   find   ride   hear

1 Mike _____ a horse, but he can ride a bike.

2 Did you see my puppy? I _____ it anywhere.

3 I don't think I _____ out for dinner tonight. I have to babysit my brother Dwight.

4 Shh! You're talking too loud. I _____ the violinist.

3 用 **can't** 或 **couldn't**，搭配下列綠色詞彙的動詞填空，完成句子。

use   speak   smoke   understand   see   ask

1 Lenore _____ or read any German until she moved to Berlin.

2 Sue wants to graduate from our high school, but she _____ a computer.

3 The doctor _____ you right now. How about three this afternoon?

4 The President of America came to our university to make a speech, but unfortunately I _____ much of what he said.

5 Sorry, you _____ or drink on this campus.

6 She has never studied physics, so she _____ any questions about Einstein's theories.

4 自右欄中選出正確的詞語，完成左欄的句子。

1 Can I have a _____ • • a the phone, please?

2 Could you pass _____ • • b with my friends tonight, Mom?

3 Could you answer _____ • • c that word, please?

4 Could I go out _____ • • d fish burger, please?

5 Can you spell _____ • • e me the sugar, please?

6 Can I sit _____ • • f here?

Chapter

44 may 和 might 的用法

I **may 和 might 句型的構成方式**

may 和 might 都是表示「未來可能會發生的事」的情態動詞（may = might），
用來表示「推測」，意為「也許，可能」，用於**肯定句**和**否定句**中。

主詞 + may / might + 原形動詞

肯定句		否定句	
I		I	
You		You	
He		He	
She	may stay.	She	may not stay.
It	might stay.	It	might not stay.
We		We	
They		They	

＊縮寫詞 mayn't 和 mightn't 比較罕見。

＊在疑問句裡，通常不用 may 或 might
　來表示「未來可能會發生的事」。

2

may 和 might 表示「未來可能會發生的事」。
可能性比較**高**的，就用 **may**；可能性比較**低**的，
就用 **might**。

* It might snow **again tonight.** (= Perhaps it will snow again tonight.) 今晚可能又要下雪了。

　┌→ = Perhaps she won't call you this afternoon.
* She might/may not **call you this afternoon.** 她今天下午可能不會打電話給你。

　┌→ = Perhaps we will see each other again someday.
* We might/may see **each other again someday.** 也許我們有一天還會再見面。

Ted What are you going to do tonight? 你今晚打算做什麼？

　┌→ = Perhaps I will go to visit Sue.
Vicki I'm not sure. I might/may go **to visit Sue.** 我也不知道，可能會去找蘇吧。

Lucy Where are you going for your vacation? 你要去哪裡度假？

　┌→ = Perhaps I will go to Paris.
Julio I'm not sure. I might/may go **to Paris.** 我還不確定，可能會去巴黎吧。

3

may、**might** 的用法，和**現在進行式**、**be going to** 的比較：

現在進行式 →	用於「肯定」、「確定」的事。	• I'm going swimming tomorrow. 我明天要去游泳。
may 和 might →	用於表達「有可能做某事」。	• I might/may go swimming tomorrow. 我明天可能會去游泳。
be going to →	用於「肯定」、「已經決定」的事。	• Mom is going to buy a new electric car next month. 媽媽下個月要買一輛新的電動車。
may 和 might →	用於表達「有可能做某事」。	• Mom might/may buy a new electric car next month. 媽媽下月可能會買一輛新的電動車。

4

may 使用**疑問句**的時機，是用來「**請求許可**」或「**向對方索取某物**」，這時候主詞只能用**第一人稱代名詞**（I或we）。在這個用法上，使用「May I ...」，比「Could I ...」、「Can I ...」更正式〔參見 Chapter 43〕。

May + **I / we** + **原形動詞**

┌→ = Could I see = Can I see，但使用 May 比較正式。

May I see your driver's license, please?

• "May I see your driver's license, please?" asked the police officer. 警察要求說：「請出示你的駕照。」

┌→ = Could I have = Can I have，但使用 May 比較正式。

• May I have the bill, please? 我要結帳，麻煩您了。

5

用來「**請求許可**」或「**向對方索取某物**」時，如果主詞不是**第一人稱代名詞**（I或we），那就要改用 can 或 could。

Can / Could + **非第一人稱** + **原形動詞** → • Could/Can Coco pay you tomorrow?
可可能明天付你錢嗎？

6

「**請求他人幫忙**」要用 can 或 could，不用 may〔參見 Chapter 43 第 4 條〕。

• Can/Could you help me wash the dishes? 你能幫我洗碗嗎？

 └→ 不可以使用 may。

1 依照範例，用 **may** 或 **might** 改寫句子。

1 Perhaps we will get a snowstorm tomorrow. (may)
We may get a snowstorm tomorrow.

2 Perhaps next month I will visit my friend Ann in Japan. (might)

3 Perhaps Dwight will be late for the party tonight. (might)

4 Perhaps Kay won't go to work on Monday. (may)

5 Perhaps Ann will change her mind and decide to move to Iran instead of Japan. (may)

6 Perhaps June and Ray will go to Norway for their honeymoon. (might)

7 Perhaps tonight I won't have time to chat with Joan on my cellphone. (may)

2 依據下列關於 Tia 的說明，用 (not) going to 或 might (not) 造句。

Tia is going to Florida for a 6-day trip. There are lots of things she wants to do and see and some things she hasn't decided about yet.

一定會做，或
一定不會做的事

1. Stay at Disney World for two days
2. Not eat at any expensive restaurants
3. Visit the Kennedy Space Center
4. Meet Sue at Clearwater Beach

是否會不會做，
並不一定

5. Not go to Miami
6. Go for a submarine ride at Sea World
7. Always eat at The Sub Shop
8. Not have time to visit museums

1 _____

2 _____

3 _____

4 _____

5 _____

6 _____

7 _____

8 _____

3 選出正確的答案。

1 _____ Lily have a cookie?

a May
b Might
c Could

2 Kay is not in school today.
She _____ sick.

a maybe
b may
c may be

3 Dan Mom, may I go to the movie
theater with Dwight tonight?
Ann I am afraid _____ .

a you cannot
b you may
c you might

4 _____ you help me carry this
table to the living room?

a Could
b May
c Might

Chapter

45 must, mustn't, needn't 的用法

I — must 句型的構成方式 —

主詞 + **must** + 原形動詞

肯定句		疑問句	
I		I	
You		you	
He		he	
She	must go.	she	go?
It	Must	it	
We		we	
They		they	

＊ must 表示「義務、必要」的時候，不用在否定句。

2

must 是表示「**義務、必要性**」的情態動詞，說明「**現在或未來必須做的事**」。

　　　　　┌─ 表示現在必須去做
• You must clean up your messy bedroom.
你必須把你亂七八糟的臥室整理好。

　　　　　　　　　　　　　　　┌─ 表示將來必須去做
• Kay and I had such a great time in Egypt—we must go there again someday.
我和凱在埃及玩得非常快樂──有一天我們一定還會再去那裡。

3

如果是「**過去必須做的事**」，不會用 must，要用 **had to**〔參見 Chapter 47〕。

• I had to clean up my room yesterday. 我昨天得打掃我的房間。

• Mom is not at home. She had to go to the hospital.
媽媽不在家，她得去醫院。

4

疑問句中「詢問對方是否必須做某事」時，英式英語使用 must，美式英語使用 have to〔參見 Chapter 47〕。

🇺🇸 美式英語 "Do I have to clean all the rooms?" cried Paul.

🇬🇧 英式英語 "Must I clean all the rooms?" cried Paul.
　　　　　　保羅大叫：「我一定要打掃所有的房間嗎？」

Note
用 must 引導的一般疑問句，
肯定回答用：
→ Yes, . . . must.

否定回答用：
→ No, . . . needn't.
→ No, . . . don't have to.
→ No, . . . doesn't have to.

5

mustn't 是 must not 的縮寫，這個否定句型用來表達「**對方不可以做某件事**」。

┌─ mustn't 表示「禁止」。

- You mustn't smoke if you want to be on this basketball team.
  如果你們想留在籃球隊裡，就不准吸菸。」

- If I show you the picture I painted, you mustn't laugh.
  如果我把我畫的畫給你看，你不可以笑喔。

6

英式英語用「I mustn't」、「We mustn't」表示「**說話者不可以做某事**」；美式更常用「I shouldn't」、「We shouldn't」〔參見 Chapter 46〕。

| 美式英語 | I shouldn't eat junk food. |

| 英式英語 | I mustn't eat junk food. 我不應該吃垃圾食物。 |

7

must 表示「**推測**」，意為「一定、肯定」，用於**肯定句**中。否定的推測要用 **can't**，意為「不可能」。

- It's late. You must be hungry. 有點晚了，你一定餓了吧。

- Jim, you just ate a whole pizza. You can't still be hungry.
  吉姆，你才剛吃下一整個披薩，不可能還餓。

8

needn't 是 need not 的縮寫，意思是「**沒有必要做某件事**」，在美式英語中較不常用，美式英語多用 don't have to 來表達〔參見 Chapter 47〕。

┌─ need 做情態動詞

→ You needn't tell Mom that I flunked the English test.

┌─ need 做一般動詞

needn't do something
= don't need to do something
= doesn't need to do something

= You don't need to tell Mom that I flunked the English test.
你沒必要告訴媽媽說我英文不及格。

| 美式英語 | You don't have to go to work tomorrow if you don't want to. |

| 英式英語 | You needn't go to work tomorrow if you don't want to.
你如果不想，明天就不用去上班。 |

9

mustn't 是「禁止」，**needn't** 是「並非必要」，兩者意思不同。

┌─ mustn't 用來表示「禁止做某事」。

- You mustn't stay here. You must leave now. 你不准待在這裡，你必須馬上離開。

┌─ needn't 用來表示「沒有必要做某事」。

- You needn't stay here. You can leave now if you want.
  你不必待在這裡。如果你想離開，現在就可以走。

1 連接左欄和右欄。依照左欄所示的狀況，用 **must** 或 **mustn't** 完成右欄的句子。

☐ That movie is fantastic.

_____

☐ You are late for dance class.

_____

☐ That dog is not friendly.

_____

☐ You have a fever.

_____

☐ Tomorrow is your mom's birthday.

_____

☐ The baby is sleeping.

_____

ⓐ you | get | too close to | it
ⓑ you | see | the doctor
ⓒ you | forget | to give her | a gift
ⓓ you | make | any noise
ⓔ you | hurry
ⓕ you | see | it

2 用 **must** 或 **had to** 填空。

☐ I was so tired last night that I _____ go to bed early.

☐ You and Lily _____ come and visit us in Italy.

☐ I _____ walk for an hour to get to school when I was in high school.

☐ You _____ be here by 8 a.m. tomorrow.

3 用 needn't、mustn't、must 或 had to 填空。

1. You _____ drive at more than 25 mph in the downtown area.

2. Be quiet. You _____ talk so loud in the library. People are trying to read.

3. You can write the report tomorrow. You _____ do it now.

4. It's a secret just between you and me. You _____ tell anybody.

5. You _____ decide now. You can tell me your decision next week.

6. You _____ tell Sue what happened to me yesterday. She already knows.

7. We can find our way there. You _____ wait for us.

8. You _____ play with that knife. You might get hurt.

9. She _____ prepare her science presentation last night.

10. I _____ hurry or I'll miss the school bus.

11. I'm getting too heavy. I _____ lose some weight.

12. Dan Why were you so late yesterday?
    Ann My mom was sick, and I _____ take her to the hospital.

Chapter 46 should 的用法

1 should 句型的構成方式

主詞 + should + 原形動詞

肯定句	否定句	疑問句
I You He She should go. It We They	I You He She should not go. It = shouldn't go. We They	I you he Should she go? it we they

2

should 用來談論「什麼是恰當的、正確的」。

┌─ 徵求他人的建議。

Ron **What** should I wear **to the party?** 我應該穿什麼衣服去參加派對？

┌─ 對他人提出建議。

Lynn **You** should wear **your colorful Chinese traditional dress.**
你應該穿你那件鮮豔的中式旗袍。

┌─ 徵求他人的建議。

Sally **I need some money for my trip to Australia next year. What** should I do?
我明年想去澳洲，需要一些錢，我該怎麼辦？

Cecil **You** should get **a summer job.** 你應該利用暑假去打工。

└─ 對他人提出建議。

3

should not（= shouldn't）表示「做某事是不好的」。

- **Dear, you** shouldn't drive **so fast here.** 親愛的，在這裡你不應該開那麼快。

- **I** shouldn't stay **up late every night.** 我不應該每晚熬夜。

- **We** shouldn't eat **too much meat.** 我們不應該吃太多肉類。

4

think 常與 should 連用，常見用法如：

肯定句	I think . . . should . . .
否定句	I don't think . . . should . . .
疑問句	Do you think . . . should . . .?

┌─ 肯定句：我認為這是個好的想法。

- I think **you** should write Sue an email to say thank-you.
  我想你應該給蘇寫封電子信件，表示一下謝意。

┌─ 肯定句：我認為這是對的作法。

- It's getting late. I think I should go **now**. 天色已晚。我想我應該走了。

┌─ 否定句：我認為不應該這樣做。

- I don't think you should wait **to write to Lulu**. 我想你不應該拖延給露露寫信。

┌─ 否定句：我認為不應該這樣做。

- I don't think Kim should depend **on Jim**. 我覺得金姆不應該依賴吉姆。

┌─ 疑問句：詢問對方是否認同。

- Do you think I should buy **this mini-skirt?** 你覺得我應該買這件迷你裙嗎？

┌─ 疑問詞 what 開頭的疑問句：詢問看法。

- What do you think **Margo and I** should do? 你認為瑪歌和我應該怎麼辦？

┌─ 疑問詞 when 開頭的疑問句：詢問時機。

- When do you think **we** should leave **for Chicago?** 你覺得我們應該什麼時候前往芝加哥？

5

must 比 should 的語氣更強烈〔must 的用法參見 Chapter 45〕。

┌─ 談論應當做的事。

- **This is an interesting book. You** should read it. 這本書很有趣，你應該讀一讀。

┌─ 談論必須做的事。

- **This is a wonderful book. You** must read it. 這本書寫得太好了，你一定要看。

Cathy Should I tell **her the truth about Mel?** 我應該老實告訴她梅爾的事嗎？

Brad Yes, you should. 是的，你應該老實說。 → 應該

Erin Yes, you must. 是的，你一定要老實說。 → 必須

6

should 也可用 ought to 表達，意思一樣（should 比 ought to 更常用）。在疑問句中，通常用「Should . . .?」

- **You** ought to call Mom more often. = You should call Mom more often.
  你應該更常打電話給媽媽。

- I ought to quit **smoking**. = I should quit **smoking**. 我應該戒菸。

| 🇺🇸 美式英語 | Such things shouldn't be allowed. → 英式英語也會用這個句型。 |
| 🇬🇧 英式英語 | Such things ought not to be allowed. 這種事情不應該被允許。 |

└─ 否定句英式可以用 ought not to，但美式一般用 should not/shouldn't。

1 從下列的綠色詞組中選出適當的詞語，使用「You should . . .」或「You shouldn't . . .」的句型，為圖中人物提出好建議。

go to see a doctor
try it on first
play computer games so much
work so hard

1

Look, how beautiful!
I think I'll buy this dress.

2

How I love to play these games!

_____

_____

3

Recently I often feel very tired.

4

I've a high fever.

_____

_____

2 用「I think . . . should . . .」或「I don't think . . . should . . .」的句型，重組句子，說出你對下列問題的看法。

1. people | drive | only | electric vehicles

   _____

2. we | stop | animal testing

   _____

3. everyone | have the right to | a free education

   _____

4. men and women | retire | at the same age

   _____

5. people | be terribly worried about | this swine flu

   _____

3 選出適當動詞，用 **Do you think I should . . .** 的句型，寫出向朋友請教的句子。

read   find   tell   invite   dye   take

1. My baby sister won't eat anything. _____ her to see Doctor Wood?

2. I like Sue White very much. She is friendly, cheerful, and hardworking. But I am too shy to ask her out for lunch. _____ her how I feel?

3. Mom says Brooke wrote an interesting book. _____ it while we are camping in Europe?

4. I don't like my house because it's too small. _____ a bigger house?

5. I'm going to have my birthday party here tomorrow. _____ Lily to the party?

6. I don't like my hair style. _____ my hair blond?

Chapter 47 have to 的用法

---

1 | **have to 句型的構成方式**

主詞 ＋ **have to** ＋ 原形動詞

		肯定句		否定句		疑問句	
單數	I You	have to go.	I You	do not have to go.	Do	you	
	He She It	has to go.	He She It	does not have to go.	Does	he she it	have to go?
複數	We You They	have to go.	We You They	do not have to go.	Do	we you they	

* 縮寫：do not have to → don't have to
does not have to → doesn't have to

2

have to 用來表示「做某件事情的必要性」。

- You have to wear a seat belt when you drive a car. 你開車時一定要繫上安全帶。

- My wife has to quit smoking if she wants to live a healthy life.
我太太要是想活得健康，就一定要戒菸。

3

have to 的過去式「had to」，用法為：

肯定句 **had to** + 原形動詞
否定句 **didn't** + **have to** + 原形動詞
疑問句 **did** + 主詞 + **have to** + 原形動詞

- I was absent from school yesterday, because I had to go to the hospital.
我昨天沒有上學，因為我得上醫院。

4

疑問句用法，用來表示「**一定要做某事嗎？**」

do
does ＋ 主詞 ＋ **have to** ＋ 原形動詞
did

- Do I have to have a haircut before I go for that interview?
  我去面試之前應該要先剪個頭髮嗎？

- Does he have to wear a tie at work? 他上班需要打領帶嗎？

- Why did Kay have to work late yesterday? 凱昨天為什麼一定要工作到那麼晚？

5

否定句用法，用來表示「**不需要做某件事**」。

- You don't have to wear a new suit when you go
  for the interview tomorrow.
  你明天去面試時不用穿新西裝。

- Mike doesn't have to wear a uniform at his school. He can wear whatever he likes.
  邁克在學校不用穿制服，他想穿什麼就可以穿什麼。

- I didn't have to get up early yesterday morning. 我昨天早上不用早起。

6

must 與 **have to** 都是「必須」（美式英語更常用 have to），但有以下用法的差異：

❶ 如果是表達個人意見「**我認為有必要做某事**」，must 與 have to 兩者皆可使用。
  ┌─→ = have to drive
- You must drive more carefully. 你開車要更小心一點。

❷ 如果不是表達個人意見，而是「**在規定上必須做的事**」或「**客觀上需要必須做某事**」，
  通常用 **have to**。
  ┌─→ 並非個人意見，而是法律規定。（非正式用語中，也可以用 must。）
- You have to drive on the left side of the road in Singapore. 在新加坡，開車必須靠左。
                                    ┌─→ 並非個人意見，而是工作所需，只能用 have to/has to。
- As a part of his job, Scot has to travel a lot. 因為工作的需要，史考特需要常常旅行。

- Mary won't be in the office next week. She has to go to a conference in Hawaii.
  瑪麗下星期不會進辦公室，她必須去夏威夷開會。 └─→ 並非個人意見，而是工作需
                                         要，只能用 have to/has to。

7

don't have to/doesn't have to（不用……）和 **mustn't**（不可以……）意思完全不同。
  ┌─→ 表示「禁止做某事」。
- "You must not smoke in any of the university's buildings," warned Sue.
  蘇警告說：「你不准在這所大學的任何一棟建築裡吸菸。」

- Coco hopes she doesn't have to get up early tomorrow. 可可希望她明天可不用早起。
  └─→ 表示「沒有必要做某事」。

1 選出正確的答案。

1 He _____ walk home last night after the party. There weren't any buses or taxies.
  a has to   b must   c had to   d didn't have to

2 I usually _____ get to work at eight.
  a must   b have to   c must not   d have not to

3 In our country, children _____ start attending school when they are five.
  a must not   b had to   c have to   d didn't have to

4 You _____ be eighteen to vote in some countries.
  a have to   b had to   c mustn't   d didn't have to

5 This is a great book. You _____ read it.
  a had to   b must   c don't have to   d didn't have to

6 If you want to become a first-class user of English, you _____ read extensively.
  a have to   b must not   c had to   d didn't have to

7 Players _____ wear anything that might injure another player.
  a must not   b must   c do not have to   d have to

8 Your skin _____ become wrinkled as you get older.
  a must not   b must   c doesn't have to   d don't have to

9 If you really want me to help you, you _____ tell me what happened.
  a must   b mustn't   c don't have to   d had to

10 Yesterday Mary and I _____ wait long for the taxi.
  a must   b mustn't   c didn't have to   d don't have to

2 用 have to 的現在式或過去式，搭配括弧裡的動詞填空，完成下列的肯定句、疑問句或否定句。

1 You cough a lot. You _____ smoking. (quit)

2 She is not in her office right now. She _____ home. (go)

3 Ann My husband is not at home. He is on a business trip to Brazil.
Dan _____ on business trips? (often, travel)
Ann Yes, he does. He often has to fly to Brazil and Mexico.

4 Ann I hate carrots.
Dan That's OK. I'll eat them. You _____ them. (eat)

5 Ann Look, the sign says, "CREDIT CARDS WELCOME!"
Dan Great! I _____ cash. (pay)

6 Ann I had to take the driving test five times. How about you? How many times _____ the driving test? (take)
Dan Only twice.

7 Judy I'm sixteen and I'm learning to drive. How old _____ to drive in your country? (be)
Lee In my country, you have to be eighteen to drive.

8 Mary I had to wear a uniform when I was in school. How about you? _____ a school uniform when you were young? (wear)
Mike I went to six different schools. Two of them required students to wear a uniform.

9 Mary Did Emma cry when you told her the news that she failed both the math and English exams?
Mike She already knew it, so I _____ her. (tell)

10 Personnel Manager How old are you? Are you single or married?
Job Seeker _____ these personal questions? Are these questions related to the position? (answer)

Chapter 48 表達意願、提出支援、物品或邀請的用語：would like, will, shall

1 would you like 的句型

would you like + 名詞 → 招待、提供物品時的用語

Stewardess What would you like, fish or chicken? 請問您要吃魚肉還是雞肉？

Passenger I'd like fish, please. 我要魚肉。→ I'd like = I would like

Stewardess Would you like tea or coffee? 請問您要喝茶還是咖啡？

Passenger I'd like coffee, please. 我要咖啡。

└→ 「I'd like something」表示「希望得到某物」，比「I want something」更為客氣。

2 would you like to 的句型

would you like to + 原形動詞 → 邀請他人來從事某個活動

Andrew Would you like to go to a concert with me on Saturday night?
你星期六晚上可以跟我去聽音樂會嗎？

Claire Yes, I'd love to. 好啊。

└→ = I would love to go . . .

3 比較 would you like 與 do you like

Would you like . . .? → 你想要……嗎？

└→ would like = want（想要）

→ 肯定句 I'd like/I'd love . . .

Do you like . . .? → 你喜歡……嗎？

└→ like = enjoy（喜歡）

→ 肯定句 I like . . .

Joe Would you like to dance with me?
你想跟我跳舞嗎？

Amy Yes, I'd love to. 好啊。

Ruby Would you like some milk tea?
想喝點奶茶嗎？

Gary Yes, please. 好啊，麻煩你了。

Tim Do you like to dance? 你喜歡跳舞嗎？

Lisa Yes, I do. I go dancing every Sunday.
喜歡，我每個星期天都會去跳舞。

Jose Do you like milk tea? 你喜歡喝奶茶嗎？

Anna Not really. I like coffee. 不太喜歡，我喜歡喝咖啡。

- I'd like **a mango, please.** 我想吃芒果。

- I like **mangoes.** 我喜歡芒果。

- I would like **to eat at a nice restaurant tonight.** 今晚我想去吃高級餐廳。

- I like **to eat at nice restaurants.** 我喜歡吃高級餐廳。

4　　would you like me to 的句型

| Would you like me to | + | 原形動詞 | → | 詢問對方要我做什麼事
（= Do you want me to . . .?） |

↳ would like = want（想要）

- Would you like me to pick **you up from the airport?** 你想要我去機場接你嗎？

- Would you like me to email **this message to Sue Wood?**
  你要我把這個訊息用電子郵件寄給蘇・伍德嗎？

- **What** would you like me to write **about?** 你想要我寫什麼？

5　　I'll 的句型

| I'll
(= I will) | + | 原形動詞 | → | **will** 可以是**助動詞**，用在未來式，表示「預測未來」〔參見 Chapter 41〕；也可以是**情態助動詞**，表示「願意幫忙做某事」。 |

- **Wait!** I'll open **the door for you.** 等等！我幫你開門。

- I'll wash **the dishes if you make supper.** 如果你做晚餐，我就洗碗。

6　　Shall I 的句型

| Shall I | + | 原形動詞 | | 情態助動詞 **shall** 常用在疑問句中，表示「提供幫助」，意思是「**要不要我……？**」。 |

> = Should I get **you some aspirin or** should I call **for the doctor?**
> = Do you want me to get **you some aspirin or call for the doctor?**

- **Oh, no! You have a fever.** Shall I **get you some aspirin or shall I call for the doctor?**
  唉呀，糟糕！你發燒了。要不要我幫你拿阿斯匹靈或是叫醫生來？

1 依據圖片，用「Would you like + 名詞」的句型，根據圖中的物品寫出問句。

tea   **1** _____

sandwiches   **2** _____

apple juice
orange juice   **3** _____

cheesecake   **4** _____

2 依據圖片和提示，用「Would you like to + 原形動詞」的句型，寫出邀請的問句。

basketball
play
this Sunday
afternoon   **1** _____

opera
watch
tonight   **2** _____

horse race
watch
next Saturday   **3** _____

on Skype
chat with me
tomorrow night   **4** _____

3 選出正確的答案。

1. Rose _____ green tea?
   James Yes, I do.
   - ⓐ Would you like
   - ⓑ Do you like

2. What _____ to do this Sunday?
   - ⓐ would you like
   - ⓑ do you like

3. Rose _____ some milk tea?
   James No, thanks. Not now.
   - ⓐ Do you like
   - ⓑ Would you like

4. _____ to get you some orange juice?
   - ⓐ Shall I
   - ⓑ Would you like me

5. _____ call for a taxi?
   - ⓐ Shall I
   - ⓑ Would you like me

6. _____ to teach?
   - ⓐ What do you like me
   - ⓑ What would you like me

7. _____ carrots, but I don't eat them very often.
   - ⓐ I like
   - ⓑ I'd like

8. James I would like to go to the Mozart Concert at the City Plaza tomorrow night.
   Rose OK. _____ get you a ticket.
   - ⓐ I shall
   - ⓑ I'll

9. Rose It's very cold in this room.
   James _____ turn on the electric heater?
   Rose Oh, yes! Thank you!
   - ⓐ Will I
   - ⓑ Shall I

10. _____ to learn 50 Greek words by next week.
    - ⓐ I like
    - ⓑ I'd like

11. Next week Sue and I _____ to visit Hollywood.
    - ⓐ would like
    - ⓑ like

Chapter

49 表達提議的用語：shall, let's, why don't we, how about

I — shall

what
where
+ shall we + 原形動詞 → shall 可用來「徵求意見」。
（美式英語更常用 should。）

What should we do now?

┌→ = What should we do now?
- **What shall we do** now? 我們現在該怎麼辦？

┌→ = Where should we go?
- **Where shall we go**? 我們應該去哪裡？

---

2 — 「提出建議」的各種句型

shall we + 原形動詞 → 建議我們來做某事
- **Shall we dance** a tango? 我們來跳探戈嗎？
- **Shall we go** for a swim? 我們去游泳好嗎？

let's + 原形動詞 → 建議我們來做某事（let's = let us）
- Jerome, let's fly to Rome.
  傑羅姆，我們坐飛機去羅馬吧。
- **Let's go** fishing tomorrow. 我們明天去釣魚吧。

why don't we + 原形動詞 → 我們何不來做……
- **Why don't we watch** a movie tonight with Dwight? 不如我們今晚跟杜威特一起去看電影吧？
- **Why don't we go** home and play some chess? 我們回家下棋好不好？

how about + 動詞 -ing / 名詞 → 提出建議做某事

┌→ = How about some apple juice?
- **How about having** some apple juice?? 要不要喝點蘋果汁？

┌→ = How about a chat on the Internet with Ken?
- **How about chatting** on the Internet with Ken? 我們上網跟肯聊天好不好？

1 選出正確的答案。

_____ **1** Rae, _____ to church this Sunday.
　　　　　　ⓐ let's to go　　ⓑ let's go　　ⓒ why don't we go

_____ **2** Lori　What should we do this morning?

　　　　　　Marc _____ some fun under the sun?
　　　　　　ⓐ How about having　　ⓑ Shall we　　ⓒ Why don't we having

_____ **3** _____ to eat tonight with Pete and Dwight?
　　　　　　ⓐ How about go out　　ⓑ When shall we going out　　ⓒ Why don't we go out

_____ **4** Lori　Where shall we go this Sunday?

　　　　　　Marc _____ go to Kim Lake for a swim and picnic.
　　　　　　ⓐ Why don't we　　ⓑ Shall we　　ⓒ Let's

_____ **5** _____ a teaching job in Japan?
　　　　　　ⓐ How about getting　　ⓑ Why don't we getting　　ⓒ Let's get

2 Dan 和 Ann 正計畫一起去度假。請用下面的綠色詞語，完成他們的對話。
（有些空格可以有兩個正確答案。）

Let's　　Why don't we　　How about　　shall we　　Shall we

Ann **1** _____ make a plan for our vacation.

Dan All right. So, where **2** _____ go?

Ann **3** _____ go somewhere warm and sunny. I'm
really tired of the snowstorms in Michigan.

Dan OK. **4** _____ go to sunny Florida?

Ann That's a good idea. But which part of Florida?

Dan **5** _____ Miami?

Ann We went there three years ago. **6** _____ go to
a different place this year.

Dan OK. **7** _____ going to Orlando?

Ann Orlando? Let me see the Disney World website. All right.

8 _____ do that. We can visit Disney World and
the Kennedy Space Center.

Dan Yes! So, when **9** _____ go there?

Ann **10** _____ February 15?

Dan February 15 is fine with me.

Ann **11** _____ go for ten days?

Dan Ten days? Mmm. Ten days sounds great.

Chapter

50 感官動詞當作一般行為動詞的用法

感官動詞可以當作**行為動詞**（描述我們的動作），也可以當作**連綴動詞**（描述外觀、狀態），本章節將介紹感官動詞當作行為動詞的用法。

1 — look 和 listen

look	→	意味（有意識）努力或專注地去「看」，強調動作的過程，所以**可以用於進行式**。

┌─ look 常和 at 連用。

- I looked at him angrily.
  我憤怒地看著他。 └─ 要用副詞修飾，不用形容詞。
- Sue is looking at the blue sea.
  蘇正在望著蔚藍的大海。

listen	→	意味（有意識）努力或專注地去「聽」，強調動作的過程，所以**可以用於進行式**。

Del What were you doing at nine last night?
昨天晚上九點你在做什麼？

┌─ listen 常和 to 連用。

Eve I was listening attentively to the VOA.
我很專心地在聽美國之音的廣播。

要用副詞修飾，不用形容詞。

2 — see 和 hear

see	→	指「看見」，強調「動作的完成，或動作的結果」，因此**不用於進行式**〔後面常接不帶 to 的不定詞或動名詞，參見 Unit 11〕。

- Did you see her leave the house?
  你看見她離開房子了嗎？

hear	→	指「聽見」，強調「動作的完成，或動作的結果」，因此**不用於進行式**〔後面常接不帶 to 的不定詞或動名詞，參見 Unit 11〕。

- I woke up and heard a bird singing.
  我醒來後聽見一隻小鳥在歌唱。

3 — watch

watch	+	受詞	→	指「觀看；留神觀察」，可以用於進行式。

- Why are you watching me eating?
  你為何看著我吃飯？
- Watch my dog jump over the log.
  你看我的狗跳那塊圓木。
- Dwight is going to watch a soccer game tonight. 杜威特今晚要去看一場足球賽。

watch 和 TV 連用，但 watch 和 see 都可以用來談論觀看電視節目和電影。

┌─「spend + time + V-ing」表示花時間做某事。

- Do not spend too much time watching TV.
不要花太多時間看電視。　└─「watch TV」是固定用語。

┌─ 觀看電視節目或電影。

- We [watched / saw] *Harry Potter and the Goblet of Fire* on TV last night.
昨晚我們看了電視上播的《哈利波特：火盃的考驗》。

4　feel 的用法

feel ＋ 受詞 →　feel 指「感知」時，不用於進行式；指「觸摸」時，可以用於進行式。

┌─ 當「感覺」時，不可以用進行式。

- Suddenly Meg felt a flea crawling up her leg.
梅格突然感覺有一隻跳蚤往她腿上爬。

┌─ 當「觸摸」時，可以用進行式。

Gus What are you doing? 你在做什麼？

Kay I'm feeling the silk cloth to determine its quality.
我在摸這絲綢料子，看看它的品質如何。

5　taste 的用法

taste ＋ 受詞 →　指「品嚐」，可以用於進行式。

- Pete tasted the fish and decided it was too salty to eat.
彼特嚐了一下魚，覺得太鹹了，不能吃。

Pam What are you doing? 你在做什麼？

Mat I am tasting the chicken soup to see if it has enough salt in it.
我在喝看看雞湯裡的鹽巴放得夠不夠。

6　smell 的用法

smell ＋ 受詞 →　smell 指「聞出、覺察出」時，不用於進行式；指動作「聞」時，可以用於進行式。

當「聞出」時，不可以用進行式。─┐

- As he walked into the house, Bing smelled something burning.
賓走進房子時，聞到有東西在燒。

┌─ 當「嗅」時，可以用進行式。

Tess What is she doing? 她在做什麼？

Sid She's smelling the flowers. 她在聞花。

7　sound 的用法

sound ＋ 受詞 →　sound 指「使響起」，可以用於進行式。

Peg Why are you sounding the alarm?
你為什麼要按警報？

Ted Because a tornado is coming.
因為龍捲風要來了。

1 自下列綠色詞中選出適當的動詞，用正確的動詞形式填空。

see   watch   hear   smell   listen to   look

1. Could you speak a little bit louder? I can't _____ you.
2. She opened the door and _____ a dead rat lying on the porch.
3. Dan picked up the socks and _____ them.
4. I _____ them arguing in the hall, but I didn't _____ what they were arguing about.
5. **Rita** Did you _____ the woman in a red mini-skirt and pink blouse?
   John Yes. That woman is Emma.
6. Do you spend lots of time _____ TV?
7. She _____ at him with her eyes full of excitement.
8. Dan usually _____ a basketball game on Sunday afternoon.

2 請判斷下列句子是否正確，正確打 ✓，不正確打 ×，並寫出正確句子。

1. I am smelling some kind of chemical in this neighborhood.
2. I tasted the milk this morning, and it was definitely sour.
3. Did you listen to someone knock on the door?
4. I'm hearing somebody coming into the house.
5. Why are you smelling your toes?
6. Were you feeling the house shake?
7. You should spend more time hearing English.
8. What is Pat looking?
9. Suddenly Lenore was hearing a strange noise outside the door.
10. When I woke up, I was smelling something rotten.
11. Please close your books and look at me.

Chapter

51 感官動詞作連綴動詞的用法

連綴動詞除了 be、appear、seem 等，下面幾個感官動詞也可以作連綴動詞。作連綴動詞時，這些詞通常是非進行式動詞〔參見 Chapter 33：不能用於進行式的動詞〕。

---

1 — look 的用法

look → look 作連綴動詞時，指「**看起來；好像是**」，後面常接形容詞，**通常不用進行式**。

• She always looks happy and healthy.
她總是神情愉快，看起來很健康。└→ look 後面接形容詞。

如果談論暫時的表情，look 可以用於簡單式或進行式，意思沒有區別。

┌→ = looks
• Your dad is looking very sad.
What's the matter with him?
你爸爸看起來很傷心，他怎麼了？

look like + 名詞 → 意思是「**看起來像……**」，不使用進行式。

┌→ look like + 名詞
• It looks like snow.
= It looks as if it's going to snow.
看起來好像要下雪了。└→ look as if + 子句

look as if + 子句 → 意思是「**看起來像……**」，不使用進行式。

---

2 — feel 的用法

feel → feel 作連綴動詞時，指「**覺得；摸上去給人某種手感**」，後面常接形容詞，**通常不用進行式**。

指「覺得」，不可用進行式。
• I'm beginning to feel chilly.
我開始感到寒冷了。

指「觸感」，不可用進行式。
• My new blanket feels so soft.
我的新毯子摸起來好柔軟。

feel fine/sick/tired 等，可以用於簡單式或進行式，意思沒有區別。

Ruth **How are you feeling?** → = How do you feel?
你覺得怎麼樣？

┌→ = I feel sick.
Paul **I'm feeling sick.** 我覺得不舒服。

fell like (= want) + 名詞 / 動名詞 → 意思是「**想要**」，不使用進行式。

┌→ feel like 後面可接名詞或動名詞。
• I feel like a cup of coffee. 我想喝一杯咖啡。
= I feel like having a cup of coffee.
• Bing feels like crying. 賓想哭。

3　taste 的用法

taste → taste 作連綴動詞時，指「嚐起來」，後面常接形容詞，不使用進行式。

┌─ taste + 形容詞
• The fish tasted awful. 這個魚很難吃。

taste like ＋ 名詞 → 意思是「嚐起來像⋯⋯」，不使用進行式。

┌─ taste like + 名詞
• The juice tasted like sugar water.
這個果汁喝起來像糖水。

taste of ＋ 名詞 → 意思是「嚐起來有⋯⋯的味道」，不使用進行式。

┌─ taste of + 名詞
• These cookies taste of ginger.
這些餅乾有薑的味道。

4　smell 的用法

smell → smell 作連綴動詞時，指「聞起來」後面接形容詞，不使用進行式。

┌─ smell + 形容詞
• This soup smells so good.
這個湯聞起來好香。

smell like ＋ 名詞 → 意思是「聞起來像⋯⋯」，不使用進行式。

┌─ smell like + 名詞
• It smells like a rotten egg.
它聞起來像一個臭掉的雞蛋。

smell of ＋ 名詞 → 意思是「聞起來有⋯⋯的味道」，不使用進行式。

┌─ smell of + 名詞
• The shop smells of fresh paint mixed with some chemicals.
這家店有油漆夾雜某些化學製品的氣味。

5　sound 的用法

sound → sound 作連綴動詞時，通常指「聽起來」，後面接形容詞，**通常不使用進行式。**

┌─ sound + 形容詞
• A cup of coffee sounds great.
喝杯咖啡聽起來不錯。

sound like ＋ 名詞 → 意思是「聽起來像⋯⋯」，不使用進行式。

┌─ sound like + 名詞
• Bali sounds like a great place for a relaxing vacation.
峇里島聽起來是一個適合放鬆的度假勝地。

sound as if ＋ 子句 → 意思是「聽起來像⋯⋯」，不使用進行式。

┌─ sound as if + 子句
• It sounds as if you've had a wonderful day.
聽起來你好像過了非常愉快的一天。

sound 如果有「有某種變化」的含意時，**可以用**進行式。

┌─ = sounds
• My car is sounding a bit strange these days.
我的車子這幾天聽起來有點怪怪的。

PRACTICE

1 選出正確的答案。

1 He ▨▨▨▨ very funny in that cowboy hat.
  a looks as if b looks like c looks

2 Gus Would you like some more chicken?
  Kay No, thanks. The chicken ▨▨▨▨, but I'm really full.
  a tasted delicious b tasted deliciously c was tasting delicious

3 Dwight ▨▨▨▨ going to the theater tonight.
  a feels like b is feeling like c feels as if

4 Things are beginning to look ▨▨▨▨.
  a gloomily b gloomy c gloom

5 It ▨▨▨▨ wonderful to be home again.
  a felt b was feeling c felt like

6 Your room ▨▨▨▨. You should open the window and air the room.
  a smells damply b is smelling damp c smells damp

7 Sally ▨▨▨▨ she was going to cry.
  a was looking as if b looked as if c was looking like

8 Mabel started to ▨▨▨▨.
  a feel miserable b feel miserably c feel misery

9 Gus How about going for a swim this afternoon?
  Kay That ▨▨▨▨.
  a sounds perfectly b sounds perfect c is sounding perfect

10 That ▨▨▨▨ Clair's children coming down the stairs.
  a sounds as if b is sounding like c sounds like

2 依據提示，填空完成句子。

1 My girlfriend's voice ＿＿＿＿＿＿＿＿＿ very pleasant. （聽起來總是）

2 The milk ＿＿＿＿＿＿＿＿＿. （喝起來是酸的）

3 Sue and Lulu feel like ＿＿＿＿＿＿＿＿＿. （唱歌和跳舞）

4 It ＿＿＿＿＿＿＿＿＿ you have caught a cold. （聽起來好像）

5 This room ＿＿＿＿＿＿＿＿＿. （有玫瑰花的氣味）

Chapter

52 使役動詞

當一個人不直接做某個動作，而是讓另一個人去做時，就要用使役動詞，表示「叫某人做某事」。常見的使役動詞有四個：make、have、let、get。

───── I ───── **make 的用法** ─────

主詞 ＋ **make** ＋ 人 ＋ 原形動詞 → 讓某人去做某件事
（make 的後面接「不帶 to 的不定詞」）

• make **me** work 讓我工作

• make **him** tell **the truth** 讓他講實話

• **Ms. Black** makes **us** read **ten storybooks a week.** 布萊克先生要我們每週讀十本故事書。

┌─ 使役動詞 make 如果用於被動語態，要接帶 to 的不定詞。

比較 **We** are made to read **ten storybooks a week.**

主詞 ＋ **make** ＋ 人／物 ＋ 形容詞 → 讓某人感到……
讓某物變得……

• make **someone** happy 讓某人開心　　• make **something** pretty 使某物變美好

• make **someone** angry 惹某人生氣　　• make **something** difficult 使某件事很難做

• make **something** nice 使某物變好　　• make **something** easy 使某件事容易做

• **Building a sand castle** made **me** happy. 堆沙堡讓我很開心。

• **Don't** make **things** more difficult **than they already are.**
事情已經夠難了，別再把它搞得更難。

主詞 ＋ **make** ＋ oneself / it ＋ 過去分詞 → 讓某人被……
讓某事被……

└─ 用過去分詞表示「被動」。

• make **yourself** heard 讓別人聽見你　　• make **it** known 使之公諸於眾

• make **yourself** understood 讓別人聽懂你　　• make **it** understood 使之被理解

• **I knew enough English to** make myself understood **while traveling across Australia last year.** 我去年在澳洲旅行時，我的英文程度夠我表達我的意思了。

• **Lily** made it known **that she came from a hardworking family.**
莉莉讓大家知道，她來自一個勤奮的家庭。

2 | **have 的用法**

主詞 + **have** + 人 + 原形動詞 → 讓某人去做某件事

- have her clean the house 要她打掃房子
- have him talk to the principal 要他和校長談談
- Claire always has her boyfriend do her hair. 克萊兒總是要她的男朋友幫她弄頭髮。

主詞 + **have** + 物 + 過去分詞 → 讓某物接受某個動作（含有被動的意思）

- have your hair cut 把你的頭髮剪了
- have the carpet cleaned 把地毯清洗乾淨
- Kay is going to have her truck tires changed today. 今天凱要換她的卡車輪胎。

主詞 + **have** + 人／物 + 動詞 -ing → **have** 後面如果接動詞 -ing 形式，則是用來「強調正在進行」。這個結構的 **have**，意指「**經歷了某事**」，而不是「讓某人做某事」。

- Last week I had so many guests that I had some of them sleeping on the floor.
  上個星期我因為客人太多，一些客人不得不睡在地板上。

3 | **let 的用法**

主詞 + **let** + 人／物 + 原形動詞 → 讓某人或某物去做某件事

- let him pass 讓他通過
- let my imagination run wild 讓我的想像力天馬行空
- Let Sue teach you how to behave. 讓蘇教你正確的行為舉止。
- Let the game begin. 遊戲開始吧。

Let the game begin.

4 | **get 的用法**

主詞 + **get** + 人 + 帶 to 的不定詞 → 讓某人去做某件事

- get her to write some emails 讓她寫電子郵件
- get him to give me a call 請他打電話給我
- Please get Kay to read five English storybooks today.
  今天請讓凱閱讀五本英文故事書。

主詞 + **get** + 物 + 過去分詞 → 讓某物接受某個動作（含有**被動**的意思）

- get **your hair** cut 把你的頭髮剪了
- get **the first chapter** finished 完成第一章節
- Kay, please don't forget to get **my motor scooter** fixed today.
  凱，請不要忘記今天要把我的速可達摩托車修好。

主詞 + **get** + 物 + 動詞 -ing → 讓某物做某個動作（含有**主動**和**正在進行**的意思）

- get **my computer** working **again** 使我的電腦重新開始運作
- get **her car** running 使她的車子運轉起來
- Bing worked on his car for five hours but failed to get **it** running.
  賓花了五個小時修他的車，但車子還是沒辦法運轉。

PRACTICE

1 選出正確的答案。

1. Did Jim make himself _____ in English while he was learning to swim?
   - ⓐ understand
   - ⓑ to understand
   - ⓒ understanding
   - ⓓ understood

2. Margo, you should have your van _____ before you go on your trip to Chicago.
   - ⓐ check
   - ⓑ to check
   - ⓒ checked
   - ⓓ checking

3. Pam wants to get her electric car _____ so that it will be easy to visit Sam.
   - ⓐ fix
   - ⓑ to fix
   - ⓒ fixed
   - ⓓ fixing

4. The professor had her students _____ five papers in one week.
   - ⓐ write
   - ⓑ to write
   - ⓒ written
   - ⓓ writing

5. Ben managed to get my clock _____ again.
   - ⓐ work
   - ⓑ to work
   - ⓒ worked
   - ⓓ working

_____ **6** How could the professor let her students _____ the final exam?
- a skip
- b to skip
- c skipped
- d skipping

_____ **7** Dirk was made _____ his homework.
- a do
- b to do
- c done
- d doing

_____ **8** I couldn't get them _____ what I was doing.
- a understand
- b to understand
- c understood
- d understanding

_____ **9** Lulu made it _____ that she was mad at you.
- a know
- b to know
- c known
- d knowing

---

2 將括弧內的詞彙以正確形式填空，完成句子。

1 Mom's new hairstyle makes her _____ ten years younger. (look)

2 Did I make it _____ that I did not want to see Lenore any more? (understand)

3 Are you going to let Ann _____ your jet to Pakistan? (fly)

4 Aunt Kay had her houseboat _____ in Monterey. (build)

5 Can you get Joe _____ me a ride to Chicago? (give)

---

3 自下列的綠色字中選出正確的詞彙填空，完成句子。

bring   sick   get   had   clean   redecorated

1 Mom made Dirk _____ his room today after he came home from work.

2 Our apartment looks much better since we had it _____.

3 I need to _____ my airplane refueled before I leave for Mumbai.

4 I'll have someone _____ your baggage to your room.

5 That chemical smell made her _____.

6 The clown _____ the audience smiling and laughing for the whole show.

Chapter

53 不定詞

1

有些**動詞**（see, watch, hear, feel, let, make, have, help）後面會先接**受詞**，再接不帶 to 的不定詞，這類動詞包含一些**感官動詞**和**使役動詞**〔參見 Chapter 52〕。

感官動詞 ＋ 受詞 ＋ 原形動詞

- Two minutes ago I felt the earth move a little.
  兩分鐘前，我有感到一點地震。
  └ 感官動詞　└ 原形動詞　└ 受詞
- Be quiet and just watch her play the chess game.
  安靜看她下棋。
- I didn't see Lynn come in. 我沒看到玲走進來。

使役動詞 ＋ 受詞 ＋ 原形動詞

- The teacher had everyone make something out of sand.
  老師要每個人都用沙子做一樣東西。
  └ 使役動詞　└ 受詞　└ 原形動詞
- Please help me (to) unload the car.
  請幫我把車子上的貨物卸下來。
  └ help 後面可接帶 to 的不定詞，也可接原形動詞。

2

有些**動詞**後面必須接帶 to 的不定詞。

動詞 ＋ 不定詞

afford 買得起	learn 學會	refuse 拒絕
decide 決定	need 需要	seem 似乎
expect 期待	offer 願意	want 想要
fail 失敗；忘記	plan 計畫	would like 想
hope 希望	promise 允諾	

- We can't afford to buy that house. 我們買不起那間房子。
  └ 動詞 └ 不定詞
- Kate again failed to be on time for her date. 凱特又沒有準時赴約了。
- Sue Star decided to buy an electric car. 蘇・斯塔爾決定要買一輛電動汽車。
- When did Clive learn to drive? 克里夫是什麼時候學開車的？

4

有些**動詞**後面可以先接**受詞**，再接帶 to 的不定詞。 ➔

allow 允許	teach 教
ask 請求	tell 告訴
expect 期待	want 想要
invite 邀請	would like 想
need 需要	

動詞　＋　受詞　＋　不定詞

- ┌ 動詞 ┌ 受詞
- Jim asked Sue to help him. 吉姆請蘇幫他。
  └➔ 不定詞
- I want you to be happy. 我要你快樂起來。
- What do you expect me to do? 你期待我做些什麼？
- Our boss would like us to work late today. 我們的老闆希望我們今天加班。

5

有些**形容詞**後面要接帶 to 的不定詞。 ➔

anxious 渴望的	eager 急切的	lucky 幸運的
ashamed 難為情的	easy 容易的	pleased 高興的
careful 小心的	expensive 昂貴的	proud 驕傲的
certain 確信的	glad 樂意的	ready 準備好的
content 滿足的	happy 高興的	reluctant 不情願的
crazy 瘋狂的	hard 艱難的	sad 傷心的
determined 下決心的	hesitant 猶豫的	shocked 震驚的
difficult 困難的	important 重要的	sorry 感到難過的
disappointed 失望的	likely 很可能的	surprised 吃驚的

形容詞　＋　不定詞

- ┌ 形容詞 ┌ 不定詞
- Is Japanese difficult to learn? 日文很難學嗎？
- It's important to do your homework. 做家庭作業很重要。
- She's easy to get along with. 她很好相處。
- I'm sorry to be so late. 很抱歉我遲到了。

I'm sorry to be so late.

6

有些**名詞**後面要接帶 to 的不定詞。 ➔

decision 決定	order 命令	refusal 拒絕
desire 渴望	permission 許可	request 請求
motivation 動機	plan 計畫	tendency 傾向
opportunity 機會	proposal 提議	wish 願望

名詞　＋　不定詞

- ┌ 名詞
- I have no desire to see him again. 我不想再見到他。
  └➔ 不定詞
- He has a tendency to sing his own praises. 他很愛吹捧自己。
- Her childhood wish to live in the jungle and study the monkeys has finally come true.
  她終於實現了童年的願望——住在森林裡研究猴子。

too 和 enough 這兩個字搭配帶 to 的不定詞，有特定的用法和意思〔參見 Chapter 57〕。

too + 形容詞 + 不定詞 → 太……，以致於不能……

- It's too <u>hot</u> <u>to work</u> today. 今天熱得無法工作。
  - 形容詞
  - 不定詞

- This car is too small for six people to sit in.
  這輛車太小，坐不下六個人。

形容詞 + **enough** + 不定詞 → 夠……，因而可以……

- She isn't <u>old</u> **enough** <u>to vote</u>. 她還不到投票的年齡。
  - 形容詞
  - 不定詞

- Mary was <u>foolish</u> **enough** <u>to believe</u> his story.
  瑪麗居然相信他講的事，真是太傻了。

PRACTICE

1 依據提示，填空完成句子。

1 Please _____ you. （讓我幫）

2 I didn't _____ in. （看見她進來）

3 Should we _____ every game we play? （期待贏）

4 He _____ our book club. （想加入）

5 Are you _____ go? （準備好）

6 I am _____ my master's degree in education.
（決心要獲得）

2 請判斷下列句子是否正確，正確打 ✓，不正確打 ×，並寫出正確句子。

1. She won't be happy live in her home village forever.
   ☐ _____

2. Two minutes ago I felt the earth to move a little.
   ☐ _____

3. I want to be healthy and happy.
   ☐ _____

4. I would like to have a cup of tea.
   ☐ _____

5. Mom was disappointed learning that I had failed the English exam.
   ☐ _____

6. Mom made me to clean up my room this morning.
   ☐ _____

7. My sister has a tendency in exaggerating things.
   ☐ _____

8. He was lucky to survive that car accident.
   ☐ _____

9. She refused go out with Mark last night.
   ☐ _____

10. Please help me open this window.
    ☐ _____

11. Grandma often says, "A person is never so old to learn."
    ☐ _____

12. Someone named Mark Wu wants to talk to you on the phone.
    ☐ _____

13. That smell made me to feel sick.
    ☐ _____

14. Dwight is too tired finish his book report tonight.
    ☐ _____

Chapter

54 動名詞（與不定詞的用法比較）

1

有些動詞後面要用動名詞。 →

dislike 不喜歡	mind 介意	resist 忍住
enjoy 喜歡	miss 免於	suggest 建議
finish 完成	practice 練習	
imagine 想像	prevent 預防	

動詞 ＋ 動名詞

動詞
- Why do you dislike playing Facebook games? 你為什麼不喜歡玩臉書遊戲？
  動名詞
- How can I practice playing the drums quietly? 我要怎樣小聲地練習打鼓？
- June will finish fixing her car by noon. 茱恩在中午之前會修好她的車。
- She suggested going for a swim in Clear Lake. 她提議去「清水湖」游泳。

2

有些動詞後面可以先接**受詞**，再接動名詞。 →

dislike 不喜歡	imagine 想像	see 看見
feel 感覺	mind 介意	watch 觀看
hear 聽	miss 免於	

動詞 ＋ 受詞 ＋ 動名詞

動詞　受詞　動名詞
- I dislike people telling me what to do and what to think.
  我不喜歡別人告訴我該做什麼、該想什麼。
- Can you imagine Dan working overtime? 你能想像丹加班嗎？
- An hour ago, I saw her walking in the City Plaza. 一小時前，我看見她在市廣場散步。

3

go 後面接動名詞的句型，經常用來談論休閒娛樂和運動。

go ＋ 動名詞

動詞　動名詞
- Kay goes swimming every other day. 凱每隔一天去游泳一次。
- She loves to go shopping on Sundays. 她喜歡星期天去購物。

go jogging	go skiing	go sailing	go swimming	go shopping
去慢跑	去滑雪	去航海	去游泳	去購物

接在**介系詞**後面的動詞，要用動名詞。

介系詞 + 動名詞

介系詞 ─┐   ┌─ 動名詞

* He's tired of listening to her empty talk. 他不想聽她無聊的談話。

* Kay got the job finished by working 14 hours a day for two weeks.
凱連續兩個星期每天工作十四個小時，完成了那份工作。

* I look forward to visiting Paris. 我很期待去巴黎。
➜ look forward to（盼望）：to 是介系詞，不是不定詞的 to，所以後面要接動名詞。

* I'm not used to driving in Singapore. 我不習慣在新加坡開車。
➜ be used to（習慣於）：to 是介系詞，不是不定詞的 to，所以後面要接動名詞。

比較　used to 指「過去時常做的一件事，而現在不再做了」，後面要接不帶 to 的**不定詞**。

* I used to walk for three hours a day, but now I only walk for an hour a day.
我以前常一天走路三小時，現在只走一小時。

* When Claire was a child, she used to have long hair. 克萊兒小時候是長髮的。

* I used to be a taxi driver, but now I'm a nurse. 我以前開過計程車，不過現在在當護士。

5

有些動詞後面接**動名詞**或**不定詞**都可以，
其意思完全相同。

begin 開始	like 喜歡	start 開始
continue 繼續	love 愛	
hate 討厭	prefer 偏好	

動詞 + 動名詞 / 不定詞

┌─ 動名詞　　　　┌─ 不定詞

* It began snowing. (= It began to snow.) 開始下雪了。

* I hate being bossed around. (= I hate to be bossed around.) 我不喜歡被人指揮來指揮去。

* She loves singing and dancing. (= She loves to sing and dance.) 她喜歡唱歌和跳舞。

Lisa　Should we take a taxi home? 我們坐計程車回家好不好？

Teddy　I would prefer walking home. (= I would prefer to walk home.) 我比較想走路回家。

6

有些動詞後面接**動名詞**或**不定詞**都可以，
但是意思不同。

forget 忘記	feel 感覺	watch 觀看
remember 記得	see 看見	
stop 停	hear 聽見	

主詞 + forget + 不定詞 → 忘記要去做某事（事情還未做）

動名詞 → 忘記已經做過某事（事情已經做過）

┌─「忘記去刮鬍子」，亦即沒有做刮鬍子這件事。
- **Bing** forget to shave **this morning.** 賓今天早上忘記刮鬍子了。

┌─「forget + V-ing 形式」常用在「will never forget + V-ing 形式」的結構中。
- **I will never** forget meeting **Erica on a trip to South Africa.**
└─已經遇見過艾芮卡。
我永遠也不會忘記在南非之旅遇見了艾芮卡。

主詞 + remember + 不定詞 → 記得要去做某事（事情還未做）

動名詞 → 記得已經做過某事（事情已經做過）

┌─ 記得要做某事（窗戶還沒有關）。
- **Please** remember to close **the window before you leave.** 離開之前記得關窗戶。

┌─ 記得已經做過了某事（曾經見過她）。
- **I** remember meeting **her at church last year.** 我記得去年在教會見過她。

主詞 + stop + 不定詞 → 結束一個行為，以開始另一個行為（不定詞用來表示「目的」= in order to）

動名詞 → 停下手邊正在的事

┌─ stop to + 原形動詞，表示停下來去做 to 之後所接的那件事。
- **She** stopped to sign **autographs for her fans.** 她停下來幫粉絲簽名。
- **I yelled at her, and then she** stopped running. 我對她吼叫，然後她停下來不跑了。
└─ stop + 動名詞，表示停下後面的動名詞那個動作。

主詞 + see / watch / hear / feel + 受詞 + 原形動詞 → 「看見、聽見或感覺」整個動作的完成

動名詞 → 「看見、聽見或感覺」某個動作正在進行

┌─ 使用原形動詞，表示在我看的時候，癩蛤蟆從公路的一邊爬到了另一邊。
- **This morning I** saw a toad cross **the road.** 今天早上我看見一隻癩蛤蟆穿越馬路。

┌─ 使用動名詞，表示在我看的時候，癩蝦蟆正在穿越馬路。
- **This morning I** saw a toad crossing **the road.** 今天早上我看見一隻癩蛤蟆在穿越馬路。

┌─ jump over 因為是短暫、瞬間完成的動作，所以不會有 see + 受詞 + jumping over 的用法
- **Did you** see her jump **over the doghouse?** 你看見她跳過了那個狗屋嗎？

PRACTICE

1 將括弧內的動詞以正確的不定詞或動名詞形式填空，完成句子。

1 I can't go now. I still have some work to do. Do you mind _____ (wait) for fifteen minutes?

2 Are you happy _____ (live) in this city?

3 Did you enjoy _____ (dance) with Sue last night?

4 I look forward to _____ (see) you in India.

5 I don't want to get up early on Sundays. I prefer _____ (stay) in bed.

6 What do you want me _____ (do) tomorrow?

7 When did Trish start _____ (learn) Spanish?

8 How could I get good at _____ (catch) fish?

9 Could you please help me? The TV is too heavy for me _____ (carry) to the living room by myself.

10 Do you hope _____ (travel) around the world in the future?

11 I shouted, "Please let me _____ (go)."

12 I would like you _____ (try) this grapefruit juice I just made.

13 I'm trying to sleep. Please stop _____ (talk).

14 Yesterday Kim was angry with Jim, and she refused _____ (talk) to him.

15 How many languages can Ms. Day _____ (speak)?

16 The berries are ripe enough _____ (pick).

17 The weather is so nice. I suggest _____ (go) for a swim in the lake.

18 She looked up briefly at me and then continued _____ (read).

2 自框內選出正確的動詞，以不定詞或動名詞的形式填空，完成句子。

take	get	read	rain	be	swim
wear	talk	play	jog	love	learn

1. She likes _____ blue jeans and tennis shoes.

2. Do you think it's easy _____ Greek?

3. My aunt is very much worried about _____ old.

4. Did he really teach herself _____ the violin?

5. She has lots of storybooks in English. She enjoys _____ for fun.

6. Bing likes _____ lots of pictures when he is traveling.

7. When it stops _____, we'll go to the beach.

8. She likes to get up early and go _____ along the river bank.

9. I used to _____ her, but not anymore.

10. Am I foolish _____ in the lake in such bad weather?

11. I tried to avoid _____ to her.

12. She's not used to _____ bossed around.

3 選出正確的答案。

_____ **1** Sue thanked the psychologist for _____ her to deal with her depression after the earthquake.
  a help
  b to help
  c helping

_____ **2** I'm young enough _____ the energy the job needs.
  a have
  b to have
  c having

_____ **3** They enjoy _____ on the boat.
  a live
  b to live
  c living

_____ **4** She agreed _____ a short speech before the summer camp's swimming competition.
  a make
  b to make
  c making

_____ **5** Stop _____ at me. I can hear you.
  a yell
  b to yell
  c yelling

_____ **6** I remember _____ Jim not to go to that party, but he went anyway.
  a tell
  b to tell
  c telling

_____ **7** Don't forget _____ your anti-virus software.
  a update
  b to update
  c updating

_____ **8** Would you mind _____ the dishes?
  a wash
  b to wash
  c washing

Chapter 55 形容詞的用法

1

用來形容人或物的描述性詞彙，叫做**形容詞**，即用來形容名詞或代名詞。在句子裡，形容詞通常可以放在以下兩個不同的位置：

1 放在「名詞」的前面；**2** 放在「be 動詞」或「連綴動詞」的後面。

形容詞 **+** 名詞 →

- **Roy is a** happy boy. 羅伊是一個快樂的男孩。
- **Tess is wearing her** new dress. 黛絲穿著她的新洋裝。
- **Have you ever talked to any** famous people? 你有沒有跟名人說過話？
- **Claire, I love your** lovely hair. 克萊兒，我喜歡你漂亮的頭髮。
- **Kay fed the** hungry ducks **today.** 凱今天餵過饑餓的鴨子了。
- **I don't like** spicy food. 我不喜歡辛辣的食物。

be 動詞 **+** 形容詞 →

↓
is, am, are 等

- **Roy** is happy. 羅伊很快樂。
- **Please** be quiet. 請安靜。

連綴動詞 **+** 形容詞 →

↓
look, feel, smell,
taste, sound, get 等

- **Your hair** looks lovely. 你的頭髮好漂亮。
- **Pete, don't eat that meat. It** smells bad. 彼特，不要吃那塊肉，它聞起來壞掉了。
- **Do you** feel bored? 你覺得無聊嗎？
- **It is OK to** get old. 變老沒有關係。
- **There is nothing wrong with** getting old. 變老沒有什麼不正常啊。

2

無論形容詞修飾的是**單數名詞**還是**複數名詞**，形容詞的拼寫都**不需要變化**。

- **a** fast **train**
一輛快速火車

- **two** fast **trains**
兩輛快速火車

- **a** quiet **village** 一個靜謐的村莊
- **two** quiet **villages** 兩個靜謐的村莊

- **an** electronic **dictionary** 一台電子字典
- **four** electronic **dictionaries** 四台電子字典

情緒形容詞（即分詞形容詞）：情緒形容詞指「情緒動詞」的 -ing 和 -ed 形式。描述「**某人的感覺、表情**」，要用 **-ed 形式**（即過去分詞）；描述「**引起這種感覺的人、物、環境、事件**」，要用 **-ing 形式**（即現在分詞）。

情緒動詞	過去分詞　V-ed	現在分詞　V-ing
描述感覺和情緒的動詞	描述一個人的感覺或表情	描述引起這種感覺的人、物、環境或事件
bore 使厭煩	bored 感到厭倦的	boring 令人感到厭倦的
confuse 使困惑	confused 感到困惑的	confusing 令人感到困惑的
embarrass 使尷尬	embarrassed 感到尷尬的	embarrassing 令人感到尷尬的
excite 使興奮	excited 感到興奮的	exciting 令人感到興奮的
frighten 使害怕	frightened 感到害怕的	frightening 令人感到害怕的
interest 使感興趣	interested 感到有趣的	interesting 引起興趣的；有趣的
satisfy 使滿意	satisfied 感到滿意的	satisfying 令人滿意的
surprise 使驚訝	surprised 感到驚訝的	surprising 令人感到驚訝的
tire 使疲倦	tired 感到疲倦的	tiring 令人感到疲倦的

- The news about Paul surprised us all. → 情緒動詞的過去式
  = The news about Paul was surprising to all of us. → 現在分詞形容詞
  = All of us were surprised at the news about Paul. → 過去分詞形容詞
  保羅的這則消息讓我們所有的人都大吃一驚。

┌→「人」感覺疲倦（tired）。
- She was tired from her exciting visit to the International Space Station.
  └→「旅程」令人興奮（exciting）。
  她去了一趟令人興奮的國際太空站之旅，非常疲倦。

┌→「人」感覺厭煩了（bored）。
- I was bored with his boring story. 我厭倦了他乏味的故事。
  └→「故事」乏味、令人生厭（boring）。

4

-ed 結尾的形容詞，常與特定的介系詞（at, by, in, from 等）搭配。

be bored with/by	對⋯⋯感到厭煩
be confused about	對⋯⋯弄不清楚
be embarrassed about	對⋯⋯感到尷尬
be excited about	對⋯⋯感到興奮
be frightened at/by	對⋯⋯感到害怕
be interested in	對⋯⋯感興趣
be surprised at	對⋯⋯感到驚訝
be tired of	對⋯⋯感到厭倦

- He is embarrassed about his huge credit card debt.
  他的信用卡負債累累，他感到很難為情。

- I was surprised at her angry reply to my innocent remark.
  我很意外她會對我一句無心的話怒言相向。

1 請將左欄的形容詞與其所修飾的右欄名詞連接。（搭配須符合語言習慣。）

1	severe •	• a	soup
2	illegal •	• b	trip
3	tasty •	• c	city
4	fragrant •	• d	injuries
5	muddy •	• e	country roads
6	tiring •	• f	possession of firearms
7	prosperous •	• g	roses

2 將下列詞彙重組為正確的句子。（句首須大寫，並在句尾加上正確的標點符號。）

1 is | cooking | some | fish | Trish | tasty

_____

2 blue | dress | her | is | Bess | wearing | old-fashioned

_____

3 you | are | why | in | position | this | interested

_____

4 was | we saw last night | very | the movie | interesting

_____

5 nothing to do | bored | I | with | am

_____

6 never feels | because | exciting | bored | she reads | Ms. Brooks | books

_____

7 saw | whale's | the | tail | big | Gail

_____

8 very | room | is | cold | this

_____

3 自框內選出可以互相搭配的形容詞和名詞，填空完成句子。

> weather   vacation   scissors
> water   fruit   job

> fresh   stormy   dangerous
> sharp   long   hot

1 I need a pair of _____ to cut this leather.

2 The Community Storm Shelter is always open during _____ .

3 Is journalism sometimes a _____ ?

4 Hardworking Tom looks very tired. I think he needs a _____ .

5 The company is one of the world's largest producers of _____ and vegetables.

6 Can a cup of _____ freeze faster than cold water?

4 由 ⓐ 和 ⓑ 的選項中，選出正確的答案。

1 Is Sue ⓐ interested ⓑ interesting in you?

2 Fighting that water balloon battle was ⓐ excited ⓑ exciting.

3 She got ⓐ bored ⓑ boring by the slow bumper car ride.

4 He told us an ⓐ interested ⓑ interesting story about Lady Gaga.

5 Mom was ⓐ concerned ⓑ concerning when Mike was riding that big elephant.

6 I was ⓐ disappointed ⓑ disappointing at my exam results.

7 He felt too ⓐ excited ⓑ exciting to fall asleep.

8 Bing thinks his present job is ⓐ bored ⓑ boring.

9 She loves to read stories ⓐ concerned ⓑ concerning UFOs and visitors from outer space.

10 My little brother was ⓐ frightened ⓑ frightening by the firecrackers.

11 She was ⓐ shocked ⓑ shocking by the bang as the left front tire on her truck went flat.

12 It turned out to be a ⓐ disappointed ⓑ disappointing dinner.

13 The lightning and thunder last night were ⓐ frightened ⓑ frightening.

14 Teaching 4-year-old kids is very ⓐ tired ⓑ tiring.

15 He asked her some ⓐ embarrassed ⓑ embarrassing questions.

16 After the earthquake, our apartment building was in a ⓐ shocked ⓑ shocking state.

17 It is a very ⓐ satisfied ⓑ satisfying result, but there is still a long way for us to go.

18 It was ⓐ surprised ⓑ surprising to see how many buildings survived the terrible earthquake.

19 I am ⓐ confused ⓑ confusing about why Amy hates me.

20 Anna felt ⓐ embarrassed ⓑ embarrassing about her daughter's bad table manners at the party last night.

21 Dan said he felt sick and ⓐ tired ⓑ tiring of her empty talk.

22 After hearing that I got 5 A's on the final exams, my dad gave me a ⓐ satisfied ⓑ satisfying smile.

23 Some of the questions on the test were very ⓐ confused ⓑ confusing.

24 I was ⓐ surprised ⓑ surprising at how fast Sally could run.

Chapter

56 副詞的種類、用法和詞序

副詞用來說明一件事情發生的情況細節，例如事情發生的時間、地點、方式、程度、條件等。可以用來修飾**動詞**、**形容詞**、**副詞**或**整個句子**。

1 表示地點和時間的副詞

主詞 + 動詞 + 受詞 + 地點副詞 + 時間副詞 →

↳ 說明事件發生的地點（Where?）。

↳ 說明事件發生的時間點（When?）或持續時間（How long?）。

表示地點（**place**）的副詞和副詞片語（如：here, abroad, home, to school），用來回答「**where**」。

表示時間（**time**）的副詞和副詞片語（如：at 7 am., this morning, all day, for five years），用來回答「**when**」或「**how long**」。

┌─ 地點副詞　┌─ 時間副詞

- **Kay arrived** home yesterday. 凱昨天抵達家。

┌─ 介系詞片語 in the same house 是地點副詞，修飾動詞 has lived。

- **He has lived** in the same house for over 40 years.
他這棟房子已經住了四十多年了。 └─ 介系詞片語 for over 40 years 是時間副詞，修飾動詞 has lived。

- **Coco is leaving** tomorrow. 可可明天離開。

- **Bing's father takes the subway to work** in the mornings.
賓的父親早上都會搭捷運去上班。

- **I haven't seen you** for ages. 我好久沒看到你了。

- **Dwight didn't sleep** all night. 杜威特整晚都沒睡。

> home 當作副詞的時候，前面不能加介系詞：
> - **She will come home soon.**
> 她很快就要回家了。

2 表示頻率的副詞

❶ 表示**頻率**（frequency）的副詞和副詞片語（如：always, sometimes, never, once a year），用來回答「how often」，又可分為「不確定頻率副詞」和「確定頻率副詞」。

❷ **不確定頻率副詞**：有兩種位置，(1) 位於一般主動詞之前；(2) 位於 be 動詞之後。

不確定頻率副詞	頻率 100-51%	always, constantly, usually, normally, frequently, regularly, often
	頻率 50-1%	sometimes, occasionally, rarely, infrequently, seldom, hardly, ever
	頻率 0%	never

主詞 + 助動詞 + 不確定頻率副詞 + 主動詞 →

↳ 說明事件發生的頻率（How often?）。

表示頻率的副詞和副詞片語，用來回答「**how often**」。

┌─ 不確定頻率副詞放在動詞之前。

- **Sally** often **feels** lonely. She needs to make some new friends.
莎莉常感到孤單，她需要結交一些新朋友。

┌─► 不確定頻率副詞放在助動詞之後，主動詞之前。

- She has never met my parents. 她沒見過我父母。

- She always gives me the same friendly smile. 她總是給我那一臉友善的微笑。

> **Note** sometimes、often、frequently 和 usually 除了放在述語動詞前，也可以放在句首或句尾。
>
> Lily sometimes comes to visit me. →放在述語動詞之前
>
> = Sometimes Lily comes to visit me. →放在句首
>
> = Lily comes to visit me sometimes. →放在句尾　　莉莉有時會來看我。

> **Note** seldom 和 rarely 本身就具有否定含意，不能用在否定句型裡。
>
> She seldom talks to me. 她很少跟我說話。
>
> She doesn't talk to me. 她不跟我說話。

┌─► 不確定頻率副詞接在 be 動詞之後。

主詞 ＋ be 動詞 ＋ 不確定頻率副詞

- He is often unhappy on Mondays. He has a drinking problem. 他星期一常感到痛苦。他有酗酒的問題。

- Labor Day is always the first Monday of September. （美國）勞動節一直是在九月的第一個星期一。

> **Note** 還有一些副詞的位置跟不確定頻率副詞的位置一樣，如：all, already, also, both, just, still。
>
> Jerome has already gone to Rome. 傑羅姆已經去羅馬了。
>
> They both live in Norway. 他倆都住在挪威。
>
> Ted is still in bed. 泰德還在床上。
>
> My two sisters are both astronauts. 我的兩個姊姊都是太空人。

❸ **確定頻率副詞**：確定頻率副詞（包括副詞片語和副詞）一般放在句尾，但有時為了強調，副詞片語也可以放在句首。

> **確定頻率副詞** ┃ 頻率確定 ┃ hourly, daily, weekly, monthly, yearly, every day, once a minute, twice a year, every morning, once, twice, once or twice, three times

┌─► 放在句尾　┌─► 放在句首

- Kay walks to school every day. = Every day Kay walks to school. 凱每天走路上學。

- She goes shopping once a week. = Once a week she goes shopping. 她每週去購物一次。

3　表示方式的副詞

❶ 表示「**方式**」的副詞和副詞片語（如：badly, carefully, cheerfully, loudly, proudly, well），稱為**方式副詞**或**情狀副詞**。

$$\boxed{主詞} + \boxed{動詞} + \boxed{受詞} + \boxed{情狀副詞} \rightarrow$$ 方式副詞或情狀副詞用來表示「方式」，情狀副詞通常以 -ly 結尾，用來回答「how」。

┌─→ well 要放在「動詞 + 受詞」後面，不放在
│   動詞之前，也不能放在動詞和受詞之間。

- **Dell plays the violin very** well**.** 戴爾的小提琴拉得很好。

❷ 以 -ly 結尾的情狀副詞位置比較靈活，可以放在動詞之前，可以放在「動詞 + 受詞」之後。有時為了強調也可以放在句首。但不能放在動詞和受詞中間。

┌─→ 放在「動詞 + 受詞」之後
- **The pig ate his food** greedily**.**

┌─→ 放在動詞之前
  = **The pig** greedily **ate his food.** 那頭豬貪婪地吃光了牠的食物。

┌─→ 放在「動詞 + 受詞」之後
- **The principal addressed the teaching staff** solemnly**.**

┌─→ 放在動詞之前
  = **The principal** solemnly **addressed the teaching staff.**

┌─→ 放在句首
  = Solemnly **the principal addressed the teaching staff.**
  校長嚴肅地向全體教員們發表演說。

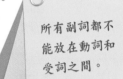

所有副詞都不能放在動詞和受詞之間。

──── **4** ──┤ 表示程度的副詞

表示「**程度**」的副詞（如：almost, completely, extremely, too, very），用來回答「to what extent」（到何程度），放在形容詞或其他副詞之前。

┌─→ 程度副詞 + 形容詞
- **Dan is** absolutely **sure that he wants to marry Ann.** 丹百分之百確定自己想要娶安。

┌─→ 程度副詞 + 形容詞
- **Maybe this skirt is** too short **for me.** 也許這條裙子我穿太短了。

┌─→ 程度副詞 + 情狀副詞
- **Sam did** quite well **on the English exam.** 山姆的英文考試考得很好。

──── **5** ──┤ 表示目的的副詞

「**目的副詞**」說明「某人做某事的目的」，用來回答「**why**」的問題。「**不定詞片語**」常做目的副詞用。

┌─→ 此不定詞片語用來表達目的
- **Sally flew to Singapore** to see her boyfriend**.** 莎莉飛去新加波找她的男朋友了。

- **He ran fast** to catch the bus**, but it was already gone.**
  他快步跑去趕公車，但車子已經開走了。

Note 數個副詞的排列順序一般為：

程度 → 方式 → 地點 → 時間

She behaved very badly in school yesterday**.**
她昨天在學校很不守規矩。

PRACTICE

1 用下面的詞來描述自己，正確地完成下列句子。

always   usually   often   sometimes   rarely   never

1. I'm hardworking.   *I'm always hardworking.*
2. I'm polite.   _____
3. I get upset.   _____
4. I get nervous.   _____
5. I'm happy.   _____
6. I yell at my parents.   _____

2 用括弧裡的副詞改寫下面句子。

1. When do you get up? (usually)   _____
2. Pete doesn't eat meat. (rarely)   _____
3. The boss is in the office. (still)   _____
4. Jim talks to Kim. (often)   _____
5. I will remember the first day I met you. (always)   _____
6. Are you late for school? (ever)   _____
7. Mary doesn't get angry. (seldom)   _____
8. I haven't been to Egypt. (never)   _____
9. My friends are married. (all)   _____
10. They are at home in the evenings. (usually)   _____
11. He has been to Rome twice. (already)   _____
12. Does Margo live in Chicago? (still)   _____

3 請將下列詞語排列成正確的句子。

1. champion | boxed | the | in the closing rounds | well

2. go | didn't | Kay | Because she was sick, | yesterday | to school

3. misses | to explore | a | never | she | chance

4. in 2002. | born | Sue | in Honolulu | was

5. late | often | Kate | at night | works

6. morning. | saw | a | Bing | bird | in his backyard | beautiful | this

7. his keys, | find | can | he | wallet, or jacket | never

8. Ken | before ten | in bed | always | is

9. reads | evening. | the news on the Internet | she | every

10. goes | often | on weekends. | to the movies | she

11. thought about | for a minute | Janet | Before her bungee jump, | it

4 改錯。

1 　We often play on the beach volleyball.

2 　Bob is going to start next week his new job.

3 　Bobby exclaimed, "This is an exciting hobby extremely!"

4 　Ms. Rice and her daughter Lulu explored carefully the tropical paradise.

5 　The choir sang last night beautifully at the concert.

6 　My father drives often to work.

7 　She can remember never my name.

8 　We love all to watch football games.

9 　They since 2008 have lived here.

10 　Will you be this evening at home?

11 　My parents very much love me.

12 　Dell speaks very well English and Spanish.

Chapter

57 too, enough, still, yet 的用法

I ── too 的用法

too 是**副詞**，用來修飾形容詞或另一個副詞，意思是「太……」。

too + 形容詞／副詞 + **for** + 人／物 → 「對……來說，太……」

- This apartment is too small for a big family. 這間公寓對一個大家庭來說，太小了。
- I'm too old for sports like surfing. 我這種年紀的人來玩衝浪這類的運動，年紀太大啦。

too + 形容詞／副詞 + **to** + 原形動詞 → 「太……，以致於不……」

- You're never too old to learn something new. 活到老，學到老。
- It's too hot to walk to school today. 今天熱得不能走路去上學。

too + 形容詞／副詞 + **for** + 人／物 + **to** + 原形動詞 → 「太……，以致於不……」

- You walk too fast for me to keep up with you. 你走得太快了，我跟不上你。

too + **much** + 不可數名詞／**many** + 複數名詞 → 「……太多了」

- Let's go somewhere else. There is too much air pollution here.
 我們去別的地方吧，這裡的污染太嚴重了。
 ┌─ air pollution 是不可數名詞。
- I don't like to live in the city. There are too many people and too much traffic.
 我不喜歡住在城裡頭，人太多，交通太擁擠。
 ┌─ people 是複數名詞。
 traffic 是不可數名詞。

---

2 ── enough 作副詞和形容詞的用法

❶ enough 作副詞時，置於形容詞、另一個副詞或動詞之後。enough 作形容詞時，
 置於名詞之前。

形容詞／副詞／動詞 + 副詞 **enough** → 「夠……」

- "Her English sounds awful."
 "I think she hasn't practiced enough."
 「她的英文聽起來很不好。」
 「我想她是練習得不夠多。」
 └─ 副詞 enough 放在動詞（practiced）後面。

• I didn't run fast enough. 我跑得不夠快。

┌── 副詞 enough 放在另一個副詞（fast）的後面。

• She is old enough to learn how to drive. 她已經到了可以學開車的年齡。

┌── 副詞 enough 放在形容詞（old）的後面。

| 形容詞 enough | + | 名詞 | → | 「夠……」 |

┌── 形容詞 enough 放在名詞（sugar）的前面。

• Is there enough sugar in your coffee?
  你咖啡裡的糖放這樣夠嗎？

❷ 形容詞或副詞 enough 常用於下面短語：

| enough | + | for | + | 人 / 物 | → | 「對……來說，夠……了」 |

• This hat isn't big enough for me. 這頂帽子我戴小了一點。

• I don't have enough money for a house. 我的錢不夠買一間房子。

| enough | + | to | + | 原形動詞 | → | 「做……，夠……了」 |

• This computer is small enough to put into your pocket.
  這台電腦小得可以裝進你的口袋裡。

| enough | + | for | + | 人 / 物 | + | to | + | 原形動詞 | → | 「對……來說，去做……，是夠……」 |

• The water in the lake isn't warm enough for us to go for a swim.
  湖水不夠暖和，我們不能去游泳。

---

3   比較 too 與 not enough

• This dress is too long for me.
  這件洋裝我穿太長了。

→ This dress isn't long enough for me.
  這件洋裝我穿長度不夠。

• She's too old to drive.
  她年齡太大，不能開車。

→ He isn't old enough to drive.
  他還不到開車的年齡。

• There is too much sugar in my tea.
  我茶裡的糖放太多了。

→ There isn't enough sugar in my tea.
  我茶裡的糖放不夠。

She threw up because she ate too much.
她因為吃太多，都吐了。

→ I'm still hungry. I didn't eat enough.
  我還餓，沒吃夠。

yet →	常位於句尾。用於**否定句**中時，意思是「**還沒有**」；用於**疑問句**中時，意思是「**已經**」。	still →	常用於肯定句和疑問句中（有時也可於否定句中），意思是「**還；依舊**」。

Karen — Has Jim finished his homework yet?　吉姆的功課寫完了嗎？
┌ yet 用於疑問句中。

Jose — No, he is still working on it. → still 用於肯定句中。　沒有，他還在寫。

Karen — What are you going to do during this summer vacation?　你今年暑假要做什麼？
┌ yet 用於否定句中。

Jose — I haven't decided yet. I'm still thinking about it.　我還沒有決定，還在考慮。

Karen — Are you ready to go now?　你準備好沒？現在可以走了嗎？

Jose — Not yet. I'm still replying to a work-related text message.　還沒有準備好，我還在回一個跟工作有關的手機簡訊。

• Are you still there? 你還在那裡嗎？ → still 用於疑問句中。

PRACTICE

1 用 too 或 enough 與括弧裡的詞語完成句子。

1. Could you please turn the TV down? It's _____. (loud)

2. I want to go to bed right now. I'm _____ to stay up any longer. (tired)

3. The boss can't see you now. She's _____. (busy)

4. Don't tell me when I should go to bed. I'm _____ to decide my bedtime. (old)

5. When you speak to a group of elderly people, please remember to speak _____. (loudly)

6. Did your boss give you _____? (vacation time)

7. I run _____ to enter this race. (slowly)

2 用「too . . . (for somebody) to do something」結構完成句子。

1. (I can't fall asleep/excited) I'm *too excited to fall asleep* .

2. (she can't carry the box/heavy) The box _____.

3. (I couldn't understand what Lee was saying/fast) Lee spoke _____
_____.

4. (I'm not going for a walk/windy) It's _____.

5 (large airplanes can't land here/short) This runway is _____.

6 (she can't get a driver's license/young) She's _____.

3 用 too/too much/too many/enough 填空。

1 There is _____ salt in the soup. I don't want to eat it.

2 That violent movie was _____ scary for my five-year-old son.

3 That's all for today. You have already asked _____ questions.

4 You look really tired. Don't work _____ hard.

5 "Would you like some more steak?" "No, thanks. I've had _____."

6 I don't like living in Iceland. There is _____ wind.

7 There isn't _____ time to get all these things done.

8 This dress is very pretty, but it's not big _____ for me.

4 參照例子為每個情景寫三句話。

1 (an hour ago) The baby *was asleep.*
   (still) She*'s still asleep.*
   (yet) She *hasn't woken up yet./She isn't awake yet.*

2 (an hour ago) It was _____
   (still) It _____
   (yet) The rain _____

3 (an hour ago) Mom _____
   (still) She _____
   (yet) Dinner is _____

5 用 yet 或 still 填空。

1 She has been thinking for two hours, but she _____ can't decide.

2 Is breakfast ready _____?

3 Flight 88 from Boston has not arrived _____.

4 Is your daughter _____ going out with that playboy Mat?

Chapter 58 quickly, badly, angrily, well 等情狀副詞的用法

---

1 以 -ly 結尾的情狀副詞

形容詞 ● + -ly 字尾 → 許多情狀副詞是以「形容詞 + -ly」構成的。
以下是加 -ly 的變化方式：

形容詞 +ly 字尾	-ful 結尾：直接 + -ly	-y 結尾：y 變 i + -ly	-e 結尾：去 e + -ly
clear → clearly	cheerful → cheerfully	angry → angrily	terrible → terribly
cheap → cheaply	hopeful → hopefully	easy → easily	simple → simply
proud → proudly	careful → carefully	lucky → luckily	true → truly
brave → bravely	truthful → truthfully	heavy → heavily	gentle → gently
clever → cleverly	grateful → gratefully	hungry → hungrily	sensible → sensibly
glad → gladly	skillful → skillfully	merry → merrily	possible → possibly

┌─ gracefully 是情狀副詞，表示那隻天鵝游泳的方式。
• The swan is swimming gracefully. 那隻天鵝悠游的姿勢很優美。

• He often speaks proudly about his successful daughter.
他常驕傲地談起他事業有成的女兒。

• All the students are listening attentively to Professor Black.
所有的學生都在專心地在聽布萊克教授講課。

• Lee left the house hurriedly. 李匆匆忙忙地出門。

> **Note** 有些以 -ly 結尾的詞是形容詞，如：daily, friendly, lively, lonely, lovely。其中 daily 和 lively 可作形容詞，也可以作副詞。

---

2 形容詞和以 -ly 結尾的情狀副詞比較

形容詞用來修飾**名詞**，或是放在連綴動詞後面，當作主詞補語；**副詞**用來修飾**動詞**、**形容詞**或**副詞**。

┌─ 形容詞 sweet 放在 be 動詞之後，當作主詞補語。
形容詞用法 Sue is very sweet. 蘇很可愛。

副詞用法 She smiled sweetly at me. 她給我一個甜甜的笑容。
└─ 情狀副詞 sweetly 放在動詞 smiled 之後，用來修飾 smiled。

形容詞用法 He is always patient with his students. 他對學生一直很耐心。

副詞用法 I waited patiently for the bus. 我耐心地等公車。

┌─ 形容詞 simple 修飾名詞 life。

形容詞用法 Lily lives a simple life. 莉莉過著簡單的生活。

副詞用法 I live very simply and don't spend lots of money. 我生活簡單，花錢不多。
└─ -e 結尾的形容詞，去 e + ly，變成副詞。
└─ very 是副詞，修飾另一個副詞 simply。simply 修飾動詞 live。

形容詞用法 She is a gentle girl. 她是一個文靜的姑娘。

副詞用法 Row your boat gently down the stream. 沿著小河，輕輕地划著你的船。
└─ 情狀副詞置於「動詞 + 受詞」（Row your boat）後面。

形容詞用法 They live a happy life. 他們過著幸福的生活。

副詞用法 They got married and wanted to live happily ever after.
他們結婚了，想從此過著幸福的生活。 └─ -y 結尾的形容詞，y 變成 i + -ly，變成副詞。

---

3 **同形的形容詞和副詞**

有些字的詞性既可以當形容詞，也可以當副詞，例如 hard、fast、late、early。

┌─ 形容詞 hard 位於繫動詞 is 後，作主詞補語。

形容詞用法 Susan is very hard to get along with. 蘇珊很難相處。

副詞用法 Kim works very hard. 金姆工作很努力。
└─ 副詞 hard 修飾動詞 works。

┌─ 形容詞 fast 修飾名詞 reader。

形容詞用法 Are you a fast reader? 你閱讀的速度快嗎？

副詞用法 Sally reads very fast. 莎莉的閱讀速度很快。
└─ 副詞 fast 修飾動詞 reads。

形容詞用法 You are late/early. 你遲到了／早到了。

副詞用法 He usually goes to bed late/early. 他通常很晚才／很早就上床睡覺。

---

4 **形容詞 good 和副詞 well 的用法**

┌─ 形容詞 good 修飾名詞 friend。

形容詞用 good • Trish is my good friend. 翠希是我的好朋友。

副詞用 well • I know Trish very well. 我跟翠希很熟。
└─ 副詞 well 修飾動詞 know。

形容詞用 good • How good is her English? 她的英文又多好？

副詞用 well • Trish speaks English very well. 翠希的英文講得很好。

Note well 也可作形容詞，但意思不同，表示「**身體健康的；安好的**」。
Lisa How are you? 你好嗎？
Brian I'm not feeling well. 我感覺不太舒服。我頭痛。
I have a headache. → 這裡的 well 是形容詞，接在感官動詞 feel 後面，意思是「安好的」。〔參見 Chapter 51〕

Note 比較意義不同的的同根副詞：

deep 深地	deeply 深刻地
hard 努力地	hardly 幾乎不
high 高	highly 非常
late 遲	lately 最近

1 把下列的形容詞改寫成副詞。

1 willing	_____	**5** poor	_____	**9** bitter	_____
2 lazy	_____	**6** noisy	_____	**10** kind	_____
3 miserable	_____	**7** noble	_____	**11** careless	_____
4 fatal	_____	**8** sad	_____	**12** frequent	_____

2 連連看。

1 fought •   • **a** Spanish fluently

2 arrived •   • **b** generously

3 spoke •   • **c** monsters bravely

4 danced •   • **d** heatedly

5 gave •   • **e** punctually

6 argued •   • **f** ballet gracefully

3 用下列的副詞完成下列句子。

correctly *fearlessly* *respectfully* *stealthily*
sleepily *dangerously* *heavily* *comfortably*

1 Ted felt quite exhausted, and he _____ nodded his head twice before he began to snore.

2 With her rifle ready, Susan _____ faced the pack of wolves.

3 My husband was seated _____ in his armchair.

4 Lily answered all the questions _____.

5 Kay always speaks to her boss _____, and he talks to her in the same way.

6 He often drives _____. Sooner or later he will get into big trouble.

7 Yesterday it rained _____.

8 Tom was late for class, so he crept _____ into the classroom.

4 選出正確答案。

1 Sam and Trish are (well/good) readers, and they are doing very (well/good) with English.

2 She is very (proud/proudly) of her new house.

3 Lily and Mat danced (beautifully/beautiful) last night at the Christmas party.

4 Kay is (quickly/quick) at learning languages, and she (quickly/quick) learned 30 new Spanish words today.

5 Clive (easily/easy) learned how to drive.

6 I know Dell very (well/good).

7 Why are you (madly/mad) at me? I didn't do or say anything wrong.

8 Hurry up! We will be late for class. Why are you always so (slowly/slow)?

9 "What are you doing?" "I'm working (hardly/hard) at practicing my English by using a computer program."

10 This problem is (easily/easy) to solve.

Chapter 59 形容詞的原級、比較級和最高級

1 形容詞的原級、比較級和最高級

原級 → 形容詞所修飾的人或物，如果未與別的人或物進行比較，那形容詞就要用原級。

- Mike is a **tall** boy, measuring 170 centimeters at the age of twelve.
  邁克是一個高大的男孩，**12** 歲身高就有 **170** 公分。

比較級 → 如果要比較**兩個人或物**，表達其中一個比另一個「更……」，那形容詞就要用比較級。

- Mark is 175 centimeters in height, so he is 5 centimeters **taller** than Mike.
  馬克身高 **175** 公分，因此他比邁克高五公分。

最高級 → 如果要比較**三個或更多的人或物**，表達其中一個「最……」，那形容詞就要用最高級。

- Jerry is 184 centimeter tall, so he is the **tallest** of the three boys.
  傑瑞身高 **184** 公分，因此他是三個男孩中最高的。

2 形容詞的比較級和最高級之構成

❶ 大多數的單音節形容詞
- + -er 字尾 → 比較級
- + -est 字尾 → 最高級

單音節形容詞 +-er/-est	以 -e 結尾的單音節形容詞 +-r/-st	字尾是「一個母音字母 + 一個子音字母」的單音節形容詞 重複字尾字母 + -er/-est
old → older → oldest	nice → nicer → nicest	big → bigger → biggest
fast → faster → fastest	safe → safer → safest	hot → hotter → hottest
few → fewer → fewest	wide → wider → widest	thin → thinner → thinnest

❷ 雙音節和多音節形容詞

以 -y 結尾
- 變 y 為 i + -er → 比較級
- 變 y 為 i + -est → 最高級

非以 -y 結尾
- more + 原級 → 比較級（比較……）
- most + 原級 → 最高級（最……）
- less + 原級 → 比較級（比較不……）
- least + 原級 → 最高級（最不……）

以 -y 結尾 變 y 為 i +-er/-est
busy → busier → busiest
easy → easier → easiest
unhappy → unhappier → unhappiest

字尾非 -y 的雙音或多音節形容詞 more/most + 原級／ less/least + 原級
careful → more/less careful → most/least careful
capable → more/less capable → most/least capable
expensive → more/less expensive → most/least expensive

* more 的反義詞是 less；most 的反義詞是 least。

❸ 少數以 -er，-ow 結尾的雙音節形容詞

+-er/-est
clever → cleverer → cleverest 聰明的
narrow → narrower → narrowest 狹窄的

❹ 不規則變化的形容詞

good	→ better	→ best（好的）
bad	→ worse	→ worst（壞的）
well	→ better	→ best（身體好的）
ill	→ worse	→ worst（病的）
far	→ farther	→ farthest（遠的）〔指距離〕
far	→ further	→ furthest（遠的）〔指程度；英式英語也可指距離〕
little	→ less	→ least（少的）〔修飾不可數名詞〕
many	→ more	→ most（多的）〔修飾複數名詞〕
much	→ more	→ most（多的）〔修飾不可數名詞〕

注意

應避免雙重比較，例如：

✓better	✗more better
✓cheaper	✗more cheaper
✓older	✗more older
✓safer	✗more safer

有些形容詞沒有比較級，如：**right, wrong, prefect, excellent** 等。

3　比較級的用法（than）

❶ 表示「**不相等**」的比較句型：進行比較的「**兩種事物或兩個人不相等**」（表示「更……」）時，用比較級，比較級後面常跟著 than。比較級前面可加上 much、far、a little、two years 等，用來強調程度。

• Mom's English is better than her Spanish. 媽媽的英語比她的西班牙語好。

• I'm taller than Pam. 我比潘姆高。

　　　　　　　　　　┌─ 比較級前面可以加上 much，用來強調程度。
• Is Japanese much more difficult than Chinese? 學日文比學中文難得多嗎？

• My aunt's dress was a little more expensive than my pants.
我姑姑的洋裝比我的褲子要貴一點。

• Harry is two years older than his brother Jerry. 哈利比他弟弟傑瑞大兩歲。

❷ than 是連接詞，後面應該接「主詞 + 述語動詞」，但在口語中可以接「受詞代名詞」（than me, than her, than us）。

• Lee is a better reader than me.
= Lee is a better reader than I am. 李的閱讀能力比我好。

• I'm healthier than her. = I'm healthier than she is. 我比她健康。

❶ 進行比較的兩者**相等**時，用「as + 形容詞原級 + as」；否定句型
「not as + 形容詞原級 + as」，可以用比較級句型來替換。

- Is Drake Pond as deep as Weep Lake? 公鴨池塘跟哭湖一樣深嗎？

- She is as busy as before. 她跟以前一樣忙。

- Dan is not as tall as his sister Ann. 丹沒有他姐姐安高。
  = Dan is shorter than his sister Ann. 丹比他姐姐安矮。
  = Ann is taller than her brother Dan. 安比她弟弟安高。

- I don't have as many friends as you do. 我的朋友沒有你的朋友多。
  = I have fewer friends than you do. 我的朋友比你的朋友少。
  = You have more friends than I do. 你的朋友比我的朋友多。

❷ 句型「the same (+ 名詞) as . . .」也可以表示「相等」。

- The two sisters look exactly the same as each other. 這兩姊妹長得一模一樣。

- The temperature today is the same as yesterday. 今天的氣溫跟昨天一樣。

- My father is the same age as my mother. = My father is as old as my mother.
  我父親跟我母親的年紀一樣大。

5 最高級的用法

比較「**三種或三種以上**」的事物或人時，要用**最高級**；如果是要將某個人、事、物，「與
其所屬的整個團體」做比較，也要用最高級。最高級的前面要加 the。

三人之間的比較。

- Which girl has the strongest will, Liz, Jane, or Jill?
  哪一個女孩最有意志力，莉茲、珍，還是潔兒？

與其所屬的整個團體做比較。

- Mr. Wood is the friendliest person in our neighborhood.
  伍德先生是我們街坊最友善的人。
  最高級後面如果是接地名，用介系詞 in
  （in school, in Europe）。

最高級後面接的地名若是 farm、island、earth 或團體名 team，要用 on。

- Lisa is the fastest swimmer on our swimming team.
  在我們的游泳隊裡，麗莎游得最快。　最高級的後面所接的團體名稱，若是複數代名詞或
  名詞（them, players），就要用 of。

- Paul is the fastest runner of them all. 在他們所有人當中，保羅跑得最快。

- She is the most hardworking student I've ever known. ── 最高級可用「I've ever . . .」、
  「you've ever . . .」等修飾
  = She is the hardest working student I've ever known.
  在我認識的學生當中，她是最用功的學生。

  在兩者之間比較，要用比較級。

  > **Note** Both exercises are easy, but the first one is the easier of the two.
  > 兩個練習題都容易，不過第一題還要容易一些。

PRACTICE

1 寫出下列形容詞的比較級和最高級形式。

1	clever _____	**8**	jealous _____	**15**	bad _____
2	sad _____	**9**	friendly _____	**16**	good _____
3	heavy _____	**10**	nice _____	**17**	dirty _____
4	rude _____	**11**	patient _____	**18**	thin _____
5	ignorant _____	**12**	wealthy _____	**19**	sunny _____
6	noisy _____	**13**	little _____	**20**	much _____
7	slim _____	**14**	wide _____		

2 寫出反義詞。

1	younger _____	**4**	worse _____	**7**	richer _____
2	more expensive _____	**5**	closer _____	**8**	less _____
3	warmer _____	**6**	more difficult _____		

3 用括弧裡的形容詞的正確形式，完成下列句子。（使用含肯定意義的 **more** 或 **most**，不用含否定意義的 **less** 或 **least**。）

1 Dan is not as _____ as Ann. (talkative)

2 It was _____ yesterday, but today it's even _____. (hot)

3 This is the _____ cat I've ever had on my lap. (heavy)

4 This church is the _____ building in our small town. (old)

5 Which is the _____ country in Asia? (small)

6 Dan is _____ than his sister Ann. (friendly)

7 What is the _____ mistake you've ever made? (bad)

8 I guessed that she was hungry and _____, so I invited her out for a pizza. (depressed)

9 Today's weather is _____ than yesterday. (bad)

10 Whose karate kicks are the _____, Vic's, Dick's, or Rick's? (good)

11 Do you think Sir Winston Churchill was the _____ Englishman during World War II? (famous)

12 Sue is the _____ student in my class. (hardworking)

13 I have a small car, and I want a _____ one. (big)

14 Sally is the _____ dancer in the ballroom. (graceful)

15 Trish is not very interested in geography and history. She's _____ interested in literature and English. (much)

16 Paul occupied the _____ armchair in the big living room. (comfortable)

17 The farmer said this was the _____ pig on the farm. (fat)

18 She is not only brilliant but also _____. (diligent)

19 Of all the dresses in this shop, I like this one the _____. (much)

20 My father is _____ than my mother. (patient)

4 選出正確答案。

_____ 1 These are probably the _____ hats in the store.
ⓐ most fancy　ⓑ fanciest　ⓒ fancy　ⓓ fancyest

_____ 2 We were all home for the holiday season. What could make for _____ Christmas than that?
ⓐ a merrier　ⓑ the merriest　ⓒ merry　ⓓ the merrier

_____ 3 *Diehard* is the _____ movie Jean has ever seen.
ⓐ most excited　ⓑ more excited　ⓒ most exciting　ⓓ more exciting

_____ 4 Of all the students in the class, Daisy is surely _____.
ⓐ less diligent　ⓑ more diligent
ⓒ the less diligent　ⓓ the least diligent

_____ 5 His flu seems to be _____ today than yesterday.
ⓐ worst　ⓑ the worst　ⓒ worse　ⓓ badder

_____ 6 The project was much _____ complicated than I had expected.
ⓐ so　ⓑ most　ⓒ more　ⓓ too

_____ 7 Jenny always gets the best job evaluations, so I guess she must be _____ employee in our small company.
ⓐ the more valuable　ⓑ a valuabler
ⓒ a more valuable　ⓓ the most valuable

_____ 8 Ted is almost _____ his older brother Ed.
ⓐ taller as　ⓑ as tall as　ⓒ the tallest of　ⓓ tall than

_____ 9 Dawn is even _____ than her brother Jon.
ⓐ smarter ⓑ more smart ⓒ smartest ⓓ more smarter

_____ 10 Liz Pool is the _____ talented dancer _____ our school.
ⓐ more, in ⓑ most, of ⓒ most, in ⓓ more, of

_____ 11 Tom is _____ basketball player _____ the island of Guam.
ⓐ the better, in ⓑ a better, on ⓒ the best, in ⓓ the best, on

_____ 12 Sue is the _____ one of the Robinson twins.
ⓐ pretty ⓑ prettiest ⓒ prettier ⓓ more pretty

5 請判斷下列句子是否正確，正確打 ✓，不正確打 ×，並寫出正確句子。

1 This castle is the oldest in the country. ☐ _____

2 Is it more cheaper to travel by car or by train? ☐ _____

3 Linda is the better student in the class. ☐ _____

4 Kay made less mistakes than Trish on the English exam yesterday. ☐ _____

5 Jane is the more generous of the twins. ☐ _____

6 根據實際情況回答下列問題。

1 Who is the funniest student in your class? _____

2 What's the best thing that has ever happened to you? _____

3 What's the worst thing that has ever happened to you? _____

4 What's the most exciting movie you have ever seen? _____

5 What's the most difficult thing you would like to do? _____

6 When is the best time of the year to visit your city? _____

7 Which class is your most boring one? Why? _____

8 Which class is your most interesting one? Why? _____

Chapter

60 副詞的原級、比較級和最高級

---

1 副詞的原級、比較級和最高級

原級 → 如果兩個人或物或兩個以上的人或物,彼此之間**沒有進行比較**,用副詞的**原級**來修飾動詞。

- Claire, Lenore, and Lily sang beautifully in the clear mountain air. 克萊兒、蕾諾兒和莉莉的歌聲,在潔淨的高山空氣中優美動聽。

比較級 → 如果要比較**兩個人或物**,表達其中一個比另一個「更……」,就要用副詞的**比較級**來修飾動詞。

- Claire sang more beautifully than Lenore. 克萊兒唱得比蕾諾兒還要動聽。

最高級 → 如果要比較**三個或更多**的人或物,表達其中一個「最……」,就要用副詞的**最高級**來修飾動詞。

- Of the three girls, Lily sang the most beautifully. 在三個女孩中,莉莉唱得最動聽。

---

2 副詞比較級和最高級的構成

❶ 大多數的單音節副詞
- + -er 字尾 → 比較級
- + -est 字尾 → 最高級

> **單音節副詞**
> **+-er/-est**
>
> fast → faster → fastest
> slow → slower → slowest
> high → higher → highest

❷ 雙音節和多音節副詞
- more + 原級 → 比較級(比較……)
- most + 原級 → 最高級(最……)
- less + 原級 → 比較級(比較不……)
- least + 原級 → 最高級(最不……)

> **兩個音節以上的副詞**
> **more/most + 原級/ less/least + 原級**
>
> slowly → more/less slowly → most/least slowly
> loudly → more/less loudly → most/least loudly
> rapidly → more/less rapidly → most/least rapidly

❸ 不規則變化的副詞 → 參看不規則變化的形容詞(例如:well → better → best)。
〔參見 P. 233〕

❹ 一些以 -y 結尾的**雙音節副詞**，比如 early 和 lively 等，這些詞也可以**做形容詞**，這類副詞的比較級和最高級不要用 more/less，而是要把 y 改成 i，然後加 -er 和 -est。

> early → earlier → earliest
> lively → livelier → liveliest

3 　**副詞比較級的句型（表示兩者不相等）**

主詞 A ＋ 動詞 ＋ 副詞比較級 ＋ **than** ＋ 主詞 B

- Can Kim run faster than Jim? 金姆跑得比吉姆快嗎？

- I go to the movies a lot, but Sue goes to the movies much more than I do.
  我常去看電影，但蘇比我還要常去看電影。

  ┌→ = than it was yesterday
- Today the water in the river is flowing slower than yesterday.
  今天的河水沒有昨天流得那麼急。

  ┌→ than me = than I did
- Today Amy arrived at the school earlier than me. 艾咪今天比我早到達學校。

4 　**表示「相等」的比較句型（as . . . as）**

主詞 A ＋ 動詞 ＋ **as** ＋ 副詞原級 ＋ **as** ＋ 主詞 B

- Sally can dance a ballet as gracefully as me. 莎莉的芭蕾舞可以跳得跟我一樣優美。

- I don't see Sue as often as you do. 我沒有像你那樣常見到蘇。
  = I see Sue less often than you do. = You see Sue more often than I do.

5 　**副詞最高級的句型**

主詞 ＋ 動詞 ＋ **the** ＋ 副詞最高級 ＋ | in / on / of | →

❶ 在最高級後面，通常在地名的前面用介系詞 in、on 等。

❷ 在最高級後面，如果有複數代名詞或複數名詞，這個複數詞前面要用介系詞 of。

- Lily works the hardest in our family. 在我們家裡，莉莉工作最勤奮。

- Grace and Tim moved the least rapidly of all the teams in our class's three-legged race.

- = Grace and Tim moved the slowest of all the teams in our class's three-legged race.
  在我們班級舉行的「兩人三腳」競賽中，葛蕾絲和迪姆是所有組當中前進最慢的一組。

- Liz runs the fastest of all the girls on the track team. 在田徑隊所有女孩中，莉茲跑得最快。

- This turtle moves the fastest of all the turtles in the pet store.
  在寵物店所有的烏龜中，這隻烏龜的行動最快。

1 用副詞 high 的正確形式，完成下列歌謠。

How ① _____ can a butterfly fly?

A butterfly can fly as ② _____ as it wants to fly.

Can a bee fly ③ _____ than a butterfly?

Please go and ask Lorelei or Eli.

2 用括弧裡的副詞的正確形式，完成下列句子。

① Lee often drives very _____ (carefully).

② Who practices the _____ in your swimming class? (hard)

③ Who swims _____, Arthur or Stew? (fast)

④ Of all my friends, Amy has traveled the _____. (far)

⑤ Kay danced _____ today than yesterday. (lively)

⑥ I think Kay has a cold and is swimming a little _____ today than yesterday. (slowly)

3 選出正確答案。

_____ ① Coco sings _____ Margo.

ⓐ more often as   ⓑ as often as   ⓒ the most often than

_____ ② Lily, could you please tap dance _____?

ⓐ loudlier   ⓑ more loudly   ⓒ most loudly

_____ **3** Mr. Spurs climbed _____ all the explorers.

ⓐ the higher of　ⓑ the highest in　ⓒ the highest of

_____ **4** I arrived at school at _____ Pat.

ⓐ the same time as　ⓑ as the time as　ⓒ the same as

_____ **5** My ballet teacher dances much _____ Fay or Kay.

ⓐ as gracefully than　ⓑ gracefully than　ⓒ more gracefully than

_____ **6** Sue runs _____ than I do.

ⓐ more fast　ⓑ more faster　ⓒ faster

_____ **7** She is eating _____ fast.

ⓐ unusual　ⓑ unusuallier　ⓒ unusually

_____ **8** Margo and Lily may win the three-legged race, because they are now moving _____ than Coco and Joe.

ⓐ most rapidly　ⓑ more rapidly　ⓒ rapidlier

_____ **9** Coco and Joe are moving _____ than a turtle.

ⓐ more slower　ⓑ most slow　ⓒ slower

_____ **10** Jean runs _____ all the runners I've ever seen.

ⓐ the faster of　ⓑ faster than　ⓒ the fastest of

_____ **11** Lily snores _____ my family.

ⓐ the loudest in　ⓑ louder than　ⓒ the loudest of

_____ **12** Roger always arrives at band practice _____ than Esther.

ⓐ late　ⓑ more late　ⓒ later

Chapter

61 表示地方的介系詞：in, at, on

1

介系詞 + 名詞 / 代名詞 → 介系詞通常出現在**名詞**或**代名詞**之前 →
- in the sky 在天空
- on the bed 在床上
- about you 關於你

2

介系詞把其後的名詞或代名詞，與句中的另一成分連接起來，例如：

| 連接動詞 | → | lie on **the bed** 躺在床上 |

| 連接名詞 | → | the sound of **loud music** 大聲音樂的聲響 |

| 連接形容詞 | → | bad for **you** 對你有壞處 |

3 | in（在……裡）〔指三度空間〕

- "Where is Jane?" "She's in the bathroom." 「珍在哪裡？」「她在浴室裡。」

- "Is Milan in the north of Italy?" "Yes, it is." 「米蘭在義大利的北部嗎？」「是的。」

- Mary lives in a big busy city, but she would prefer to live in the quiet countryside.
瑪麗住在一個繁華喧鬧的大城市裡，但她寧願住在寧靜的鄉村。

┌ 片語 in the middle of，表示「在……中間」。
- In the middle of the Garden of Eden was the tree of knowledge.
「知識樹」就在在伊甸園的中央。

┌ in the hospital 在這裡表示「住院」，英式英文用 in hospital。
- Tom is sick. He's in the hospital. 湯姆生病了。他在住院。

→ in the sky 在天空裡	in a taxi 在計程車裡	in a picture/photograph 在照片上
in the water 在水裡	in a book 在書裡	in the world 在世界上
in the garden 在花園裡	in a newspaper 在報紙裡	in Kuwait 在科威特
in bed 在床上	in the living room 在客廳裡	in prison 在監獄裡
in a car 在車子裡	in the hospital 在住院／在醫院	in jail 在牢房裡

4 | at（在……地點）〔指在一點上〕

- There's someone at our door. 我們門口有人。

- The post office is at the end of Fourth Street. 郵局在第四街的盡頭。

- While I was waiting at the traffic lights, a woman bumped her car into mine.
我在等紅綠燈時，一位女子的車撞上我的車了。

- Kay is not at work today. She's at home. 凱今天沒有來上班。她在家裡。
  └→ at work 是慣用語，表示「在上班中」。
  └→ at home 是慣用語，表示「在家裡」。

"Is Rae at school today?" "No, she's not."「芮今天來上學沒有？」「沒有。」
  └→ at school 是慣用語，表示「在上學中」。

"Where were you last night?" "I was at a concert."
「你昨晚在哪裡？」「我去聽音樂會。」
  └→ at a concert 是慣用語，表示「去聽音樂會」。

→ at home 在家
  at work 在上班
  at school 在學校
  at college 在大學
  at Sally's (house) 在莎莉家
  at the dentist's 在牙科診所
  at a party 在聚會上

  at a concert 在音樂會上
  at a basketball game 在看籃球賽
  at the top (of the page)
     在（頁面的）頂端
  at the bottom (of the page)
     在（頁面的）下端
  at the bus stop 在公車站

  at the door 在門口
  at her desk 在她的書桌旁
  at the end of Tenth Street
     在第十街的盡頭

1 in school 或 at school 都可表示講話的此刻正在學校上課。
  "Where is Claire?" 克萊兒在哪裡？
  "She is at school." 她在學校。
  （ = She is in school. ）

2 但提及「具體的學校」，要用 at，例如：
  at Michigan State University 在密西根大學

1 in 或 at 都可用於建築物（飯店、餐館等）的名稱之前。
  We stayed at the Holiday Inn.
  = We stayed in the Holiday Inn.
  我們住在假日飯店。

2 但如果強調在建築物裡面，只用 in：
  There are 500 rooms in the Holiday Inn. 假日飯店有 500 個房間。

比較 arrive in 與 arrive at
Yesterday I finally arrived in London.（到達大地點）我終於在昨天到達了倫敦。
Sue arrived at the airport at two.（到達小地點）蘇在兩點時到達了機場。

5 on（在……上）〔指在表面上，或是在一線上〕

比較

sit on a chair 坐在椅子上
sit on a sofa 坐在沙發上
sit in a sofa chair 坐在沙發椅上
lie on the bed 躺在床上
lie in bed 躺在床上
（in bed 指被毯子等覆蓋著）

- "Where is my backpack?" "That's funny. It's on your back."
  「我的背包在哪裡？」「真滑稽。就在你的背上啊。」

- "Is Washington, D.C. on the Potomac River?" "Yes, it is."
  「華盛頓位於波托馬克河畔嗎？」「是的。」

- Look, there's a huge spider running on the floor.
  瞧，有一個大蜘蛛在地板上跑。

- Did you come here on a cruise ship? 你是搭遊輪來這裡的？

- My office is located on the first floor of the Administration Building.
  我的辦公室在行政大樓一樓。

- I saw a car accident on the way home. 我在回家的路上看到一起車禍。
  └→ home 之前不用介系詞 to。

- I saw a motor scooter accident on the way to work. 我在上班的路上，看見一起摩托車車禍。

- In America people drive on the right side of the road, not on the left side.
  在美國，人們在馬路上行車是靠右邊行駛，而不是靠左邊。

on a bus 在公車上	on a horse 在馬匹上	on the way home 回家的路上
on a train 在火車上	on the first floor 在一樓	on the left 在左邊
on an airplane 在飛機上	on the second floor 在二樓	on the right 在右邊
on a ship 在船上	on the way to 去 . . . 的路上	

6　in、at、on：描述居住地點的用法差異

in ＋ 城市或城鎮 → ・ Margo lives in Chicago. 瑪歌住在芝加哥。

┌ 英式英語用 in ＋ 街道

on ＋ 街道 → ・ Pete lives on Washington Street. 彼特住在華盛頓大街。

at ＋ 門牌號碼 → ・ Pete lives at 1018 Washington Street.
彼特住在華盛頓大街 1018 號。

PRACTICE

1　使用 in/at/on，配合圖片右邊裡的詞語，看圖回答問題。

the lake

Where is she swimming?

1 _____

the desk

Where is he sitting?

2 _____

the bus stop

Where are those people standing?

3 _____

the airplane

Where is Jane?

4 _____

2 請從提示字中選出正確答案。

(in) (on) **1** ⓐ "I'll put some green tea _____ your cup."
"Thank you. That's just what I need."
ⓑ "Is Sydney _____ the southeast coast of Australia?" "Yes, it is."

(at) (on) **2** ⓐ There are lots of beautiful pictures _____ the walls in the living room.
ⓑ Mabel sat down _____ the table and began to eat.

(at) (in) **3** ⓐ She lives _____ Hawaii.
ⓑ Sue lives _____ 86 West Fourth Avenue.

(in) (on) **4** ⓐ Look, a kite is flying high _____ the sky.
ⓑ A big black bear was sitting _____ the road.

(at) (on) **5** ⓐ "Where are your friends Dan and Ann?" "They are _____ work."
ⓑ "Where is your apartment?" "It's _____ the second floor."

3 改錯：請將下列句子改寫為正確的句子。

1 Ted is reading on bed.
_____

2 There is a supermarket on the end of this street.
_____

3 Her name is on the bottom of the page.
_____

4 There are four police officers in our door.
_____

5 There's a small church at the top of the hill.
_____

6 "Is there a mall near here?"
"Yes, turn right on the next set of traffic lights. You won't miss it."
_____
_____

Chapter

62 表示地方的介系詞：beside, between 等

---

beside, under, over, behind, in front of

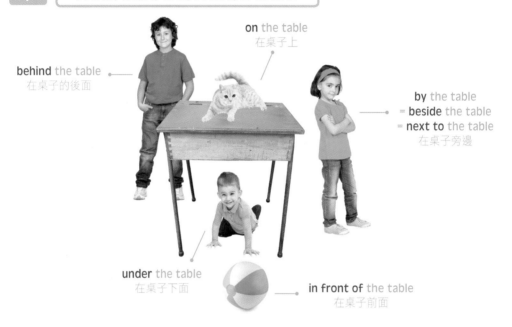

behind the table
在桌子的後面

on the table
在桌子上

by the table
= beside the table
= next to the table
在桌子旁邊

under the table
在桌子下面

in front of the table
在桌子前面

❶ **beside** 和 **by** 指「在……旁邊；在……附近」，相當於 **next to** 和 **near**。

　　　　└• = next to = by = near

• Tom sat down beside Mom. 湯姆在媽媽身邊坐下來。

❷ **under**（在正下方）　　反義詞 **over**（在正上方）

• under the bridge 橋下方　　over the bridge 橋上方

• Who is that girl sitting under the tree? 坐在樹下的那個姑娘是誰？

• An owl is sitting on the tree branch over my head. 一隻貓頭鷹坐在我頭頂上的樹枝上。

❸ **behind**（在……的後面）　　反義詞 **in front of**（在……的前面）

• A crowd of angry people gathered in front of the city hall.
一群憤怒的人群聚集在市政廳前面。

• Who is sitting behind Mark? 坐在馬克後面的是誰？

❹ **in front of**（在……的前面）：表示在某一空間外部。
in the front of（在……的最前部）：表示在某一空間內部的前面。

• in the front of the car 汽車的前座　　in front of the building 大樓前面

> **Note** beside (= next to; near; by) 指「在……旁邊」。
> besides (= in addition to) 指「在……之外、除……之外」。
>
> He knelt beside the dead soldier and began to say a prayer. 他在那名陣亡戰士的旁邊跪下來，開始祈禱。
> Did Kim talk to anyone else besides Jim? 金姆除了跟吉姆說話外，還有跟別人說話嗎？

2 —— above 和 below

→ **above** the table
在桌子上面

→ **below** the clock
在時鐘的下面

above 表示「在……上面」，通常用來
說明某樣東西的位置比另一樣東西高，
但並非在正上方（有時也指正上方）。

below 表示「在……下面」，通常用來說明某樣
東西的位置比另一樣東西低，但並非在正下方。
below 與 **above** 互為反義字。

- **My new blue skirt ends just above my knees.**
  我的藍色新短裙只到膝蓋上方。

- **Dee's dress extends below her knees.**
  蒂的洋裝長過膝蓋。

- **below sea level** 低於海平面
- **below the horizon** 地平線下

- **above sea level** 高於海平面
- **above the horizon** 地平線上

3 —— among 的用法

→ **among** the toys
在玩具的中間

among 指某人或某物「被包括
在特定的一群人或物之中」。

- **Is she popular among her classmates?** 她在同學中人緣好嗎？

- **Is Claire among the students who are sitting over there?**
  克萊兒是否坐在那邊的那些學生裡頭的？

4 —— between 的用法

→ **between** the trees
在兩棵樹中間

between 表示某人或某物「位
於兩個人或物之間」。注意：如
果指定了具體**兩個實體**（人或
物），就只能用 **between**。

- **Who is that man standing between Ann and Nan?**
  站在安和南之間的那個男子是誰？

1 看圖完成下列句子。

1 There is a boat _____ the bridge.

2 The post office is _____ the school.

3 There is a big tree _____ our house.

4 The airplane is flying _____ the clouds.

5 Grace is sleeping _____ the fireplace.

6 A butterfly is flying _____ my cat.

2 選出正確答案。

_____ **1** The new Italian restaurant is _____ the Holiday Inn and the movie theater.
　　ⓐ among　　ⓑ between　　ⓒ beside

_____ **2** She lives in the apartment _____ mine.
　　ⓐ between　　ⓑ above　　ⓒ in front of

_____ **3** The sun is now _____ the horizon.
　　ⓐ beside　　ⓑ behind　　ⓒ below

_____ **4** She is always shy about speaking _____ a large audience.
　　ⓐ in front of　　ⓑ between　　ⓒ behind

_____ **5** Who is standing _____ Susan?
　　ⓐ beside　　ⓑ between　　ⓒ among

_____ **6** About half of New Orleans is _____ sea level.
　　ⓐ between　　ⓑ below　　ⓒ beside

_____ **7** Trish is studying three other languages _____ Spanish.
　　ⓐ beside　　ⓑ among　　ⓒ besides

Chapter

63 表示方向／動向的介系詞

---

1 — up 和 down

up

He's climbing up the hill. 他在上山。

down

He's walking down the hill. 他在下山。

→ up（向……上）
down（向……下）

- Sue headed up the stairs to the fifth floor. 蘇上樓梯朝五樓去了。
- Before sunset, we went down the mountain. 我們在日落之前下山了。

---

2 — to 和 from

to

I'm going to the beach. 我要去海灘。

from

They are coming back from the beach. 他們正從海灘回來。

→ to（往，去）
from（從……來）

- How long does it take to walk from your home to school?
從你家到學校，走路要多久時間？

---

3 — on 和 off

get on the bus 上公車

get off the bus 下公車

→ on（上公車、火車、飛機等；放……上面）
off（離開……）

- Don't put your feet on the coffee table. 不要把你的腳放在咖啡桌上。
- Please take your feet off the coffee table.
請把你的腳從咖啡桌上移開。

- Kay put some postcards on our classroom's bulletin board yesterday.
凱昨天把一些明信片貼在我們教室的布告欄上。

- Today she took the postcards off the bulletin board. 她今天把明信片從布告欄上取了下來。

比較 jump/hop onto → onto（到 ... 之上）
的反義詞也是 off

Can your frog hop onto that big log?
你的青蛙能跳到那塊大圓木上嗎？

Sue, don't jump off that wall. It is too high.
蘇，不要從那個牆上跳下來。牆太高了。

4 — into 和 out of

→ into（到……裡）
out of（自……離開）

get into the car 進入汽車　　get out of the car 從汽車出來

- Sue is going into the hospital. She hurt her arm while jumping off a high wall.
  蘇正走進醫院。她從一道高牆跳下來，傷到了手臂。

- Sue's coming out of the hospital. She has a broken arm.
  蘇正從醫院走出來。她的手臂骨折了。

- Kim dove into the swimming pool and began to swim. 金姆跳進游泳池裡，游了起來。

- Dwight took the old batteries out of the flashlight. 杜威特把舊電池從手電筒裡取出來。

> 比較 put something in . . . → 比較少用：put something . . . into
> He put the new batteries in the flashlight. 他把新電池裝進手電筒裡。

5 — over 和 under

→ over（越過……）
under（在……下面）

His dog jumped over the fence. 他的狗跳過柵欄。

My cat went under the fence. 我的貓從柵欄下面走出去。

> 比較
> The jet airplane was flying above Miami.
> 噴射機正飛在邁阿密的上空。

- The jet airplane was flying over Miami. 噴射機正飛過邁阿密。

- Midge rowed her boat under the bridge. 米姬划船從橋下過去。

6 — through, around/round, across, along

through

around/round

→ through（穿過、通過）
around/round（繞過；
在……四處；在……附近）

She's sliding through the large pipe.
她滑行通過大管道。

A monkey came around/round the corner.
一隻猴子從轉角走過來。

- **drive** around **the town** 開車繞過城鎮
- **travel** around **Australia** 在澳大利亞各地旅遊
- around **the corner** 在拐彎處；在附近

- **We didn't drive** around **Tampa; we drove** through **it.**
  我們開車沒有繞過坦帕市；我們穿過了坦帕市。

- **Why is your dog running** around **and** around **that merry-go-round?**
  你的狗為什麼繞著旋轉木馬轉來轉去？

- **The sunlight came** through **the big window and made the living room warm.**
  陽光透過大窗戶使客廳暖和起來。

→ **along**（沿著）
across（橫越，穿過）

She's walking her dog along **the sea.** 她正沿著海邊溜狗。

They are walking across **the road.**
他們在穿過馬路。

- **Is that a big toad hopping** along **the road?** 那是一隻大癩蛤蟆在沿著馬路跳躍嗎？

- **Can you swim** across **this lake?** 你能游過這個湖嗎？

[比較] across 強調穿過某一平面；through 強調從某一空間內部通過。

She's walking across **the street.** 她正在過街。

Is Sue going to the other side of the avenue through **the tunnel?**
蘇要通過地下道去大街的另一邊嗎？

---

7 **past**

→ **past**（經過）

- **Lily ran** past **me and didn't even say "Hi" to me.**
  莉莉從我身邊跑過去，甚至沒跟我打聲招呼。

He drove past **the bus stop.**
他開車經過了公共汽車站。

[比較] **The parade slowly passed us.** 遊行隊伍緩慢地從我們身邊走過。
  → passed us = went past us（passed 是 pass 的過去式）
Mom, please pass me the salt. 媽媽，請把鹽遞給我。
  → pass me the salt = hand me the salt

1 請寫出下列詞彙的反義字。

1 up _____
2 under _____
3 into _____
4 on _____
5 from _____
6 behind _____

2 看圖並用介系詞完成下列句子。

1 Gus got _____ the bus.
2 The burglars got _____ the house _____ the open window.
3 Jane got _____ the car.
4 The cat jumped _____ the table.

3 填入表「方向」的介系詞。

1 Was Louis Bleriot the first pilot to fly an airplane _____ the English Channel?
2 Bing went _____ school very early this morning.
3 He fell _____ the tree and _____ the river.
4 Jill and Bill are driving their jeeps _____ the top of that mountain.
5 The moon goes _____ the earth.
6 There was a terrible traffic jam on Route 78 this morning. A stream of slow moving traffic stretched _____ the southbound lane for about four miles.
7 Joe looked _____ the window and watched people on the street.
8 The dog jumped _____ the fence and _____ the garden.
9 Would you like to come to my home and have a cup of coffee? My house is very close. It's just _____ the corner.
10 She took $100 _____ her purse and put it in my left hand.
11 We walked _____ the art gallery for almost two hours and saw lots of amazing paintings.
12 How far is it _____ here _____ the train station?
13 Kay drives _____ work almost every day.
14 The cat jumped _____ the roof of my car, stayed there for a few minutes, and then jumped _____ the roof and into my garden.
15 Will Ms. Rule dive _____ the swimming pool?
16 Amy is looking at a boat on the river. The boat is going _____ the bridge.
17 Midge is looking at a balloon that is flying _____ the bridge.

Chapter

64 表示時間的介系詞：at, on, in

---

1 at

at 用於「某一具體時間點」、「年齡」、「某些節日」之前。

at + 一天中的特定時間 →
- Our store closes at 9:30 p.m. 我們商店晚上九點半關門。
- She usually goes to bed at midnight. 她通常是半夜上床睡覺。
- Pop will come home at noon. 爸爸會在中午時回家。
- The Little Mermaid plays in the day and sleeps at night.
  那個小美人魚白天玩耍，晚上睡覺。

at + 年齡 →
- She started to learn English at the age of three.
  她三歲那年開始學英文。

at + 節日名稱 →
- We give each other cards and gifts at Christmas.
  耶誕節期間，我們互相贈賀卡和禮物。

at the end of 在……末尾 →
- Coco is going to quit her job at the end of this month and move to Tokyo. 可可月底要辭職，然後搬去東京。

at the moment 在此刻 →
- The manager can't see you now. She's very busy at the moment. 經理現在不能見你，她目前很忙。

---

2 on

on 用於「星期幾」、「具體的日期」、「具體的某一天」。

on + 日期／某日 →
- on Children's Day 在兒童節那一天
- on New Year's Day 在元旦那一天
- Kate will come to visit me on March 8. 凱特三月八號要來看我。
- See you on Saturday. 星期六見。
- Kay always goes to church on Christmas Day.
  每逢耶誕節那天，凱都要去教堂做禮拜。

> at Christmas 在耶誕節期間
> at Easter 在復活節期間　比較

on + 星期幾 + 一天中的某段時間 →
- Mom goes shopping on Sunday mornings.
  媽媽星期天上午去購物。 └ 表示具體一天的早上、下午、晚上時，要用介系詞 on。

---

3 in

in 用於「世紀」、「月分」、「年分」、「季節」等或「泛指上午、下午、傍晚」的詞（morning, afternoon, evening）之前；in 還可用於一段時間之前，表示「……之後」。

in + 月份／年份／季節／世紀 →

- in the 21st century 在 21 世紀
- in the 19th century 在 19 世紀
- **Her birthday is** in May. 她的生日在五月。
- **Kate was born** in 2008. 凱特出生於 2008 年。
- **I don't like to go to Alaska** in the winter. **It's too cold.**
  我不喜歡冬天去阿拉斯加州。那裡太冷了。

in + 一天中的特定時間 →

- In the evening, Bing often reads the news on the Internet. 賓晚上常在網上閱讀新聞。

> 但 night 要與 at 連用：
> at night
> 注意

比較

in the morning 在上午	on Monday morning 在週一上午
in the afternoon 在下午	on Tuesday afternoon 在週二下午
in the evening 在晚上	on Saturday evening 在週六傍晚
in the day 在白天	on Friday night 在週五晚上

- **Bing often feels good** in the morning. 賓在早上時通常感覺很好。
- **Are you going out to eat** on Saturday evening? 你星期六晚上要上館子嗎？
- **Kay is seldom at home** in the day. 凱白天很少在家。

in + 一段時間 →

- **I will be ready** in five minutes. 我會在五分鐘後準備好。
- **What do you think you will be doing** in ten years?
  你想你十年後會在做什麼？

↳ 表示「在……之後」。

4

weekend
週末

🇺🇸 美式英語 通常用 on：
on the weekend
on weekends

- **I usually spend some time chatting with my friends on the Internet** on weekends.

🇬🇧 英式英語 通常用 at：
at the weekend
at weekends

- **I usually spend some time chatting with my friends on the Internet** at weekends.

我週末通常要花一些時間在網上與朋友們聊天。

5

當表示時間的名詞前有 this, next, last, every, tomorrow, yesterday, tonight（**表示某特定時間**）時，就不可以用 at, on, in。

- **Are you going out to eat** this evening? 你今晚要上館子吃飯嗎？
- **See you** tomorrow morning. 明天早上見。
- **Where were you** last night? 你昨天晚上在哪裡？
- **Kay is going on vacation** next Monday. 凱下星期一要去度假。
- **Usually I am not busy** on weekends, **but I am very busy** this weekend.
  我週末時通常不忙，但這週末我會很忙。

1 在空格處填上 at、on、in。

1	_____ night	**10**	_____ Christmas
2	_____ the evening	**11**	_____ Friday night
3	_____ 2020	**12**	_____ the fall
4	_____ Sunday morning	**13**	_____ 10:25 a.m.
5	_____ the moment	**14**	_____ March
6	_____ April 15	**15**	_____ the weekend
7	_____ New Year's Day	**16**	_____ ten minutes
8	_____ midnight	**17**	_____ Friday
9	_____ the end of July	**18**	_____ the winter

2 在空格處填上 at、on、in。句首字母要大寫。

1 _____ 5:30 a.m., Eve was ready to leave.

2 Our class about robots exploring the moon begins _____ 2:30 _____ the afternoon.

3 Does Dwight have a part-time job _____ night?

4 I will start my new job _____ July.

5 _____ the spring, birds are singing and flowers are blooming.

6 Dwight enjoys looking at the stars _____ night.

7 After Mike got up _____ six this morning, he fed the cats and then went out for a long walk.

8　Does Kay usually have a party _____ her birthday?

9　Do you have a festival in your country _____ October?

10　Do you go skiing _____ the winter?

11　Do you go to church _____ Sunday mornings?

12　My daughter Kate was born _____ July 16, 2008.

13　I usually surf the Internet _____ the evening.

14　Where were you _____ March 25?

3　在空格處填上 at、on、in。句首字母要大寫。

Kay usually gets up (1)_____ 6:30. She eats breakfast while watching the morning news on TV. She goes to school from Monday through Friday. (2)_____ the morning, she has four hours of classes. (3)_____ the afternoon, she plays soccer from 2:00 to 3:00. Kay does her homework (4)_____ the evening, and she does not watch TV (5)_____ night. She doesn't go to school (6)_____ Saturdays and Sundays, but she usually reads novels, does homework on her computer, or goes hiking, swimming, or camping. She usually goes to church (7)_____ Sunday morning and plays soccer (8)_____ Sunday afternoon. Sometimes she visits her friends or relatives (9)_____ the weekend. (10)_____ Christmas Day, New Years Day, and July 4th, Kay always has a big dinner with her relatives.

Chapter

65 其他表示時間的介系詞

I — **from . . . through/to（從……直至）**

| 美式英語 | • Do you work from Monday through Friday? |

| 英式英語 | • Do you work from Monday to Friday? |

你的工作時間是從週一到週五嗎？

• Kate lived in Kuwait from January 2002 to the end of 2008.
凱特從 2002 年 1 月到 2008 年底，居住在科威特。

---

2 — **until/till . . .（直到……時）**

❶ 用於肯定句中時，意為「直到……為止」。述語動詞要用**延續性動詞**，如：stayed up, work 等。

❷ 用於否定句，表示「直到……才」。述語動詞要用**非延續性動詞**，如：stop, fall asleep 等。

❸ until 和 till 可通用，但位於句首時，只能用 until。

• until tomorrow 直到明天
• until 3:00 in the morning 直到早上三點
• until the end of the year 直到年底

• Last night I stayed up reading a novel until/till two in the morning. 我昨晚熬夜看一本小說，一直看到凌晨兩點。

• Last night I didn't fall asleep until/till three in the morning.
昨晚我睡不著覺，一直到凌晨三點才入睡。

| until / till | + 子句 | → | until/till 在此作**連接詞**，後面接子句〔參見 Unit 13〕。 |

• Please wait here until/till I come back. 請在這裡等候我回來。

比較 till/until（直到）和 by（不遲於）（= not later than）

Dwight and I danced until/till midnight. 杜威特和我一直跳舞跳到半夜。
You must come back home by 9 p.m. 你一定要在晚上九點之前回到家。

3 | before, after, during

❶ **before**
在……以前

• There are only two hours left before the exam. 離考試只剩兩小時了。

after
在……以後

• After the meal, he helped his mom to do the dishes. 飯後，他幫媽媽洗了碗。

during
在……期間

• Please don't talk so loud during lunch.
吃飯時，講話不要這麼大聲。

❷ before 和 after 也可以作連接詞，後面接子句；during 只能作介系詞，後面接名詞。

• They started to quarrel during the meal.
= They started to quarrel while they were eating. 他們在飯桌上開始爭吵起來。
└─ while 是連接詞。

• Say your prayers before you go to bed.
= Say your prayers before going to bed. 睡覺前要祈禱。
└─ 介系詞 before 和 after 之後可以接動詞 -ing 形式。

• Last Sunday after we did the shopping, we went to the movie theater.
= Last Sunday after doing the shopping, we went to the movie theater.
上個星期天，我們購物後去了電影院。

4 | since, for

since 丅 開始的時間 → since + 過去某一時刻，表示「自……以來」、「從……至今」。

• since 2009 從 2009 之後
• since March 從三月起
• since two in the morning 從凌晨兩點開始
• since I was a little girl 從我小時候開始

• Kate has lived here since 2008. 凱特從 2008 年到現在都住在這裡。

• It has been snowing since seven in the morning. 從早上七點起就一直在下雪。

• It has been raining since I arrived home. 從我回到家後就一直在下雨。
└─ since 可以作連接詞，後面接子句，子句要用過去式，主句要用完成式。

for + 時間長度 → for + 某一段時間，指「時間的長度」。

• for two hours 兩個鐘頭
• for three years 三年了
• for five months 有五個月
• for a long time 好長一段時間了

• I played a game on Facebook for two hours last night. 我昨晚在臉書上玩了兩小時的遊戲。

• Kay's boyfriend has been in the hospital for three days. 凱的男朋友住院有三天了。

> 比較　Kate lived in Kuwait from 2002 to 2008. 凱特從 2002 年到 2008 年，都住在科威特。
> Kate lived in Kuwait until 2008. 凱特住在科威特一直住到 2008 年。
> Now Kate lives in Rome. She moved to Rome in December 2008.
> 凱特現在住在羅馬。她是 2008 年 12 月搬到羅馬的。
> Kate has lived in Rome since December 2008. 從 2008 年 12 月起，凱特就一直住在羅馬。

1 請判斷下列句子是否正確，正確打 ✓，不正確打 ×，並寫出正確句子。

1 They have been married since three years.

⬚ _____

2 Dad often falls asleep during he is watching TV.

⬚

_____

3 After graduation from high school, he travelled around the country in his car.

⬚ _____

4 She always feels nervous before exams.

⬚ _____

5 Last night I fell asleep during the movie.

⬚ _____

6 I was late for school today because I waited for the bus during half an hour.

⬚ _____

2 用 until, since, for 填空。

1 Next week Jane is going to the Philippines _____ five days.

2 Dwight is tired today. He didn't go to bed _____ midnight.

3 I have known Kay _____ grade school.

4 The boss is not in her office. She has gone away on a business trip. She won' be back _____ Thursday.

5　I'm going to take a short nap _____ 15 minutes.

6　I haven't heard from Amy _____ last July.

3　用 to, during, while 填空。

1　Gwen lived in Austria from 2005 _____ 2010.

2　Do not argue _____ you're having dinner.

3　Do not argue _____ the meal.

4　Kay took care of my children _____ I was away.

5　Thousands of homes were bombed _____ World War II.

4　用「before +-ing」形式和「after + -ing」形式造句。

1　Dirk finished his homework. He was tired. (After)

_____

2　Let's have a discussion about this issue. Then we make a decision. (Before)

_____

3　 Rick ate too much cheesecake. Then he felt sick. (After)

_____

4　Think carefully. Then answer my next difficult question. (Before)

_____

Chapter 66 on, at, by, with 以及「形容詞/動詞 + 介系詞」

1 與 on 搭配的慣用語

on a trip 在旅途中
on fire 著火
on the Internet 在網路上
on the phone 在電話上
on the radio 在廣播中
on time 準時
on TV 在電視上
on vacation 在度假

• The building is on fire. Call 911! 大樓起火了。快打 911！
• Will her flight be on time? 她的航班會準時到達嗎？
• Bing watches the news on TV every evening.
賓每天晚上都要看電視新聞。

2 與 at 搭配的慣用語

at war 交戰
at 65 miles an hour
一小時 65 英里的速度
at 38 degrees Centigrade
在攝氏 38 度時

• You should drive at 5 miles an hour or less in a school zone.
在文教區，你應該以每小時 5 英里或 5 英里以下的速度駕駛。
• Water freezes at zero degrees Centigrade.
水在攝氏零度時結冰。
• America and Japan were at war from 1941 to 1945.
美國和日本在 1941 年到 1945 年期間交戰。

3 與 by 搭配的慣用語

by car 搭汽車
by bus 搭公車
by train 搭火車
by airplane (= by air)
搭飛機
by ship 坐輪船
by bike 騎自行車

• Do you like to travel by train or by airplane?
你喜歡坐火車還是坐飛機旅行？
• Gus usually goes to work by bus. 加斯通常搭公車上班。

注意

「步行」要用 on foot (= walk)：
    She usually goes to school on foot. 她通常走路上學。
「搭校車」要用 on the school bus：
    He usually goes to school on the school bus. 他通常搭校車上學。

a book by . . .
由……寫的書
a painting by . . .
由……畫的畫

• Have you read *The Old Man and the Sea* by Ernest Hemingway? 你讀過海明威的《老人與海》沒有？
• *Boy With a Pipe* is a painting by Pablo Picasso.
油畫《拿煙斗的男孩》是畢卡索畫的。

> be influenced by . . . 受……影響
> be painted by . . . 被……油漆
> （by 用在被動語態裡）

- All the rooms in our house were recently painted by Mom and Dad.
  最近我們家所有的房間都被媽媽和爸爸粉刷過。

  → 被動語態的用法請參看 Unit 15。

4 with 和 without

with（與……一起；有……的；用……工具）的反義詞是 without（沒有）。

- You should discuss this problem with your parents. 你應該跟你父母討論這個問題。
- Would you like your coffee with or without sugar? 你的咖啡要加糖還是不加糖？
- Do you know that girl with red hair? 你認識那個紅頭髮的女孩嗎？
- He stirred the chicken soup with a big spoon. 他用一個大湯匙攪拌雞湯。

5 介系詞的固定搭配

| 形容詞 | ＋ | 介系詞 | ＋ | 名詞 |
| 分詞 | | | | |

- The teacher was angry with/at Dan and Ann.
  老師很生丹和安的氣。

- She is always angry about some little things.
  她總是為一些小事生氣。

- Trish is not good at Spanish. 翠希的西班牙語不太好。

- She is full of anger about her divorce.
  她對自己的離婚充滿怨恨。

- My opinion about this issue is similar to yours.
  我對這個問題的看法和你一樣。

- We're sorry about your loss.
  我們對你的損失感到很難過。

- I'm really sorry for/about yelling at you last night.
  我昨天晚上對你大喊大叫，實在很抱歉。

> 注意 介系詞後面可以接「動名詞」（介系詞＋-ing 形式）。
> Kay is fed up with doing the same thing day after day.
> 對日復一日做同樣的事，凱感到很厭倦了。
> Larry's sister Pat is very good at telling stories.
> 賴瑞的妹妹派特很會講故事。
> She entered without knocking on the door.
> 她沒有敲門就走進去了。

according to 根據
afraid of 害怕
amazed at 對……感到驚奇
angry about something
　　因某事生氣
angry with/at somebody
　　生某人的氣
bad at 不擅長
different from 與……不同
famous for 因……而出名
fed up with 對……厭倦
full of/filled with 充滿……的
good at 擅長
good for 對……有好處
interested in 對……感興趣
made of/from 由……製成的
married to 和……結婚
nice/kind of somebody to do
　　某人做……令人感激
nice/kind to somebody
　　對某人友好
opposed to 反對
proud of 對……感到驕傲
satisfied with 滿意
similar to 類似的
sorry about something
　　對某事感到遺憾
sorry for/about doing something
　　為做過某事而感到抱歉
strict with somebody
　　對某人要求嚴格

動詞 + 介系詞	happen to 發生於	speak/talk to somebody about something

	happen to 發生於	speak/talk to somebody
	hear about 聽說	about something
	interfere with 妨害；干預	跟某人談論某事
agree with 同意	know about 知道	talk about 談論
arrive in/at 到達	laugh at 嘲笑	thank somebody for
ask (somebody) for 請求；要求	listen to 聽	為……感謝某人
belong to 屬於	look after 照顧	think about 考慮
deal with 處理	look at 看	think of 想到
depend on 依靠；信賴	look for 尋找	wait for 等待
disagree with 與……意見不一	pay for 支付	worry about 擔心
get to 到達	run after 追趕	

- **Can we** depend on **Bob to finish the job?** 我們能依靠鮑勃完成這項工作嗎？

- **What** happened to **Pat? She seems to be very angry.** 派特發生了什麼事？她好像很生氣。

- **What is she** looking at? 她在看什麼？

- **"What are you doing?" "I'm** looking for **my wallet."** 「你在做什麼？」「我在找我的錢包。」

- **I'll be away for a week. Can you** look after **my little dog?** → look after = take care of 照顧
  我要離開一個星期，你能幫我照顧一下我的小狗嗎？

- **She was** running after **me.** 她在我的後面跑。

PRACTICE

1 在下列詞彙後面補充介系詞。

1 according _____	5 opposed _____	9 different _____
2 disagree _____	6 listen _____	10 full _____
3 similar _____	7 depend _____	11 interested _____
4 interfere _____	8 afraid _____	12 married _____

2 用下面的介系詞，完成下列句子。（有些句子會有兩個答案。）

about   after   at   for   from   in   of   on   to   with

1 Health depends _____ good food, fresh air, and enough exercise and sleep.

2 Nan is quite different _____ her twin sister Ann.

3 You are trying to avoid me. Are you angry _____ me?

4 She is married _____ an astronaut.

5 It was very nice _____ you to help Sue.

6 I really feel sorry _____ yelling at you just now.

7 Is she good _____ fixing cars?

8 Are you interested _____ sports or music?

9 I'm sorry _____ the misunderstanding.

10 Who will look _____ your children when you are on your business trip next week?

---

3 | 用括弧裡的提示，完成句子。

1 Bob is _____ his job. (think/quit)

2 _____ you very much _____ me the truth. (thank/tell)

3 I'm leaving. I'm _____ to her empty talk. (fed up/listen)

4 I'm _____ you. (sorry/blame)

5 She is _____ costs. (bad/control)

---

4 | 使用介系詞來完成下列句子。

1 Does she talk _____ her parents about her marriage problems?

2 Whenever he doesn't listen _____ me, we get into trouble.

3 I strongly disagree _____ you on this issue.

4 Does she know a lot _____ the International Space Station?

5 Don't interfere _____ my business.

6 My little sister is afraid _____ the dark.

7 Sue is out of town this week. She's _____ vacation.

8 This necklace belongs _____ Alice.

9 I'm leaving now. I'm tired of waiting _____ Pam.

10 Do you go to school _____ foot or _____ bike?

11 She's listening to the news _____ the Internet.

12 I hope the flight will be _____ time.

Chapter

67 對等連接詞 and, but, or, so 及並列句

對等連接詞連接的成分必須是對等的，如：

名詞 ⟷ 名詞　　　介系詞片語 ⟷ 介系詞片語

形容詞 ⟷ 形容詞　　簡單句 ⟷ 簡單句

動詞 ⟷ 動詞

> **注意**
>
> 在美式英語中，連接三個或三個以上的成分時，在 **and, but, or** 的前面，通常要加逗號。

1　連接字或短語

對等連接詞 and, but, or 用來連接句中平行的字或短語。

- **Jake and Mary both love my strawberry cake.** 傑克和瑪麗都很喜歡我的草莓蛋糕。

  └─ and 的意思是「和、以及、又」。這句的 and 連接兩個對等的名詞。

  ┌─ and 連接三個對等的形容詞。
- **Sally is** intelligent, hardworking, and friendly. 莎莉聰明、勤奮又友善。

  名詞　　　　　名詞
- **She has lots of money** but **can't find** happiness and peace. → 一個句子中可以有一個以上的連詞：but 連接兩個對等的動詞片語；and 連接兩個對等的名詞。

  動詞片語　　　　　　動詞片語

  她很有錢，但卻找不到幸福和平靜。

- **Does Gus go to school** on foot or by bus? 加斯是走路還是搭公車去上學的？

  → or 用來連接可供選擇的人或物，表示「或者」。這句的 or 連接兩個對等的介系詞片語。

- **Sue or Andrew will pick you up at the airport at two.** 蘇或安德魯會在兩點時去機場接你。

  └─ or 連接兩個對等的名詞。

2　連接兩個獨立子句

對等連接詞 and, but, or, so 用來連接兩個獨立子句（即，兩個簡單句），構成一個並列句。並列句中的各獨立子句意義同等重要，相互之間沒有從屬關係，是**平行並列**的關係。在美式英語中，連接詞 and, but, or, so 前面通常會用逗號把兩個子句分開。

Kay kissed Ted on his bald head. →獨立子句

They decided to get married this Sunday. →獨立子句

┌─並列句

 Kay kissed Ted on his bald head, and they decided to get married this Sunday. 凱在泰德的禿頂上親吻了一下，然後他們決定這個星期天結婚。

• Dee is smart and arrogant, but her sister Sally has a pleasant personality.
蒂精明而傲慢，不過她的妹妹莎莉性格和藹可親。

• I love orange juice, but Dee loves tea and coffee. 我愛喝柳橙汁，但蒂愛喝茶和咖啡。

• We can go out to eat tonight, or we can just eat leftovers at home.
今天晚上我們可以上館子，或是在家裡吃剩飯。

• I had no money that night, so I had to stay at the train station.
我那天晚上身上沒帶錢，所以只好睡火車站。

→ 對等連接詞 so 只用於連接兩個獨立子句，
so 引導的獨立子句表示「結果」。

> 注意
>
> 「or」還可以指「否則；要不然」，常用於「祈使句 + or + 簡單句」的結構中。
>
> Get out of my house, or I'll call the police. 從我家出去，否則我就叫警察。

---

3 比較 so 和 because

比較對等連接詞 so 和從屬連接詞 because：

❶ so 是**對等連接詞**，表「結果」，連接兩個獨立子句。

❷ because 是**從屬連接詞**，表「原因」，連接一個主句和從屬子句。 → 從屬連接詞參見
　　　　　　　　　　　　　　　　　　　　　　　　　　　　　　　　Chapter 68。

❸ so 和 because 不能同時使用，只能選擇其一。

• It was raining, so we didn't go climbing. 在下雨，所以我們沒有去爬山。
　　　　　　　└─► so 的前面要用逗號。

• We didn't go climbing because it was raining.　→ because 引導的子句位於主句後面時，
　　　　　　　　　　　　　　　　　　　　　　　　　　通常不用逗號與前面的主句分開。

　= Because it was raining, we didn't go climbing.　→ because 引導的子句置於句首時，
我們沒有去爬山，因為在下雨。　　　　　　　　　　　需要逗號與後面的主句分開。

• Ted didn't go to school today because he had a fever. 泰德今天沒去上學，因為他發燒。

• Ted had a fever, so he didn't go to school today. 泰德在發燒，所以今天沒有去學校。

PRACTICE

1 用左欄的獨立子句配搭右欄的獨立子句，然後用 **and, but, or** 構成並列句。

1 You can study hard for this entrance exam.

2 Amos has already bungee jumped twice.

3 Are you married?

4 The apples were so red.

5 Sally lost a fortune in the stock market.

6 Ms. Wu was reading a newspaper.

7 I wanted to call you.

8 Jim likes me.

a Her husband was changing their baby's diaper.

b I forgot your cellphone number.

c She still seems to live quite comfortably.

d You can fail.

e He is still very nervous.

f Are you single?

g I like him.

h They tasted good to Ted.

1
_____

2
_____

3
_____

4
_____

5
_____

6
_____

7
_____

8
_____

2 用左欄的獨立子句配搭右欄的獨立子句，使用 **so** 或 **because** 連接成一個句子。

1 Be faithful in small things.

2 She has always been nervous in public.

3 June isn't very healthy.

4 Her alarm clock didn't go off.

5 Jim failed to appear.

6 She refused to give up her dream of being in the movies.

a Kate was late for school.

b We went to the beach without him.

c She loved acting.

d It is in them that your strength lies.

e It is no surprise that she avoids large gatherings.

f She tries to swim or jog for an hour every afternoon.

1 _____

2 _____

3 _____

4 _____

5 _____

6 _____

3 用 **and, but, or** 填空。

1 Ted Skinner came home early, took a quick shower, _____ went to bed without eating his dinner.

2 Is Gus going up the mountain on foot, by car, _____ by bus?

3 Bruce loves coffee, tea, _____ orange juice.

4 "This horse is thin _____ very strong," explained Mr. Brown.

Chapter 68 從屬連接詞 when, while, as, before, after, if, though 等與從屬子句

從屬連接詞連接「從屬子句」和「主句」，子句本身不能獨立存在，必須依賴主句才能表達完整的意義。從屬連接詞引導的子句放在主句的前面時，要用逗號分開；子句在主句後面時，通常不用逗號。

I

從屬連接詞 when, while, as, before, after, if, though 等連接主句和從屬子句，即副詞子句。

when → 當……時

從屬子句放在主句的前面時，要用逗號分開。

從屬子句　　主句
When Bing went out this morning, it was snowing.

主句　　從屬子句
= It was snowing when Bing went out this morning.

賓今早出門時，正在下雪。 →如果動詞是非延續動詞（arrive, come in, go out, stop），從屬連接詞只能用 when，不能用 while。

while → 當……時
- While I was away, Clair took care of my daughter Kay.
  = Claire took care of my daughter Kay while I was away.
  我出門在外時，克萊兒在照顧我女兒凱。 →這句也可以用 When。

as 表示兩個動作同時發生。

as → 當……時
- As Sue and I were sitting down to dinner, there was a knock on the door.
  = There was a knock on the door as Sue and I were sitting down to dinner. 蘇和我剛坐下來吃飯，就有人在敲門。

before → 在……之前
- Before you cross the street, look both ways.
  = Look both ways before you cross the street.
  在過街之前，左右兩邊都要看看。

after → 在……之後
- After her husband died, Gwen never got married again.
  = Gwen never got married again after her husband died.
  葛雯的先生去世後，她就再也沒有結婚。

miss the bus　　take a taxi

| if | → | 如果 |

- If I miss the last bus, I'll have to take a taxi or walk home.
  = I'll have to take a taxi or walk home if I miss the last bus.
  如果錯過了最後一班公車，我就要搭乘計程車或走路回家。

| though/ although | → | 雖然 |

- Though/Although I was exhausted, I could not fall asleep.
  = I could not fall asleep though/although I was exhausted.
  我雖然累壞了，但還是睡不著。
  └→ although 和 though 都可以指「雖然」。

2

when, before, if, unless 等連接詞引導的**副詞子句**，要「**用現在式表示未來**」。

└→ 不可以使用未來式。

- We won't climb the mountain if it rains tomorrow. 明天如果下雨，我們就不去爬山。
  → 時間為未來「tomorrow」時，主句用未來式（won't climb），但 if 子句要用簡單現在式（rains）。

- Don't worry. I'll lock the door before I go to bed. 不要擔心。我上床之前會鎖門的。

- We will have our candlelight dinner after Eve and Nancy leave.
  等伊芙和南西離開後，我們就要開始吃燭光晚餐。

- Kay will look after my dog while I'm away.
  我出門在外時，凱會照顧我的狗。

3 — when 和 if 的比較

❶ 當「**確定事情將發生**」時，用 **when** 表示。

- I'll play a Facebook game when I finish my math homework.
  寫完數學作業後，我就要玩一個臉書的遊戲。
  → I'm sure I'll finish my math homework.（我確定我一定會寫完數學作業。）

❷ 當「**不確定事情是否將發生**」時，用 **if** 表示。

- I'll play a Facebook game if I finish my math homework by 9 p.m.
  如果我在晚上九點之前寫完數學作業，我就要玩一個臉書遊戲。
  → Perhaps I'll finish my math homework by 9 p.m. I'm not sure.
  （我也許能在九點之前寫完數學作業，但我不是很確定。）

1 選用 A 欄和 B 欄的詞語，並以 when 開頭造句。

When +

A	B
he is at work	she smiled and waved
your plane arrives	I was at a friend's house
I'm on vacation	he always wears a tie
Amy saw us	Sue will stay at my apartment
the accident occurred	I'll be at the airport

1
2
3
4
5

2 選用 A 欄和 B 欄的詞語，並以 if 開頭造句。

If +

A	B
you eat all the cookies	I'll buy it for you
you're busy now	you'll miss your flight
I still feel sick tomorrow	you'll get as sick as a dog
you like this skirt	I won't go to school
you don't hurry	I can talk to you later

1
2
3
4
5

3 用 if 或 when 填空。

1 _____ she was young, she lived with her mother and stepfather.

2 "Are you going to visit Paris this summer?" "Perhaps. _____ I go, I'll let you know."

3 I'm thinking of going to a movie tonight. _____ I go, will you come with me?

4 I'm going for a swim _____ I get home from school this afternoon.

5 I'm going to attend a conference in Mexico City during the first week in April. I'll contact you _____ I'm in Mexico City.

6 _____ we hurry, we can catch the bus.

7 Do you mind _____ I sit here?

8 _____ Mom comes back home, I'll give her a big surprise.

Chapter

69 相關連接詞

- both ... and
- either ... or
- not only ... but also
- neither ... nor

I　相關連接詞連接對等的成分

相關連接詞不能單獨使用，必須**成對使用**，可以看成是「成對的並列連接詞」。相關連接詞連接兩個在語法上平行的結構。

both ... and　→　兩者都；既……又……

┌─ 連接兩個主詞（Sue, I）。
- Both Sue and I are attending the conference in Washington D.C. next week.
  = Sue and I are attending the conference in Washington D.C. next week.
  蘇和我下星期都要去參加華盛頓的會議。

  → 上面兩個句子的意思一樣，用 both 是強調「兩者都……」。

連接兩個名詞，用 both 強調
┌─ 「既……又……」。
- Your attorney is well respected for both her honesty and intelligence.
  = Your attorney is well respected for her honesty and intelligence.
  = Your attorney is well respected for her honesty as well as intelligence.
  你的律師備受尊重，因為她既誠實又聰慧。
  └─ 由 as well as 連接的成分也必須是平行的結構。

not only ... but also　→　不僅……也是……；既是……，也是……

- She is not only a great magician but also a great musician.　→ 連接兩個名詞短語。
  = She is both a great magician and a great musician.
  = She is a great magician and a great musician.
  她不僅是一個很厲害的魔術師，也是一名傑出的音樂家。

either ... or　→　或者；不是……就是……（只有其中一個是）

┌─ 連接兩個時間副詞短語。
- I am going to visit my sister in India either this summer or next summer.
  = I am going to visit my sister in India this summer or next summer.
  不是今年夏天就是明年夏天，我要去印度看望我妹妹。

  → 上面兩個句子意思一樣，用 either 有強調作用。

neither . . . nor → 既不……，也不……（兩個都不是）

- She is neither friendly nor honest. 她既不友善，也不誠實。 → 連接兩個形容詞。

- My little brother Dwight can neither read nor write. → 連接兩個動詞。
  我小弟弟杜威特既不會閱讀，也不會寫字。

not . . . but → 不是……，而是……

- My boss declared, "It is a time not for words but for action."
  = My boss declared, "It is not a time for words but a time for action.
  我的老闆表示說：「這不是光說不練的時候，而是要拿出具體行動的時候。」
  → 第一句連接兩個 for 介詞短語；第二句連接兩個名詞短語。

2

相關連接詞連接「並列主詞」時，**動詞**要用**單數**還是**複數**？

❶ 「**both . . . and**」要接「複數動詞」。

- Both my daughter and son are attending the Reading Experimental School.
  = My daughter and son are attending the Reading Experimental School.
  我女兒和兒子都在念「閱讀實驗學校」。

❷ 其餘的相關連接詞連接並列主詞時，「**動詞要與第二個主詞的單複數一致**」。

→ 第二個主詞（my son）是單數，
動詞用單數。

- Not only my daughter but also my son is attending the Reading Experimental
  School. 不只是我女兒，我兒子也在讀「閱讀實驗學校」。

→ 第二個主詞（his parents）
是複數，動詞用複數。

- Either Dwight or his parents are going to visit me tonight.
  今天晚上，不是杜威特就是他的父母會來找我。

第二個主詞是複數，
動詞要用複數。

- Neither Trish nor her children speak English.
  翠希和她的孩子們都不會講英文。

在「**主詞 + as well as . . .**」的結構中，as well as 只是一個**插入成分**，句子的述語動詞要與前面的主詞的單複數一致，而不是與插入成分一致。「as well as . . .」前後要用逗號把主詞和動詞分開。

···· 主詞 ···· 這是額外補充的訊息

• Amy's habit of reading for fun, as well as her computer skills, is going to help her to do well in college.
艾咪喜歡看書的嗜好，還有她的電腦技巧，都會有助於她在大學裡求學順利。

➜ 重點強調的是主詞（habit），「as well as her computer skills」只是一個插入成分，對主詞補充額外的訊息，因此，述語動詞應該與主詞 habit 一致。

PRACTICE

1 選出正確答案。

_____ **1** Both my daughter and son _____ to play Facebook games.
ⓐ like　　ⓑ likes　　ⓒ are liking　　ⓓ is liking

_____ **2** Neither my sister Kim nor my brother Jim _____ responsible for the accident.
ⓐ were　　ⓑ was　　ⓒ have　　ⓓ has

_____ **3** We will go on a trip to _____ Australia _____ Norway. We have only a 10-day vacation and therefore can visit only one place.
ⓐ both, and　　　　ⓑ not only, but also
ⓒ neither, nor　　　ⓓ either, or

_____ **4** We usually don't eat desserts because _____ Pete _____ I like to eat anything sweet.
ⓐ either, or　　　　ⓑ not only, but also
ⓒ neither, nor　　　ⓓ both, and

_____ **5** Louise is very good at language learning, and she leads her class in _____ English _____ Chinese.
ⓐ both, and　　ⓑ either, nor　　ⓒ neither, nor　　ⓓ both, or

_____ ⑥ She is interested _____ in sports _____ in art.
　ⓐ either, nor　ⓑ not only, but also
　ⓒ neither, or　ⓓ both, or

2 改錯。有些句子可能會有兩個錯。

① Either the manager nor the treasurer were going to attend the meeting.

_____

② Her trip to Nepal was both exciting or tiring.

_____

③ Neither Lilly or Amy live in Italy.

_____

④ She is not only a fast runner but also plays the piano very well.

_____

⑤ Either Louise or her two younger sisters needs to make supper.

_____

3 用相關連接詞翻譯下列句子或短語。

① Ms. Bridge 昨天既沒有給我打過電話也沒有給我發過手機簡訊（a text message）。

_____

② 她想修建一棟新房子或者改建（remodel）她的舊別墅（cottage）。

_____

③ Ms. Bridge 想修建一棟房子或者一棟別墅（cottage）。

_____

④ Mike 和我都喜歡歌劇（opera）。

_____

277

Chapter 70 連接詞

- whether . . . or
- so . . . that
- no matter what
- such . . . that

1

---

whether . . . or → 相關連接詞「不管是……還是……」

└→ whether 與 or 連用，引導一個副詞子句。

- Whether you win this speech contest or lose, it doesn't matter as long as you do your best.

  只要你盡力而為，無論你在這次講演比賽中是贏是輸，都不重要。

whether 與 or 連用，引導一個名詞子句，
└→ 作動詞 ask 的直接受詞。

- When you see Scot tomorrow, ask him whether he can come to our party or not.
  = When you see Scot tomorrow, ask him whether or not he can come to our party.
  = When you see Scot tomorrow, ask him whether he can come to our party or he can't.

  你明天見到史考特時，問問他是否能來參加我們的聚會。

  → 當 or 後面的部分是否定式時，可以有上面三種不同的表達方式。

2

以下片語引導副詞子句。

no matter who → 不管誰
- No matter who calls, don't answer the phone.
  └→ whoever 是關係代名詞。
  = Whoever calls, don't answer the phone.
  不要接電話，不管是誰打來的。

no matter what → 不管什麼
- No matter what Jim says, don't trust him.
  └→ whatever 是關係代名詞。
  = Whatever Jim says, don't trust him.
  無論吉姆說什麼，都不要相信他。

no matter where → 不管哪裡
- No matter where you are, I'll always miss you.
  └→ wherever 是連接詞。
  = Wherever you are, I'll always miss you.
  無論你在哪裡，我都會常常想念你。

no matter when → 不管何時
- No matter when Amy gets home, she always has some ice cream.
  └→ whenever 是連接詞。
  = Whenever Amy gets home, she always has some ice cream. 艾咪不管什麼時候回到家，她都要吃冰淇淋。

no matter how	→ 不管怎樣

- No matter how hard I try, I can't stop her from marrying that drunk tomorrow.

┌─ however 是副詞。

= However hard I try, I can't stop her from marrying that drunk tomorrow.

無論我再怎麼阻擋，也阻擋不了她明天嫁給那個酒鬼。

3

「so . . . that」、「such . . . that」（如此……以致於……）引導結果副詞子句，其中 that 是連接詞。

> so 是副詞，修飾另一個副詞 much，與連接詞 that 連用，that 引導「結果副詞子句」。

so many so much so few so little	+ 名詞 ↳that 在口語中常省略	+ **that**	+ 子句	→

↳so many 等片語有時會修飾名詞（如：so many changes），有時會修飾動詞（如：has changed so much）。

- My home village has changed so much (that) I can hardly recognize it.

我的故鄉變化如此之大，我幾乎認不出來了。

> 副詞 so + 形容詞（sick）+ that 引導的「結果副詞子句」。

so	+ 形容詞	+ **that** ↳that 有時可省略	+ 子句	→

- This morning I was so sick (that) I could not even drink my milk.

今天早上我噁心得很厲害，連牛奶都喝不下去。

> such 是形容詞，修飾名詞 liar，與連接詞 that 連用，that 引導「結果副詞子句」。

such	+ a/an	+ 名詞	+ **that**	+ 子句	→

↳ 如果 such 修飾單數可數名詞，需要在名詞前加不定冠詞 an 或 a。

- He is such a liar that nobody believes a word of what he says.

他是這麼愛說謊，他講的話沒有人會相信。

比較 比較「so . . . that」和「too . . . to」〔參見 Unit 11 不定詞〕。

I was so upset that I could not fall asleep. → that 後面接子句。

= I was too upset to fall asleep. → too 後面接不定式。

我難過得睡不著覺。

1 用下面所提示的連接詞填空。

whether . . . or   so . . . that   too . . . to
such . . . that   no matter what   no matter how
no matter when   no matter who

1 It was _____ a strong earthquake _____ the shocks were felt in three nearby countries.

2 It is wonderful that my dinner is always ready _____ I come home.

3 The storm was _____ strong _____ send in rescue helicopters.

4 I'm leaving _____ you like it _____ not.

5 It's _____ hot _____ sit in the sun.

6 I don't know _____ Lily is still in Canada _____ she has gone to Italy.

7 You are not allowed to smoke here, _____ you are.

8 _____ I do, she's not happy with me.

9 _____ long I sleep, I don't want to get up in the morning.

10 Susan was _____ sick _____ she was ready to give up on living.

11 After she heard the news that her son died in a car accident, Susan was _____ sad _____ she could not eat anything for two days.

12 _____ smart he was, he failed to graduate from high school because he was too lazy.

13 I don't care _____ you go _____ stay.

14 _____ she says to me, I'll forgive her.

2 用第一題所提示的連接詞，翻譯下面的句子。

1 不管你喜歡不喜歡，你都要把那些胡蘿蔔吃了。

_____

2 風太大，不能坐在戶外。

_____

3 她太生我的氣了，兩個月都不跟我說話了（refuse to talk）。

_____

4 不管是誰，都得遵守交通規則。

_____

5 不管你何時向我告別，我都不會哭。

_____

6 路途漫長又艱難，我花了一個星期的時間才恢復體力（get over it）。

_____

7 Kay 激動得不知道該說什麼。

_____

8 天氣很不好，Kay 決定整天都待在家裡。(awful weather)

_____

Chapter

71 句子的元素

I 主詞和述語

主詞 → 執行某個動作的人、地點或事物,通常是**名詞**或**代名詞**,或是用「相當於名詞的詞或短語」來充當。

述語 → 用來說明主詞「做什麼」、「是什麼」或「怎麼樣」,以動詞及其他詞擔任。一組詞裡如果沒有「主詞」和「述語動詞」,就不能成為一個句子。

　　　　　　主詞　述語動詞
- Brooke wrote a funny book. 布魯克寫了一本有趣的書。
  → 這是一個句子,有一個主詞和述語動詞。

主詞	述語	
Ann and May	ran away.	→ 動詞(ran)+ 副詞(away)
She	can dive.	→ 主要動詞(dive)及其助動詞(can)
Lulu and Sue	walked and talked.	→ 複合動詞

安和梅跑走了。
她會跳水。
露露和蘇邊散步邊聊天。

run away

---

2 主詞補語

主詞補語又稱**表語**,出現在**連綴動詞**(be、seem、appear、look、become 等)後面的名詞、形容詞、動名詞、子句、介系詞片語或不定詞片語,都叫作主詞補語,用來對主詞做補充說明〔連綴動詞參見 Chapter 22〕。

主詞	連綴動詞	主詞補語	
Art	is	smart.	→ 這裡的主詞補語是形容詞。
Scot's two sisters	are	(both) astronauts.	→ 這裡的主詞補語是名詞。
Joan	is	on the phone.	→ 這裡的主詞補語是介系詞片語。

亞特很聰明。
史卡特的兩個姐姐(都)是太空人。
裘恩在講電話。

astronauts

❶ 「直接或間接接受動詞之動作」的名詞、代名詞、短語或子句，就叫做**受詞**；
「跟在**介系詞**後面」的名詞、代名詞或短語，也是受詞。

主詞	述語動詞	受詞
• Mr. Oat	loves	his boat.
• Jade	played	tennis **with** Ms. Venice.
• Uncle Dennis	would like	to play some tennis.

→ 主詞是 Jade，述語動詞是 played，用來說明主詞做了什麼，tennis 是動詞 played 的受詞，Ms. Venice 是介系詞 with 的受詞。

→ 主詞是 Uncle Dennis，述語是 would like，用來說明主詞打算做什麼，不定詞片語 to play some tennis 作受詞。

歐特先生很愛他的船。
潔德跟威尼斯小姐打了網球。
鄧尼斯叔叔想打打網球。

❷ 直接受詞和間接受詞的用法，參見 Chapter 77 第一點的「簡單句」。

4 定語

定語「用來修飾名詞和代名詞」。定語可以由形容詞、代名詞、名詞、數詞、不定詞片語、介系詞片語、子句以及現在分詞或過去分詞擔任。定語放在主詞的前面時，稱為「前置定語」，放在主詞的後面時，稱為「後置定語」。

❶ **前置定語**：前置定語多是形容詞、代名詞、名詞、動名詞和數詞。

• Merle is a pretty girl. 梅兒是一個美麗的女子。→形容詞作定語。

• What's your name? 你叫什麼名字？→代名詞作定語。

• Is Gus Diver a bus driver? 加斯・戴弗是公車司機嗎？→名詞作定語。

• Is that crying boy called Roy? 正在大哭的那個男孩叫羅伊嗎？→現在分詞作定語。

• I'll stay here for two hours. 我會在這裡待兩個小時。→數詞作定語。

❷ **後置定語**：後置定語多是不定詞、介系詞片語和形容詞子句。

• Bess has no wish to move back to the U.S.
貝絲一點都不想搬回美國。→不定詞片語作定語。

• Who is that weird man with a big beard?
那個留著大鬍子的奇怪男子是誰？

→ 形容詞 weird 作定語，要前置；介系詞短語 with a big beard 作定語，要後置。

狀語「用來修飾動詞、形容詞或副詞」，表示時間、地點、條件、原因、目的、程度和方式等。狀語通常由副詞、介系詞片語、副詞子句或相當於副詞的詞或短語來擔任。

• **My mom snored** very loudly **last night**. 我媽昨天的打呼聲很大聲。

  → 副詞 loudly 用來修飾動詞 snored，表示「方式」；
     副詞 very 則用來修飾另一個副詞 loudly，表示「程度」。

• **Gus is standing** over there **waiting for the bus**. 加斯正站在那邊等公車。

  → 副詞短語 over there 與分詞短語 waiting for the bus，都用來修飾
     動詞 is standing，前者表示「地點」，後者表示「目的」。

• **Ted sleeps** on the bed. 泰德睡在床上。

  → 介系詞片語作狀語，修飾動詞（sleeps），表示「地點」。

• If it is a fine day tomorrow, **I'll go swimming in Deer Lake.**
  如果明天天晴，我就會去鹿湖游泳。

  → if 引導的子句作狀語，修飾後面的主句，表示「條件」。

受詞補語用來補充說明受詞，與受詞一起構成複合受詞。受詞補語通常由名詞、形容詞或起名詞和形容詞作用的詞或短語來擔任。

• **Please keep the classroom** clean and tidy.

  ┌─▶ 形容詞作受詞補語。

  請保持教室的整潔。

• **They named their daughter** May.

  ┌─▶ 名詞作受詞補語。

  他們把女兒取名為梅。

• **I caught Pam** cheating **on the English exam.**

  ┌─▶ 動名詞作受詞補語。

  我在英文科的考試上抓到潘在作弊。

1 下列句子是不是完整的句子呢？請將完整的句子打 ✓，不正確打 ×，
並寫出正確句子。

1 Does Robby have a hobby?

☐ _____

2 Elaine her doll Jane.

☐ _____

3 Claire long brown hair.

☐ _____

4 Does Mary know Gary?

☐ _____

5 Mary smiled at Gary.

☐ _____

6 Mike his bike.

☐ _____

2 根據提供的中文意思，完成下列句子。

1 Eli climbs _____. 伊萊爬得高。

2 Jake ate _____. 傑克吃了那條蛇。

3 That guy _____ a _____. 那個傢夥是間諜。

4 Clair's teddy bear is _____. 克蕾兒的玩具熊在樓梯上。

5 Karen Wang _____ studied the _____ about
Hong Kong.

凱倫・王仔細地研究了那個有關香港的網站。

6 Jill loves _____ with Clyde. 吉兒喜歡跟克萊德一起騎一匹馬。

（請使用不定詞寫出答案）

Chapter

72 肯定句、否定句、一般疑問句

I 肯定句

肯定句用以陳述「肯定」的事實。

• She is an excellent student. 她是一名優秀的學生。

• Coco will come to visit me tomorrow. 可可明天要來找我。

---

2 否定句

❶ 否定句在 **be 動詞**（am, is, are, was, were）、**助動詞**（has, have）、**情態動詞**（will, can, could, must, should, would）的後面，加上否定詞「**not**」。

→ be 動詞 / 助動詞 / 情態動詞 ＋ not

肯定句	否定句 → be 動詞 / （情態）助動詞 ＋ not
I'm tired. 我累了。	I'm not tired. 我不累。→ be 動詞 + not
He was angry. 他生氣了。	He wasn't angry. 他沒有生氣。→ wasn't = was not
She has finished her holiday shopping. 她已經完成了節日購物。	She hasn't finished her holiday shopping. 她還沒有完成節日購物。 → has+ not + 過去分詞；hasn't = has not
I will cook tonight. 我今晚要做飯。	I will not cook tonight. 我今晚不做飯。 → will + not + 動詞原形；will not = won't

❷ 需要用 don't, doesn't, didn't 的否定句：

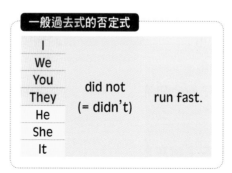

肯定句	否定句 → do / does / did + not
I like to play Facebook games. 我喜歡玩臉書遊戲。	I don't like to play Facebook games. 我不喜歡玩臉書遊戲。
She builds houses. 她修建房屋。	She doesn't build houses. 她沒有修建房屋。
I arrived in time for my father's birthday party. 我及時趕到了父親的壽宴。	I didn't arrive in time for my father's birthday party. 我沒有及時趕到父親的壽宴。

❸ 「not」與 all、every，或是「由 every 構成的複合代名詞」連用，表示**部分否定**。

• She explained, "Not all Canadians speak English well."
她解釋說，「並非所有加拿大人的英語都講得好。」

• Today not everything went well. 今天不是事事順利。

❹ 除 not 外，還有其他的否定詞可以用來構成否定句。以下是常用的否定詞或短語：

few/little 幾乎沒有	none 一點也沒有
hardly 幾乎不	nothing 什麼也沒有
never 從不	seldom 很少；難道
no 不	

→ • She seldom smiles or laughs.
她很少微笑或是開口笑。

3 ┤ 一般疑問句 ├

❶ 疑問句是用來提問的句子，句尾須使用**問號**（？）。需要用 yes 或 no 來回答的疑問句是「**一般疑問句**」。在一般疑問句中，**be 動詞**（am, is, are, was, were）、**助動詞**（has, have）、**情態助動詞**（will, can, could, must, should, would）要放在主詞的前面。

Is it . . .?	Have . . . you?	Can . . . she?

肯定句 → 主詞 + be 動詞 / 述語動詞	疑問句 → be 動詞 / （情態）助動詞 + 主詞 (+ 主動詞)
Arthur is an excellent singer. 亞瑟是一名優秀的歌手。	Is Arthur an excellent singer? → be 動詞（Is）要放在主詞（Arthur）前。 亞瑟是一名優秀的歌手嗎？
She has finished her homework. 她已經寫完功課了。	Has she finished her homework? 她寫完功課了嗎？ └ 助動詞（Has）要放在主詞（she）前。
Kim can swim. 金姆會游泳。	Can Kim swim? 金姆會游泳嗎？ └ 情態助動詞（Can）要放在主詞（Kim）的前面。

❷ 需要用「Do ...?」、「Does ...?」、「Did ...?」的一般疑問句：

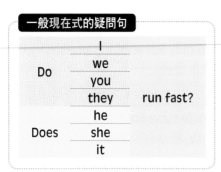

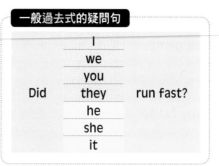

肯定句	疑問句
They live in a small village. 他們住在一個小村莊裡。	Do they live in a small village? 他們住在一個小村莊裡嗎？
Trish works hard at her English. 翠希學習英文很努力。	Does Trish work hard at her English? 翠希學習英文很努力嗎？
Kate felt great. 凱特感覺很好。	Did Kate feel great? 凱特感覺很好嗎？

PRACTICE

1 改錯：請將下列句子改寫為正確的句子。

1 It doesn't snows in Miami.

2 Joe and I do know not how to get to Tokyo.

3 Has arrived Coco in Chicago?

4 Are going you to sing with Sue and Pete?

5 Did Erika moved to South Africa last year?

6 Should we go now.

7 It has rained not for a month.

8 She likes not her job.

2 用否定縮寫形式，把下列句子改為否定句。

1 I saw her talking to the principal. _____

2 Lynn has read the novel *Dinosaurs Before Dark*. _____

3 Joe became a lawyer two years ago. _____

4 Tonight Sue and Lulu will fly to Honolulu. _____

5 She is playing a computer game. _____

6 It snowed last night. _____

7 He is going to keep on smoking. _____

8 Neal always washes his hands before each meal. _____

9 Dwight can go with you to see a movie tonight. _____

10 She was born in Hawaii. _____

3 將下列的疑問句寫出正確的詞序。

1 on the phone | tired | after talking to her boyfriend | often | is | Joan?

_____

2 waited | you | for Sue | have | long?

_____

3 sleep | Kate | eight | till | sometimes | does?

_____

4 flying | Sue | Honolulu | to | is?

_____

5 she | her toes | touch | can?

_____

6 loudly singing | was | she | happy Hong Kong song | a?

_____

Chapter

73 特殊疑問句 (1)：用疑問詞提問

I **八個疑問詞**

用疑問詞來提問的問句叫「**特殊疑問句**」。回答特殊疑問句時不能用 yes 或 no。

1 **Who ...?** → 疑問代名詞 who 指人，意思是「誰？」。

who is = who's

- Who's **your favorite NBA basketball player?** 你最喜歡的 NBA 隊員是誰？
- Who **took my key?** 是誰拿了我的鑰匙？

    Mom Jan is talking on the phone. 簡正在講電話。
    Dad Who is she talking to? 她在跟誰講電話？

    → 在口語中，who 也可以用作受詞。在此句中，who 是介系詞 to 的受詞。
    → 用 who 等疑問詞開始的疑問句，介系詞（to, from, with 等）常位於句尾。

2 **What ...?** → what 指動物或事物，意思是「什麼？」。

what is = what's

❶ what + 名詞（what 在此句型中作疑問形容詞）

- What **time is it?** 現在是幾點？
- What **kind of animal is that?** 那是什麼動物？
- What **day is today?** 今天是星期幾？

What kind of animal is that?

❷ what 後不帶名詞（what 在此句型中作疑問代名詞）

- What's **your favorite subject?** 你最喜歡的科目是什麼？
- What **did you say?** 你說什麼？
- What **does she want to talk to me about?** 她想跟我說什麼？ ┌ 介系詞 about 位於句尾。

What is it like?

Pam I ate at the new French restaurant on Tenth Street last night.
我昨晚去吃了第十街新開的那家法國餐廳。
Mat What's **it** like? 那家餐廳如何？→ like 是介系詞，意思是「……怎麼樣？」。
Pam It's superb. 很讚。

Sid I had a wonderful vacation in Bali. 我去峇里島度假玩得很開心。
May What **was the weather** like? 那裡的天氣怎樣？
Sid It was lovely. 很好。

3 **Which . . . ?** → which 用來在「少數的事物或人」當中做選擇，詢問「哪一個」、「哪一些」。

❶ which + 名詞（which 在此句型中作疑問形容詞）

- Which <u>one</u> is my seat? 哪一個是我的位子？

- Which <u>President</u> ended the Vietnam War—Richard Nixon or Gerald Ford? 哪一個總統結束了越戰，理查·尼克森還是吉羅德·福特？

❷ which 後不帶名詞（which 在此句型中作疑問代名詞）

- Which do you prefer—tea or coffee? 你比較喜歡喝哪一個，茶還是咖啡？

- Which is bigger—the Earth or Mars? 哪一個比較大，地球還是火星？

> 比較　用 which 時，想到的是具體的小數字；泛指時，則用 what。
>
> - Which university did she go to—Harvard or MIT?
>   她上的是哪一所大學，哈佛還是麻省理工學院？
> - What university did you go to? 你上的是哪一所大學？
> - Which do you like more, modern music or classical music?
>   你更喜歡哪一種音樂，現代音樂還是古典音樂？
> - What kind of music does Mike like? 邁克喜歡什麼樣的音樂？

4 **When . . . ?** → 疑問副詞 when 指時間，表示「什麼時候？」。

when is = when's
- When's the best time to visit Disney World and the Kennedy Space Center? 什麼時候是參觀迪士尼世界和甘迺迪太空中心的最佳時間？

- When did Coco visit Chicago? 可可是什麼時候去遊歷了芝加哥的？

- When do you usually get up? 你通常什麼時候起床？
  = What time do you usually get up? 你通常幾點起床？

5 **Where . . . ?** → 疑問副詞 where 指地點，表示「在哪裡？」。

where is = where's
- "Where's my backpack?" "It's on your back."
  「我的背包在哪裡？」「在你的背上。」

- Where shall we go? 我們要去哪？

- Where are you from? 你是從什麼地方來的？
  └ 介系詞 from 位於句尾。

6 **Why . . . ?** → 疑問副詞 why 用來詢問「原因、理由、目的」，意思是「為什麼？」。

why is = why's
- Why's everyone picking on me? 為什麼大家都在找我的碴兒？

- Why are you always in a hurry? 你為何總是匆匆忙忙？

- "Why are you still in bed?" "Because I studied until midnight."
  「你為什麼還在床上？」「因為我昨晚讀書讀到半夜。」

7 **Whose . . . ?** → 疑問形容詞 **whose** 用來詢問「所有權」，意思是「是誰的？」。

- "Whose cellphone is this?" "It's mine." 「這是誰的手機？」「是我的。」

- "Whose dirty socks are on my bed?" "Those are Jane's socks."
  「是誰的髒襪子放在我的床上？」「那是珍的襪子。」

  whose 和 who's 的比較

  - Who's that young woman over there on the grass? → Who's = Who is
    那邊草地上的那位年輕女子是誰？

  - "Whose wallet is this?" "It's Mike's." 「這是誰的錢包？」「是邁克的。」

8 **How . . . ?** → 疑問副詞 **how** 是用來詢問「狀況怎麼樣？」或是「怎麼？」。

how is = how's

- "How's your friend Jill?" "She's sick with the flu."
  「你朋友潔兒還好嗎？」「她患了流感。」

- "How do you spell your first name?" "J-A-Y-N-E."
  「你的名字怎麼拼寫？」「J-A-Y-N-E。」

- "How do you usually go to school?"
  "Most of the time I ride my electric motor scooter."
  「你通常是怎麼去上學的？」「我大部分都是騎電動摩托車去上學。」

---

2 how 構成的疑問詞組：how + 形容詞 / 副詞

how old . . . ?
- "How old are your twin sisters, Amy and Emily?" "They are three."
  「你的雙胞胎妹妹艾咪和艾米莉有多大了？」「他們三歲了。」

how tall . . . ?
- "How tall is your brother Paul?" "He's about 1.89 meters."
  「你的兄弟保羅有多高？」「他大概有 189 公分。」

how big . . . ?
- How big is the universe? 宇宙有多大？

how far . . . ?
- How far is it from your home to your school? 從你家到你學校有多遠？

how much . . . ?
- "How much are those blue jeans?" "They are twenty dollars."
  「那條藍色牛仔褲多少錢？」「20 塊美金。」
  → how much 詢問價錢，意思是「多少」、「多少錢」。

- "How much money do you want to borrow?" "Only $10."
  「你想借多少錢？」「只借 10 塊美金。」 → how much + 不可數名詞（money）

how many . . . ?

how many + 複數名詞
- "How many people do you want to invite to your birthday party?"
  "About 20." 「你想邀請多少人參加你的生日派對？」「大概二十。」
  → how many + 複數名詞（people）

- How many times have you been late for class during this semester?
  這學期你上課遲到了幾次？ → how many + 複數名詞（times）

how often . . .?	• "How often do you Tweet on Twitter?" "Many times a day."
詢問頻率	「你多久上 Twitter 網站一次？」「一天好幾次。」

• "How often do you go to see a movie in a theater?" "About once a month." 「你多久去電影院看一次電影？」「大概每月一次。」

how long . . .?	• "How long has Coco lived in Chicago? "About three years."
詢問持續時間	「可可在芝加哥住了多長時間？」「大概有三年。」

• "How long does it take you to walk from your home to school?" "Half an hour." 「從你家走路去上學，要走多久？」「半小時。」

PRACTICE

1 選填 Who, What, When, Where, Why, How, Whose, Which 來完成下列句子。

1 _____ is your name?

2 _____ do you spell your name?

3 _____ are you from?

4 _____ do you live?

5 _____ old are you?

6 _____ tall are you?

7 _____ toy train is this?

8 _____ is your mom's birthday?

9 _____ long have you studied English?

10 _____ kind of music do you like?

11 _____ is your favorite movie star?

12 _____ is your favorite song?

13 _____ are you studying so hard?

14 _____ is the Sears Tower?

15 _____ do you prefer, music or sports?

16 _____ are my keys?

17 _____ long have you studied in this school?

18 _____ do you and Rae usually do on Saturdays?

19 _____ is older, Lynne or Liz?

20 _____ nationality are you?

2 選出正確答案。

Who : What

1 a _____ is your favorite sport?
  b _____ is your favorite singer?

How often : How long

2 a _____ do you shop online?
  b _____ can a human live without water?

Which : What

3 a _____ is the longest river in the world?
  b _____ is the longest river, the Yangzi River, the Nile River, or the Amazon River?

Who's : Whose

4 a _____ dancing with Sue Crews?
  b _____ money is this?

Which : What

5 a _____ is the capital of Australia?
  b _____ way should we go, left or right?

3 在空白處填上下列文字選單中的疑問詞，完成下列的小對話。

How often   Who   What   When   How long
How many   How far   Where   How   Why

1 **Elaine** _____ does Ann Pool get to school?

Dwayne Ann often walks to school with Sue McCool.

2 **Elaine** _____ do they have to walk?

Dwayne They have to walk more than two miles, but they love to walk and talk.

3 **Elaine** _____ does it take them?

Dwayne They are neighbors, and they usually leave home at 7:10 and get to school by 7:50. So, it takes them about forty minutes.

4 **Elaine** _____ is the Moon?

Dwayne It is in space and orbits the Earth. The Earth orbits the Sun, and the Sun orbits the core of the Milky Way Galaxy.

5 **Elaine** _____ pages in English have you read today?

Dwayne Today I've read about 80 pages in *The Diary of a Wimpy Kid*. It's an interesting novel.

6 **Elaine** _____ do you usually eat in the morning?

Dwayne I usually have some cheese and strawberries with milk.

7 **Elaine** _____ do you love English?

Dwayne Because I love to read American comic books and novels.

8 **Elaine** _____ does your brother Dwight play computer games?

Dwayne Dwight plays educational computer games every night.

9 **Dwayne** _____ lives in that cabin?

Elaine Clair lives there.

10 **Dwayne** _____ are you going to visit Norway?

Elaine I'm going to visit Norway in May.

4 請判斷下列對話是否正確，正確打 ✓，不正確打 ×，並加以更正。

1 **Ben** How long do you practice modern ballet? ☐

May I practice modern ballet every day. ☐

294

2 Ben What kind of dessert do you like? ☐

May I dream about chocolate ice cream. I also ☐
love vanilla ice cream on a piece of apple pie.

3 May Who's your brother's favorite subject? ☐

Ben My brother Lee loves P.E. ☐

4 Ben Where does Gwen have time to visit her ☐
friends?

May Gwen often spends time with her friends ☐
on Sunday afternoons.

5 Ben How do you go to bed so early? ☐

May I want to be healthy and look my best. ☐

6 Ben What do you think of Ike and Mike? ☐

May I like them. They are gentlemen. ☐

7 Ben Which do you like better, Ann or Nan? ☐

May I like them both. ☐

8 Ben Why is Jerome? ☐

May Jerome is in Rome. ☐

5 用「How + 形容詞或副詞」（old、long 等）完成下列的問句。

1 "_____ is your home to the airport?" "It's about 50 kilometers."

2 "_____ is Kate?" "She's twenty-eight."

3 "_____ has Kay worked in Taipei?" "Nearly five years."

4 "_____ do you chat with your friend Mat on the Internet?" "Once a week."

5 "_____ are you?" "I'm fifteen."

6 "_____ have you studied English?" "Three years."

7 Ann Mount Everest is the highest mountain in the world.

Dan _____ is Mount Everest?"

Ann "It's 8,848 meters."

8 "_____ is Japan?" "It's about 377,835 square kilometers."

9 "_____ is Kelly? "She's about six feet tall."

10 "_____ is the Mississippi River?" "It's 3,779 kilometers long."

Chapter

74 特殊疑問句 (2)：特殊疑問句的詞序

I ── **用 who, what 來詢問主詞**

在特殊疑問句中，**who** 和 **what** 用來詢問「**主詞**」時，疑問句和陳述句的詞序一樣（主詞＋動詞），動詞形式也是一樣，不能用助動詞 do、does 和 did。

陳述句 → 主詞 ＋ 動詞	特殊疑問句 → 主詞(Who, What) ＋ 動詞
• <u>Joe</u> broke the window. 喬打破了窗戶。	• <u>Who</u> broke the window? 誰打破了窗戶？
• <u>Sue</u> wants to see Mr. Brown. 蘇想見布朗先生。	• <u>Who</u> wants to see Mr. Brown? 誰想見布朗先生？
• <u>Something</u> happened this morning between Sue and Lulu. 今早在蘇和露露之間發生了一些事。	• <u>What</u> happened this morning between Sue and Lulu? 今早在蘇和露露之間發生了什麼事？
• <u>The traffic jam</u> made Paul late for school. 塞車使得保羅上學遲到了。	• <u>What</u> made Paul late for school? 是什麼造成保羅遲到？

---

2 ── **用 who, whom, what 來詢問受詞**

who、**whom** 和 **what** 用來詢問「**受詞**」時，要用「疑問句」的詞序。在非常正式語中用受格 whom，一般情況下可以用 who 作受詞。

陳述句 → 主詞 ＋ 動詞	特殊疑問句 → 受詞(Who, What) ＋ 助動詞 ＋ 主詞 ＋ 主動詞
• Kay saw <u>Sue</u> yesterday. 凱昨天見到了蘇。	• <u>Who</u> did Kay see yesterday? 凱昨天見到了誰？
• Ann likes <u>Dan</u>. 安喜歡丹。	• <u>Who</u> does Ann like? 安喜歡誰？
• Mom is going to make <u>fish</u> for dinner. 媽媽晚餐要做魚肉吃。	• <u>What</u> is Mom going to make for dinner? 媽媽晚餐做什麼吃？ → What 是不定式動詞 make 的受詞。
• Kay bought <u>an electric car</u> yesterday. 凱昨天買了一輛電動汽車。	• <u>What</u> did Kay buy yesterday? 凱昨天買了什麼？

❶ be 動詞或助動詞（is、are、have、has、can 等）位於主詞的前面。

陳述句 → 主詞 + 動詞	特殊疑問句 → 疑問詞 + be 動詞 + 主詞 / 疑問詞 + 助動詞 + 主詞 + 主動詞
• The Stature of Liberty is **in New York Harbor.** 自由女神像位於紐約港。	• **Where** is the Stature of Liberty? 自由女神像在哪裡？
• Mary was **angry.** 瑪麗生氣了。	• **Why** was Mary **angry?** 瑪麗為什麼生氣？
• She is **surfing the Internet.** 她正在網上瀏覽。	• **What** is she **doing?** 她正在做什麼？
• They have **been married for two years.** 他們結婚有兩年了。	• **How long** have they **been married?** 他們結婚多久了？
• She will **go to India next week.** 她下個星期要去印度。	• **When** will she **go to India?** 她什麼時候要去印度？
• Joe can't **come to the meeting tomorrow.** 喬明天不能來參加會議。	• **Why** can't Joe **come to the meeting tomorrow?** 喬明天為什麼不能來參加會議？

❷ 用助動詞「do . . .?」、「does . . .?」、「did . . .?」構成的特殊疑問句：

陳述句 → 主詞 + 動詞	特殊疑問句 → 疑問詞 + do/does/did + 主詞 + 主動詞
• She went **to the library this morning.** 她今天早上去了圖書館。	• **Where** did she go **this morning?** 她今天早上去了哪裡？
• Mary didn't call **Henry.** 瑪麗沒有打電話給亨利。	• **Why** didn't Mary call **Henry?** 瑪麗為什麼沒有打電話給亨利？
• Sue lived **in Miami for two years.** 蘇在邁阿密住了兩年。	• **How long** did Sue live **in Miami?** 蘇在邁阿密住了多久時間？
• She drinks **her coffee with milk.** 她喝咖啡加牛奶。	• **How** does she drink **her coffee?** 她喝什麼樣的咖啡？
• Dwight went **to bed late last night.** 杜威特昨晚很晚才睡覺。	• **When** did Dwight go **to bed last night?** 杜威特昨晚是什麼時候睡覺的？
• Kay didn't go **to school yesterday.** 凱昨天沒有去上學。	• **Why** didn't Kay go **to school yesterday?** 凱昨天為什麼沒有去上學？

1 | 請判斷下列對話是否正確，正確打 ✓，不正確打 ×，並加以更正。

1. When is Mary and Joe's wedding anniversary? ☐
2. What time Ted usually goes to bed? ☐
3. Why Sue is angry with Lulu? ☐
4. How often Bing goes mountain climbing? ☐
5. How long have lived you in Honolulu? ☐
6. How are you doing with your English grammar? ☐
7. Why are you often late for English class? ☐
8. How much sugar you want in your coffee? ☐
9. How much Mat paid for that cat? ☐
10. Where are Linda and Sue from? ☐

2 | 根據下面劃線部分的文字提問。

1. Last night Jane listened to an English story for an hour.
2. Steve bought an antique car on Christmas Eve.
3. Erica Bar traveled across America by car.
4. Your puppy is in the backyard.
5. Tom's birthday is on April 1.
6. The sun is the center of our solar system.
7. Kay has learned twenty-five new English words today.
8. She goes swimming almost every day.
9. Paul is 1.90 meters tall.
10. Kay's electric car cost $25,000.
11. This is her cellphone.

Chapter

75 選擇疑問句、附加問句和感嘆句

I ── 選擇疑問句

「提供兩種或兩種以上的情況」要對方進行選擇的疑問句，稱「**選擇疑問句**」。
回答時不能用 yes 或 no。供選擇的部分，要用 **or** 連接。

> **Jan** Which city do you like better, Chicago or New York?　→ 這個問句既是特殊疑問句，
> 你比較喜歡哪一個城市，芝加哥還是紐約？　　　　　　也是選擇疑問句。

> **Del** I don't like either of them. 我兩個都不喜歡。

> **Joe** Is she American or Canadian? 她是美國人還是加拿大人？

> **Jill** She's Canadian. 她是加拿大人。

---

2 ── 附加問句

❶ 附加問句（question tag），用來「**確認某事的真實性**」，或「**請求贊同**」。

> **Jan** Davy isn't going to marry Lulu, is he? 大衛不會跟露露結婚，對嗎？
> ↳ 附加問句，用來「詢問某事的真實性」。

> **Del** No, he isn't. Last week he married Amy. 對，不會。他上星期已經娶了艾咪。

❷ 附加問句是由 **be 動詞**或**助動詞**（have、will、can 等）和**代名詞**（I, you, he 等）
構成。附加問句的**主詞**必須使用**代名詞**，且和陳述句的「**人稱**」和「**時態**」要保
持一致。

肯定的陳述句	+	否定的附加問句	→	❶ 前面的陳述句是肯定句時，附加問句就要用否定的。

❷ 否定附加問句通常要用縮寫形式（isn't it,
aren't you, won't you, can't she）。

• Dee will fly to Rome tomorrow, won't she? 蒂明天早上要飛去羅馬，對嗎？

• She is from Iran, isn't she? 她是伊朗人，對嗎？

• Claire, there is something wrong with your DVD player, isn't there?
克萊兒，你的 DVD 播放機出了毛病，是不是？
→ there is 的句型，附加問句要用「be 動詞 + there」。

• I am a little bit overweight, aren't I? 我的體重有點超重，是不是？
→ I am 的否定附加問句是「aren't I?」。

• It is impossible for Sue to finish her English assignment tonight, isn't it?
→ 「impossible」不能視為否定詞，附加問句仍要用否定形式。

否定的陳述句 ＋ 肯定的附加問句 → 前面的陳述句是否定句時，附加問句就要用肯定的。

- Lee can't speak Chinese, can he? 李不會講中文，對嗎？
- You haven't finished your math homework, have you?
  你還沒有寫完你的數學作業，對嗎？
- Claire, there isn't anything wrong, is there? 克萊兒，沒出什麼問題吧，對嗎？
- I am not late, am I? 我沒有遲到，對嗎？

❸ 如果句子裡沒有 be 動詞，也沒有助動詞（have、will、can 等），那麼附加問句裡就要用 do, don't, does, doesn't, did, didn't。

- Lulu, you like your new hairstyle, don't you? 露露，你喜歡你的新髮型，對嗎？
- Lily doesn't like sugar in her coffee, does she? 莉莉不喜歡在咖啡裡加糖，對嗎？
- Lulu, you talked to our new Canadian teacher today, didn't you?
  露露，你今天有跟我們新來的加拿大老師說過話，對嗎？
- Sue, you did not talk to our new Canadian teacher today, did you?
  蘇，你今天沒有跟我們新來的加拿大老師說過話，對嗎？

❹ 陳述句有 no, never, hardly, seldom, few, little 等否定詞時，附加問句要用肯定形式。

- She can never remember my name, can she? 她永遠記不住我的名字，不是嗎？
- Your parents seldom scolded you, did they? 你的父母親很少罵你，對嗎？

❺ 以 let's 開頭的祈使句，附加問句用 shall we。其餘的祈使句可用 will you。

- Let's go fishing on Sunday morning, shall we? 我們星期天上午去釣魚，要不要？
- Sue, please turn off the TV, will you? 蘇，可以請你把電視關掉嗎？

❻ 若陳述句部分的主詞是指示代名詞 this, that 或是**動名詞**（如：walking, jogging）時，疑問部分的主詞用 it。

- Paul, this is a cute doll, isn't it? 保羅，這是個可愛的玩偶，不是嗎？
- Playing ping-pong in the World Cup championship is her favorite fantasy, isn't it?
  在世界盃錦標賽打乒乓球是她最大的夢想，不是嗎？

❼ 陳述句的述語動詞是**行為動詞 have**，附加問句要用助動詞 do/did。如果陳述句中的述語動詞 have 作**狀態動詞**，表示「擁有」時，附加問句既可用 do/did，也可以用 have/has/had。

• You have a nap every afternoon, don't you? 你每天下午都要午睡，是嗎？

$\overbrace{}$ 行為動詞

• She has a new car and a new house, doesn't she?

$\overbrace{}$ 狀態動詞

= She has a new car and a new house, hasn't she?

她擁有一輛新車和一棟新房子，不是嗎？

❽ 附加問句的回答：前面的陳述句是**肯定句**時，附加問句的回答與一般疑問句的回答一樣，yes 表示「是」，no 表示「不」。但陳述句是**否定句**時，其答語 yes 意為「不」，no 則意為「是」。

Judy　Kate always feels great, doesn't she? 凱特一直感覺很好，是嗎？

Pete　Yes, she does. → 陳述句為肯定句： 　　是的，她一直感覺很好。

Pete　No, she doesn't. 答語 yes 意為「是」； 　　並沒有，她並非一直感覺很好。
　　　　　　　　　　no 則意為「不」。

Judy　You are not from New York, are you? 你不是紐約人，是嗎？

Pete　Yes, I am. → 陳述句為否定句： 　　不，我是紐約人。

Pete　No, I am not. 其答語 yes 意為「不」； 　　是，我不是紐約人。
　　　　　　　　　no 則意為「是」。

3　感嘆句

感嘆句通常由感嘆詞 **what** 或 **how** 引導，表示「讚美、驚歎、喜悅」等感情。

What + a/an + 形容詞 + 名詞 + 主詞 + 動詞 → **what** 引導的感嘆句

• What an honest guy he is! 他是一個多麼誠實的小夥子啊！
→ 單數可數名詞（guy），一定要加不定冠詞（a/an）。

• What lovely roses! = What lovely roses they are! 這些玫瑰花好漂亮啊！
→ 主詞 + 動詞（they are），可以省略。

How + 形容詞／副詞 + 主詞 + 動詞 → **how** 引導的感嘆句

How + 陳述句 → **how** 引導的感嘆句

• How fast she is typing! 她打字好快啊！

$\overbrace{}$ 副詞

• How disappointed Lily will be! 莉莉將會非常失望啊！

$\overbrace{}$ 形容詞

• How I wish to be beautiful, healthy, and wealthy!
我多麼希望能夠美麗、健康、富有！

$\overbrace{}$ 陳述句

How fast she is typing!

1 把下列的陳述句改成附加問句。

1 This issue is very important.

_____

2 You are a big coffee drinker.

_____

3 Gwen shouldn't start smoking again.

_____

4 You went to a movie with Sue last night.

_____

5 Bing should quit drinking and smoking.

_____

6 Kay and Fay can't do any of the martial arts.

_____

7 Jogging is the best way to remain fit.

_____

8 I am supposed to come back home before 10 p.m.

_____

9 Lily can speak Spanish fluently.

_____

10 It didn't snow yesterday in Tokyo.

_____

11 Let's go now.

_____

12 There were too many people in the mall.

_____

2 請判斷下列對話是否正確，正確打 ✓，不正確打 ×，並加以更正。

1 What noisy you are making!　☐

2 What a great idea!　☐

_____

3 What nice music it is! ☐

4 Look, what a mess have you made! ☐

5 What exciting movie! ☐

6 What terrible the earthquake was! ☐

3 | 把下列由 **What** 引導的感歎句，更改成由 **How** 引導的感歎句。

1 What a friendly girl Liz is!

2 What a hardworking student you are!

3 What beautiful flowers!

4 What a sad story it is!

4 | 用感嘆句完成下列句子。

1 She walks very fast. _____ she walks!

2 My trip to Tibet was very exciting. _____ my trip to Tibet was!

3 Paris is a very beautiful place. _____ place Paris is!

4 We are having lovely weather these days. _____ weather we are having these days!

5 I miss my friend Gwen very much. _____ I want to see her again!

Chapter

76 祈使句

Ⅰ 祈使句使用的時機和場合

1 指示 instructions

- Look at **the picture on page 25.**
  看第 25 頁的插圖。

2 警告 warnings

- Watch **out!** 小心！

3 邀請 invitations

- Gus, come **and** join us.
  加斯，過來加入我們

4 建議 advice

- Stay **in bed. Don't go to school today.**
  待在床上。今天不要去上學。

5 招待 offers

- **Please** have **some lemonade.**
  請喝點檸檬飲料。
  └→ * 加上 please，可以讓祈使句
    聽起來比較客氣、禮貌。
    *please 可以放在句首或句尾。

6 請求 requests

- Pass **me the salt, please.**
  請把鹽巴遞給我。

肯定句 → 通常直接以原形動詞開頭，主詞 you 通常被省略。有時候也可以用一個名詞或代名詞開頭，清楚表明我們是在對誰說話。

- Dwight, turn on the light. 杜威特，把燈打開。
- Tell Mr. Oak that joke. 把那個笑話講給歐克先生聽。
- Sit down and be quiet. 安安靜靜坐下來。
- Ms. Long, please sing us a song. 龍先生，請給我們唱首歌。

否定句 → 一般是在原形動詞前加「**don't**」或否定副詞「**never**」。

Don't
Do not + 原形動詞 →
Never

- Do not tell Mr. Oak that joke.
  = Don't tell Mr. Oak that joke.
  不要把那個笑話講給歐克先生聽。

- Dwight, do not turn on the light.
  = Dwight, don't turn on the light.
  杜威特，不要開燈。

- Don't write on the desks.
  = Never write on the desks.
  不要在書桌上寫字。

- Ellen and Ben, never argue with each other like that again! 艾倫，班，永遠不要再這樣爭吵了！

- Don't park here! It says "No parking."
  不要在這裡停車。牌子上寫的是「禁止停車」。

以 no 開頭的祈使句

no + 名詞
      動名詞 →

- No parking! 禁止停車！
- No smoking! 禁止吸菸！

第一、三人稱的祈使句，通常是以 let 開頭的祈使句。

- Let's go for a swim. 我們去游泳吧。→ 第一人稱 us
- Let her go. 讓她走吧。→ 第三人稱 her

1 把下列的肯定祈使句改成否定祈使句。

1 Please sit down, Louise. _____

2 Tell her to study math. _____

3 Open your books. _____

4 Kay, go away. _____

5 Run, boys. _____

6 Take off your shoes. _____

2 自括弧中選出正確的答案，畫上底線。

1 Dwight, (not watch/do not watch) TV tonight.

2 Pat, (speak never/never speak) to your mom like that!

3 (Reads/Read) a lot of interesting English storybooks.

4 Please (don't smoke/no smoke), Louise.

5 Please (be/is) quiet, Abby!

6 "(Have/Has) some green tea," I said to the dean.

7 (Don't be/Be not) late to meet Pete.

8 Louise, (be/are) silent, please.

3 把下面的單詞組成句子。注意句首字母要大寫

1 right | mess | sweep up | the | now.

_____

2 Steve! | flight | to leave. | is going | your | quick, | be

_____

3 light. | read | don't | dim | in

_____

4 me | your | show | please | Tess, | red blouse. | new

_____

5 street. | run | don't | Pete, | the | on

_____

6 get | to take a bath | a haircut. | don't | and | me | tell

_____

Chapter 77 簡單句、並列句和副詞子句

I 簡單句

簡單句只包含一個獨立子句，內含一個主詞和一個述語動詞，表達一個完整的概念。簡單句的基本句型如下：

1 主詞 ＋ 述語動詞 ＋ 介系詞片語 → • Sue dove **into the cool pool.**
蘇跳進了冰涼的游泳池。

2 主詞 ＋ 述語動詞 ＋ 受詞 ＋ 介系詞片語 → • Lynne married **Ray in May.**
琳在五月時和瑞結婚了。

3 主詞 ＋ 連綴動詞 ＋ 主詞補語 → • Brook is **a cook.** 布魯克是一個廚師。
　　　　　　　　　　　　　　└→ 名詞作「主詞補語」。
• Ann is **in Japan.** 安在日本。
　　　　　　　└→ 介系詞片語作主詞補語。

4 主詞 ＋ 述語動詞 ＋ 間接受詞（名詞／受格代名詞） ＋ 直接受詞（名詞） →

ⓐ **直接受詞**是直接受到動詞行為影響的人或事物，是行為動詞的接受者。

ⓑ **間接受詞**是間接受到動詞行為影響的人或事物，可以是一個名詞或一個代名詞，表明及物動詞所做的行為是為誰而做的。用作受詞的**代名詞**須使用**受格**形式。

　　　　　┌─ 間接受詞
• **Kay** showed **me the way.**
凱給我指了路。　　└→ 直接受詞

5 主詞 ＋ 述語動詞 ＋ 間接受詞 ＋ 直接受詞（疑問詞＋不定詞） →

　　　　　　┌─ 間接受詞
• I told **Sue what to do.**
　　　　　　　└→「疑問詞 + 不定詞」，當作直接受詞
我告訴蘇該做什麼。

6 主詞 ＋ 述語動詞 ＋ 受詞 ＋ 動詞 ＋ 受詞

• I heard **you yell at Del.**
我聽到你對戴爾吼叫。

2 ── 並列句

並列句是由兩個或兩個以上的簡單句（即獨立子句），由**並列連接詞**（and、but、or、nor、so 等）連接而構成。在美式英語中，當並列句是由連接詞連接起來的兩個獨立子句時，在連接詞前面要加逗號〔參見 Chapter 67〕。

- Mary is a very smart girl. Sometimes she gets crazy with her friend Daisy. → 兩個簡單句（即獨立子句），每一個簡單句各有一個完整而獨立的「主詞＋述語」結構。

- Mary is a very smart girl, but sometimes she gets crazy with her friend Daisy. → 兩個獨立子句（即簡單句）由並列連接詞 but 連接，but 前面要加逗號。
  瑪麗是一個聰明的女孩，但是她跟朋友黛絲在一起時，有時會變得很瘋狂。

3 ── 副詞子句

除了簡單句、並列句外，還有複合句。**複合句**「由一個主句（即獨立子句），再加上一個或一個以上的附屬子句」所組成。子句在句子裡承擔各種職責。有三種基本的子句（**副詞子句、形容詞子句、名詞子句**），根據子句在句中的作用來分類。

副詞子句在與主句的關係中扮演副詞（即狀語）的角色，為主句（即獨立子句）裡發生的事情提供更多的訊息，根據所傳達的內容，可分為時間、地點、原因、條件、目的、結果、比較、讓步等種類〔參見 Chapter 68 和 Chapter 70〕。

用來回答問題「When?」，由連接詞引導，如：

❶ 時間副詞子句 →

when（在……什麼時）	after（在……以
while（在……什麼時候）	後）
as soon as（一……就）	since（自從）
before（在……之前）	till/until（直到）

······ 時間副詞子句

- After she buys this rocket plane, Coco will be able to fly from San Francisco to Chicago. 可可買了這架火箭飛機後，就能夠從三藩市飛到芝加哥。
  → 如果主句是簡單未來式（will be），時間副詞子句要用簡單現在式（buys）表示未來的時間。

❷ 地點副詞子句 → 以 where（哪裡）或者 wherever（無論哪裡）開始，回答問題「Where?」。

······ 地點副詞子句

- Wherever you go, I'll be with you. 無論你去哪裡，我都要和你在一起。

❸ 條件副詞子句 → 指出某事發生的條件或環境，通常由 if（如果）和 unless（除非）引導。

······ 條件副詞子句

- Make sure to get enough sleep if you want to be healthy and wealthy.
  如果你想健康、富有，就一定要有足夠的睡眠。

4 原因**副詞子句** → 說明事件發生的原因，通常用來回答「Why?」的問題，常以 because（因為）、as（因為）、since（既然；由於；因為）開頭。

┌····· 原因副詞子句
• Uncle Buzz fired Daisy because she was often angry and lazy.
因為黛絲常常發脾氣，而且又懶惰，所以被巴斯叔叔解雇了。

5 結果**副詞子句** → 由「so ... that」、「such ... that」（如此……以致於……）來引導。

┌····· 結果副詞子句
• Astronaut Andrew Boon was so tired that he fell asleep while going to the moon.
太空人安德魯‧布恩因為太累了，結果在前往月球的途中睡著了。

6 目的**副詞子句** → 說明主句的目的，通常以 so that、in order that 或 so 引導，意為「以便……」，用來回答「What for?」（為了什麼）的問題。目的副詞子句與主句之間不要逗號隔開。

┌····· 目的副詞子句
• Dad quickly put the milk in the fridge so (that) it wouldn't go sour.
爸爸趕快把牛奶放進冰箱，這樣就不會發酸。➜ so that 中的 that 在口語中可省略。

┌─ 比較 ──────────────────────────────────────┐
│   so 是表「結果」的並列連接詞，意為
│   ┌─「因此；所以」，需要用逗號隔開。
│ • Uncle Lee loves photography, so he has taken a lot of
│   pictures of his friends and family.
│   李叔叔很喜歡攝影，所以他拍了很多親友的照片。
└──┘

7 情狀**副詞子句** → 亦即「方式副詞子句」，說明事件發生的方式，常用來回答「How?」的問題。情狀副詞子句通常以 as（依照）、exactly as（完全依照）、just as（正如）、as if/as though（就好像）來引導。

┌····· 情狀副詞子句
• Please just do as you are told, and you'll find something better than gold.
請依指示去做吧，那樣你就會找到比黃金還更好的東西。

8 讓步**副詞子句** → 表示「雖然、儘管」，通常以 although/though（雖然）、even though/even if（即使）、whether（無論）開頭。

┌····· 讓步副詞子句
• Whether I win or lose, I will fight. 無論輸贏，我都要奮戰。

9 比較**副詞子句** → 是用來做比較的子句，通常以 than（比）、as（像……一樣）、as ... as（像……一樣）開頭。

┌····· 比較副詞子句
• The rain ended sooner than I expected. 這場雨比我預料的還快結束。

1 自括弧中選出正確的答案，畫上底線。

_____ **1** I enjoy living in Antarctica, _____ it is very cold.
ⓐ before　ⓑ even though　ⓒ so that　ⓓ whether

_____ **2** Trish has the world at her fingertips _____ she has excellent English.
ⓐ till　ⓑ even though　ⓒ whether　ⓓ as

_____ **3** Ann acts _____ she could easily win this beauty contest.
ⓐ as if　ⓑ than　ⓒ after　ⓓ because

_____ **4** _____ the hurricane gets here, Jane will fly her jet plane to Spain.
ⓐ In order that　ⓑ Wherever　ⓒ Before　ⓓ But

_____ **5** _____ a road is bumpy mile after mile, you can either get grumpy or put on a smile.
ⓐ Unless　ⓑ When　ⓒ Because　ⓓ Where

_____ **6** Listen to Uncle Lars carefully _____ you will know everything about how to get to Mars.
ⓐ before　ⓑ where　ⓒ so that　ⓓ after

_____ **7** Do _____ you are told, and don't be so bold.
ⓐ even though　ⓑ in order that　ⓒ so　ⓓ as

_____ **8** Mother's Day is in May, _____ Father's Day is in June.
ⓐ nor　ⓑ or　ⓒ and　ⓓ so

2 指出錯誤並更正。

1 I'll get a comb <u>from</u> Rome <u>when</u> Papa in a rocket <u>will get</u> home.
　　　　　　A　　　　　B　　　C　　　　　　　　　　D

2 <u>Flying</u> a spaceship is not <u>as</u> difficult <u>so</u> Amy <u>told</u> me.
　　A　　　　　　　　　　B　　　　C　　　D

3 My advice to Sue is <u>to live</u> <u>when</u> the weather <u>is</u> great for <u>flying</u> rocket planes.
　　　　　　　　　　　A　　　B　　　　　　　　C　　　　　D

4 <u>As soon as</u> she <u>was</u> sick, Mary <u>could</u> not come to our <u>wedding</u>.
　　　A　　　　　B　　　　　　　C　　　　　　　　　D

Chapter

78 名詞子句作主要動詞的受詞

名詞子句可以當作主句動詞的受詞，這類名詞子句叫「**受詞子句**」。連接受詞子句的「從屬連接詞」，主要有 that, whether, if，以及疑問詞 who, whom, whose, which, what, when, where, why, how 等。

I 連接詞 that 引導的名詞子句作動詞的受詞

陳述句作**受詞子句**時，用從屬連接詞 **that** 連接。that 在子句中不充當任何成分，只起連接主句和子句的作用，可以省略。

- **Do you think (that) Sam cheated on the math exam?** 你認為山姆數學考試作了弊嗎？

  → 名詞子句是一個陳述句，作主句裡的動詞 think 的受詞。

- **Sally told me (that) her family was going to move to Italy.**
  莎莉告訴我，她們全家人要搬到義大利去。

  → 名詞子句是主句動詞 told 的直接受詞。

- **She announced (that) Pam received an A on yesterday's chemistry exam.**
  她宣布，潘姆在昨天的化學考試中得到了 A。

  → 名詞子句是主句動詞 announced 的受詞。

2 由疑問詞引導的名詞子句作動詞的受詞

特殊疑問句作**受詞子句**時，由疑問詞 when, who, what, where, whatever, how, which, why 等引導。注意：受詞子句的詞序一律用**陳述句的詞序**，即「**主詞 + 述語**」。

❶ 帶有 be 動詞（作連綴動詞）的特殊疑問句：

主句	名詞子句	
Do you know	**how old Liz is?**	你知道莉茲幾歲嗎？
I know	**how old Liz is.**	我知道莉茲幾歲。
I don't know	**how old Liz is.**	我不知道莉茲幾歲。

How old is Liz?
莉茲幾歲了？

→ 名詞子句是主句裡的動詞 know 的受詞。
注意子句的順序，主詞在動詞前（Liz is）。

❷ 帶有（情態）助動詞 is, am, are, have, has, can, should 等的特殊疑問句：

When is Ann **going to Iran?**
安什麼時候去伊朗？
	→	• **Do you know** when Ann is **going to Iran?**
		  你知道安什麼時候去伊朗嗎？
		• **I don't know** when Ann is **going to Iran.**
		  我不知道安什麼時候去伊朗。

What should I **do?**
我該怎麼辦？
	→	• **Can you tell me** what I should **do?**
		  你能告訴我，我該怎麼辦嗎？
		• **Please tell me** what I should **do.**
		  請告訴我，我該怎麼辦。

Where has Ron **gone?**
朗去了哪裡？
	→	• **Do you know** where Ron has **gone?**
		  你知道朗去了哪裡嗎？
		• **I don't know** where Ron has **gone.**
		  我不知道朗去了哪裡。

❸ 帶有助動詞 do, does, did 的特殊疑問句：

Where did I put **my wedding ring?** 我把我的結婚戒指放到哪裡去了？	→	• **Do you know** where I put **my wedding ring?** 你知道我把我的結婚戒指放去哪裡了嗎？ • **I don't remember** where I put **my wedding ring.** 我不記得我把我的結婚戒指放在哪裡了。

What does Sue think **about Lulu?** 蘇對露露的看法是什麼？	→	• **Do you know** what Sue thinks **about Lulu?**
		  你知道蘇對露露有何看法嗎？
		• **I know** what Sue thinks **about Lulu.**
		  我知道蘇對露露的看法。

---

3 連接詞 whether 或 if 引導的名詞子句作動詞的受詞

❶ 「Is . . .?」、「Do . . .?」、「Can . . .?」等句型的**一般疑問句**，要用 whether 或 if 引導名詞子句作動詞的受詞。

Is Kay **getting better today?** 凱今天有好一點嗎？	→	• **Do you know** whether Kay is **getting better today?** 你知道凱今天有好一點嗎？ • **I don't know** whether Kay is **getting better today.** 我不知道凱今天是不是有好一點。 → 也可以用 if 代替 whether

Can Kim **swim?**
金姆會游泳嗎？
	→	• **Do you know** if Kim can **swim?**
		  你知道金姆會不會游泳嗎？
		• **I don't know** if Kim can **swim.**
		  我不知道金姆會不會游泳。
		  → 也可以用 whether 代替 if

❷ 只能用 whether 不能用 if 的情況：

| 受詞子句在介系詞之後時 | → | **Judy** Shall we go camping this Saturday?
我們這個星期六要去露營嗎？

Pete It depends on whether it will rain on Saturday.
看星期六會不會下雨再決定。 |

與 or 連用時　→　• I'll ask Scot whether he can come tomorrow or not.
　　　　　　　　　我會問史考特，看他明天會不會來。

受詞子句前移時　→　• <u>Whether Joe will go to Australia or America this summer</u>, I really don't know.
　　　　　　　　　喬今年夏天會去澳洲還是去美國，我真不知道。

---

4 ｜ 否定前移 ｜

當主句的主詞為第一人稱（**I, we**），述語動詞為 **think, believe, imagine, suppose, guess** 等時，如果表示否定意義，應把主句變成否定句，即「否定前移」。

• I don't think (that) everyone could learn to fly an airplane.
　我認為**不是每個人**都可以學會駕駛飛機的。

> 在受詞子句中，否定前移的句子翻譯成中文時，要否定後移。

PRACTICE

1 ｜ 用「**Do you know if . . . ?**」句型提問。

1 Does Ms. Bridge live in this cottage?　Do you know if ＿＿＿＿＿＿＿＿＿
＿＿＿＿＿＿＿＿＿＿＿＿＿＿＿？

2 Is Susan an Egyptian?　Do you know if ＿＿＿＿＿＿＿＿＿
＿＿＿＿＿＿＿＿＿＿＿＿＿＿＿？

3 Did Sam and I pass the English exam?　Do you know if ＿＿＿＿＿＿＿＿＿
＿＿＿＿＿＿＿＿＿＿＿＿＿＿＿？

4 Will oil prices go up or down?　Do you know if ＿＿＿＿＿＿＿＿＿
＿＿＿＿＿＿＿＿＿＿＿＿＿＿＿？

5 Did he talk to Kay on the Internet yesterday?　Do you know if ＿＿＿＿＿＿＿＿＿
＿＿＿＿＿＿＿＿＿＿＿＿＿＿＿？

2 用「Do you know . . .?」句型提問。

1. Why is Kay absent today?   Do you know _____?

2. How long did Dwight play "Happy Farm" on Facebook last night?   Do you know _____ _____?

3. Is Bret Wu's cellphone connected to the Internet?   Do you know _____ _____?

4. What does Sue Pool want to do after her graduation from high school?   Do you know _____ _____?

5. Does Amy like me?   Do you know _____?

6. Where is the bathroom?   Do you know _____?

7. Who is piloting that plane?   Do you know _____?

3 根據提示把下面句子改成名詞子句。

1. You didn't do your homework.   Mom said _____.

2. Clair lost her teddy bear.   Who told you _____?

3. How old are you?   Don't ask me _____.

4. Dan ran his bicycle into Ted.   Dan felt sorry _____.

5. Milk is good for you.   They say _____.

6. What can I do for you?   I don't know _____.

7. Can we finish this job on time?   I don't know _____.

8. Where did you park my van?   Could you tell me _____?

4 從括弧裡選出正確的表達方式，劃上底線。

1. Why (didn't you go/you didn't go) to school today?

2. Please tell me why (does Amy dislike/Amy dislikes) me.

3. Could you tell me (what did Kay do/what Kay did) yesterday?

4. What (Eve wants/does Eve want) from Steve?

5. Why (do you want/you want) to live in Hawaii?

6. Could you tell Kitty (how pretty is she/how pretty she is) and then take her to the best pizza cafe in New York City?

Chapter

79 名詞子句作主句的主詞、主詞補語或置於主句的形容詞後

---

1 主詞子句（名詞子句作主句的主詞）

❶ 名詞子句可以由從屬連接詞 **that** 引導放在句中作主詞，充當**主詞子句**。從屬連接詞 that 在子句中不充當任何成分，只起連接主句和子句的作用，但 **that 不能省略**。

- **That Gus loved Kate** came as a great surprise to us. 加斯愛上凱特，這讓我們大吃一驚。
  → 名詞子句「That Gus loved Kate」作句子的主詞。從屬連接詞 that 不能省略。

  > 注意 此表達方式更常使用「**it** 形式主詞」，把真正的主詞子句放在句尾。
  >
  > **It came as a great surprise to us that Gus loved Kate.**
  > 加斯喜歡凱特，這消息令我們大吃一驚。

❷ 名詞子句也可以由**疑問詞**（why, when 等）引導在句中作**主詞子句**。

　　　　　　名詞子句

- **Why Amy loves her noisy parrots** puzzles me. 我搞不懂艾咪為什麼會喜歡嘰嘰喳喳的鸚鵡。
  → 名詞子句是句子的主詞。why 是子句中的副詞，指「為什麼」。
  子句的詞序是「疑問詞 + 主詞 + 動詞」。

---

2 名詞子句用在連綴動詞後面作主詞補語

❶ 名詞子句可以由從屬連接詞 **that** 引導，置於主句連綴動詞之後，對主句的主詞作補充說明。從屬連接詞 that 在子句中不充當任何成分，只起連接主句和子句的作用。

- **The trouble was that he didn't want to work.** 麻煩的是，他不想工作。
  → 名詞子句置於主句連綴動詞 was 之後，對主句的主詞作補充說明。
- **The problem was that she didn't put on her seat belt.** 問題是，她沒有繫上安全帶。

❷ 名詞子句也可以由**疑問詞**（why, when 等）引導，作句子的主詞補語。

- **That's why Claire went there.** 那就是為什麼克萊兒去了那裡。
  → 名詞子句是句子的主詞補語。
  = **That's the reason why Claire went there.** 那就是克萊兒會去那裡的原因。
  → 形容詞子句修飾名詞 reason〔參見 Chapter 80 形容詞子句〕。

---

3 名詞子句放在主句的「形容詞」後

名詞子句由從屬連接詞 **that** 引導（that 可省略），接在主句的「形容詞」之後，用以描述主句的主詞對子句所描述內容的感受。

- I am glad (that) we can take a long vacation. 我很高興，我們能度一個長假。
- We felt sad (that) so many people died during the huge earthquake and tsunami in Japan. 我們感到很難過，在日本的大地震和海嘯中有那麼多人罹難。
- Kay was disappointed (that) Tom didn't take her out for dinner on Friday. 凱很失望，湯姆星期五沒有帶她上館子。

PRACTICE

1 根據括弧裡的提示，完成下面句子。

1. He didn't show up at the party. (disappointed me)

2. You wear your tie and white shirt to the wedding. (his request)

3. Kay likes to play with her pretty kitty. (what Kay likes to do)

4. She didn't win the English speech contest. (I'm disappointed)

5. Amy and Tom's marriage ended in divorce. (surprised me)

6. Both of you have been in love with each other for years. (the best thing)

7. We have become friends. (I'm glad)

8. Why does Sally dislike Larry? (it's a mystery)

2 選出正確答案。

1. Whatever _____ yesterday is none of my business. ⓐ did you do ⓑ you did

2. The problem is _____ Ann refuses to sell her giraffe because it often makes her laugh. ⓐ that ⓑ what

3. _____ you thought about that politician is correct. ⓐ What ⓑ That

4. The saddest thing is _____ many people still live in poverty. ⓐ why ⓑ that

5. Joan is glad _____ she paid off all of her student loan. ⓐ whether ⓑ that

6. Her wish is _____ her children will grow up to be honest, hardworking, and friendly. ⓐ that ⓑ how

Chapter

80 關係代名詞和關係副詞引導的形容詞子句

在複合句中，修飾名詞或代名詞的子句叫作「**形容詞子句**」。被形容詞子句修飾的名詞或代名詞叫作「**先行詞**」。形容詞子句由「**關係代名詞**」或「**關係副詞**」引導，**接在所修飾的詞（即先行詞）的後面**。

---

1 | 關係代名詞 who 和 that 作形容詞子句的主詞

關係代名詞 who 和 that 指「人」，作形容詞子句的**主詞**，**不能省略**：
ⓐ **who** 只能指代「人」，不能指代「物」。
ⓑ **that** 可以指代「人」或「物」。

| **兩個簡單句** | • I know an adventurous woman. She has traveled to 180 countries. |

ㄴ she 指人，關係代名詞要用 who 或 that 來指代。

┌ 先行詞
| **一個複合句** | • I know an adventurous woman who/that has traveled to 180 countries. |

ㄴ who 和 that 在此皆可作子句的主詞。

我認識一個喜愛冒險、周遊了 180 個國家的女子。

---

2 | 關係代名詞 that 和 which 作形容詞子句的主詞

注意：作主詞的關係代名詞都不能省略。

關係代名詞 **that** 和 **which** 指「物」，作形容詞子句的**主詞**，**不能省略**。**which** 只能指代「物」，不指代「人」。

┌ it 指物，關係代名詞要用 that 或 which 來指代。
| **兩個簡單句** | • Susan is wearing a skirt. It is too short for her. |

┌ 先行詞
| **一個複合句** | • Susan is wearing a skirt that/which is too short for her. |

ㄴ that 和 which 在此皆可作子句的主詞。

蘇珊穿了一件對她來說顯得太短的裙子。

❶ 關係代名詞 **who, whom, that** 都可以用來作形容詞子句的**受詞**，指代「人」，指代「物」則用 **that** 或 **which**。who 既可作主詞，也可作受詞，而 whom 只能作受詞。who (whom), that, which 在形容詞子句中作**受詞**時，**常可省略**。

⌐→ who, whom 或 that 是形容詞子句動詞 met 的受詞，指代「人」（girl）。

• The Egyptian girl (who/whom/that) I met on the cruise ship to Mexico could speak five languages.
我在去墨西哥的大型遊輪上認識的那位埃及女孩會講五種語言。

→ 不要同時使用關係代名詞（who, whom, that）和人稱代名詞（her）。

⌐ that 是形容詞子句動詞 gave 的直接受詞，
⌐→ 指代「物」（dress）。

• The dress (that) I gave Linda as a birthday gift looks fantastic on her.
我送給琳達當生日禮物的那件衣服，她穿起來很好看。

→ 不要同時使用關係代名詞（that）和人稱代名詞（it）。

⌐ that 是形容詞子句介系詞 in 的受詞，指代「物」（hotel）。
⌐→ 介系詞 in 不可以省略。

• The hotel (that) Jake stayed in last week is on a beautiful lake.
傑克上星期住的那家飯店，就座落在一座美麗的湖濱上。

→ 不要同時使用關係代名詞（that）和人稱代名詞（it）。

• Who's the young man (that) Emma is playing ping-pong with?
在和艾瑪一起打桌球的那個年輕男子是誰？

→ 主句裡已經有 who，所以形容詞子句要嘛省略作受詞的關係代名詞（who, whom, that），要嘛用 that，但不用 who，也不用 whom。

❷ 在形容詞子句中，who 雖然可以作受詞，與 whom 通用，但是**接在介系詞後面時只能用 whom**，不能用 who。

⌐→ who 和 whom 作子句的受詞時，可通用。

• Is that the woman whom/who you introduced to Harry Bloom?
那位就是你介紹給哈利·布魯姆的女子嗎？

⌐→ 介系詞後面，只能用 whom。

• That is the woman with whom Joe ate breakfast in the dining room.
那位就是和喬一起在餐廳吃早餐的女子。

❸ 在形容詞子句中，that 和 which 雖然都可以作指代「物」，當作子句的主詞或受詞，但在下面兩種情況下，**只能用 which**，不能用 that：

接在介系詞後面時，只能用 which →	• This is the cottage <u>in which</u> I was born. 我就在這棟別墅裡出生的。

┌→ which had a broken leg 是非限定形容詞子句。

非限定性形容詞子句 →	• Joe Wu's chair, <u>which</u> had a broken leg, fell on my big toe. 喬·吳的椅子斷了一條腿，椅子倒下來壓到我的大腳拇趾了。

━━ 4 ━━ 關係代名詞 whose 引導形容詞子句 ━━━━━━━━━━━━━

whose 用來指代「人」或「物」，亦即，先行詞可以是「人」，也可以是「物」。whose 在子句中修飾名詞。

┌→ 整個子句修飾先行詞 woman。

指代「人」 • I know a woman <u>whose</u> son just won one million dollars in a lottery.
我認識一個女子，她的兒子剛贏了一百萬美金的樂透。
→ 關係代名詞 whose 在此指「她的」，子句中修飾 son。

┌→ 整個子句修飾先行詞 toy dinosaur。

指代「物」 • The toy dinosaur <u>whose</u> legs are broken is behind the door. 斷了兩條腿的那個玩具恐龍就放在門後面。
→ 關係代名詞 whose 在此指「它的」，在子句中修飾名詞 legs。

━━ 5 ━━ 關係副詞 where, when, why 引導形容詞子句 ━━━━━━━━━

關係副詞 **where** 指「地點」，**when** 指「時間」，**why** 修飾先行詞 reason，表「原因」。

┌→ 整個子句修飾先行詞 places。

• I like to visit places <u>where</u> I can get a feel for the local culture and everyday life.
我喜歡參觀那些能讓我感受到當地文化和日常生活的地方。
關係副詞 where，指代「地方」（在那裡、往那裡）。

┌→ 整個子句修飾先行詞 day。

• I still remember the day <u>when</u> I first met Kay. 我還記得我第一次見到凱的那天。
→ 關係副詞 when，指代「時間」（當……時）。

┌→ 整個子句修飾先行詞 reason。

• Do you know the reason <u>why</u> she dislikes me? 你知道她為什麼不喜歡我的原因嗎？
→ 關係副詞 why，指代「原因」（為什麼）。

比較 Do you know <u>why she dislikes me</u>? 你知道她為什麼不喜歡我嗎？
→ 「why she dislikes me」是名詞子句，作主句動詞 know 的受詞〔參見 Chapter 78〕。

❶ 當先行詞是表「**時間**」的名詞時，在形容詞子句中，用 which 或 that 作受詞（可省略），用 when 作副詞。

- 先行詞

• I'll never forget the happy **time** (that/which) we had on the cruise ship to Mexico.
  我永遠都不會忘記我們坐在遊輪上前往墨西哥時的那一段愉快時光。

  ➜ 關係代名詞 that 或 which 作形容詞子句動詞 had 的受詞。

先行詞

• I'll never forget the day when I first arrived in Chicago.
  我第一次去芝加哥的那天，我畢生難忘。

  ➜ 關係副詞 when 作形容詞子句的副詞，相當於 on which。

❷ 當先行詞是表「**地點**」的名詞時，在形容詞子句中，用 which 或 that 作受詞（可省略），用 where 作副詞。

先行詞

• This is the ancient **town** (that/which) I visited three years ago with Margo.
  這座古城，就是我和瑪歌三年前一起去玩的地方。

  ➜ 關係代名詞 that 或 which 作形容詞子句動詞 visited 的受詞。

先行詞

• This is the house where Sue was born. 這間房子就是蘇出生的地方。

  ➜ 關係副詞 where 作形容詞子句的副詞，相當於 in which。

7 ── 形容詞子句中的述語要與先行詞的人稱和單複數一致

關係代名詞在形容詞子句中作主詞時，子句中的**述語動詞**在「人稱」與「單複數形」上，要與**先行詞**保持一致。

先行詞單數名詞

• This is Sally Brown, who works with Sue. 這位是莎莉‧布朗，她是和蘇共事的人。

  ➜ who 作形容詞子句的主詞，子句中的述語動詞用單數形 works。

先行詞複數名詞

• The two girls who are cooking are my sisters Sue and Lulu.
  正在煮菜的那兩個女孩，是我的姊妹蘇和露露。

  ➜ who 作形容詞子句的主詞，子句中的述語動詞用複數形 are。

1 將兩句合併為一句。

1 She gave me a cellphone yesterday. It has lots of functions and provides access to the Internet anywhere in the world.
The cellphone _____.

2 The principal is talking to a woman. She is our new English teacher from Canada.
The woman _____.

3 Lars showed me some pictures of the planets. The planets orbit distant stars.
Lars _____.

4 I met an Italian woman in the park today. She was wearing a funny purple hat.
The Italian woman _____.

5 Our family has a maid. She's very good at making cookies.
Our family _____.

2 用 who, which, whose, when, where, why 填空。

1 I know a woman _____ daughter will soon visit the International Space Station.

2 Is that the police officer _____ helped us find our lost robot?

3 Do you know the reason _____ Kay isn't in school today?

4 Is this the village _____ you grew up?

5 What's the name of the river _____ flows through the village?

6 Are you looking forward to the day _____ your summer vacation begins?

3 請判斷下列句子是否正確，正確打 ✓，不正確打 ×，並寫出正確句子。

1 Jim loves all the interesting storybooks his teacher reads to him.

◯ _____

2 She likes movies who can make her laugh and cry.

◯ _____

3 My favorite month is always December, when we celebrate Christmas.

◯ _____

4 The movie that I saw last night was scary.

◯ _____

5 Everything she said it was not true.

◯ _____

6 Do you know the reason why most men like motorcycles?

◯ _____

7 The restaurant I am working is called "The Double Happiness Cafe."

◯ _____

8 Sue prefers music that she can dance.

◯ _____

9 Kay lost the necklace her boyfriend gave it to her last Saturday.

◯ _____

10 Most of the people which we invited to our party didn't show up.

◯ _____

11 The dinner we had in that restaurant was very delicious.

◯ _____

12 The boots I am wearing them are beautiful and comfortable.

◯ _____

Chapter

81 間接引語的用法

I ── 直接引語和間接引語

用引號「直接引用講話者原本的談話」，稱為「**直接引語**」（direct speech）。
若是轉述原講話者說過的話，叫做「**間接引語**」（indirect speech）。

直接引語　Lily said, "I am really glad to have met Sally."　莉莉說：「我很開心遇到了莎莉。」

間接引語　Lily said (that) she was really glad to have met Sally.
莉莉說她很開心遇到了莎莉。

→ 將直接引語改寫為間接引語時，有時須改變直接引語裡的代名詞（I、you 等）。
例如：I 可能要改成 he 或 she，my 可能要改成 his 或 her。

---

2 ── 轉述時不同句式的連接詞

❶ **陳述句（that）** → 直接引語是陳述句，變為間接引語時，由連接詞 **that** 引導。**that** 在口語中常可省略。

直接引語　Dad said, "My shirt smells bad."
爸爸說：「他的襯衫聞起來有怪味。」

間接引語　Dad said (that) his shirt smelled bad.
爸爸說他的襯衫聞起來有怪味。

→ 代名詞變化：直接引語中的主詞是第一人稱（I, we, my, our），變為間接引語時，
人稱變化要與主句的主詞一致（如：Dad → his）。
→ 時態變化：現在式 smells 變成過去式 smelled〔參見第三點：動詞時態的變化〕。

❷ **一般疑問句
（whether, if）** → 直接引語是一般疑問句，要變為間接引語時，由連接詞 **whether** 或 **if** 引導。
注意：在間接疑問句中，主詞通常放在動詞前面，與陳述句的句型一樣。間接引語一般疑問句的句型如下：

| whether
if | + | 主詞 | + | 動詞 | → | 一般情況下，**whether** 和 **if**
可以通用，但與 **or not** 連
用時，只能用 **whether**。 |

直接引語　I asked, "Mary, are you hungry?" 我問：「瑪麗，你餓了嗎？」

間接引語　I asked Mary whether/if she was hungry. 我問瑪麗她會不會餓。

→ 代名詞變化：直接引語裡的代名詞 you（第二人稱），在間接引語中改成
she，與主句的受詞一致（Mary → she）。
→ 時態變化：現在式 are 要變成過去式 was〔參見第三點：動詞時態的變化〕。

③ **特殊疑問句 (who, what, how 等)** → 直接引語是特殊疑問句，要變為間接引語時，由特殊疑問詞引導。間接引語特殊疑問句如下：

疑問詞 **+** 主詞 **+** 動詞

直接引語 **Kay asked, "How old are you?"** 凱問：「你幾歲了？」

間接引語 **Kay asked me how old I was.** 凱問我幾歲了。

→ 代名詞變化：直接引語裡的代名詞 you（第二人稱），在間接引語中改成 I，與主句的受詞一致（me → I）。

→ 時態變化：現在時 are 要改成過去式 was〔參見第三點：動詞時態的變化〕。

④ **祈使句** → 直接引語是祈使句，要變成間接引語時，一般轉換成如下的結構：

tell
ask **+** somebody (not) to do something
order

直接引語 **Mr. Black told us, "Be quiet."** 布雷克老師跟我們説：「安靜！」

間接引語 **Mr. Black told us to be quiet.** 布雷克老師叫我們安靜。

---

3 — **動詞時態的變化**

直接引語變間接引語時，除了人稱代名詞要變化外，時態也會變化。如果使用的轉述動詞是**過去式**，如：said（說）、stated（陳述）、reported（報導），這些動詞後面的間接引語，常需要改變原直接引語的動詞時態。時態變化規則如下：

1 **簡單現在式** → **簡單過去式**

直接引語 **Lily stated, "I have to leave early."** 莉莉聲明，「我得早走。」

間接引語 **Lily stated she had to leave early.** 莉莉聲明，她得早走。→ have/has → had

直接引語 **He declared, "I don't like chicken or turkey."**
他聲明：「我不喜歡雞肉，也不喜歡火雞肉。」

間接引語 **He declared he didn't like chicken or turkey.**
他聲明，他不喜歡雞肉，也不喜歡火雞肉。→ do/does → did

直接引語 **Kate said, "I feel great."** 凱特説：「我感覺很好。」

間接引語 **Kate said she felt great.** 凱特説，她感覺很好。→ 現在式 feel → 過去式 felt

直接引語 **She stated, "I can finish the job on time."** 她表示，「我能按時完成工作。」

間接引語 **She stated she could finish the job on time.** 她表示，她能按時完成工作。
→ can → could

2 現在進行式 → 過去進行式

[直接引語] Bob said, "I am enjoying my new job." 鮑勃說：「我喜歡我的新工作。」

[間接引語] Bob said he was enjoying his new job. 鮑勃說，他喜歡他的新工作。

→ am/is/are → was/were

3 現在完成式 → 過去完成式

[直接引語] Lulu said, "I've never been to Honolulu." 露露說：「我沒去過檀香山。」

[間接引語] Lulu said she had never been to Honolulu. 露露說她沒去過檀香山。

→ 現在完成式 have been → 過去完成式 had been

4 簡單過去式 → 過去完成式

[直接引語] She said, "Jerome gave me a ride home." 她說：「傑羅姆送我回家。」

[間接引語] She said that Jerome had given her a ride home. 她說傑羅姆送她回家。

→ 過去式 gave → 過去完成式 had given

5 簡單未來式 → 過去未來式

[直接引語] Ann said, "I'll visit you someday in Japan."
安說：「有一天我會去日本看你。」

[間接引語] Ann said she would visit me someday in Japan.
安說，她有一天會來日本看我。 will → would

4 動詞時態不變化的情況

❶ 如果使用的**轉述動詞**（表示「說……」的動詞）是**簡單現在式**，如：says（說）、states（陳述）、reports（報導），這些動詞後面的間接引語就**不需要改變**原直接引語的**動詞時態**。

[直接引語] Kate often tells me, "You look great." 凱特常對我：「你看起來棒極了。」

[間接引語] Kate often tells me that I look great. 凱特常告訴我，我看起來棒極了。

❷ 直接引語是「**客觀真理**」、「**自然現象**」或「**名言警句**」時，變為間接引語，子句的時態不變化。

[直接引語] My mom said, "Actions speak louder than words."
我媽媽說：「事實勝於雄辯。」

[間接引語] My mom said that actions speak louder than words.
我媽媽說，事實勝於雄辯。

❸ 直接引語中有「**確定的過去時間**」（in 2002, two years ago 等）時，子句的時態不變化。

[直接引語] She asked, "Were you in New York in 2012?"
她問我：「你 2012 年的時候在紐約嗎？」

[間接引語] She asked me whether I was in New York in 2012.
她問我，我 2012 年的時候是否在紐約。

❹ 直接引語中「所談論的動作或狀態**仍在繼續**」時，子句的時態不變化。

[直接引語] Kay said, "I am sick today."
凱說：「我今天生病了。」

[間接引語] Kay said she is sick today.
凱說她今天生病了。

➜ 轉述時，時間仍然在今天，
「生病」的狀態仍在繼續。

---

5 ── say, said 與 tell, told 比較 ──────

| tell
told | + | somebody（受格代名詞或名詞） | + | that 受詞子句 |

| say to
said to | + | somebody（受格代名詞或名詞） | + | that 受詞子句 |

| say
said | + | that 受詞子句 |

- Ann said (that) she would soon go to Japan.
  安說，她很快就要去日本了。

- Ann told me that she would soon go to Japan.
  安告訴我，她很快就要去日本了。

- Ann said to me that Mr. King was a hardworking man.
  安對我說，金先生工作勤奮。
  Ann told me that Mr. King was a hardworking man.
  安告訴我，金先生工作勤奮。

➜ 「said to somebody + that 子句 /told somebody + that 子句」
結構中，常保留 that。

1 把下面的直接引語改成間接引語。

1 "I'm paid once a week," explained the maid.

_____

2 Kate said, "We will come home late."

_____

3 He said, "Kay enjoys daydreaming about her wedding."

_____

4 Mat said, "I can't find my hat."

_____

5 I asked, "Trish, do you like English?"

_____

6 Smiling happily, she said, "I'm going to have a baby in May."

_____

7 Lily said to me, "I don't like turkey."

_____

8 He asked, "Kay, when are you going to open up your new coffee and sandwich cafe?"

_____

2 看圖並用 **say, said** 或 **tell, told** 填空，完成下列對話。

Jim is not good at studying.

June and her brother Mike are going to visit Libya soon.

Billy is good at juggling.

Dwight may be late for the party.

1 [Judy] What did Kim _____ about Jim?

[Pete] She _____ me that he was not good at studying.

2 [Judy] What did Lily _____ you about Billy?

[Pete] She _____ that he was good at juggling.

3 [Judy] What did June _____ in her text message?

[Pete] She _____ that she and her brother Mike were going to visit Libya soon.

4 [Judy] What did Dwight _____ to you this morning?

[Pete] He _____ he might be late for the party on Saturday night.

---

3 更正錯誤。（有些句子可能會有一個以上的錯誤。）

1 Did Paul say you that he might call me?

_____

2 She asked did I like to play farm games on Facebook.

_____

3 Jill said she will write a song about Hong Kong.

_____

4 Nan asked me when was I going to Pakistan.

_____

5 [Mary] Bob quit his job yesterday.

[Pete] Really? I saw Bob last week, and he told that he is enjoying his job.

_____

_____

Chapter

82 被動語態的用法

---

1 ── 主動語態和被動語態

英語有兩個語態：主動（active）和被動（passive）。**主動語態**表明「主詞做某事」，即，主詞是動詞的執行者，而**被動語態**表明「主詞是動作的承受者」。

當「**動作的執行者未知或不重要**」時，常用**被動語態**。在被動語態中，如果想表明誰是動作的執行者時，需要用介系詞 **by**。

主動語態 • Australians speak English. 澳洲人講英文。 ➜ 主動語態強調動作的執行者。
　　　　　行為者　　　　　　承受者

被動語態 • English is spoken by Australians. ➜ 被動語態強調動作的承受者。
　　　　　承受者　　　　　　　行為者

被動語態 • English is spoken in Australia. ➜ 動作的執行者「未知或不重要」時，
　　　　　承受者　　　　　　　　　　　常用被動語態。

主動語態 • Has Lenore painted the door? 蕾諾兒已經漆過門了嗎？

被動語態 • Has the door been painted (by Lenore)?
門已經漆過了嗎？／門是蕾諾兒漆的嗎？

➜ 在被動語態句子中，動詞的執行者（Lenore）可以被提及，也可以省略。

---

2 ── 被動語態的句型

| 助動詞 be | + | 過去分詞 | ➜ | 助動詞 be 包括 is, am, are, was, were, will be, has been, have been 等。 |

時態	主詞	be（單／複數）	過去分詞
簡單現在式	1. The robotic soldier/soldiers	is/are	destroyed.
情態動詞 (can, should 等)	2. The robotic soldier/soldiers	can be/can be	destroyed.
	3. The robotic soldier/soldiers	should be/should be	destroyed.
簡單過去式	4. The robotic soldier/soldiers	was/were	destroyed.
現在進行式	5. The robotic soldier/soldiers	is being/are being	destroyed.
過去進行式	6. The robotic soldier/soldiers	was being/were being	destroyed.
簡單現在完成式	7. The robotic soldier/soldiers	has been/have been	destroyed.
簡單未來式	8. The robotic soldier/soldiers	will be/will be	destroyed.

1. 機器人戰士被消滅了。　　4. 機器人戰士被消滅了。　　7. 機器人戰士已經被消滅。
2. 機器人戰士能夠被消滅了。　5. 機器人戰士正在被消滅。　　8. 機器人戰士將被消滅。
3. 機器人戰士應該被消滅。　　6. 機器人戰士那時正在被消滅。

- I am seldom invited to parties. 我很少被邀請參加聚會。→簡單現在式

- I was not invited to Mark's birthday party last week.
  我上星期並未受邀參加馬克的生日派對。→簡單過去式

- Pam is being questioned about cheating on the exam.
  潘姆因考試作弊正在受到訊問。→現在進行式

- At eleven last night, Kate was being scolded for coming back home too late.
  昨晚 11 點時，凱特因回家太晚被責罵。→過去進行式

- I'm not going to the welcome-home party for Pam. I haven't been invited.
  我不會去參加潘姆的接風派對。我並沒有受到邀請。→ 簡單現在完成式

- Will a cherry pie be made for Jill and Bill? 會給潔兒和比爾做一個櫻桃派嗎？→簡單未來式

- Is this old house going to be sold? 這棟舊房子要被賣掉嗎？→ be going to 未來式

- Traffic laws should be followed to avoid accidents. 應遵守交通規則，以防範事故發生。
  → 情態動詞的被動語態由「情態動詞 + be + 過去分詞」構成。

- Your assignment needs to be finished before our next class.
  你的報告要在下堂課開始之前完成。→ 不定詞的被動結構由「to + be + 過去分詞」構成。

- Our teacher made us read fourteen short storybooks in English this week. → 主動
  = We were made to read fourteen short storybooks in English this week. → 被動
  我們老師要我們這星期讀 14 本短篇的英文故事書。→ 使役動詞變被動語態時，要用不定詞 to。

---

3 | **主動語態不能改成被動語態的情況**

❶ 只有「表示**動作**的及物動詞」可以被改成被動結構，而**「不及物動詞」沒有被動形式。**

　　☒ This fish is tasted really delicious.

　　☑ This fish tastes really delicious. 這魚嚐起來真好吃。
　　　　　　└→ tastes 在這個句子裡是不及物動詞，沒有被動形式。

❷ 表示「**狀態**」的及物動詞，例如 have（擁有）、own（擁有）、last（使得以維持下去）
等，不能用於被動語態。

- Our community has a big swimming pool. 我們的社區有一個大泳池。

- My sister Mary owns a five-star hotel on the beach in Florida.
  我妹妹瑪麗擁有一家五星級的飯店，開在佛羅里達州的海邊。

❸ 「反身代名詞」或「相互代名詞」作受詞時，不能用於被動語態。

- Please enjoy yourself at the party. 請好好享受這個派對。

- You should help each other to learn English. 你們應該互相幫助彼此學習英語。

- **Kevin** was born **in London on April 18, 2011.**
  凱文於 2011 年 4 月 18 日生於倫敦。

- **In America, you** are supposed **to call before you visit a friend.**
  在美國，你去拜訪朋友之前應該先打個電話。

- **Our cottage** is situated/located **on a beautiful lake.**
  我們的別墅座落在一個美麗的湖濱上。

- **What** is **love** made of? 愛情是由什麼構成的？

PRACTICE

1 更正錯誤。

1 When was invented the printing press?

2 Dan is greatly influenced from his hardworking girlfriend Ann.

3 She supposes to go with me to a conference in Hawaii.

4 Where is she born?

5 "English teaches in almost every school in the world," said Trish.

6 Emma knows that her loan has paid off by her grandma.

7 The telephone has been invented by Alexander Bell in 1876.

8 This room messed up by Lily, not me.

2 用括弧裡的詞彙補全句子。

1. "Where's your electric motor scooter, Lily?"
   "It _____ at the garage." (repair)
2. "How old is your house?" "It _____ sixty years ago. (build)
3. Kay's taking a vacation next week, and her coffee and sandwich shop _____ for six days. (close)
4. Kay said, "Supper _____ at 5 p.m. every day." (serve)
5. Ann said her robotic doll _____ in Japan. (make)
6. At the moment he _____ for a college position to teach both Chinese and Japanese. (interview)
7. My cellphone was broken yesterday, but it's OK now.
   It _____. (repair)
8. "What _____ for?" inquired Lenore. (solar cells/use)
9. What _____ to bring to the party? (we/suppose)
10. _____ to park here? (we/allow)

3 把下面的句子改成被動語態。

1. A loud noise woke up the boys.

   _____

2. The Amana Corporation introduced the first personal microwave in 1967.

   _____

3. Somebody told Kate what had happened to her alcoholic classmate.

   _____

4. The plane crash killed twenty people.

   _____

5. I can't find my wallet anywhere. I think somebody has stolen it.

   _____

動詞第三人稱單數形式的構成

〔參見 Chapter 28 簡單現在式：肯定句的用法。〕

▇1 構成方法

☆ 動詞原形後面直接加 -s：

drink → drinks（喝）　　　take → takes（拿取）　　　walk → walks（走）
eat → eats（吃）　　　say → says（說）

☆ 以 -s, -sh, -ch, -x, -o 結尾的動詞，加 -es：

pass → passes（經過）　　teach → teaches（教導）　　do → does（做）
push → pushes（推）　　　fix → fixes（修理）

☆ 以子音字母 + y 結尾的動詞，先變 y 為 i，再加 -ies：

copy → copies（拷貝）　　hurry → hurries（趕快）
fly → flies（飛）　　　　marry → marries（結婚）

▇2 -s/-es 的的讀音規則

☆ -s 接在無聲子音（除 [t] 以外）之後，要讀 [s]：

help → helps [s]　　work → works [s]

☆ -s 接在母音或有聲子音（除 [d] 以外）之後，要讀 [z]：

play → plays [z]　　feel → feels [z]

☆ -s 接在 [t]、[d] 之後時，與 [t]、[d] 連起來讀成 [ts]、[dz]：

want → wants [ts]　　stand → stands [dz]

☆ 以子音字母 + y 結尾的動詞，先變 y 為 i，再加 -es，此時 -es 讀成 [z]：

cry → cries [z]worry → worries [z]

☆ 以 -s, -x, -ch, -sh, -o 結尾的動詞，加 -es，-es 讀 [ɪz]：

miss → misses [ɪz]　　fetch → fetches [ɪz]　　　go → goes [ɪz]
mix → mixes [ɪz]　　　finish → finishes [ɪz]

規則動詞過去式和過去分詞的構成

參見 Chapter 35 簡單過去式,以及 Chapter 37 簡單現在完成式。

1 構成方法

☆ 一般由原形動詞直接加 **-ed**:

accept → accepted → accepted　　　help → helped → helped
happen → happened → happened

☆ 以 **-e** 結尾的動詞加 **-d**:

blame → blamed → blamed　　　hate → hated → hated
confuse → confused → confused

☆ 以子音字母 + **y** 結尾的動詞,先變 y 為 i,再加 **-ed**:

apply → applied → applied　　　reply → replied → replied
copy → copied → copied　　　study → studied → studied

☆ 以一個子音字母結尾的重讀閉音節,先雙寫該子音字母,再加 **-ed**:

grab → grabbed → grabbed stop → stopped → stopped
nod → nodded → nodded　　　prefer → preferred → preferred

☆ 少數以 **-l** 結尾的動詞,在英式英語中需要雙寫 l,再加 **-ed**,但在美式英語中則不要雙寫。如:**travelled**(英式)→ **traveled**(美式)

2 **-ed** 的讀音規則

☆ **-ed** 接在無聲子音(除 [t] 以外)之後,要讀 [t]:

looked [t]　　　helped [t]

☆ **-ed** 接在母音或有聲子音(除 [d] 以外)之後,要讀 [d]:

played [d]　　　changed [d]

☆ **-ed** 接在發音為 [d]、[t] 之後,要讀成 [ɪd]:

decided [ɪd]　　　waited [ɪd]

3 現在分詞的拼寫規則 〔參見 Chapter 30 現在進行式：肯定句的用法。〕

1 大多數原形動詞 + -ing = 現在分詞

cook → cooking 做飯	sing → singing 唱歌	talk → talking 談話
look → looking 看	sleep → sleeping 睡覺	throw → throwing 扔；投
play → playing 玩耍	speak → speaking 講話	wait → waiting 等待
read → reading 閱讀	study → studying 學習	watch → watching 觀看

2 字尾 -e 的動詞，去掉 -e 後，再加 -ing。

arrive → arriving 到達	make → making 製造	take → taking 拿；取
come → coming 來	move → moving 移動	write → writing 寫
dive → diving 跳水	rise → rising 上升	
drive → driving 駕駛	smile → smiling 微笑	

3 字尾 -ie 的動詞，先把 -ie 變成 y，再加 -ing。

lie → lying 躺
die → dying 死

4 以「一個母音 + 一個子音」結尾的單音節動詞，先重複字尾子音，再加 -ing。

☆ 只要具有下列所有條件的動詞，就要重複字尾子音：

ⓐ 短音動詞。
ⓑ 單音節的動詞。
ⓒ 以 b、d、g、m、n、p、r、t 這些子音字母結尾的動詞。
ⓓ 在子音前面只有一個母音（a、e、i、o、u）。

cut → cutting 切；割	run → running 跑	swim → swimming 游泳
get → getting 變成；成為	shop → shopping 購物；逛街	tap → tapping 輕拍
jog → jogging 慢跑	stop → stopping 停止	
nod → nodding 點頭	sit → sitting 坐	

★ 如果字尾的子音前面有兩個母音，就不要重複字尾子音：

sleep → sleeping 睡覺

wait → waiting 等待

★ 如果字尾是連續兩個子音字母，就不要重複最後一個子音：

want → wanting 想要

help → helping 幫助

5 以「一個母音 + 一個子音」結尾的雙音節動詞，如果重音在最後一個
音節，則要重複字尾的子音，然後再加 **-ing**。

begin → beginning
[bɪˋgɪn]　　[bɪˋgɪnɪŋ]

→ begin 有兩個音節，並以「一個母音 + 一個子音」結尾，
重音在最後一個音節上，因此重複子音 n。

happen → happening
[ˋhæpən]　　[ˋhæpənɪŋ]

→ happen 也有兩個音節，也是以「一個母音 + 一個子音」結尾，
但重音在第一個音節上，因此最後一個音節的子音 n 不重複。

不規則動詞表 〔參見 Chapters 34, 35, 37〕

❶ 以下字序由左至右為：原形 → 過去式 → 過去分詞
❷ 藍色字表示三態同型。
❸ 具有兩種變化型且表不同意義者，以編號標示。

原形	過去式	過去分詞	中文
am (be)	→ was	→ been	be 動詞 am
are (be)	→ were	→ been	be 動詞 are
awake	→ awaked/awoke	→ awoken/awaked	喚醒；醒來
beat	→ beat	→ beaten	打；擊
become	→ became	→ become	變成；成為
begin	→ began	→ begun	開始
bend	→ bent	→ bent	彎曲；轉彎
bite	→ bit	→ bitten	咬；啃
bleed	→ bled	→ bled	流血
blow	→ blew	→ blown	吹；刮
break	→ broke	→ broken	打破；折斷
bring	→ brought	→ brought	帶來；拿來
build	→ built	→ built	建築；建造
burn	→ burned/burnt	→ burned/burnt	燃燒；著火
buy	→ bought	→ bought	買
catch	→ caught	→ caught	接住；抓住
choose	→ chose	→ chosen	選擇；挑選
come	→ came	→ come	來
cost	→ cost	→ cost	花費
cut	→ cut	→ cut	切；割
deal	→ dealt	→ dealt	處理；對付
dig	→ dug	→ dug	掘（土）；挖（洞）
dive	→ dived	→ dived	潛水（美式英語過去式可用 dove）
do	→ did	→ done	做
draw	→ drew	→ drawn	畫
dream	→ dreamed/dreamt	→ dreamed/dreamt	做夢
drink	→ drank	→ drunk	飲；喝
drive	→ drove	→ driven	駕駛（汽車等）
eat	→ ate	→ eaten	吃；喝
fall	→ fell	→ fallen	落下；降落
feed	→ fed	→ fed	餵養；飼養
feel	→ felt	→ felt	摸；觸；感覺
fight	→ fought	→ fought	打架

find	→ found	→ found	找到
fly	→ flew	→ flown	飛
forget	→ forgot	→ forgotten	忘記
forgive	→ forgave	→ forgiven	原諒
freeze	→ froze	→ frozen	結冰
get	→ got	→ gotten/got	獲得（美式英語中，過去分詞用 gotten，英式英語用 got）
give	→ gave	→ given	給
go	→ went	→ gone	走
grow	→ grew	→ grown	成長
hang	① → hanged	→ hanged	絞死；吊死
	② → hung	→ hung	懸掛
have (has)	→ had	→ had	擁有
hear	→ heard	→ heard	聽見
hide	→ hid	→ hidden	隱藏
hit	→ hit	→ hit	打擊
hold	→ held	→ held	握著
hurt	→ hurt	→ hurt	使受傷
is (be)	→ was	→ been	是（第三人稱單數現在式）
keep	→ kept	→ kept	持有；保有
kneel	→ knelt	→ knelt	跪著（美式英語中，過去式和過去分詞也可用 kneeled）
know	→ knew	→ known	知道
lay	→ laid	→ laid	放；擱
lead	→ led	→ led	引導
leap	→ leaped/leapt	→ leaped/leapt	跳躍
learn	→ learned/learnt	→ learned/learnt	學習（過去式和過去分詞 learnt 主要為英式用法）
leave	→ left	→ left	離開
lend	→ lent	→ lent	借給
let	→ let	→ let	允許；讓
lie	→ lay	→ lain	躺
light	→ lit/lighted	→ lit/lighted	照亮
lose	→ lost	→ lost	丟失
make	→ made	→ made	製造
mean	→ meant	→ meant	意指；意味
meet	→ met	→ met	遇見；碰上
mistake	→ mistook	→ mistaken	弄錯；誤解
misunderstand	→ misunderstood	→ misunderstood	誤會；曲解

output	→ output	→ output	生產；輸出
overcome	→ overcame	→ overcome	戰勝；克服
overeat	→ overate	→ overeaten	吃得過飽
overhear	→ overheard	→ overheard	無意中聽到
oversleep	→ overslept	→ overslept	睡過頭
overthrow	→ overthrew	→ overthrown	打倒；推翻
pay	→ paid	→ paid	支付
proofread	→ proofread	→ proofread	校對
prove	→ proved	→ proved/proven	證明（proven 主要為美式用法）
put	→ put	→ put	放
quit	→ quit	→ quit	離開；放棄；辭職（英式用法：quit/quitted → quit/quitted）
read	→ read	→ read	閱讀
rebuild	→ rebuilt	→ rebuilt	重建
redo	→ redid	→ redone	再做；改裝
retell	→ retold	→ retold	再講；重述
rethink	→ rethought	→ rethought	重新考慮
rewrite	→ rewrote	→ rewritten	重寫
ride	→ rode	→ ridden	乘坐
ring	→ rang	→ rung	成環形；包圍
rise	→ rose	→ risen	上升
run	→ ran	→ run	跑
say	→ said	→ said	說
see	→ saw	→ seen	看見
seek	→ sought	→ sought	尋找
sell	→ sold	→ sold	銷售
send	→ sent	→ sent	發送
set	→ set	→ set	放置
shake	→ shook	→ shaken	搖動
shine	→ shone	→ shone	發光、出眾（規則動詞 shine → shined → shined，意思是「擦亮」）
shoot	→ shot	→ shot	發射
show	→ showed	→ shown	顯示
shrink	→ shrank/shrunk	→ shrunk/shrunken	收縮
shut	→ shut	→ shut	關上
sing	→ sang	→ sung	唱
sink	→ sank	→ sunk	下沉
sit	→ sat	→ sat	坐
sleep	→ slept	→ slept	睡覺

smell	→ smelled/smelt	→ smelled/smelt	嗅;聞(過去式和過去分詞 smelt 主要為英式用法)
sow	→ sowed	→ sowed/sown	播種
speak	→ spoke	→ spoken	說話
speed	→ speeded/sped	→ speeded/sped	迅速前進
spell	→ spelled/spelt	→ spelled/spelt	拼字
spend	→ spent	→ spent	花錢;花時間、精力
spill	→ spilled/spilt	→ spilled/spilt	溢出(過去式和過去分詞 spilt 主要為英式用法)
spoil	→ spoiled/spoilt	→ spoiled/spoilt	寵壞(過去式和過去分詞 spoilt 主要為英式用法)
spread	→ spread	→ spread	使伸展
stand	→ stood	→ stood	站立
steal	→ stole	→ stolen	竊取
stink	→ stank/stunk	→ stunk	發惡臭
strike	→ struck	→ struck/stricken	攻擊(美式用法中過去分詞也用 stricken)
swear	→ swore	→ sworn	發誓
sweat	→ sweat/sweated	→ sweat/sweated	出汗
sweep	→ swept	→ swept	清掃
swim	→ swam	→ swum	游泳
take	→ took	→ taken	拿走
teach	→ taught	→ taught	講授
tear	→ tore	→ torn	撕開
tell	→ told	→ told	告訴
think	→ thought	→ thought	思索
throw	→ threw	→ thrown	投;擲
undergo	→ underwent	→ undergone	經歷
understand	→ understood	→ understood	理解
undertake	→ undertook	→ undertaken	從事
undo	→ undid	→ undone	解開;取消;破壞
upset	→ upset	→ upset	弄翻;使心煩意亂
wake	→ woke	→ woken	醒來
wear	→ wore	→ worn	穿著
weep	→ wept	→ wept	哭泣
wet	→ wet/wetted	→ wet/wetted	淋濕
win	→ won	→ won	獲勝
withdraw	→ withdrew	→ withdrawn	收回;取消
write	→ wrote	→ written	寫

1 數詞可分為基數和序數。基數詞是用來計數或表示「多少」的數詞。

one	1	a/one hundred and one	101
two	2	a/one hundred and two	102
three	3	a/one hundred and fifty	150
four	4	two hundred	200
five	5	two hundred and twenty	220
six	6	three hundred	300
seven	7	a/one thousand	1,000
eight	8	four thousand and ten	4,010
nine	9	five thousand	5,000
ten	10	five thousand and thirty	5,030
eleven	11	a/one million	1,000,000
twelve	12	two million four hundred thousand	2,400,000

☆ **and** 放在最小單位或十位數字的前面：

→ 表示千位數以上的數字：不管數字有多大，只有百位數與十位數之間加 and；若十位數是零，則百位與個位之間加 and；若百位數是零，則在千位後面加 and。

thirteen	13
fourteen	14
fifteen	15
sixteen	16
seventeen	17
eighteen	18
nineteen	19
twenty	20

102 → a/one hundred and two → and + 個位數

412 → four hundred and twelve → and + 十位數

5,279 → five thousand two hundred and seventy-nine
→ 百位數和十位數之間加 and。

3,088 → three thousand and eighty-eight
→ 百位數是零，在千位數後面加 and。

thirty	30
forty	40
fifty	50
sixty	60
seventy	70
eighty	80
ninety	90
a/one hundred	100

☆ **hundred, thousand, million** 等後面不加 -s：

500 → five hundred (Not: five hundreds)
6,000 → six thousand (Not: six thousands)

→ 但可以說：hundreds of . . . （數百……）
thousands of . . . （數千……）

→ 表示幾十幾（20 以上的十位數）時，在十位數和個位數之間加連字號號，如：

· twenty-one
· sixty-nine

☆ 年份的說法： 1852 → eighteen fifty-two
1995 → nineteen ninety-five
2011 → two thousand eleven
= twenty eleven

☆ 表示「在……世紀……年代」，用「in + the + 年代 s/'s」。

in the 1990s = in the 1990's (in the nineteen nineties) 20 世紀 90 年代
Did Tom live in New Zealand in the 1980s/1980's？
湯姆一九八〇年代的時候住在紐西蘭？

☆ 年齡的說法：

① 表示年齡時，常用「**at the age of + 基數詞**」。

He was a smoker and died of lung cancer at the age of 46. 他抽菸，46 就死於肺癌。

② 表示某人幾十歲時用複數 → in her thirties 在她三十幾歲時

☆ 電話號碼的說法： 87390116 → eight seven three nine zero one one six

2 基數詞表示編號。

☆ 用「名詞 + 基數詞」表示：名詞和基數詞都要大寫，但基數詞也可用阿拉伯數字表示（比如：**Chapter Three/Chapter 3, Book 2/Book Two**）。

Room 108	Class Two	page 40	Gate 2	Building 5
Volume Six	Platform 3	Lesson One	Exercise 9	Flight 876

☆ 名詞 **line, note, page, paragraph, size, verse** 不大寫，如：**paragraph 5**。

3 序數詞是用來表示順序的詞。

first	第一	ninth	第九	seventeenth	第十七	seventieth	第七十
second	第二	tenth	第十	eighteenth	第十八	eightieth	第八十
third	第三	eleventh	第十一	nineteenth	第十九	ninetieth	第九十
fourth	第四	twelfth	第十二	twentieth	第二十	hundredth	第一百
fifth	第五	thirteenth	第十三	thirtieth	第三十	three hundredth	第三百
sixth	第六	fourteenth	第十四	fortieth	第四十		
seventh	第七	fifteenth	第十五	fiftieth	第五十		
eighth	第八	sixteenth	第十六	sixtieth	第六十		

☆ 表示「第幾十幾」（21－99）時，只需將「個位數」改為「序數詞」，在十位數和個位數之間用連字號號。

第 32 → thirty-second　　　　第 141 → one hundred and forty-first

☆ 序數詞表示「順序」時，通常要與「定冠詞」（**the**）連用。

the second picture 第二幅畫　the first lesson 第一課　the fifth exercise 第五題練習題
My office is on the second floor. 我的辦公室在二樓。

☆ 序數詞前有所有格代名詞或名詞所有格時，序數詞前不用冠詞。

my twentieth birthday →我的二十歲生日　　Mary's second child →瑪麗的第二個孩子

☆ 比較基數和序數的用法：

Sue knew that jet fighters were developed during the Second World War.
= Sue knew that jet fighters were developed during World War Two.
蘇知道噴射戰鬥機是在第二次世界大戰期間發明的。

Jane Vine is an eager ninth grade cheerleader.= Jane Vine is an eager cheerleader in Grade Nine. 簡·魏是九年級一位熱情洋溢的啦啦隊隊長。

Amy, please turn your book to page 25, and read the second paragraph.
艾咪，請把書翻到 25 頁，然後朗讀第二段落。→ 表示編號時，基數詞與序數詞可以綜合應用。

1 時間的讀法

☆ 美式和英式英語之間讀時刻的區別：

🕐 美式先讀小時，後讀分鐘。(英式現在也採用這種讀法了。)

🕐 英式先讀分鐘，後讀小時，中間加介詞，在三十分鐘以內用「分鐘 +past+ 小時」，
超過 30 分鐘時用「分鐘 +to+ 下一小時」。

① **It's 8:30 a.m.** 現在是早上 8 點半。

> 美式／英式讀法 **It's eight-thirty a.m.**
>
> 英式讀法為主 **It's half past eight in the morning.**

→ 注意：在書面用語中，a.m. 和 p.m. 前面一定要用數字（8:30），
不能寫成「eight-thirty a.m.」。

② **It's 6:15 p.m.** 現在是晚上 6 點 15 分。

> 美式／英式讀法 **It's six-fifteen p.m.**
>
> 英式讀法為主 **It's a quarter past six in the evening.**

③ **It's 7:40.** 現在是 7 點 40 分。

> 美式／英式讀法 **It's seven-forty.**
>
> 英式讀法為主 **It's twenty to eight.**

④ **It's 9:30.** 現在是 9 點 30 分。

> 美式／英式讀法 **It's nine-thirty.**
>
> 英式讀法為主 **It's half past nine.**

2 o'clock 的用法

☆ 英式英語談論「整點」時，喜歡用 o'clock 這個字，如：

four o'clock in the morning 凌晨四點鐘　　seven o'clock in the morning 早上七點鐘
4 o'clock in the afternoon 下午四點鐘　　7 o'clock in the evening 晚上七點鐘

→ 使用數字（2, 3, 4 等）是為了強調；拼寫出英文數字（two, three, four 等）是慣用法。

☆ 美式英語不常用 o'clock，而喜歡簡單說 a.m. 或 p.m.。如果從上下文可以清楚
知道是在講上午還是下午，那麼美國人連 a.m. 和 p.m. 都會省略，只說數字。

① **It's 11 a.m.** 現在是早上 11 點。

> 美式／英式讀法 **It's eleven a.m.**
>
> 英式讀法為主 **It's eleven o'clock in the morning.**

② **Clive asked, "June, is it noon?"** 克萊夫問：「茱恩，現在是正中午嗎？」
June replied, "No, Clive, it's 11:55." 茱恩回答：「不是，克萊夫。現在是 11 點 55 分。」

> 美式／英式讀法 **"No, Clive, it's eleven fifty-five."**
>
> 英式讀法為主 **"No, Clive, it's five to twelve."**

3 「a.m.」、「p.m.」和「o'clock」的用法

☆ 「a.m.」和「p.m.」不能跟「o'clock」連用。

three o'clock 三點鐘
3 a.m. 凌晨三點
three o'clock in the morning 凌晨三點
→ 不能寫成 3 a.m. o'clock

ten o'clock 十點鐘
10 p.m. 晚上十點
ten o'clock at night 晚上十點
→ 不能寫成 10 p.m. o'clock

☆ o'clock 只和「整點」連用。閱讀或寫作時，不要讀或寫成 nine-thirty o'clock、
ten-twenty o'clock 等，應該使用下列正確的形式：

① 非整點（書面寫法）：8:30　書面/口語　eight-thirty
　　　　　　　　　　　　　書面/口語　half past eight

② 整點（書面寫法）：2:00　書面　2 o'clock　→ 使用數字（2, 3……）是為了強調。
　　　　　　　　　　　書面/口語　two o'clock　→ 拼寫出英文數字（two, three . . .）是慣用法。

☆ a.m. 和 p.m. 不能和表示時間的片語（in the morning、in the afternoon、
in the evening 和 at night 等）連用。

at 11 p.m. = at eleven at night
晚上十一點 → 不能寫成 at 11 p.m. at night

at 10:30 a.m. = at ten-thirty in the morning
早上十點半 → 不能寫成 at 10:30 a.m. in the morning

☆ 在書寫的時候，a.m. 和 p.m. 前面要用數字，不用英文拼寫；如果遇到整點（九點整、
十點整）的情況，不需要把零寫出來（如：3 p.m.）。

2:55 a.m. 凌晨 2 點 55 分 → 不能寫成 two fifty-five a.m.
7:35 p.m. 晚上 7 點 35 分 → 不能寫成 seven thirty-five p.m.
9:20 a.m. 早上 9 點 20 分 → 不能寫成 nine-twenty a.m.

2 a.m. 凌晨 2 點 → 不能寫成 two a.m.
7 p.m. 晚上 7 點 → 不能寫成 seven p.m.
9 a.m. 早上 9 點 → 不能寫成 nine a.m.

☆ 如果沒有提到 a.m.、p.m. 或 o'clock，就要把時間的數字全部用英文字拼寫出來（five,
five-thirty），或者把所有的數字（包括零）寫出來（5:00, 5:30）。用連字號連接小
時和分鐘，例如：nine-thirty（九點三十分）。但如果分鐘之間已經有了連字號，就
不用連字號連接小時和分鐘，例如：nine twenty-five（九點二十五分）。

arrive at ten　　　　　　　= arrive at 10:00　　十點到達
arrive at ten-thirty　　　　= arrive at 10:30　　十點半到達
leave at ten fifty-two　　　= leave at 10:52　　十點五十二分離開
leave at two forty-five　　　= leave at 2:45　　兩點四十五分離開

Clive said, "My shoe store is always open
until 5:00."
→ 如果省略了 a.m. 或 p.m.，整點後面用數字
時，就需要把零寫出來（5:00, 8:00）。

= Clive said, "My shoe store is always open
until five."
→ 如果省略了 a.m. 或 p.m.，整點後面用數字時，
也可以用英文字拼寫出來（five, eight）。

= Clive said, "My shoe store is always open
until 5 p.m."
→ 如果有 a.m. 或 p.m.，整點後面常省略零（5
p.m., 8 a.m.）。

克萊夫說：「我的鞋店一直都是開到五點。」

Unit 1 名詞和冠詞

Chapter 1

❶

1. sheep
2. copies
3. birthdays
4. leaves
5. heroes
6. videos
7. dresses
8. brushes
9. children
10. churches
11. boxes
12. buses
13. zoos
14. goldfish
15. pianos

❷

2. Lori's mom told us two Christmas stories.
3. Your children are in my house./
   Your child is in my house.
4. She has three wishes.
5. Grandpa has two bad teeth.
6. There are a lot of fish in the pond.
7. Where are my blue pajamas?

❸

1. teeth
2. foxes, boxes
3. boys, toys
4. lives
5. potatoes, tomatoes
6. yo-yos, pianos

❹

1. (babies) baby
2. (bodies) body
3. (children) child
4. (copies) copy
5. (dresses) dress
6. (foxes) fox
7. (heroes) hero
8. (knives) knife
9. (leaves) leaf
10. (libraries) library
11. (oxen) ox
12. (pianos) piano
13. (potatoes) potato
14. (quizzes) quiz
15. (radios) radio
16. (thieves) thief
17. (tomatoes) tomato
18. (videos) video
19. (wishes) wish
20. (wives) wife
21. (women) woman

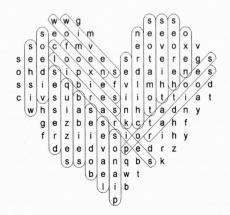

Chapter 2

❶

1. an (engineer)
2. a (businessperson)
3. an (editor)
4. a (singer)
5. a (doctor)
6. an (artist)
7. a (firefighter)
8. a (waiter)
9. an (actress)
10. a (ballet dancer)

❷

1. a	6. a	11. an	16. an
2. a	7. a	12. a	17. a
3. an	8. an	13. an	18. an
4. a	9. an	14. an	19. an
5. an	10. an	15. an	20. an

❸ 1. an   2. an   3. a   4. a   5. a   6. an

❹

1. one passenger
2. a cup
3. An FBI
4. a university
5. an hour
6. an Egyptian
7. an X-ray, a one-horned
8. a bookstore

❺

2. Her mom is an engineer.
3. I'd like to play a computer game.
4. Jenny never wears a bikini.
5. They live in an old house.
6. He works at a university.

Chapter 3

❶

1. snow
2. a tie
3. bread
4. a table
5. a student
6. milk

❷

1. ✓
2. × ("Would you like a glass of apple juice?" asked Mike./"Would you like some apple juice?" asked Mike.)
3. × (Lily, your hair looks lovely.)
4. ✓
5. × ("Does Mom have a lot of butter?" asked Tom.)
6. × (Knowledge is power. — Sir Francis Bacon)
7. ✓
8. × (Time flies when we're having fun under the sun!)
9. × ("Are there any students absent today?" asked Kay.)
10. × (My parents are going to visit Norway in May.)
11. × (Mort saw heavy traffic near the airport.)

❸

1. is	4. is	7. is a	10. is an
2. is a	5. is a	8. are	
3. are	6. are	9. is	

Chapter 4

❶ 1. a, the 2. a, the 3. an, the 4. an, the

❷

1. a) the picture	b) a picture
2. a) the sofa	b) a sofa
3. a) a shower	b) the shower
4. a) a dog	b) the dog
5. a) a gate	b) the gate
6. a) the ocean	b) an ocean

❸

1. Margo locked **the** door and closed **the** window.
2. I have to pick up Mort at **the** airport.
3. The BBC report was about the huge new wind farm in **the** North Sea.
4. Mary learned a lot about **the** world in the library.
5. Why do **the** stars twinkle in **the** dark sky?

Chapter 5

❶

1. I like pop music./I don't like pop music.
2. I like soccer./I don't like soccer.
3. I like golf./I don't like golf.
4. I like computer games./
   I don't like computer games.
5. I like Japanese food./
   I don't like Japanese food.
6. I like fast-food restaurants./
   I don't like fast-food restaurants.
7. I like ice cream./I don't like ice cream.
8. I like pears./I don't like pears.

❷

1. a) carrots	b) the carrots
2. a) French toast	b) the French toast
3. a) The children	b) children
4. a) the salt	b) salt
5. a) The bread	b) bread
6. a) Pandas	b) The pandas
7. a) the country	b) a country
8. a) rain	b) the rain
9. a) the city	b) a city
10. a) people	b) the people/those people

11. a) the（the sea 泛指所有的大海）
    b) a/the（a wild sea 用於泛指。當 sea 前面有形容詞時，可用 a；the wild sea 是特指。）

Chapter 6

❶

1. /, /, /	4. the	7. the	10. /, /
2. the, /, /	5. the	8. /, the	11. /
3. /	6. /, /	9. /	12. /, /

❷

1. the guitar	6. the movie theater
2. home	7. the eleventh
3. the police	8. TV
4. breakfast, the morning	9. prison
5. midnight	10. bed

Chapter 7

❶ 1. f 2. c 3. a 4. b 5. e 6. d

❷ 1. d 2. f 3. a 4. c 5. b 6. e

❸

1. Africa, North America
2. Germany, the Netherlands
3. Dubai, Tokyo
4. the Atlantic, the Indian Ocean
5. the Arabian Sea, the Mediterranean
6. the Mississippi, the Rhine
7. the British Museum, the National Gallery
8. the Hilton, the Holiday Inn
9. Mount Everest, the Himalayas
10. the Gobi Desert, the Sahara

❹

1. /	4. the	7. the
2. /, /, /	5. /	8. /
3. The, the, /	6. the	

Chapter 8

❶

1. women's magazines
2. my grandma's glasses/
   my grandmother's glasses
3. Liz's computer
4. Doris's school
5. the rabbit's head
6. the top of her head
7. my parents' house
8. the farmer's wife
9. my math teacher's name
10. the name of my hometown

2

1. the boss's
2. children's
3. the women's
4. the Coxes'
5. Peter's
6. Jane's birthday party
7. the end of the street

3

1. another person's
2. aunt's love stories
3. Dawn Knox's two cats
4. Joy's pocket
5. bird's cage
6. Jane's toys
7. Sherlock Holmes's hat
8. Mona's trunk

Unit 2 數量形容詞

Chapter 9

1 1. d　2. a　3. e　4. c　5. b

2

1. There's no good news about our nation's economy.
2. There aren't any hangers in the closet.
3. There's no evidence to prove she was involved in the crime.
4. She hasn't put any money in the bank.

3

1. some
2. some/no
3. any
4. any
5. some/no
6. any
7. some
8. some, no
9. some
10. any

4

1. every
2. Every
3. all
4. all
5. Every
6. all

Chapter 10

1

1. a
2. d
3. b
4. d
5. d
6. c
7. a
8. c
9. a
10. c

2

1. a lot of/many
2. too much
3. A few/Some/Several
4. a little
5. many/a lot of
6. enough
7. How many
8. little
9. There are
10. too much

Chapter 11

1

1. Both my brothers are
2. Neither man has
3. Both buses are
4. Neither answer is
5. Both refrigerators are
6. Neither leg is

2 1. c　2. b　3. d　4. a　5. d　6. a　7. d　8. d　9. d

Unit 3 人稱代名詞

Chapter 12

1

1. you/they
2. It
3. She
4. He
5. They
6. It

2

1. It
2. It
3. We/They
4. I
5. She
6. They
7. He
8. You/They

Chapter 13

1 1. my　2. his　3. her　4. its　5. our　6. her, their

2

1. My
2. My
3. Their
4. Their
5. Their
6. your
7. your
8. your

3 1. d　2. c　3. b　4. a　5. e

4

1. a) it's　b) its
2. a) He's　b) His
3. a) her　b) my
4. a) Its　b) his

Chapter 14

1

1. I like her./I don't like her.
2. I like it./I don't like it.
3. I like it./I don't like it.
4. I like them./I don't like them.
5. I like him./I don't like him.
6. I like it./I don't like it.

2 1. me　2. I　3. He　4. us　5. her　6. him

3

1. me, him
2. you, them
3. me
4. my, me, their
5. I
6. him
7. them
8. her
9. We, he, us
10. I, you, me

4

1. I need copies of those pictures of the International Moon Base. Please email them to me. Thank you!

2. Ann doesn't like dogs. She is afraid of them.
3. I want to talk to Gus, but he doesn't want to talk to me.
4. That's my money. Please give it back to me.
5. "Does Bob like his new job?"
   "No, he doesn't like it."

Chapter 15

1 1. his 2. mine 3. ours 4. hers 5. yours

2
1. This apartment is ours.
2. "This new house is mine," said the dog.
3. That backpack is not mine. I left mine at home.
4. This room isn't ours. Ours is 504, not 404.
5. Those cows are hers.
6. Is this coat yours? —No, it isn't mine.

3
1. × (Sue went out for dinner with some friends of hers.)
2. × (It's your problem, not mine.)
3. × (I'm going on a trip to Australia with a friend of mine.)
4. ✓

Unit 4 其他代名詞

Chapter 16

1 1. c 2. e 3. b 4. a 5. d

2
1. This   3. those   5. Those   7. those
2. That   4. This   6. These   8. This

Chapter 17

1 1. ones, ones, ones   2. one, one, one, one

2
1. ones (= dresses)   3. one (= singer)
2. one (= envelope)   4. one (= movie star)

3
1. ✓
2. ✓
3. × (I prefer artificial fur. I never get my wife anything made of real fur.)
4. × ("Would you like to have a sports car?" "No, I don't need one.")

5. × ("Waitress, these cups are not clean." "Oh, sorry! Here are some clean ones.")
6. × (She asked for some more coffee, but there was none left.)

Chapter 18

1
1. ✓
2. × (There is nothing in our fridge./ There isn't anything in our fridge.)
3. × (I don't want to talk to anybody right now.)
4. ✓
5. × (Is everything OK with Kay?)
6. ✓
7. × (She is nowhere to be seen./ She isn't anywhere to be seen.)
8. × (I don't have anything important to do today./
   I have nothing important to do today./
   I have something important to do today.)

2
1. nowhere   3. anywhere
2. everywhere   4. somewhere

3
1. something   3. anything   5. Everything
2. anything   4. nothing   6. something

4
1. somebody   3. Everybody   5. anybody
2. nobody   4. somebody

Chapter 19

1
1. Most people
2. All the students
3. Some of the questions
4 all the people, any of these people
5. most of the night
6. was
7. most of you
8. All of them

2
1. Most of them.   3. Some of them.
2. All of them.   4. None of them.

3
1. most of   4. all   7. no
2. any of   5. None of   8. Some of
3. Some   6. most of

349

Chapter 20

❶

1. either of
2. several of
3. Neither
4. many
5. Both/Both of
6. Neither of
7. either
8. Many of
9. Several
10. both of

❷

1. Both/Both of
2. Either
3. either of
4. Neither of
5. both of

❸

1. Both of my sisters like reading and motorcycle riding.
2. Both these oranges are bad.
3. Neither of them is coming tomorrow.
4. She doesn't like either of her math teachers.
5. Either of the children is good at playing the piano. = Both of the children are good at playing the piano.
6. Neither of my sisters can dance.
7. Both of us saw it happen.

Chapter 21

❶

1. herself
2. myself
3. themselves
4. ourselves
5. himself
6. yourself
7. yourselves
8. itself

❷ 1. a 2. c 3. b 4. a 5. d 6. c 7. b 8. d

❸

1. ✓
2. × (On the long dinner table is the sign "Please help yourself.")
3. ✓
4. × (Why are you laughing at yourself/ yourselves?)
5. × (The students themselves invited Marty and me to their party.)
6. ✓

Unit 5 動詞

Chapter 22

❶

1. b
2. a
3. b
4. a
5. b
6. a
7. a
8. b
9. b
10. a

❷

1. × (The red meat tasted bad and caused me to vomit in my bed.)
2. ✓
3. ✓
4. × (The little girl first got mad and then later became sad.)
5. ✓

❸

1. smell good/smell delicious
2. smell these flowers
3. taste the fish
4. taste good/taste delicious
5. feel soft

Chapter 23

❶

1. open the door
2. gave me a headache
3. give me the money
4. runs a hotel
5. gave $5,000 to the church
6. has left me some food

❷

1. is walking her dog
2. is walking happily
3. is flying a kite
4. is flying high in the sky
5. is driving a new sports car
6. is driving carefully
7. are playing basketball
8. are playing in the park

❸

1. ✓
2. × (Ray bought Kay some roses for her birthday.)
3. ✓
4. ✓
5. × (Mom is reading a funny story to my little brother Tom.)

Chapter 24

❶ 1. C 2. A 3. B 4. C 5. B 6. C 7. A 8. C

2

1. looking for
2. called off
3. agree with
4. bring up
5. handed in
6. took off
7. turned away
8. find out
9. hung up
10. look it up
11. keep up with
12. get up
13. Watch out/Look out
14. ran into
15. make fun of

Unit 6 現在式

Chapter 25

1

1. is
2. are, are, are
3. are
4. are
5. is
6. am, am
7. is
8. are

2

1. b 3. b 5. c 7. b 9. a
2. a 4. c 6. b 8. c 10. a

3

1. Are, are
2. Are, am not (No, I am not. = No, I'm not.)
3. Are, are not (No, they are not.
   = No, they're not./No, they aren't.)
4. Is, is not (No, she is not. =No, she's not./
   No, she isn't.)
5. Is, is
6. Is, is not (No, he is not. = No, he's not./
   No, he isn't.)
7. Are, are not (No, they are not.
   = No, they're not./No, they aren't.)
8. Are, am

Chapter 26

1

1. There is
2. There are
3. There are
4. There is

2

1. Is there → No, there isn't.
   (There is a cat in the box.)
2. Are there → No, there aren't.
   (There is only one person in the car.)
3. Is there → Yes, there is.
4. Are there → Yes, there are.

3 1. c 2. a 3. e 4. b 5. d

4

1. is
2. is
3. Is, are
4. Is, isn't
5. Are, are
6. Are
7. are
8. Is
9. It's
10. There is

Chapter 27

1 1. have 2. has 3. have 4. have

2

1. Does, has
2. Do, have, don't have
3. Do, have, don't
4. Does, have, does
   (Yes, she does. = Yes, she has.)
5. Do, have

3 1. c 2. a 3. d 4. b 5. e

4

1. Tom has a tent.
2. Tom has knives and forks.
3. Tom doesn't have a jacket.
4. Tom doesn't have a sleeping bag.

5

1. Do rabbits have big ears?
   Or: Have rabbits got big ears?
2. Does Claire have black hair?
   Or: Has Claire got black hair?
3. Does Scot Oat have a nice houseboat?
   Or: Has Scot Oat got a nice houseboat?
4. Does the fox have a long tail? Yes, it does.
   Or: Yes, it has.
5. Do you have a headache?
   Or: Have you got a headache?
6. She usually has a sandwich for lunch.

Chapter 28

1

1. drinks
2. sits
3. goes
4. kisses
5. carries
6. cooks
7. rests
8. brushes
9. studies
10. wishes
11. marches
12. hurries

2 1. likes 2. go 3. loves 4. drinks 5. works

3

1. d (He drives a school bus.)
2. a (He plays drums.)
3. e (She makes bread.)
4. c (She teaches English.)
5. b (We sing pop songs.)

4 1. have 2. has 3. has

5

1. closes	3. teaches	5. speaks
2. loves, love	4. washes	6. sleeps

Chapter 29

1

1. Does	3. Does	5. Do
2. Do	4. Do	6. Does

2

1. doesn't	3. don't	5. don't
2. don't	4. doesn't	6. doesn't

3

1. goes → **Does** Bing **go** to church every Sunday morning? → (Yes,) he **does**.
2. wash → **Do** Kay and Lee **wash** their electric car every Sunday? → (Yes,) they **do**.
3. speaks → **Does** Trish **speak** Polish? → (No,) she **doesn't**.
4. play → **Do** Kay and May **play** basketball every day? → (No,) they **don't**.
5. go → **Do** Ming and you **go** out to eat every Friday evening? → (No,) we **don't**.
6. plays → **Does** she **play** computer games at home? → (No,) she **doesn't**./ (No,) she never **does**.

4

1. Do Mr. and Mrs. Dream like ice cream?
2. How much does it cost to fly from London to Singapore?
3. What does he want for breakfast?
4. How do you usually go to school?
5. Does it often snow here?
6. Does your brother Mike like soccer?

Chapter 30

1

1. raining	6. making	11. stopping
2. swimming	7. coming	12. controlling
3. tying	8. driving	13. running
4. jogging	9. putting	14. lying
5. dying	10. happening	15. sitting

2

1. Ted is standing on his head.
2. I'm doing the splits./I am doing the splits.
3. The baby is crying.
4. The girls are running.
5. She's cooking./She is cooking.
6. Dad is sleeping.
7. The kites are flying.
8. She is trying on her new dress.
9. I'm/I am reading a novel on my cellphone.

3

1. I am reading an English storybook.
2. The girls are swimming now.
3. She is looking at the birds in the tree.
4. She is praying for world peace.
5. He is giving Rose a red rose.
6. You are not listening to me.
7. They are chatting on the Internet.
8. You are sitting in my seat.
9. Ming and Dennis are playing tennis.
10. Uncle Pete is walking across the street.

4

1. is cooking	3. is wearing	5. is swimming
2. is doing	4. are staying	

Chapter 31

1

1. a) He is **writing** an email to Lily.
     = He's **writing** an email to Lily.
   b) **Is** he **writing** an email to Lily?
   c) He is **not writing** an email to Lily.
     = He's **not writing** an email to Lily.
     = He **isn't writing** an email to Lily.
2. a) She is **thinking** about food.
     = She's **thinking** about food.
   b) **Is** she **thinking** about food?
   c) She is **not thinking** about food.
     = She's **not thinking** about food.
     = She **isn't thinking** about food.
3. a) They **are jumping** on the big bed now.
     = They're **jumping** on the big bed now.
   b) **Are** they **jumping** on the big bed now?
   c) They **are not jumping** on the big bed now.
     = They're **not jumping** on the big bed now.
     = They **aren't jumping** on the big bed now.
4. a) She is **jogging** in the fog.
     = She's **jogging** in the fog.
   b) **Is** she **jogging** in the fog?
   c) She is **not jogging** in the fog.
     = She's **not jogging** in the fog.
     = She **isn't jogging** in the fog.

2

1. No, he is not. = No, he's not. = No, he isn't.
2. He is singing. = He's singing.

3. No, he isn't. = No, he's not. = No, he is not.
4. He is reading a newspaper.
   = He's reading a newspaper.
5. No, she isn't. = No, she's not. = No, she is not.
6. She's sleeping in our classroom.
   = She is sleeping in our classroom.
7. No, they aren't. = No, they're not.
   = No, they are not.
8. They are making cupcakes.
9. No, she isn't. = No, she's not.
   = No, she is not.
10. She's talking on the phone.
    = She is talking on the phone.
11. No, he isn't. = No, he's not. = No, he is not.
12. He's watching TV. = He is watching TV.

❸
1. Who are you waiting for?
2. Are you listening to me?
3. Are you staring at that woman in the miniskirt?/Is that woman in the miniskirt staring at you?
4. Are your relatives staying at a hotel?

Chapter 32

❶
2. (you) swim, (you) are swimming
3. (he) swims, (he) is swimming
4. (she) swims, (she) is swimming
5. (it) swims, (it) is swimming
6. (we) swim, (we) are swimming
7. (you) swim, (you) are swimming
8. (they) swim, (they) are swimming

❷
1. Why is Meg carrying
2. go
3. Is she using
4. I usually do, I'm playing

❸
2. Are you wearing sunglasses now?
   Yes, I am./No, I am not.
3. Does it often snow in your city?
   Yes, it does./No, it doesn't.
4. Is it snowing now?
   Yes, it is./No, it isn't.
5. Do you usually listen to English in the evening?
   Yes, I do./No, I don't.
6. Are you listening to English now?

Yes, I am./No, I am not.
7. Do you sometimes play chess in the afternoon?
   Yes, I do./No, I don't.
8. Are you playing chess now?
   Yes, I am./No, I am not.
9. Do you often make tea for your mom?
   Yes, I do./No, I don't.
10. Are you making tea for your mom now?
    Yes, I am./No, I am not.

❹
1. do   3. doesn't   5. does
2. is, is   4. do, don't   6. are

Chapter 33

❶
1. need   9. is Mom smelling
2. thinks   10. has
3. is looking   11. tastes
4. Do you want   12. are having
5. see   13. know
6. Does the baby smell   14. do not understand
7. are you thinking   15. want
8. does your dad think   16. prefers

❷
1. × (This flower smells so good!)
2. × (I love ice cream.)
3. ✓
4. ✓
5. × (Be quiet, please. I'm thinking hard.)
6. × (Bob has a good job.)
7. ✓
8. × (Do you know my friend Sue?)
9. × (Dan feels that time is very precious.)
10. ✓
11. ✓
12. ✓
13. × (Do you see what Mom means about Tom?)
14. × (How much do you weigh?)
15. × (I love my dog very much.)

Unit 7 過去式

Chapter 34

❶

1. was, was　3. is, is　2. is, is　4. was, was

❷

1. were → I was at the movie theater./
   I was at home.
2. Was → Yes, she was./No, she wasn't.
3. Was → Yes, it was./No, it wasn't.
4. Were → Yes, we were./No, we weren't.

❸ 1. a 2. b 3. b 4. c 5. c 6. a 7. c 8. b 9. a

❹

1. Was Jerome at home last night?
2. Why was Kay upset yesterday?
3. Why were you and Bing late for school this morning?
4. When were you born?

Chapter 35

❶

1. cut　　3. slept　　5. hit
2. set　　4. got　　6. read

❷

2. Did you have a good time last night?
   → Yes, I did. (No, I didn't.)
3. Did you study English last night?
   → Yes, I did. (No, I didn't)
4. Did you eat any pizza last night?
   → Yes, I did. (No, I didn't.)
5. Did it snow last night?
   → Yes, it did. (No, it didn't.)

❸

2. Did Jane go to see a movie?
   → Yes, she went to see a movie.
3. Did Jane do lots of homework?
   → Yes, she did lots of homework.
4. Did Jane play table tennis?
   → Yes, she played table tennis.
5. Did Jane climb a mountain?
   → No, she didn't climb a mountain.

Chapter 36

❶

1. Dee was listening to the BBC.
2. Brooke was reading a cookbook.
3. Ted was bouncing on his big bed.

4. Kim and Jim were jogging in the gym.
5. Paul was teaching his dog how to catch a ball.
6. Uncle Ed was getting ready to go to bed.

❷

1. They were playing basketball.
2. She was cooking.
3. He was practicing singing.
4. They were walking their dog.
5. I was teaching my dog Lulu how to roll over.
6. She was barking at my cat Lily.
7. He was writing an email to his friend Dee.
8. They were arguing about nothing.
9. She was building a huge sand castle.
10. They were eating by candlelight.

❸ 1. c 2. a 3. b 4. c 5. d 6. d 7. c 8. a 9. b

Chapter 37

❶

2. Has Ann arrived in Pakistan?
   → Ann hasn't arrived in Pakistan.
3. Has she (ever) told you about her vacation in Paris?
   → She hasn't told me about her vacation in Paris.
4. Have they knocked down all the old houses in this neighborhood?
   → They haven't knocked down all the old houses in this neighborhood.
5. Has Dirk finished his math homework?
   → Dirk hasn't finished his math homework.

❷

1. have been, for　　3. has not been, since
2. has worked, since　4. have lived, for

❸

1. has never smiled　3. Have, ever played
2. has never been　　4. Have, ever cheated

❹

1. been　3. gone　　5. gone　7. gone
2. been　4. been, been　6. been　8. gone

❺

1. have already done　3. has already begun
2. has not yet taken　4. Has, finished

Chapter 38

❶

1. robbed → robbed
2. helped → helped
3. nodded → nodded
4. rained → rained
5. wrote → written
6. believed → believed
7. hurried → hurried
8. took → taken
9. danced → danced
10. met → met
11. waited → waited
12. see → seen
13. said → said
14. worried → worried
15. spoke → spoken
16. stayed → stayed
17. slept → slept
18. enjoyed → enjoyed

❷

1. a   3. b   5. b   7. a   9. b
2. b   4. b   6. a   8. b   10. b

❸

1. refused
2. occupied
3. traveled
4. rang
5. studied
6. continued

❹

1. have seen
2. has broken
3. has gone
4. has explored
5. have had
6. has climbed

Unit 8 未來式

Chapter 39

❶

2. I'm meeting a friend on the Internet tomorrow night.
   → I'm not meeting a friend on the Internet tomorrow night.
3. I'm going to the multiplex movie theater on Saturday night.
   → I'm not going to the multiplex movie theater on Saturday night.
4. I'm having a private English class on Sunday afternoon.
   → I'm not having a private English class on Sunday afternoon.
5. I'm playing some computer games on Sunday morning.
   → I'm not playing any computer games on Sunday morning.

❷

1. What is Sally doing on Saturday night?
   → She is visiting Dwight on Saturday night.
2. Where is Sally going on Sunday night?
   → She is going to a dance with Vance.
3. What is Sally doing next Monday morning?
   → She is going on a business trip to Los Angeles.
4. Where is Sally flying from?
   → She is flying from New York Airport.
5. Which hotel is Sally staying at?
   → She is staying at the Holiday Inn.
6. How long is Sally staying in Los Angeles?
   → She is staying there for five days.
7. When is Sally coming back home?
   → She is coming back home next Friday night.
8. What time is Sally arriving in New York?
   → She is arriving in New York at 9:20 p.m.

❸

1. are you doing
2. am going
3. does the movie start
4. starts

Chapter 40

❶

1. is going to be
2. is going to help
3. is going to work
4. is going to teach
5. are going to travel
6. am going to move

❷

1. I am going to put some pictures on my blog. Or: I am not going to put some pictures on my blog.
2. I am going to chat with my friends on Skype. Or: I am not going to chat with my friends on Skype.
3. I am going to watch some DVD movies. Or: I am not going to watch some DVD movies.
4. I am going to play badminton. Or: I am not going to play badminton.
5. I am going to visit my friends. Or: I am not going to visit my friends.
6. I am going for a hike in the countryside. Or: I am not going for a hike in the countryside.

❸

1. She's going to church on Sunday morning.
2. She's going to fly to Paris on Sunday morning.
3. She's going to play soccer on Sunday morning.

4. She's going to chat with her parents on Skype on Sunday morning.

Chapter 41

❶

2. Will there be any global wars?
3. Will polar bears be extinct?
4. Will life be better?
5. Will the Internet be the same?
6. Will there be more schools than now?
7. Will people live longer?
8. Will humans speak the same language?
9. Will there be a big gap between the poor and the rich?
10. Will there be any cities and farms on the moon?
11. Will robots do all the farming?
12. Will there be any cars, trains, buses, and RVs on Mars?

❷

2. There will be global wars.
   Or: There won't be any global wars.
3. Polar bears will be extinct.
   Or: Polar bears won't be extinct.
4. Life will be better. Or: Life won't be better.
5. The Internet will be the same.
   Or: The Internet won't be the same.
6. There will be more schools than now.
   Or: There won't be more schools than now.
7. People will live longer.
   Or: People won't live longer.
8. Humans will speak the same language.
   Or: Humans won't speak the same language.
9. There will be a big gap between the poor and the rich. Or: There won't be a big gap between the poor and the rich.
10. There will be cities and farms on the moon. Or: There won't be any cities and farms on the moon.
11. Robots will do all the farming.
    Or: Robots won't do all the farming.
12. There will be cars, trains, buses, and RVs on Mars. Or: There won't be any cars, trains, buses, and RVs on Mars.

❸ 1. d 2. e 3. a 4. c 5. b 6. f

❹

1. Will   3. I'm working
2. will   4. it will snow a lot

Chapter 42

❶

1. am going to/'m going to
2. is going to
3. will/'ll
4. are going to/'re going to
5. will/'ll
6. will/'ll

❷

1. am going to	6. is going to
2. will	7. will
3. will	8. is going to
4. are going to	9. are going to
5. will	10. will

Unit 9 情態動詞

Chapter 43

❶

2. Can you play the violin?
3. Can you stand on your head?
4. Can you drive a bus?
5. Can you ride a horse?
6. Can you dance a ballet?

❷

1. can't ride   3. can go
2. can't find   4. can't hear

❸

1. couldn't speak   4. couldn't understand
2. can't use   5. can't smoke
3. can't see   6. can't ask

❹ 1. d 2. e 3. a 4. b 5. c 6. f

Chapter 44

❶

2. Next month I might visit my friend Ann in Japan.
3. Dwight might be late for the party tonight.
4. Kay may not go to work on Monday.
5. Ann may change her mind and decide to move to Iran instead of Japan.
6. June and Ray might go to Norway for their honeymoon.
7. Tonight I may not have time to chat with Joan on my cellphone.

2

1. She is going to stay at Disney World for two days.
2. She is not going to eat at any expensive restaurants.
3. She is going to visit the Kennedy Space Center.
4. She is going to meet Sue at Clearwater Beach.
5. She might not go to Miami.
6. She might go for a submarine ride at Sea World.
7. She might always eat at The Sub Shop.
8. She might not have time to visit museums.

3 1. c 2. c 3. a 4. a

Chapter 45

1

1. (f) You must see it.
2. (e) You must hurry.
3. (a) You mustn't get too close to it.
4. (b) You must see the doctor.
5. (c) You mustn't forget to give her a gift.
6. (d) You mustn't make any noise.

2 1. had to 2. must 3. had to 4. must

3

1. mustn't   4. mustn't   7. needn't   10. must
2. mustn't   5. needn't   8. mustn't   11. must
3. needn't   6. needn't   9. had to   12. had to

Chapter 46

1

1. You should try it on first.
2. You shouldn't play computer games so much.
3. You shouldn't work so hard.
4. You should go to see a doctor.

2

1. I think people should drive only electric vehicles. Or: I don't think people should drive only electric vehicles.
2. I think we should stop animal testing. Or: I don't think we should stop animal testing.
3. I think everyone should have the right to a free education. Or: I don't think everyone should have the right to a free education.
4. I think men and women should retire at the same age. Or: I don't think men and women should retire at the same age.

5. I think people should be terribly worried about this swine flu.
   Or: I don't think people should be terribly worried about this swine flu.

3

1. Do you think I should take
2. Do you think I should tell
3. Do you think I should read
4. Do you think I should find
5. Do you think I should invite
6. Do you think I should dye

Chapter 47

1

1. c   3. c   5. b   7. a   9. a
2. b   4. a   6. a   8. c   10. c

2

1. have to quit
2. had to go
3. Does he often have to travel
4. don't have to eat
5. don't have to pay
6. did you have to take
7. do you have to be
8. Did you have to wear
9. didn't have to tell
10. Do I have to answer

Chapter 48

1

1. Would you like a cup of tea?/ Would you like some tea?
2. Would you like a sandwich?
3. Would you like some orange juice or apple juice?
4. Would you like a piece of cheesecake?/ Would you like some cheesecake?

2

1. Would you like to play basketball this Sunday afternoon?
2. Would you like to watch an opera tonight?
3. Would you like to watch a horse race next Saturday?
4. Would you like to chat with me on Skype tomorrow night?

3

1. b   3. b   5. a   7. a   9. b   11. a
2. a   4. b   6. b   8. b   10. b

Chapter 49

1 1. b   2. a   3. c   4. c   5. a

2
1. Let's
2. shall we
3. Let's
4. Why don't we/Shall we
5. How about
6. Let's
7. How about
8. Let's
9. shall we
10. How about
11. Shall we/Why don't we

Unit 10 感官動詞和使役動詞

Chapter 50

1
1. hear
2. saw
3. smelled
4. heard, listen to
5. see
6. watching
7. looked
8. watches

2
1. × (I smelled some kind of chemical in this neighborhood./I can smell some kind of chemical in this neighborhood.)
2. ✓
3. × (Did you hear someone knock on the door?)
4. × (I can hear somebody coming into the house./I heard somebody coming into the house.)
5. ✓
6. × (Did you feel the house shake?)
7. × (You should spend more time listening to English.)
8. × (What is Pat looking at?)
9. × (Suddenly Lenore heard a strange noise outside the door.)
10. × (When I woke up, I smelled something rotten.)
11. ✓

Chapter 51

1
1. c   3. a   5. a   7. b   9. b
2. a   4. b   6. c   8. a   10. c

2
1. always sounds
2. tastes sour/tasted sour
3. singing and dancing
4. sounds as if
5. smells of roses

Chapter 52

1
1. d   3. c   5. d   7. b   9. c
2. c   4. a   6. a   8. b

2
1. look 2. understood 3. fly 4. built 5. to give

3
1. clean   3. get   5. sick
2. redecorated   4. bring   6. had

Unit 11 不定詞和動名詞

Chapter 53

1
1. let me help
2. see her come
3. expect to win
4. wants to join
5. ready to
6. determined to get

2
1. × (She won't be happy to live in her home village forever.)
2. × (Two minutes ago I felt the earth move a little.)
3. ✓
4. ✓
5. × (Mom was disappointed to learn that I had failed the English exam.)
6. × (Mom made me clean up my room this morning.)
7. × (My sister has a tendency to exaggerate things.)
8. ✓
9. × (She refused to go out with Mark last night.)
10. ✓
11. × (Grandma often says, "A person is never too old to learn.")
12. ✓
13. × (That smell made me feel sick.)
14. × (Dwight is too tired to finish his book

14. ✗ (Dwight is **too tired to finish** his book report tonight.)

Chapter 54

❶

1. waiting	10. to travel
2. to live	11. go
3. dancing	12. to try
4. seeing	13. talking
5. staying/to stay	14. to talk
6. to do	15. speak
7. learning/to learn	16. to pick
8. catching	17. going
9. to carry	18. reading/to read

❷

1. to wear/wearing	7. raining
2. to learn	8. jogging
3. getting	9. love
4. to play	10. to swim
5. reading	11. talking
6. to take/taking	12. being

❸ 1. c 2. b 3. c 4. b 5. c 6. c 7. b 8. c

Unit 12 形容詞和副詞

Chapter 55

❶

1. d (severe injuries)
2. f (illegal possession of firearms)
3. a (tasty soup)
4. g (fragrant roses)
5. e (muddy country roads)
6. b (tiring trip)
7. c (prosperous city)

❷

1. Trish is cooking some tasty fish.
2. Bess is wearing her old-fashioned blue dress.
3. Why are you interested in this position?
4. The movie we saw last night was very interesting.
5. I am bored with nothing to do.
6. Ms. Brooks never feels bored because she reads exciting books.
7. Gail saw the whale's big tail.
8. This room is very cold.

❸

1. sharp scissors   4. long vacation
2. stormy weather   5. fresh fruit
3. dangerous job   6. hot water

❹

1. a	5. a	9. b	13. b	17. b	21. a
2. b	6. a	10. a	14. b	18. b	22. a
3. a	7. a	11. a	15. b	19. a	23. b
4. b	8. b	12. b	16. b	20. a	24. a

Chapter 56

❶

2. I'm always polite.
3. I sometimes get upset./Sometimes I get upset./I get upset sometimes.
4. I often get nervous.
5. I'm usually happy.
6. I never yell at my parents.

❷

1. When do you usually get up?
2. Pete rarely eats meat.
3. The boss is still in the office.
4. Jim often talks to Kim.
5. I will always remember the first day I met you.
6. Are you ever late for school?
7. Mary seldom gets angry.
8. I have never been to Egypt.
9. My friends are all married.
10. They are usually at home in the evenings.
11. He has already been to Rome twice.
12. Does Margo still live in Chicago?

❸

1. The champion boxed well in the closing rounds.
2. Because she was sick, Kay didn't go to school yesterday.
3. She never misses a chance to explore.
4. Sue was born in Honolulu in 2002.
5. Kate often works late at night.
6. Bing saw a beautiful bird in his backyard this morning.
7. He can never find his keys, wallet, or jacket.
8. Ken is always in bed before ten.
9. She reads the news on the Internet every evening.
10. She often goes to the movies on weekends.

about it for a minute.

4

1. We often **play volleyball on the beach**.
2. Bob is going to **start his new job next week**.
3. Bobby exclaimed, "This is an **extremely exciting** hobby!"
4. Ms. Rice and her daughter Lulu **carefully explored** the tropical paradise./Ms. Rice and her daughter Lulu **explored** the tropical paradise **carefully**.
5. The choir sang beautifully at the concert **last night**.
6. My father **often** drives to work.
7. She can **never** remember my name.
8. **We all love** to watch football games.
9. They **have lived here since 2008**.
10. Will you be **at home** this evening?
11. My parents love me **very much**.
12. Dell speaks English and Spanish **very well**.

Chapter 57

1

1. too loud
2. too tired
3. too busy
4. old enough
5. loudly enough
6. enough vacation time
7. too slowly

2

2. is too heavy for her to carry it
3. too fast for me to understand what he was saying
4. too windy for me to go for a walk
5. is too short for large airplanes to land here
6. too young to get a driver's license

3

1. too much
2. too
3. too many/enough
4. too
5. enough
6. too much
7. enough
8. enough

4

2. It was raining./
   It is still raining./
   The rain hasn't stopped yet.
3. Mom was cooking./
   She's still cooking./
   Dinner is not ready yet.

5 1. still   2. yet   3. yet   4. still

Chapter 58

1

1. willingly
2. lazily
3. miserably
4. fatally
5. poorly
6. noisily
7. nobly
8. sadly
9. bitterly
10. kindly
11. carelessly
12. frequently

2

1. c (fought monsters bravely)
2. e (arrived punctually)
3. a (spoke Spanish fluently)
4. f (danced ballet gracefully)
5. b (gave generously)
6. d (argued heatedly)

3

1. sleepily
2. fearlessly
3. comfortably
4. correctly
5. respectfully
6. dangerously
7. heavily
8. stealthily

4

1. good, well
2. proud
3. beautifully
4. quick, quickly
5. easily
6. well
7. mad
8. slow
9. hard
10. easy

Chapter 59

1

1. cleverer → cleverest
2. sadder → saddest
3. heavier → heaviest
4. ruder → rudest
5. more/less ignorant → most/least ignorant
6. nosier → nosiest
7. slimmer → slimmest
8. more/less jealous → most/least jealous
9. friendlier → friendliest
10. nicer → nicest
11. more/less patient → most/least patient
12. wealthier → wealthiest
13. less → least
14. wider → widest
15. worse → worst
16. better → best
17. dirtier → dirtiest
18. thinner → thinnest
19. sunnier → sunniest
20. more → most

❷
1. older
2. cheaper/less expensive
3. colder
4. better
5. farther
6. easier/less difficult
7. poorer
8. more

❸
1. talkative
2. hot, hotter
3. heaviest
4. oldest
5. smallest
6. friendlier
7. worst
8. depressed
9. worse
10. best
11. most famous
12. most hardworking/ hardest working
13. bigger
14. most graceful
15. more
16. most comfortable
17. fattest
18. diligent
19. most
20. more patient

❹
1. b	4. d	7. d	10. c
2. a	5. c	8. b	11. d
3. c	6. c	9. a	12. c

❺
1. ✓
2. ✗ (Is it **cheaper** to travel by car or by train?)
3. ✗ (Linda is the **best** student in the class.)
4. ✗ (Kay made **fewer** mistakes than Trish on the English exam yesterday.)
5. ✓

Chapter 60

❶ 1. high   2. high   3. higher

❷
1. carefully
2. hardest
3. faster
4. farthest
5. livelier
6. more slowly

❸
1. b	3. c	5. c	7. c	9. c	11. a
2. b	4. a	6. c	8. b	10. c	12. c

Unit 13 介系詞

Chapter 61

❶
1. She's swimming in the lake.
2. He's sitting at the desk.
3. They are standing at the bus stop.
4. She's on the airplane.

❷
1. a) in   b) on
2. a) on   b) at
3. a) in   b) at
4. a) in   b) on
5. a) at   b) on

❸
1. Ted is reading **in** bed. (Or: Ted is reading **on the bed**.)
2. There is a supermarket **at** the end of this street.
3. Her name is **at** the bottom of the page.
4. There are four police officers **at** our door.
5. There's a small church **on** the top of the hill.
6. "Is there a mall near here?" "Yes, turn right **at** the next set of traffic lights. You won't miss it."

Chapter 62

❶
1. under
2. near/next to/beside/by
3. behind
4. above (也可以用 over，表示從雲的這一邊到另一邊，即「飛越過」。)
5. by/near/next to/beside
6. above

❷ 1. b   2. b   3. c   4. a   5. a   6. b   7. c

Chapter 63

❶
1. down
2. over
3. out of
4. off
5. to
6. in front of

❷ 1. on   2. into, through   3. out of   4. off

❸
1. across
2. to
3. off, into
4. to
5. around
6. along
7. out of
8. over, into
9. around
10. out of
11. around
12. from, to
13. to
14. onto, off
15. into
16. under
17. over/above

Chapter 64

❶

1. at	6. on	11. on	16. in
2. in	7. on	12. in	17. on
3. in	8. at	13. at	18. in
4. on	9. at	14. in	
5. at	10. at	15. on/at	

❷

1. At	4. in	7. at	10. in	13. in
2. at, in	5. In	8. on	11. on	14. on
3. at	6. at	9. in	12. on	

❸

1. at	3. In	5. at	7. on	9. on/at
2. In	4. in	6. on	8. on	10. On

Chapter 65

❶

1. ✕ (They have been married for three years.)
2. ✕ (Dad often falls asleep while he is watching TV.)
3. ✓
4. ✓
5. ✓
6. ✕ (I was late for school today because I waited for the bus for half an hour.)

❷

1. for	3. since	5. for
2. until	4. until	6. since

❸

1. to	3. during	5. during
2. while	4. while	

❹

1. After finishing his homework, Dirk was tired.
2. Before making a decision, let's have a discussion about this issue.
3. After eating too much cheesecake, Rick felt sick.
4. Before answering my next difficult question, think carefully.

Chapter 66

❶

1. to	3. to	5. to	7. on	9. from	11. in
2. with	4. with	6. to	8. of	10. of	12. to

❷

1. on	4. to	7. at	10. after
2. from	5. of	8. in	
3. with/at	6. for/about	9. about	

❸

1. thinking about quitting
2. Thank, for telling
3. fed up with listening
4. sorry for/about blaming
5. bad at controlling

❹

1. to	5. with	9. for
2. to	6. of	10. on, by
3. with	7. on	11. on
4. about	8. to	12. on

Unit 14 連接詞、並列句和副詞子句

Chapter 67

❶

1. (d) You can study hard for this entrance exam, or you can fail.
2. (e) Amos has already bungee jumped twice, but he is still very nervous.
3. (f) Are you married, or are you single?
4. (h) The apples were so red, and they tasted good to Ted.
5. (c) Sally lost a fortune in the stock market, but she still seems to live quite comfortably.
6. (a) Ms. Wu was reading a newspaper, and her husband was changing their baby's diaper.
7. (b) I wanted to call you, but I forgot your cellphone number.
8. (g) Jim likes me, and I like him.

❷

1. (d) Be faithful in small things because it is in them that your strength lies. (—Mother Teresa)
2. (e) She has always been nervous in public, so it is no surprise that she avoids large gatherings.
   = Because she has always been nervous in public, it is no surprise that she avoids large gatherings.

3. (f) June isn't very healthy, **so** she tries to swim or jog for an hour every afternoon.
= **Because** June isn't very healthy, she tries to swim or jog for an hour every afternoon.

4. (a) Her alarm clock didn't go off, **so** Kate was late for school.
= **Because** her alarm clock didn't go off, Kate was late for school.

5. (b) Jim failed to appear, **so** we went to the beach without him.
= **Because** Jim failed to appear, we went to the beach without him.

6. (c) She refused to give up her dream of being in the movies **because** she loved acting.
= She loved acting, **so** she refused to give up her dream of being in the movies.

❸ 1. and   2. or   3. and   4. but

Chapter 68

❶

1. When he is at work, he always wears a tie.
2. When your plane arrives, I'll be at the airport.
3. When I'm on vacation, Sue will stay at my apartment.
4. When Amy saw us, she smiled and waved.
5. When the accident occurred, I was at a friend's house.

❷

1. If you eat all the cookies, you'll get as sick as a dog.
2. If you're busy now, I can talk to you later.
3. If I still feel sick tomorrow, I won't go to school.
4. If you like this skirt, I'll buy it for you.
5. If you don't hurry, you'll miss your flight.

❸

1. When   4. when   7. if
2. If   5. when   8. When
3. If   6. If

Chapter 69

❶ 1. a   2. b   3. d   4. c   5. a   6. b

❷

1. Either the manager **or** the treasurer **was** going to attend the meeting./
Neither the manager nor the treasurer **was** going to attend the meeting.
2. Her trip to Nepal was both exciting **and** tiring.

3. Neither Lilly **nor** Amy **lives** in Italy./
Either Lilly or Amy **lives** in Italy.
4. She is not only a fast runner but also **a great pianist.**/
She **not only runs fast** but also plays the piano very well.
5. Either Louise or her two younger sisters **need** to make supper.

❸

1. Yesterday Ms. Bridge **neither** called me **nor** sent me a text message.
2. She wanted/wants **either** to build a new house **or** remodel her old cottage.
3. Ms. Bridge wanted/wants to build **either** a house **or** a cottage.
4. **B**oth Mike **and** I like opera.

Chapter 70

❶

1. such, that   8. No matter what
2. no matter when   9. No matter how
3. too, to   10. so, that
4. whether, or   11. so, that
5. too, to   12. No matter how
6. whether, or   13. whether, or
7. no matter who   14. No matter what

❷

1. You will eat those carrots **whether** you like them **or** not./
Whether you like them **or** not, you will eat those carrots.
2. It's **too** windy **to** sit outside.
3. She was **so** angry with me **that** she refused to talk to me for two months.
4. **No matter who** you are, you have to follow the traffic rules.
5. **No matter when** you say goodbye to me, I won't cry.
6. It was **such** a long and difficult trip **that** it took me almost a week to get over it./
The trip was **so** long and difficult **that** it took me almost a week to get over it.
7. Kay was **so** excited **that** she didn't know what to say.
8. It was **such** awful weather **that** Kay decided to stay at home for a whole day.

Unit 15 句子的元素和種類

Chapter 71

❶

1. ✓
2. ✗ (Elaine loves/likes/liked/loved her doll Jane.)
3. ✗ (Claire has/had long brown hair.)
4. ✓
5. ✓
6. ✗ (Mike rides/rode/likes/liked his bike.)

❷

1. high
2. the/that snake
3. is, spy
4. on the stairs
5. carefully, website
6. to ride a horse

Chapter 72

❶

1. It doesn't snow in Miami./
   It does not snow in Miami.
2. Joe and I do not know how to get to Tokyo./
   Joe and I don't know how to get to Tokyo.
3. Has Coco arrived in Chicago?
4. Are you going to sing with Sue and Pete?
5. Did Erika move to South Africa last year?
6. Should we go now?
7. It has not rained for a month./
   It hasn't rained for a month.
8. She doesn't like her job./
   She does not like her job.

❷

1. I didn't see her talking to the principal.
2. Lynn hasn't read the novel *Dinosaurs Before Dark*.
3. Joe didn't become a lawyer two years ago.
4. Tonight Sue and Lulu won't fly to Honolulu.
5. She isn't playing a computer game.
6. It didn't snow last night.
7. He isn't going to keep on smoking.
8. Neal doesn't always wash his hands before each meal.
9. Dwight can't go with you to see a movie tonight.
10. She wasn't born in Hawaii.

❸

1. Is Joan often tired after talking to her boyfriend on the phone?
2. Have you waited long for Sue?
3. Does Kate sometimes sleep till eight?
4. Is Sue flying to Honolulu?
5. Can she touch her toes?
6. Was she loudly singing a happy Hong Kong song?

Chapter 73

❶

1. What
2. How
3. Where
4. Where
5. How
6. How
7. Whose
8. When
9. How
10. What
11. Who
12. What
13. Why
14. Where
15. Which
16. Where
17. How
18. What
19. Who
20. What

❷

1. a) What   b) Who
2. a) How often b) How long
3. a) What   b) Which
4. a) Who's   b) Whose
5. a) What   b) Which

❸

1. How
2. How far
3. How long
4. Where
5. How many
6. What
7. Why
8. How often
9. Who
10. When

❹

1. (Ben) ✗ (How often do you practice modern ballet?)
2. ✓
3. (May) ✗ (What's your brother's favorite subject?)
4. (Ben) ✗ (When does Gwen have time to visit her friends?)
5. (Ben) ✗ (Why do you go to bed so early?)
6. ✓
7. (Ben) ✗ (Who do you like better, Ann or Nan?)
8. (Ben) ✗ (Where is Jerome?)

❺

1. How far
2. How old
3. How long
4. How often
5. How old
6. How long
7. How high
8. How big
9. How tall
10. How long

Chapter 74

❶

1. ✓
2. ✗ (What time does Ted usually go to bed?)

3. ✗ (Why **is** Sue angry with Lulu?)

4. ✗ (How often **does** Bing **go** mountain climbing?)

5. ✗ (How long **have you lived** in Honolulu?)

6. ✓

7. ✓

8. ✗ (How much sugar **do** you want in your coffee?)

9. ✗ (How much **did** Mat **pay** for that cat?)

10. ✓

❷

1. **How long** did Jane listen to an English story last night?

2. **What** did Steve buy on Christmas Eve?

3. **How** did Erica Bar travel across America?

4. **Where** is your puppy?

5. **When** is Tom's birthday?

6. **Where** is the sun?

7. **How many** new English words has Kay learned today?

8. **How often** does she go swimming?

9. **How** tall is Paul?

10. **How much** did Kay's electric car cost?

11. **Whose** cellphone is this?

Chapter 75

❶

1. This issue is very important, **isn't it?**

2. You are a big coffee drinker, **aren't you?**

3. Gwen shouldn't start smoking again, **should she?**

4. You went to a movie with Sue last night, **didn't you?**

5. Bing should quit drinking and smoking, **shouldn't he?**

6. Kay and Fay can't do any of the martial arts, **can they?**

7. Jogging is the best way to remain fit, **isn't it?**

8. I am supposed to come back home before 10 p.m., **aren't I?**

9. Lily can speak Spanish fluently, **can't she?**

10. It didn't snow yesterday in Tokyo, **did it?**

11. Let's go now, **shall we?**

12. There were too many people in the mall, **weren't there?**

❷

1. ✗ (What **noise** you are making! 或 How noisy you are!)

2. ✓

3. ✓

4. ✗ (Look, what a mess **you have made**.)

5. ✗ (What **an** exciting movie!)

6. ✗ (**How** terrible the earthquake was!)

❸

1. **How friendly** Liz is!

2. **How hard** you are working!

3. **How beautiful** these/those flowers are!

4. **How sad** the story is!

❹

1. How fast   4. What lovely

2. How exciting   5. How

3. What a beautiful

Chapter 76

❶

1. Please **don't** sit down, Louise.

   = Please **do not** sit down, Louise.

2. **Don't** tell her to study math.

   = **Do not** tell her to study math.

3. **Don't** open your books.

   = **Do not** open your books.

4. Kay, **don't** go away.

   = Kay, **do not** go away.

5. **Don't** run, boys.

   = **Do not** run, boys.

6. **Don't** take off your shoes.

   = **Do not** take off your shoes.

❷

1. do not watch   5. be

2. never speak   6. Have

3. Read   7. Don't be

4. don't smoke   8. be

❸

1. Sweep up the mess right now.

2. Be quick, Steve! Your flight is going to leave.

3. Don't read in dim light.

4. Tess, please show me your new red blouse.

5. Pete, don't run on the street.

6. Don't tell me to take a bath and get a haircut.

Unit 16 簡單句、並列句和複合句

Chapter 77

1 1. b 2. d 3. a 4. c 5. b 6. c 7. d 8. c

2

1. D: gets   3. B: where
2. C: as   4. A: Because

Chapter 78

1

1. Ms. Bridge lives in this cottage
2. Susan is an Egyptian
3. Sam and I passed the English exam
4. oil prices will go up or down
5. he talked to Kay on the Internet yesterday

2

1. why Kay is absent today
2. how long Dwight played "Happy Farm" on Facebook last night
3. if/whether Bret Wu's cellphone is connected to the Internet
4. what Sue Pool wants to do after her graduation from high school
5. if/whether Amy likes me
6. where the bathroom is
7. who is piloting that plane

3

1. (that) you didn't do your homework
2. (that) Claire lost her teddy bear
3. how old I am
4. (that) he ran his bicycle into Ted
5. (that) milk is good for you
6. what I can do for you
7. whether/if we can finish this job on time
8. where you parked my van

4

1. didn't you go   4. does Eve want
2. Amy dislikes   5. do you want
3. what Kay did   6. how pretty she is

Chapter 79

1

1. **That** he didn't show up at the party disappointed me.
   = **It** disappointed me **that** he didn't show up at the party.

2. His request **is that** you wear your tie and white shirt to the wedding.
3. What Kay likes to do **is** to play with her pretty kitty.
4. I'm disappointed (**that**) she didn't win the English speech contest.
5. **That** Amy and Tom's marriage ended in divorce surprised me.
   = **It** surprised me **that** Amy and Tom's marriage ended in divorce.
6. The best thing **is that** both of you have been in love with each other for years.
7. I'm glad (**that**) we have become friends.
8. It's a mystery why **Sally dislikes** Larry.

2 1. b 2. a 3. a 4. b 5. b 6. a

Chapter 80

1

1. (**that**) she gave me yesterday has lots of functions and provides access to the Internet anywhere in the world
2. (**who/whom/that**) the principal is talking to is our new English teacher from Canada
3. showed me some pictures of the planets **that** orbit distant stars
4. (**who/whom/that**) I met in the park today was wearing a funny purple hat
5. has a maid **who** is very good at making cookies

2

1. whose   3. why   5. which
2. who   4. where   6. when

3

1. ✓
2. × (She likes movies **that/which** can make her laugh and cry.)
3. ✓
4. ✓
5. × (Everything she said **was** not true.)
6. ✓
7. × (The restaurant **where** I am working is called "The Double Happiness Cafe."/ The restaurant I am working **in** is called "The Double Happiness Cafe.)
8. × (Sue prefers music that she can dance **to**.)
9. × (Kay lost the necklace her boyfriend **gave her** last Saturday.)

10. × (Most of the people (who/whom/that) we invited to our party didn't show up.)
11. ✓
12. × (The boots I am wearing are beautiful and comfortable.)

Unit 17 間接引語和被動語態

Chapter 81

❶

1. The maid explained (that) she was paid once a week.
2. Kate said (that) they would come home late.
3. He said (that) Kay enjoyed daydreaming about her wedding.
4. Mat said (that) he couldn't find his hat.
5. I asked Trish whether she liked English.
6. Smiling happily, she said (that) she was going to have a baby in May.
7. Lily said to me that she didn't like turkey.
8. He asked Kay when she was going to open up her new coffee and sandwich café.

❷

1. say, told   3. say, said
2. tell, said   4. say, said

❸

1. Did Paul tell you that he might call me?/ Did Paul say to you that he might call me?/Did Paul say that he might call me?
2. She asked whether I liked to play farm games on Facebook.
3. Jill said she would write a song about Hong Kong.
4. Nan asked me when I was going to Pakistan.
5. I saw Bob last week, and he told me that he was enjoying his job./I saw Bob last week, and he said that he was enjoying his job./I saw Bob last week, and he said to me that he was enjoying his job.

Chapter 82

❶

1. When was the printing press invented?
2. Dan is greatly influenced by his hardworking girlfriend Ann.

3. She is supposed to go with me to a conference in Hawaii.
4. Where was she born?
5. "English is taught in almost every school in the world," said Trish.
6. Emma knows that her loan has been paid off by her grandma.
7. The telephone was invented by Alexander Bell in 1876.
8. This room was messed up by Lily, not me.

❷

1. is being repaired
2. was built
3. will be closed/is going to be closed
4. is served
5. was made
6. is being interviewed
7. has been repaired
8. are solar cells used
9. are we supposed
10. Are we allowed

❸

1. The boys were woken up by a loud noise.
2. The first personal microwave was introduced in 1967 by the Amana Corporation.
3. Kate was told what had happened to her alcoholic classmate.
4. Twenty people were killed in the plane crash.
5. I can't find my wallet anywhere. I think it has been stolen.

國家圖書館出版品預行編目資料

Fun學初級英文文法 / Dennis Le Boeuf
& 景黎明著 一初版. 一[臺北市]：寂天文
化, 2020.08 面；公分.

ISBN 978-986-318-128-6 (菊8K平裝)
ISBN 978-986-318-334-1 (菊8K精裝)
ISBN 978-986-318-217-7 (25K平裝)
ISBN 978-986-318-557-4 (20K精裝)
ISBN 978-986-318-621-2 (16K平裝)
ISBN 978-986-318-738-7 (20K平裝)
ISBN 978-986-318-827-8 (16K精裝)
ISBN 978-986-318-931-2 (25K精裝)

1. 英語   2. 語法

805.16   109010978

作者 _ Dennis Le Boeuf & 景黎明

製程管理 _ 洪巧玲

出版者 _ 寂天文化事業股份有限公司

電話 _ +886-2-2365-9739

傳真 _ +886-2-2365-9835

網址 _ www.icosmos.com.tw

讀者服務 _ onlineservice@icosmos.com.tw

出版日期 _ 2020年8月 初版再刷（160104）

郵撥帳號 _ 1998620-0 寂天文化事業股份有限公司

訂購金額600（含）元以上郵資免費

訂購金額600元以下者，請外加郵資65元

若有破損，請寄回更換